Praise for *Extinction Game*

'Gary Gibson has been turning out highly readable, intriguing wide-screen space operas for almost a decade, action-adventure novels of ideas that bear comparison with the work of Peter Hamilton and Al Reynolds. With *Extinction Game* Gibson has changed tack and produced what might be his finest novel to date . . . a gripping mystery [that] can only increase Gibson's growing reputation as a master of core SF'
Guardian

'Gibson makes the most of his parallel universes, forging a strong plot with a few twists that fairly boggle the mind'
Daily Mail

'Gibson creates a vivid picture of life after an apocalypse . . . the pace is relentless, and the story twists several times before reaching a conclusion that sets up this new series. A fast-paced post-apocalyptic thriller that builds to an exciting conclusion'
SciFiBulletin.com

'The prose is vibrant with a real sense of momentum and the author manages to reach a nice equilibrium between character development and story . . . The result is a rewarding novel full to brimming with ideas, with a great story and an ever-so-easy-to-read style. I really do hope we see more'
SFBook.com

'A damn good read . . . I've simply stormed through it with that same sense of wonder and excitement that accompanied reading his other work. What more can you wish for?'
Upcoming4.me

EXTINCTION GAME

Gary Gibson has worked as a graphic designer and magazine editor, and began writing at the age of fourteen. He lives in Glasgow. His previous novels include the Shoal series (*Stealing Light*, *Nova War* and *Empire of Light*), plus the stand-alone books *Angel Stations*, *Against Gravity*, *Final Days*, *The Thousand Emperors* and *Marauder*.

You can find Gary on www.garygibson.net

By Gary Gibson

Angel Stations
Against Gravity

The Shoal Trilogy

Stealing Light
Nova War
Empire of Light

Final Days
The Thousand Emperors
Marauder

Extinction Game

Gary Gibson

EXTINCTION GAME

TOR

First published 2014 by Tor

This edition published 2015 by Tor
an imprint of Pan Macmillan
20 New Wharf Road, London N1 9RR
Associated companies throughout the world
www.panmacmillan.com

ISBN 978-1-4472-4272-7

A CIP catalogue record for this book is available from the British Library.

Typeset by Ellipsis Digital Limited, Glasgow
Printed and bound by CPI Group (UK) Ltd, Croydon, CR0 4YY

Visit **www.panmacmillan.com** to read more about all our books
and to buy them. You will also find features, author interviews and
news of any author events, and you can sign up for e-newsletters
so that you're always first to hear about our new releases.

EXTINCTION GAME

ONE

There's an old story I once read that starts like this: *The last man on Earth sat alone in a room. There was a knock on the door.* Except for me it wasn't a knock, just some muddy tracks in a field that told me I was not, as I had long since come to believe, the last living human being.

But before I found those tracks and my world changed in ways I couldn't even have begun to imagine, I stood in front of a mirror and wondered whether or not this would be the day I finally blew my brains out.

The weapon of choice was a Wesson semi-automatic I had prised from the fingers of a man named Herschel Nussbaum ten years before. This was just moments after I killed him and four days after he had nearly tortured me to death. I kept the gun in a bathroom drawer, under the basin before which I now stood. Its barrel was sleek and grey, and the grip had wooden insets of a fine, dark grain that felt warm against the skin when you picked it up. I thought about opening the drawer, how easy it would be, how quick. Click, *bam*, and no more Jerry Beche. No more last man on Earth. Just an empty house, and the wind and the trees, and the animals that had inherited the deserted cities and towns.

I'd had this same thought almost every morning for the last couple of years. Under any other circumstances this would, I admit, appear excessively morbid. But I was all alone on a world devoid of human life. I feared growing too old or too sick or so feeble I would no longer be able to make that choice, to end my life on my own terms.

The only certainty I had left was that one day I would take that gun out of its drawer and join the rest of my species in extinction. I'd push the barrel against the roof of my mouth, angled up so the bullet would blow straight through the top of my skull. I had nightmares, you see, about screwing it up. I dreamed of blowing half my face off and waking up in a pool of blood and bone fragments, still alive.

Or at least, that's what I told myself I'd do.

I didn't open the drawer. Instead, I picked up a jerrycan of water placed by the door, and poured some of it into the sink. I splashed a little on my cheeks, and when I looked up I caught a glimpse of my unshaven face in the mirror over the sink. I looked thin – gaunt, really. It had been a long winter, and I wondered, not for the first time, if some undiagnosed masochistic streak kept me from settling down somewhere warmer than England. For the first time I noticed a touch of grey at my temples that made me look like my father.

It makes you look distinguished, I imagined Alice saying.

'It makes you look distinguished,' she said from behind me.

I turned to see her leaning against the frame of the bathroom door, arms folded across her chest, one corner of her mouth turned up in amusement. She wore a thick navy cardigan over a red T-shirt that clashed violently with the ratty green scarf knotted around her neck. I never saw her wear anything else.

'Remember you have to check the wind turbines today,' she said, stepping back from the door. 'Last thing we need is another power failure.'

I nodded mutely. There had been another outage the previous evening, the lights fading to a dull brown before eventually stuttering back to life. I had a diesel generator as backup, but fuel was precious and I didn't want to use any more than was absolutely essential. I had made repairs to the transmission lines only the week before. The problem, then, could only lie with the wind turbines up the hill that were still functioning.

I dried my face and stepped back out into the corridor, then hesitated. I could hear Alice humming from the direction of the kitchen. What was it that suddenly felt so wrong? What was it that . . . ?

Of course. How *could* I have forgotten?

I made my way back to the bedroom and picked up the broken I Ching coin from the bedside table, a piece of black cord tied around it so that I could wear it around my neck. It was my lucky charm, my talisman, the last remaining link to the life I had lost long ago.

When I entered the kitchen, Alice was gone and the house was silent. I breakfasted on wheat grain milled by my own hand, softened with powdered milk and filtrated water. This was flavoured with a dribble of honey from the food stores I maintained in the cellar. I heated some water on the wood-burning stove and washed the meal down with freeze-dried coffee, then made for the hallway. I pulled on a heavy jacket and picked up my shotgun, my breath frosting in the cold air.

The past few weeks had been bitterly cold, sleet and snow tumbling endlessly from grey English skies, but over the last few days the temperature had started to crawl back up. I stepped outside, seeing the snow had begun to melt. In the distance, past the trees lining the road, I heard crows call out to each other, their voices stark and flat in the monochrome landscape. The wind turbines were visible at the peak of the hill a quarter of a mile away. Altogether a peaceful winter morning.

In the next moment, the crows exploded upwards from a small copse of poplar farther up the hill. I tensed, wondering what had spooked them. There was a real danger of encountering predators with no memory, and therefore no fear, of human beings. Over the years I had caught glimpses of bears and even lions, presumably escaped from zoos or circuses after their owners died. Several winters ago I'd had a nasty encounter with a polar bear that came charging out of an alleyway.

Dogs were undoubtedly the worst. The smaller ones had mostly died out in the years following the apocalypse, leaving the larger, fiercer specimens to dominate. After a winter like this one they would be hungry indeed, and I never stepped outside my door without a loaded shotgun under my arm.

I listened, but heard nothing more. More than likely the crows had been startled by a badger or fox. Even so, I kept watching out as I shut the door behind me. I walked past an outbuilding containing a processing tank that turned cheap vegetable oil raided from deserted supermarkets into biodiesel, then I stepped through a wooden gate leading into a field where sheep had once grazed. The place in which I now made my home was an ultra-modern affair, a boxy construction with broad glass windows, constructed, so far as I could tell, mere months before the apocalypse. I had it found it pristine and unlived in; better still, it was easy to keep warm, even in the depths of a winter such as this.

I followed a well-worn path up the side of the hill until I came to a line of twin-bladed wind turbines. There were a dozen in all, tall and graceful and rising high above me. Only three still functioned. The rest stood silent, despite my vain attempts to repair them. I had never been able to find the necessary spare parts.

The turbines were one of the main reasons I chose to settle where I did. I had driven fence posts into the hillside, paralleling the path leading to the turbines, and strung thick cables all the way down the hill to my chosen home. From the top of the hill I could see what had been the town of Wembury in the distance, still Christmas-card pretty under its blanket of snow despite the recent rain.

The blades of the remaining three turbines that still worked spun steadily under a freezing wind. I made my way inside a transformer shed next to one of them and first checked the voltmeter and then the storage batteries. I kept expecting to come up the hill and find another of the turbines dead.

'I keep expecting to come up the hill and find another of the turbines dead,' said Alice. I could just see the other half of the Chinese coin I wore around my own neck peeking out through her scarf, on its silver chain. 'I'm amazed they've lasted this long.'

I pulled a fuse box open and took a look inside. 'Always the pessimist,' I said.

'Takes one to know one.'

I glanced over at her, still wearing her blue cardigan and green scarf. *She'll catch her death dressed like that*, I thought, then quickly pushed the thought away.

I could see a streak of rust at the back of the fuse box, at the top. I looked up to the roof of the shed, to where I had cut a hole for the power cables. The weatherproofing had partly come away, letting in rain and snow; one more thing I had to fix. I pulled out the fuse nearest the rust stain and saw where it had become touched with corrosion.

No wonder the power had nearly gone the other night. I pulled a spare out of a box on the floor and replaced it.

'Job done,' I said, stepping back, but Alice had vanished once more. I went out of the shed, but there was no sign of her. It was maddening sometimes, the way she'd come and go.

I glanced down at the broad muddy patch that spanned the distance between the nearest turbine and the transformer shed and saw several sets of bootprints. I stared at them, then blinked hard, sure I was seeing things, but they were still there when I looked again. They were fresh: their outlines clear, the grooves in the mud filled with a thin layer of water, indicating they had been made some time within the last couple of hours. I stared at them numbly. It had been a couple of days since I'd last been out, and it had rained heavily. I peered more closely at them, seeing they were quite different from my own bootprints. Then I looked around, trying to make sense of it, the blood thundering in my ears.

'Alice?' I called out, the words choked. 'Have you . . . ?'

I stopped mid-sentence. Of course it hadn't been her bootprints, *couldn't* be. I looked again; there were three distinct sets of prints. They had stood here, walking back and forth across the mud, studying the turbines, the shed and presumably the cables leading down to the house.

Three people. Three living, breathing human beings.

That's when it really hit me. My heart began to thud so hard it hurt. I fell to my knees, tears rolling down my face. *I wasn't alone.*

But then something else occurred to me. If I wasn't alone . . . who, exactly, had come calling?

I thought, then, of Herschel Nussbaum, and his partner-in-genocide, Marlon Keene, both dead by my own hand. They had not been working alone.

I stood quickly, and cast a wild glance towards the poplars and the deeper woods spreading down the far slope of the hill, wondering just who might be looking back. The trees and the rusting turbines took on a menacing quality they'd never had before. I had dreamed of an improbable rescue for years, and yet I had good reason to be very afraid of being found.

My shotgun. It was still propped against the wall of the shed. I ran back in to retrieve it, but my hands were shaking so hard I fumbled with it at first.

I stepped back outside and saw Alice standing staring down at the bootprints. Her feet, I saw, were clad in cheap trainers, rather than boots.

'Where the hell were you?' I demanded, the strain evident in my voice. 'Stay where I can see you!'

When she looked up at me, her face was shining. 'Someone's found us,' she said, her tone full of astonishment. 'Oh, my God, Jerry! Do you know what this means? Someone's come to *rescue* us—'

'Then why were they wandering around here in the middle of the night instead of coming down to the goddam house?' I demanded. 'How long have they been out here, watching us?'

Alice frowned at me, pulling her cardigan closer around her narrow shoulders. 'What are you so worried about? I—'

'Don't you *understand*?' I nearly yelled at her. 'Who could they be, but Red Harvest? Who else could have the antidote? Who else could still be alive after they poisoned the entire bloody planet? Don't you *see*? Maybe they want revenge, for what I did to Nussbaum and Keene!'

'You're being ridiculous,' she scoffed. 'They're all just as dead as everyone else; you know that. You found their base and they were all—'

I had travelled to the States a few years after the apocalypse. It had taken me nearly two years to get there, where I could once have flown to my destination in a matter of hours. Red Harvest's main compound and centre of operations had turned out to be deserted, bar a few hundred corpses scattered through dormitories and basement rooms.

'No,' I said, shaking my head. 'I can't be sure. Not *really* sure. Some of them could still be alive, if they had the antidote.'

Focus. I took a deep breath, fighting off panic. I examined the bootprints again, studying the path they took. All three sets, I saw, encircled the nearest turbine. One of them had stepped away, the grass flattened where they had approached the first of the fence posts that supported the power cables extending towards my house.

I ran back down and through the gate, and for the first time saw what I had missed on the way up: a single set of prints crossing a patch of snow just metres from my front door. I had entirely failed to see them.

My blood froze as I wondered again how long they had been watching me. I needed to hide, to go to ground. I had a cache of supplies hidden in a church in Wembury; everything I would need to leave this place forever.

And there was Alice again, by my side as always.

'We need to head for the village,' I said. 'At least until we know who we're dealing with.'

'It can't be Red Harvest,' she insisted. 'Not after all these years. Maybe—'

I raised a hand to stop her. 'These people committed *genocide*. We can't take any chances!'

'But what if you're wrong, and they've come to rescue us? Then we'll never be saved!'

I looked towards the house, feeling panic's black tide prepare to pull me under again. There was no time to retrieve anything. I had to move *now*.

But what if Alice was right . . . ? What if we *could* be saved, and there was some place out there that had escaped Red Harvest's murderous attention? Somewhere with people in their dozens or hundreds or even – dared I imagine it? – *thousands*.

Some part of me, I knew, would welcome even a death squad intent on torturing and killing me, so great was my desire for human contact. But the saner part of me drove me to make my way around to the other side of the house, where a second gate gave access to a stream skirting the side of the hill. The stream was lined with trees and bushes that could give me cover as I made for the denser woods on the hill's far side. But where was—?

And then Alice was beside me, her feet crunching in the snow as we ran. I was so badly out of shape that my lungs soon began to ache. I splashed across the rocky stream, then followed an ancient bridle path that would lead me deep amongst ancient stands of oak and birch, their roots thick with concealing briars.

I stopped for a moment, to fill my heaving lungs, and in that moment glanced back. Was it only my imagination that made me think I had seen something moving at the top of the hill, where I had been only minutes before? Or . . . ?

I dived in amongst the trees and kept running, despite the growing numbness in my thighs. How could I have let myself get so unfit? I peered ahead as I pushed through the dense undergrowth until finally I came to a road leading into Wembury.

'Do you hear that?' asked Alice, looking all around.

At first I heard only the sigh of the wind, and the rustle of branches. Then it came to me – a far-off yipping that aroused a primal fear in me. A pack of dogs.

'We should turn back,' said Alice. 'We've still got miles to go, and we don't know how many there might be.'

'Let me think,' I snapped. 'We can't turn back.'

'For God's sake, Jerry – the last thing we want to do is get attacked by wild animals just when we might have a chance of rescue. We need to turn back!'

I stared towards the nearest houses, still a good fifteen minutes away on foot, then back the way we had come. I knew from experience how dangerous even a moment's hesitation could be, but a succession of days that were identical to each other had made me slow.

I pulled my shotgun from my shoulder and patted the pocket of my jacket where I always kept spare ammunition. 'We're not turning back,' I said. 'I've dealt with worse before. Now come *on*.'

One of the things I remember the most from those first months alone in the world is the sound of dogs crying out day and night. Most of them were still locked in their homes with their dead owners – unlucky for them, lucky for me. As for the rest, they wandered the streets in search of food and – once they ran out of corpses to feast on – prey.

I started to move again, ignoring the pain in my lungs and chest. I was close enough now to the houses of Wembury to see their empty windows and the cars scattered across the road. The church spire rose above the rooftops, like a beacon drawing me towards my cache of supplies.

I heard barking from somewhere behind me and knew the dogs were on my trail. I tightened my grip on the shotgun, despite the sudden dampness of my palms, and turned to see a heavyset canine that looked as if its mother had mated with a bear come barrelling towards me, low and squat with legs pumping furiously. Its jaws gaped wide, its eyes white around their edges. I came to a stop and had to fire twice before the dog finally tumbled to the ground and lay still.

I cracked the shotgun open and hurriedly fumbled two more cartridges into the barrel before snapping it shut again. There was no point in running any more; even if I tried, the rest of the pack would catch me long before I reached the nearest of the houses. The best I could do was take a stand and hope for the best.

My heart grew cold when the rest of the pack caught up with their fallen leader. There were half a dozen of them: big, mean-looking sons of bitches with murder in their eyes, flesh clinging to thin ribs. They surrounded me in a half-circle, snarling and growling.

I had, I realized, doomed myself. I had let myself panic, when under any other circumstances I would never have taken such drastic risks. I brought my shotgun to bear on the nearest of them, determined not to let them take me easily. At least Alice would have a chance to get away.

In the next moment, I heard the roar of an engine. I whirled around, thinking perhaps Alice had managed to run back to the house and get our truck. Instead, I saw an armoured van come crashing off the road leading into Wembury and onto the grass, before accelerating straight towards me. It braked to a hard stop and a figure leaned out of the passenger-side window, brandishing a rifle and shouting something at me. It sounded like, *Get down*.

I didn't need any further encouragement. I dropped flat to the ground, shots echoing overhead, thunderous in the still winter air. The dog nearest me seemed to rear back on its hind legs as the back of its skull exploded. Three more of its compatriots rapidly followed, before those remaining took the hint and fled howling into the under-brush.

I lay there trembling in the dirt and snow, watching as the rear legs of the nearest dog twitched momentarily before becoming forever still. My rescuer jumped down from the van and I saw he was dressed in a hazmat suit with a visored hood. Behind the hood I saw the face of an Asian man, with a thick handlebar moustache.

'Run, you furry bastards!' the man yelled towards the trees, firing one more shot into the air by way of punctuation. His voice was muffled slightly by his hazmat suit.

I didn't allow myself time to think. I pushed myself upright and sprinted past him and towards the road, catching sight of his startled expression as I fled. I heard shouted curses and another van door slamming open, followed by the sound of boots crunching on snow. I felt an awful terror at the thought that Red Harvest might get hold of Alice. I prayed she had done the sensible thing and made her own way into Wembury and found some place to hide.

Someone tackled me from behind just as I reached the road, slamming me face-first onto the ground. I tried to twist free, but there were two of them, and obviously in much better shape than I was. I couldn't see their faces clearly because of their hazmat suits, although I caught sight of a severe crew cut as they hauled me upright before hustling me in the direction of the van. My rescuer, his expression more sombre now, pulled open the doors at the rear as we approached. I was then half-thrown, half-pushed inside and the doors were slammed shut.

The outside world was barely visible through thick steel mesh that covered every window. Another sheet of mesh separated me from the front cabin, which was wide enough to take three seats. I knew this because in the next moment three men climbed in the front. The engine thrummed into life a second later.

'You comfortable back there, Jerry?' one of them said over his shoulder. 'You *are* aware we're trying to save your worthless skin, right?'

My name. They *knew my name*. That clinched it. I no longer had any doubt they were Red Harvest; perhaps they had learned my identity from Nussbaum and Keene before I killed them. Perhaps, then, they had spent all the years since hunting me down so they could take their revenge.

I wasn't ready to give up, not yet. I lay on my back and braced myself as best I could, despite the bumping, swaying motion of the van, and started to kick at the rear doors as hard as I could with both booted feet. The metal clanged hollowly as I battered at it with all my might.

The van lurched to a halt after half a minute. I kept kicking until the doors were suddenly yanked open.

I didn't hesitate. I threw every ounce of strength and energy I had left into hurling myself straight at the figure standing silhouetted by the bright winter sun. He stumbled backwards as I roared my anger and terror and ran past him.

The cold winter air bit at my lungs. We were still in the outskirts of Wembury, having covered barely half a mile. There were houses on all sides of me – any number of places I could hide in. I dived into the gap between two buildings, and started to clamber over a rusted heap of a car that blocked the driveway just as something punched me in the shoulder.

Or at least that was what it felt like.

I whirled around to see who had come up behind me, but there was no one. I got up on the roof of the wrecked car, in preparation for dropping down on the other side, but before I could, my legs folded beneath me. A terrible fatigue swept through my muscles with such speed that I slid backwards off the car. I lay there on the weedy gravel, panting with fear and exhaustion as shadows crowded the edges of my vision. I listened to the voices come closer, wondering what they had shot me with.

I closed my eyes for just a moment, and that was all the shadows needed to reach out and swallow me entirely.

TWO

The next time I opened my eyes, it was to see faintly buzzing strip lighting directly overhead.

I jerked upright, to find myself in a hospital bed at one end of a boxlike room, its walls painted in that particular institutional shade of pink designed to soothe and calm the violent and insane. I saw a sink to my right, white cabinets on my left. There was a single window covered over by a heavy black blind that allowed no light through. There were no clocks, or anything that might tell me what time of day or night it might be.

Just beyond the foot of the bed stood a door with a broad window to one side, through which I could see another room of the same approximate dimensions as the one I occupied. It was empty, however, apart from a row of lockers.

I looked down and saw I was wearing disposable blue paper pyjamas that crinkled as I moved. I saw also that my right hand had been handcuffed to a metal rail running along one side of the bed. My left hand, at least, remained free. I yanked experimentally at the chain a couple of times, but it was soon clear that brute force was never going to set me free.

I stared through the pane of glass at the outer chamber. I wondered if I might be inside some kind of isolation unit. If they thought I might be carrying the EVE virus with which Red Harvest had wiped out the rest of humanity, that would make sense. They had shot me with a tranquillizer dart, I felt sure, then brought me to this place . . . wherever it might be.

I leaned over the side of the bed and saw a bedpan. The sight alone filled me with an overwhelming urge to urinate. Despite my shackles, I was at least able to get both feet on the ground and make use of the pan. Then I lay back, still groggy from the effects of the tranquillizer, and fell asleep until Alice came to me.

I came awake only slowly, from a dream in which I had been swimming through an ocean of oil, desperate to reach air. She gazed down at me in alarm, her face framed by the strip lights. She mouthed something at me, and when I tried to reply, no words would emerge, despite a powerful sense of overwhelming danger. She shook her head in frustration, then darted out of sight. I tried to sit up and see where she had gone, but there was no sign of her. I hoped she could get away, escape whatever place we had been brought to, and soon enough I slid once more into unconsciousness.

I found myself ravenous with hunger the next time I opened my eyes. I rattled at the chain in frustration, wondering if their intention was to starve me to death. But only a short while passed before the door in the outer room opened, allowing two men to enter.

One was slight and bespectacled and wore the white coat of a doctor, while the second was tall and muscular and wore a grey T-shirt and cargo trousers. He pushed a metal trolley. His crew cut made me think he might have been one of the three men who captured me. I watched with fascination as they each opened a locker in the other room, withdrawing white suits from within and pulling them on, finally completing the ensemble with visored hoods.

More hazmat suits, I realized. I had been right in thinking I was in some kind of isolation chamber. But if they had the antidote to the EVE virus, as I knew Red Harvest had, was it really necessary to take such extreme precautions?

Then, I remembered: the men who captured me had also worn hazmat suits. Perhaps they didn't have the antidote after all.

They checked each other's suits before opening the inner door. As it swung open, I felt a sudden breeze, indicating a difference in pressure between the outer and inner chambers, and further confirming my virus theory. I smelled coffee and baked bread and felt my hunger grow exponentially, as the larger of the two men lifted a plastic tray of food from his trolley before depositing it on top of the white cabinet.

'Mr Beche,' said the other man, smiling at me, 'Jerry. How are you feeling?'

'Like I've been hunted, kidnapped, drugged and chained,' I answered. 'Where am I, and who the fuck are you?'

'We'll get to that,' he replied. 'First of all, we want to make sure you're well, and then we'll talk.'

'Or you can just tell me who you are, and where I am, *right now*,' I insisted. 'Otherwise, why the hell are you keeping me here?'

The little man's shoulders rose and fell. 'I'm sorry. I don't have the authority to tell you anything.'

'Are you Red Harvest?' I demanded, my heart hammering.

'No.' He brought both hands up in a gesture of placation. 'Rest assured, we're not.'

'Then why the *fuck* am I chained to the fucking bed?'

The smaller man opened and closed his mouth, then looked to his larger companion, who placed the plastic tray on the trolley standing near my bed and pushed it closer. 'You attacked some of our people when they brought you in,' he said, his voice calm but certain, 'despite them saving your life.'

'Bullshit,' I said, trembling with fear and anger. 'You're Red Harvest. Where is she?' I demanded, my voice rising in pitch. 'Where is Alice?'

'Who?' asked the smaller man, baffled.

'Alice!' I nearly screamed. 'My wife, Alice Beche. I *know* you've got her here somewhere.'

'Mr Beche—'

I lunged towards the trolley, grabbing hold of the plastic tray and flinging the food and coffee at them. The larger man ducked neatly to one side, and the tray went sailing past his head before clattering to the floor. '*Where is she?*' I screamed. 'In some other cell? *Where?*'

The two men exchanged a long glance with each other. The smaller one turned to me and opened his mouth to say something, but then I saw his companion shake his head, and he fell silent.

'You shouldn't have done that, Mr Beche,' said the larger man. 'You need to eat. You're malnourished as it is.'

'Why?' I bellowed. 'So I can be good and healthy when you torture me again? Is that it?'

I kept screaming as they rapidly retreated back the way they had come without another word. When they were gone I curled up on the bed in terrible anguish, my face damp with tears as I screamed Alice's name, hoping against hope that wherever they were keeping her, she could hear me. The smell of food while my stomach roiled with hunger was almost more than I could bear.

After enough hours had passed, I fell asleep once more, from exhaustion as much as fatigue. The next time I woke, I found another trolley beside me, laden with hot food. I gorged myself on it until I was nearly sick, then waited to see what happened next.

I learned to tell the time by the nature of my meals: first came thick porridge and coffee, then later scrambled eggs, and later still fish or chicken with salad – breakfast, lunch and dinner. The food was good, far from prison slop, and brought to me by a sallow-faced man of about middle age, based on what I could see behind his visor.

I didn't react, shout or scream, throw the tray around or anything like that. I asked him to at least open the blind, but he wouldn't do it. Why, I couldn't guess. What harm could it do, to at least see the outside world?

My initial panic had subsided, replaced by desperate cunning. I knew my best chance to escape required me to cooperate, at least for the moment. I forced myself to watch passively as the man who brought me my food and changed my bedpan went through the rigmarole of changing into a hazmat suit before wheeling a trolley into the inner chamber, then repeating the whole process in reverse. The most he ever said was, *Good morning, Mr Beche*, or *Good evening, Mr Beche*, no matter what I said or asked.

By my estimation, three days passed like this before they sent the shrink in to talk to me.

On the morning of the fourth day, someone new arrived with my breakfast. He wore a dark suit that looked curiously old fashioned, with a narrow tie and a pair of thick-rimmed glasses and a button-down white shirt; he didn't bother with the hazmat suit. Neither did the burly individual accompanying him – the same man whom I'd attempted to decapitate by throwing a plastic tray at him. This time, when the inner chamber door opened, I detected no sigh of air indicating a pressure differential between the two chambers. My quarantine, then, was over.

He wheeled a trolley inside and wordlessly handed me my tray of porridge and coffee, a look of warning in his eyes. The other man entered carrying a plastic chair in one hand and a briefcase in the other. He placed the chair near the bottom of my bed before taking a seat and opening the briefcase on his lap.

'Guess I'm safe to be around after all, huh?' I asked.

'There is no EVE virus any more, Mr Beche,' he said. 'We had to take precautions, of course, until we were absolutely sure. But there's no trace of the virus in your bloodstream. In fact, all the evidence points to the EVE virus being extinct.'

'But it was airborne . . .'

'Not any more,' the man explained. 'Not even in a dormant form. We checked.'

I stared at him, thunderstruck, still far from sure whether he was lying to me or not. 'Who are you, exactly?'

'My name is Doctor Sykes,' the man replied. 'I can imagine how frustrating it must be for you, being kept in the dark like this. I know it doesn't make any sense right now, but, rest assured, there are good reasons for it.'

'There's no good damn reason to keep me chained up like this.'

'You've been violent,' he said. 'It's for our protection.'

'Why can't I see out of the window?'

'All in good time.' He held up a card. 'Now, tell me. What's the first thing this makes you think of?'

I stared at the Rorschach card held in his hands and laughed out loud. 'You absolutely *have* to be shitting me.'

'Mr Beche, please. This won't take long.'

'I thought those things were a joke,' I said. 'What do you think I am, crazy?'

Sykes sighed, put the card down and picked up another. 'Let's try it again, Mr Beche. Let's just concentrate on the task at hand.'

I glanced at the ink blotches. 'Murdered corpse,' I said, with confidence.

Sykes exchanged a look with the other man, who shrugged almost imperceptibly. Sykes lifted another card.

'My parents fucking,' I said immediately.

'You're not taking this seriously, Mr Beche.' He held up another card.

'My pet cat Mitzy after I cut out her entrails because they wouldn't let me have any cake on my birthday,' I snarled.

Sykes gave me a baleful look, then dropped the cards back in his briefcase with a sigh.

'I don't *need* a psychological test, dammit!' I said. 'We were alone for ten years. *Ten years*, thinking everyone else was dead. I had to go foraging through streets filled with corpses.'

'You said "we".'

'Sure,' I replied. 'Me and my wife, Alice. You've got her here somewhere, right?'

Sykes licked his lips and glanced at my chained wrist. 'Mr Beche . . . you must know she died along with everyone else, from the EVE virus.'

'Bullshit,' I said thickly. 'You caught her and brought her here.' I leaned towards him as far as the chain would let me, and felt a small rush of pleasure when he ducked his head back slightly. 'I want you to know something. She had nothing to do with . . . with what

I did to Nussbaum, and Keene. That was all me, do you under-stand?'

'That doesn't quite fit with what you wrote in your diaries,' said Sykes.

I looked at him, baffled. He opened his briefcase again and lifted out something I recognized immediately. I stiffened, outraged to see something so precious in his vile, criminal hands.

'Where did you get that?' I demanded.

'From the place you made your home the past several years,' he said. 'It's your diary, isn't it? One of them, at any rate.'

I stared back at him, mute. He licked his lips and turned back to some of the earliest pages.

'Alice is the reason I'm here to talk to you,' he explained, passing the diary over to me. He tapped at the top of one page, where an entry began. I stared down at the words, then back up at him.

'Read it, please, Jerry.'

'I . . .'

The words I had been about to say caught in my throat, and my vision blurred with tears. I didn't need to read it; I knew the entry off by heart.

This morning I dug the grave, out back in the garden where Alice liked to sit on sunny days. I talked to her for a while before I put her in the hole, about the things I was going to do, and about how I'd come and visit . . .

I pushed the diary away.

'You tried to save her, but you were too late,' said Sykes.

'She was right here,' I said numbly.

And yet I had written those words. I remembered, then, for the first time in a long time, the journey I had worked so hard to sup-press: travelling across a blighted landscape filled with the bodies of the dead, the air thick and rancid with their stink, hunted by dogs already turned feral. I remembered . . .

I don't remember exactly what I said next, or what I did. All I really remember is Crew Cut wrestling me back down onto the bed, and holding me there while Sykes hurriedly stuck something in my arm. They said much later that I hit Sykes, but I don't remember that bit. Mostly, I remembered all the things I had worked so hard never to have to remember again.

Alice was sitting on the end of my bed, still wearing that same ratty green scarf she'd picked up in Toulouse during our honeymoon.

'I miss you,' I said, my throat so thick with emotion I could barely get the words out.

'I know you do, sweetheart,' she said, and glanced towards the door. 'You stay here while I get myself a coffee, okay?'

'Wait,' I said, as she got up and pulled the door open. 'Don't go.'

She turned and smiled, hair swinging around her shoulders. 'Look at you,' she said, nodding at my wrist, still cuffed to the bed. 'You never miss a chance to do your party trick, do you?'

I frowned. 'What are you talking about?'

'Take care, honey,' she said, pulling the door open and slipping out of sight.

That was the last time I ever saw her. I suppose that's the moment I started to regain my sanity. But at that moment all I could really think was, *Party trick? What party trick?*

Then I woke up for real, and realized what she meant. It had been such a very long time ago, it was hardly surprising I had forgotten.

Floyd had taught me the party trick back when we had been students together, and long before he recruited me to help him try and save the world. His love for cheap magic stunts knew no bounds, especially if any pretty girls were in the vicinity. One time at a party he got a girl to cuff his hands behind his back, before we all participated in locking him in the bathroom. We stood outside, beers in hand and counting down from sixty en masse, barely reaching twenty before he came bursting out of the door, unshackled arms raised in triumph. The last I saw of him that night, was as he disappeared into his room with the girl who'd cuffed him, and a stolen bottle of wine.

Naturally, I had to know how he did it. And since I was his roommate, he showed me, although I was never as good or as quick as Floyd.

First, he explained, you need a paperclip.

Thinking back, I must have been aware on some subliminal level of the paperclip lying on the floor. I had lashed out at Sykes, who'd made the mistake of sitting just that little bit too close to me, sending his briefcase flying, cards and papers scattering across the floor.

I pulled myself off the bed, dropping down on one side of it until I could see the paperclip, lying just beneath the sink. I had a struggle reaching it, chained to the bed as I still was, but I finally managed to scoot the paperclip under my fingertips and get a hold of it.

I unfolded one end of the paperclip, before inserting the tip into the keyhole of the cuffs. Then it was just a matter of bending the wire back, with the tip still inserted, until it was at a ninety-degree angle to the lock. The fiddly part – which I always had the most trouble with – involved carefully working the wire until the inner mechanism popped loose, thereby releasing the coiled spring which opened the lock . . .

I muttered and swore and worked at it for a lot longer than just sixty seconds. But after some minutes of muted swearing, I heard a satisfying *click*, and the cuffs slid from around my wrist.

I stood properly for the first time in days, my muscles aching as I did so. I slipped quickly through the inner chamber door, then gently eased the outer one open too. I felt a rush of relief that it hadn't been locked. But then, why lock it when I was chained up inside?

I peered up and down a corridor, seeing and hearing nothing. There was a window at one end, through which I saw the night sky. I tiptoed along the corridor to a corner where I found an empty nurse's station, a stairwell visible beyond a set of fire doors.

'Hey!'

I twisted around to see a uniformed soldier back the way I had come, his eyes wide in shock. His hand reached for the holster at his hip.

I ran through the fire doors and into the stairwell, throwing myself down the steps as fast as I could. Almost before I realized it I was on the ground level, and I battered through another set of doors until I was outside. The air was summer warm, and I tasted jasmine in the night air. Crickets chirped somewhere off in the distance; wherever we were, it was a hell of a long way from snowy old England – indeed, a lot farther, I would soon learn, than I could ever have imagined.

To one side, I saw a tall wire fence surrounding both the hospital building, its blocky exterior decorated in white stucco, and what looked to my eyes like a military barracks. I twisted around, unsure where to go next, until I saw a wide unmanned gate perhaps ten metres away, not far from the barracks. I also saw a huge hangar, light pouring from its interior.

Then I looked up, and saw something that will remain forever seared into my memory. The moon hung overhead, fat and pale – but not the moon I had known all my life. There was a jagged chunk missing from one side, as if it had been smashed with some monumental hammer that had nearly, but not quite, cracked it apart. I stared up at it, frozen, until a siren began to wail through the night air.

Suddenly I was in motion again, making my way towards a row of jeeps parked next to the barracks. I threw myself in the driver's seat of the first one I came to and found the keys in the ignition. I got it started and reversed hard, catching sight of numerous figures who had come spilling out of the hospital. One of them – the same guard or soldier I had encountered within – raised his pistol towards me in a two-handed grip.

'For Christ's sake,' I heard someone shout at him, 'don't shoot him! He's one of ours, you moron!'

I didn't hang around to ask what they meant by *one of ours*. I gunned the engine and aimed directly at the open gates. I bounced straight through and onto a road that led into the distance. I could see the sea on one side, and the dark mound of a steep-sided hill of black rock.

The road took me towards a town. At first it looked just as deserted as anywhere else I had seen in the last ten years, but as I drew closer I saw lights, and even heard music drifting on the warm, scented air.

It sounded like Springsteen. I again caught sight of the moon's cracked face. An after-effect of whatever drugs I increasingly felt sure they'd been feeding me, no doubt. Who knew what they might have been putting in the food they gave me?

I heard an engine roaring behind me, and glanced in the rear-view mirror to see headlights come bouncing after me from the direction of the barracks. Something pinged off the dashboard before me and fell clattering into the shadowy recesses of the passenger-side footwell. I hunkered down low, guessing someone was taking potshots at me. I reached the outskirts of the town, swinging past buildings that looked dark and deserted. The music and lights came from somewhere up ahead.

I took a corner at full speed, and the jeep fishtailed, its rear slamming into the trunk of a palm tree leaning drunkenly over the road. The impact sent me spinning around, and the engine cut out. When I tried to start it again, it turned over without catching.

I got out and started running. I turned another corner and found myself confronted by the source of all the light and noise: a hotel bar, like a vision from a dead world. I caught the murmur of voices and saw a figure that looked strangely familiar, standing near the steps leading into the interior of the building, a rifle held in its hands. More people appeared at the top of the steps behind the figure as I gawped.

The sound of the pursuing jeep drawing nearer galvanized me into action. I sprinted diagonally across the road, towards a shadowy alley opposite the hotel, but not fast enough. I felt something hit me in the back of the neck and I yelled from shock and pain. I reached up and plucked a dart out from my skin. I dropped it, fingers already growing numb at their tips.

I took a step forwards, and collapsed. I managed to turn to look over at the man who had shot me. He had slung his rifle back over his shoulder: it was the Asian man with the handlebar moustache, the one who had captured me. Instead of a hazmat suit, he wore a garish Hawaiian shirt and had a pink cocktail glass held delicately in one hand.

'Still a crazy son of a bitch,' he said, looking down at me. 'You've been giving us all conniptions ever since you got here, you know that?'

THREE

They moved me to a different room in the hospital. To my surprise, it had a window, through which I could clearly see the moon's fractured face. I stared out at it deep into the night, until I realized that I wasn't crazy, and it was real; and that wherever I was, I was a long, long way from home.

I might easily have accepted the notion I had been transported to some alien planet, but for the fact that aside from the monstrous gash in its face, the moon was recognizably the same one I had seen all my life.

By confronting me with my diaries, Sykes had forced me to face the madness into which I'd fallen during my long years of isolation. I had buried Alice myself. I had even written of the event, so that I would never forget, but had then worked hard to do precisely the opposite. When I thought back to my imagined conversations with her, they seemed entirely real. I could still see her in my mind's eye, standing there before me. But try as I might, I could no longer conjure her into even the illusion of objective existence. She remained a phantom, even as I curled up on the narrow bed they gave me, and I wept and cried out her name, filling myself with a grief too many years delayed.

That night, I remembered with desperate clarity my journey across a dying land to try and rescue her, only to find her dying. I remembered burying her in a shallow grave in the garden of the home we once shared. I remembered our honeymoon in Toulouse, where I had picked up a broken I Ching coin at a flea market, and joked we should each wear one half. And she, despite her derision, and her despisal of anything resembling sentimentality, had nonetheless followed my suggestion. I remembered taking her half of the coin, and pushing it into her cold and lifeless hand, before spading the dirt on top of her body.

I had failed to save her, as I had failed to save the human race. And then I had failed even to join the rest of my species in death. But at least now I knew that this place in which I found myself was, undeniably, real.

I was still, however, cuffed to the bed, and a guard had been posted outside my door, which remained open at all times. Every twenty minutes or so he would peer inside to see what I was up to.

The morning brought me a new visitor: a small, heavyset woman with short dark hair. She carried a tray loaded with coffee and toast in one hand and a plastic bag in the other. She waited as the guard uncuffed me, then she handed me my breakfast before introducing herself as Nadia Mirkowsky. There was an Eastern European lilt to her accent.

'You want to know who we are, and why you're here,' she said. 'In order to explain that, we're going on a trip. But you need to promise you won't pull any more stunts like last night.'

I rattled my chain. 'You've been holding me prisoner without explanation. Why should I trust you?'

She inclined her head, as if acknowledging the point. 'Personally, I think that was a mistake. But they had to make sure you were clear of the virus first, and we weren't allowed in to talk to you.'

Who are 'they'? I wondered. 'Go on then.'

'Everyone here works for an organization that calls itself the Authority. I'm in charge of something called a Pathfinder team. In order to explain who we are and what we do, we need to go on that trip.'

I nodded towards the window. 'Where are we, exactly?'

'Easter Island, a couple of thousand kilometres west of Chile. So if you were thinking of running away again, believe me – there is, quite literally, nowhere to run.'

'So we're still on Earth?'

I saw a flicker of a smile. 'You thought you were on some other planet, maybe, when you saw the moon's face?'

'It crossed my mind,' I said, chewing my toast, 'except it doesn't make sense that some alien planet would have the exact – well, *almost* the same exact moon as us.'

Her mouth broadened into a grin. 'It doesn't, does it? But it would all make more sense if I just showed you, instead of telling you everything.' She nodded at the remains of my breakfast. 'Just about done?'

I took a last gulp of instant coffee before putting the tray down. 'All done.'

She handed me the plastic bag, and I found it contained a pair of black jeans, a grey T-shirt, leather boots, socks, and a pair of shrink-wrapped boxers. She stepped over to the corner of the room and stared into space while I quickly got dressed.

I was then led back outside, and into the beginnings of a sunny morning. A few soldiers strolled past the barracks from where I had stolen a jeep the previous evening, and I stiffened when they glanced our way, but they merely bent their heads towards each other and muttered some exchange as they continued past us. Nadia meanwhile climbed in behind the wheel of one of the parked jeeps and gestured at me to get in.

'And that's it?' I asked, climbing in beside her. 'Just like that, I'm a free man?'

'When you see what I'm going to show you,' she said, 'you might understand us a little better. If we'd just told you everything at the start, before you saw that moon, you'd have assumed we were lying, that we were really your Red Harvest cult, trying to twist your mind. But what you're about to learn is still going to be a shock, Jerry. I want you to be prepared for that.'

I had no idea what she was talking about. 'All right then. Where are we going, exactly?'

'Not far,' she replied. 'In fact, we'll be there in less than two minutes.'

The engine throttled into life, and we drove deeper inside the fenced-off compound within which the hospital and barracks sat. The compound covered about a square mile, and also contained a training ground, several warehouses, a couple of prefab one-storey buildings and the big hangar, outside which a number of trucks were parked. Next to these were two bulbous, silvery vehicles, like props from a science fiction movie, which hadn't been there the last time I had been outside.

Nadia pulled up next to the doors of the hangar and we got out. I tensed as the same Asian man who had shot me twice emerged from just inside the entrance. He was clearly waiting for us. Nadia jumped out and clapped him on the shoulder. 'You two met already, I think?'

The Asian man chuckled and stepped towards me, one hand extended and a wary but friendly look on his face. 'No hard feelings, right?' he said. 'It wasn't personal or anything. Just following orders. My name's Yuichi.' His accent sounded West Coast, possibly from California. 'We just didn't want you to hurt yourself, the way you were charging around the place.'

'When?' I challenged him. 'The first time you shot me, or the second?'

'Whoa, there,' he said, leaning back from me with a grin that was only slightly fixed in place. 'Okay, sorry on both counts, then. I did try and tell you we were there to rescue you.'

'Gee,' I said, 'I hadn't realized. But maybe if you'd knocked on my front door, instead of chasing me halfway across the countryside with guns and vans and scaring the living shit out of me, I might have believed you.'

'Would you really?' he asked me, and in fairness I couldn't be at all sure just how I might have reacted. 'For what it's worth, we were still trying to figure out how to approach you when you fled. After that, we didn't have much choice but to go after you.'

'I saw your footprints,' I said. 'They were everywhere.'

'Yeah.' Yuichi scratched the back of his neck. 'I guess we screwed up a little.'

An awkward silence grew between us. Nadia widened her eyes at me, nodding towards Yuichi in a clear exhortation to shake his hand.

Instead, he made the first move, stepping forward and clasping one of my hands in both of his.

'I'm sorry,' he said, with what sounded like genuine conviction. 'We really, honestly, were worried you might hurt yourself. Both times.'

'Fine,' I said. I didn't really know what else to say, and I was already starting to feel far, far out of my depth. The other man's grin broadened, and despite my lingering animosity towards him, I could detect no trace of ill-will in his forthright gaze.

He let go of my hand and looked at Nadia. 'Y'all set? 'Cause there's a truck due any second now we can take right back through. I already cleared it.' He hooked a thumb towards the hangar's interior.

'Sounds good,' she said. 'Lead on.'

I followed them inside, still utterly baffled as to what was going on. Most of the interior was taken up by two broad circular platforms, each about four metres in width and resting on a forest of supporting struts and miscellaneous pieces of unidentifiable equipment. From the rim of each platform rose three metal pylons, equidistant from each other. The pylons curved in towards each other until only a narrow gap separated their tips. Each pylon was wrapped in thick bundles of steel and copper wire, while power cables connected the platforms to a pair of quietly humming generators in the rear of the hangar. I saw several men in what looked like military fatigues standing or sitting around a card table near the doors, talking quietly among themselves. A coffee machine was perched on top of the table.

'These are what we call transfer stages,' Yuichi explained, pointing to each platform in turn. 'Now watch,' he said, directing my attention towards another man in fatigues, seated before a rack of equipment. Yet more cables snaked from the rear of the rack, disappearing beneath the nearest of the two platforms.

I watched as this operator tapped at a keyboard mounted on his rack of equipment, then he reached up to flick various switches with practised efficiency. A screen set at eye level burst into life before him, data scrolling across it too rapidly for me to fathom its purpose.

A faint hum began to emanate from the nearest platform. The air between the tips of its surrounding pylons began to shiver and twist, visibly writhing. I gaped, uncomprehending, as this twisting effect expanded suddenly to encompass the entire platform. Air swept past me in a sudden gust and towards the platform, ruffling my hair.

Then, where the platform had been empty just a moment ago, it now supported a large diesel truck. I squeezed my eyes shut, then opened them again, but it was still there.

'What the hell just happened?' I gasped. A trick of some kind: a sleight-of-hand illusion, or a switch. It had to be.

The vehicle's driver reversed it down the ramp before coming to a halt. The men lounging around their card table had come forward, and they now began to unload a number of plastic and metal crates from the rear of the vehicle, stacking them next to the hangar doors. I gaped, open-mouthed, at Nadia and Yuichi. The way they grinned made it clear they were enjoying my reaction.

Yuichi stepped towards the truck and had a quick word with its driver, who had just disembarked and was in the process of lighting up a cigarette next to the open door of its front cabin. The man shrugged and stepped away, and Yuichi turned to look at me and Nadia, gesturing to us to join him.

Seconds later the three of us had crammed into the three seats in the truck's front cabin, with myself in the middle and Yuichi behind the wheel. He guided the vehicle back up the ramp and onto the platform.

A creeping, icy sensation formed in the pit of my belly at the thought of whatever might be coming next. I had to fight the urge to climb over Nadia and get the hell out of the truck again; their friendly manner be damned.

'Please,' I said finally, although it took an effort to unlock my jaw and get the words out. 'Just tell me what's going on.'

'The important thing,' said Nadia, 'is to remember that seeing is believing. Like the moon, yes?'

I leaned forward, glancing up through the windscreen at the pylons overhead. The air twisted around us, and the hangar became a smear of light.

'No,' I said, suddenly losing my nerve and leaning over Nadia to try and reach the door handle. 'I don't know what you're—'

I gasped as the ground opened beneath us and we plummeted – or so it felt. For a very brief instant, I caught sight of a grey void all around the truck, and suddenly we were somewhere else.

I stared out at a frozen wasteland. I gasped convulsively and rapidly, my heart hammering with such ferocity I feared I might be on the verge of a heart attack.

Yuichi and Nadia both climbed out, letting in blasts of freezing air. Nadia held the door open for me, an expectant look on her face. It took me a few moments to finally unlock my limbs and join them outside.

The hangar – the island – were gone. The cold bit at me, sucking every last dreg of warmth from my bones and flesh.

I could see that the truck was parked within a circle of half a dozen metal bollard-like objects. A single-storey flat-roofed building stood close by. I looked up to see a sky draped with impenetrably heavy clouds. At first I thought it must be late evening, but then I made out the faintest outline of the sun, almost directly overhead. Undulating dark hills reached out to a gloomy, barely visible horizon, their slopes studded with the corpses of trees.

'In there,' said Yuichi, guiding me towards the building. I needed no further prompting, my teeth were chattering so hard. The three of us pushed through the door and inside, and I bathed in the delicious heat within.

A short, cheerful-looking man got up from an easy chair as we entered, a book in one hand. He nodded in greeting to Nadia and Yuichi as the three of us gathered before a roaring log-fire.

His smile faltered, his eyes widening when he saw me. 'You're . . .'

'This is Jerry Beche,' said Nadia, 'our *new Pathfinder.*' She said this with what struck me as exaggerated emphasis, although she did not explain what a Pathfinder actually was. 'Jerry,' she continued, looking back at me, 'this is Tony Nuyakpuk. He helps run things around here.'

'Hi,' I said, nodding. Tony mirrored my gesture, still staring at me in a way that made me uncomfortable.

'I wasn't expecting anyone,' said Tony. His eyes narrowed. 'Is this on the record?'

'Sure,' said Nadia. 'We're just taking Jerry here on a whistle-stop tour.' She said this in a matter-of-fact way, but from the way she held his gaze, and the uneasy look on Tony's face, it was clear there was some subtext of which I was not aware.

'Nuyakpuk,' I said, wanting to break the awkward atmosphere. 'That's an Inuit name, right?'

'Sure is,' said Tony. 'Anything I can do for you people while I'm here?'

'It's just a stop-over, but we need cold-weather gear,' said Yuichi. 'We're going for a little drive, and in the meantime we need you to realign the stage for a trip to AR-21.' He hooked a thumb towards the far end of the cabin. 'Cold-weather gear still in the same place?'

Tony nodded, and Yuichi led me over to a door at the opposite end of the building. I glanced back at Tony, who muttered something under his breath to Nadia. It sounded like *Holy Mother of God*.

Behind the door was a walk-in cupboard, and I was handed a pair of heavy padded trousers, a hooded parka and thick gloves. Before long, suitably dressed for the Arctic temperatures, I was back in the truck, watching as the building dwindled behind us in the gloom. Nadia had taken the wheel, carefully guiding the truck between two of the bollards.

'Start talking,' I said, feeling cold for reasons that had nothing to do with the ambient temperature. 'How the hell did we get here, and what the hell is this place, anyway?'

'What do you know about parallel universes?' asked Yuichi.

I searched his face to see if he was joking, but he looked deadly serious. 'Outside of a couple of science documentaries on the Discovery Channel, about as much as anyone else,' I replied. 'Is that what you're saying? We're in a parallel universe?'

'Look outside,' he said, nodding out through the windscreen. 'Does this look like any place you've ever been?'

I stared at him beside me. 'I don't know,' I replied, with only a slight tremble in my voice. 'I think you're asking me to believe a lot.'

'I know we are,' Yuichi agreed. 'Which is why we came out here.'

'We're here,' said Nadia, pulling over by the side of the road.

I followed them back out of the truck, thinking again about the moon's fracture and what it implied. Nadia left the engine running, and I guessed we weren't going to be hanging around for long. From what I could see, we were in the middle of nowhere. There was no sign of anything resembling civilization, bar the cracked and broken tarmac of the highway.

A torch appeared in Yuichi's hand, and he switched it on as he stepped towards a sign by the side of the road. He played the torch's beam over the sign as the freezing wind bit at the exposed skin of my face. It read: 'WELCOME TO THE WORLD-FAMOUS WINE-GROWING REGION OF NAPA VALLEY, CALIFORNIA'.

I stared at the sign, then up at the dark and lowering skies. Frozen devastation, in all directions.

'In this particular alternate,' said Nadia, 'Yellowstone Park erupted, big time. Not everyone knows this, but beneath all those hot springs, geysers and attractive scenic routes lies a lake of molten magma the size of Long Island. And the pressure's been building and building down there for millions of years, just waiting for the right conditions to come bursting out.' She shook her head sadly. 'From what Tony and other survivors tell us, they didn't have much warning. There were a few more earthquakes than usual, as well as a sudden, in-explicable outwards migration of wildlife trying to get as far away from the park as they could run, swim or crawl.' She raised her hands. 'Then, *boom*. Enough ash and dirt got blown into the sky, in the space of a single day, to build a life-size replica of Mount Everest. It'll be still more years before anyone sees the sun.'

'And that all means that just about everything died,' added Yuichi, switching the torch back off and stepping over. 'Food cycle shattered, crops failing. Most species went extinct and the forests died. That, along with a catastrophic crash in global temperatures, pretty much did for civilization here.'

'How many survivors?' I asked, even as part of my mind refused to accept the evidence of my own eyes. I pictured them making the sign up and planting it in some remote region, in order to fool me into believing their ridiculous story. But to what possible end? And was such a notion really any less lunatic than what they were telling me?

'After the plagues and the fighting, maybe a few thousand here and there. People like Tony were better equipped to survive, but they still suffered badly. It's pretty much over for humanity in this place, and it's the same on world after world after world.'

'So there's more than just this world, and the one we just came from?'

Yuichi started to pull himself back up into the truck. 'Sure as shit, there's more,' he said. 'And you're going to see at least a couple others before we head on home. *Now* do you see what we mean by "seeing is believing"?'

We drove back the way we had come, to find Tony waiting for us with hot coffee and bowls of soup he had prepared for our return. We sat and ate by the fire, Tony insisting on squatting next to it while Nadia made use of his easy chair. Myself and Yuichi crouched on low stools taken from the kitchen nook.

Tony seemed more relaxed this time around, and as we talked, I learned he was a member of one of several Inuit communities that had made its way south from Alaska a few years before the Authority first found their way to this alternate. Even when he showed me snapshots of a New York half-buried under glaciers, the Statue of Liberty still just about recognizable despite being mostly submerged in ice, I still had trouble believing in what I was being told about parallel universes. A couple more years, Tony continued, and both the city and the statue would be ground down to dust. He explained there were other, similar communities scattered here and there across this Earth, all from cultures with long experience of dealing with harsh and frozen environments.

After we had finished eating, and as we sat by the glowing warmth of the fire, Nadia explained in precise and concrete detail the substance of my new reality.

She, Yuichi and a number of others were all, she explained, survivors of some apocalyptic event or other, on different parallel Earths. Each had come from somewhere identical in most important respects to my own – up to the point where most, if not all, of humanity was wiped out.

Yuichi, I quickly realized, despite the outward appearance of a biker outlaw, was clearly a man of deep learning and intelligence. He soon took over, delving for my benefit into the mechanics by which an infinity of parallel universes might exist. Although not a physicist, I was nonetheless still a scientist, so I wasn't entirely unfamiliar with the concepts he outlined. My comprehension, however, was at times paper thin. Whenever there were two or more possible outcomes to any event, he explained, the universe fractured, quietly and invisibly, so that each of those possible outcomes in fact took place. Creation was big enough to accommodate a near-infinity of parallel realities, each branching off the other and accommodating every possible history.

I learned some of the acronyms they used to describe certain of these worlds; NTE stood for Near-Total Extinction – meaning bad enough to kill most of humanity, but not all of it. TEA stood for Total-Extinction Alternate. The worst was TPD, or Total Planetary Destruction. Along with these acronyms were further bifurcations of classification, such as Category 3 NTE or Category 5 TEA, terms Yuichi and Nadia tossed around with apparent abandon.

I barely had time to take any of this in before we were once again back in the truck, then back at our arrival point. The air twisted around us, and I felt that same fleeting moment of weightlessness before we materialized somewhere new.

Over the next several hours, I saw things and places I can hardly describe. I no longer had any choice but to accept as absolute truth everything Nadia and Yuichi told me.

The next world we visited looked almost normal, viewed on arrival through the hermetically sealed windows of a vast dome. I saw dusty streets overgrown with weeds and trees, and buildings slowly crumbling from decades of neglect. I saw minarets and onion domes, and learned we were in the outskirts of Istanbul – although not, of course, *my* Istanbul.

To step outside, I was told, was to die. We were on an Earth that had suffered what Yuichi called a 'slow apocalypse'. It seemed that decades before, some as-yet-unidentified environmental catastrophe caused the birth rate amongst higher mammalian species first to dwindle, then drop to zero, guaranteeing extinction. Humanity soon suffered the same fate. Then it got worse: everyone under the age of thirty started to die, until the only remaining witnesses to this particular tragedy were a few doddering geriatrics.

The next world proved to be coated in ice to a depth of some miles. After that, we travelled to yet another, with a swollen sun that blazed down on desiccated ruins and oceans reduced to dusty, lifeless bowls.

When finally we returned to the hangar and the island on which it stood, it appeared infinitely more welcoming than it had that same morning.

'And this place?' I asked, following Yuichi and Nadia back out through the hangar doors. The sun had crossed the sky, and now dipped towards the ocean. 'Where does this island fit into your categories?'

'This alternate is a TEA,' said Yuichi. 'Category 1.'

'That doesn't tell me anything,' I said, not quite able to hide my exasperation.

'It means that exactly what happened here is still a mystery. We don't know where the people went, or why, or how. There are no corpses, nothing but a few smoking holes in the ground in the middle of nowhere where somebody dropped nukes. But there's nothing remotely communicable in the air or the water or the food chain, or anywhere else we can identify. Whatever did for the people here is, we hope, long gone. Besides, we've been here a good couple of years, and nothing's happened to *us*.'

'There must be records here somewhere on this alternate,' I said. 'Something that would make sense of where all the people went. *Somebody* must have written something, left some kind of clue.'

'Sure. Maybe they did, and we just haven't found it yet. But from what we can tell, it happened fast, Jerry – real fast.'

I looked at Nadia. 'You said this is Easter Island. That's the one with all the statues?'

Nadia nodded. 'They're called *moai*,' she said. I knew the island's original inhabitants had left monolithic carved stone figures of revered ancestors scattered all across their land. 'It's worth taking a drive out to see them.'

But why are we here, I wondered, on this remote island of all places? A thousand more questions crowded my lips, but I felt sure that for every one of them that might be answered, a hundred more were waiting to be born.

Even so, there was one in particular that overrode all the rest.

'Why me?' I asked. The wind blew across the island's slopes, singing through the wire fence surrounding the compound. 'Why go to all the effort of finding me and bringing me here? You told Tony I was the "new Pathfinder". What the hell does that mean?'

'The Pathfinders are advance scouts,' Yuichi explained. 'We're Pathfinders – people like you, me and Nadia. We're the first people to go in and explore new alternates and assess their dangers on behalf of the Authority. When we're not carrying out research and reconnaissance, we search for technology and data, most often from alternates more advanced than the Authority's own.'

'What if there isn't a transfer stage on the other side?' I asked.

'Depends,' said Yuichi. 'We either take a portable stage through and set that up as soon as we arrive, or we can bring someone back at a prearranged time so long as they make sure they're on the exact same spot where they arrived. That last one's a little tricky, though, so we prefer not to do it too often.'

'Okay,' I said. 'And "people like us" – what did you mean by that?'

'If there's one overriding thing we all have in common,' said Yuichi, 'it's that each of the Pathfinders is the survivor of an extinction event. We all come from alternates where the human race was nearly or completely obliterated – and one or two of us, like you, have every reason to think we might actually have been the last living people on our worlds.'

I looked between them and laughed, the sound edging towards hysteria. 'Just to be clear – you're telling me you're the last man and woman on Earth, but from *different* Earths?'

'It's not quite that simple,' said Yuichi, 'but close enough.'

'You're here,' said Nadia, 'because we're recruiting. There are about a dozen of us, and we all learned how to survive for very long periods of time in extremely hostile environments. In the eyes of the Authority, that makes us uniquely qualified for the kind of work they ask us to do.'

'And the Authority are who, exactly?'

'That's where it gets complicated,' said Nadia, folding her arms. 'We don't really know.'

I blinked, unsure at first I had heard her correctly. 'You don't *know*?'

'We know they invented the transfer stage technology,' she continued. 'But they keep their cards close to their chest about anything else. What matters is that they rescued us from our various alternates and gave us a chance at a new life, when a lot of us had every reason to believe we would never set eyes on another living human being ever again.' Her gaze fixed on mine. 'I know just how hard it can be, Jerry, to be alone for so very long. It drives you mad, pushes you over the edge, until the day you wake up and realize you'd rather end it all than suffer one more day alone on a dead world. After that, it's just a matter of time before you either lose your mind or take the easy way out.' She stepped a little closer to me. 'Does that sound familiar to you?'

'A little,' I said, unable to hide more than a hint of defensiveness. What she had said sounded so familiar, in fact, I wondered if she had spoken with Sykes, the psychiatrist who had interviewed me.

She smiled humourlessly. 'When you get a chance at a new life like that, you don't ask too many questions. You're just overjoyed not to be on your own. I'll be straight with you, Jerry – you're here because we know all about you. We know from your diaries you went all across the globe looking for the people who murdered your alternate, and that you managed to kill some of the people responsible. Most people couldn't manage a fraction of what you've done, and you did it knowing you might well be alone for the rest of your life. That,' she said, 'makes you an exceptional human being, and that is why the Authority want to recruit you to work for them.'

I looked between the both of them, unsure at first what to say. I was still struggling to absorb everything I had been told and learned in just the last few hours.

'Do I get a choice in this?' I asked at length.

'Sure,' said Yuichi. He looked at Nadia. 'Tell him.'

'The Authority can't force you to work for them,' she said. 'But the alternative is just going back where you came from.'

'Did anybody ever choose to go back?' I asked.

She laughed as if I'd said the most ridiculous thing she'd ever heard. 'Are you fucking crazy?' she said. 'Of course they didn't. Who the hell in their right mind would?'

'It's just a lot to take in,' I said, massaging my temples with both hands. 'I mean – Jesus, a few days ago I was staring at a gun in a drawer wondering if I could use it on myself, and now here I am, and you're telling me all this, and . . .'

'I know,' said Nadia with apparently genuine sympathy. She put a hand on my shoulder. 'I had to make the same choice myself. We all did.'

I realized I was crying; whether from joy, or grief, or sheer sensory shock, I couldn't tell you. Most probably some combination of all of the above. These people had kidnapped me, locked me up, shot me with darts, taken me on a roller-coaster ride to places I hadn't even imagined might exist, then asked me to work for an organization that revealed nothing about itself, in return for being rescued. There were plenty of things that didn't quite add up, and I could sense there was a lot they still hadn't told me.

Yet, despite all that, I was desperate to accept what they were offering, regardless of any conditions stated or as yet unstated, because of one single undeniable, irrefutable truth. What they were offering me was infinitely preferable to what I'd had before. I could see in their eyes that they knew this, and that they knew I knew it. It didn't matter, and I didn't care.

'Then I'll say yes,' I replied. 'Assuming somebody around here can tell me exactly what the hell it is you want me to do.'

FOUR

Barely a month later, and a few short hours before I found myself trapped in a subterranean cavern, in imminent danger of being swallowed up in a lake of fire, I found myself standing on the edge of a vast precipice.

Nadia was with me. At our feet, an enormous shaft at least a mile across had been dug deep into the Icelandic coast. The only light came from the stars above, and from Hekla, a volcano seventy miles distant that was undergoing one of its periodic eruptions. Its summit burned red, the fiery glow clearly visible on the horizon.

I was on yet another post-apocalyptic alternate. I had, as yet, seen no other kind of parallel, and yet I knew that by its very nature the multiverse must contain an enormous variety of timelines where there had been no extinction event within living memory. The Authority's peculiar obsession with dying or dead worlds was something for which I still had no explanation.

Integrated circuitry in the visor of my spacesuit compensated for the lack of light, so that I could see where a road had been cut into the walls of the shaft. It spiralled down until it finally vanished into stygian depths, where not even my suit's circuitry could compensate. On the far side of the shaft lay the war-ravaged ruins of Reykjavik, where the Icelanders had made their last stand against invading European and American forces.

According to the readout on my helmet's display, it was a chilly 268 degrees below zero, cold enough that the snow lying all around us was composed not of crystallized water, but of frozen air. As their world spiralled out of its former orbit, moving farther and farther away from the life-giving sun, the atmosphere had grown sufficiently cold that it had frozen into a thin layer clinging to the ground. Beyond my visor lay only hard vacuum, and certain death were I to remove my helmet.

Without an atmosphere to scatter the light and make them twinkle, the stars were bright and unblinking. Nadia had earlier, for my benefit, pointed towards the horizon and indicated the rough location of the sun. I saw nothing except a star a little brighter than the rest, surrounded by unending darkness.

'What is that?' I asked, seeing a dot of red light flash in one corner of my visor. A faint beeping accompanied it. The air inside the suit tasted dry and rubbery, and my throat rasped every time I swallowed. There were other readouts, projected onto the interior curve of my spacesuit's helmet, many of them as yet indecipherable to me. Part of the reason we had come to this alternate was so I could learn how to manoeuvre inside such suits as this.

'Some kind of alert,' said Nadia, her voice clipped. 'I just hope it's nothing to do with that tremor a minute ago.'

As it would soon turn out, it had everything to do with the tremor. As if in response, the ground shifted once again beneath our feet, just very slightly, and I automatically stepped back from the edge of the chasm.

I looked over at Nadia; her face was barely visible behind the visor of her spacesuit. My suit's electronics painted her face in witchy green. 'So what's it about?' I asked.

'Don't know,' she replied. 'The suit radio's a piece of crap. Hasn't got enough range even to contact our Forward Base directly.' She gestured towards the Excursion Vehicle parked nearby that had brought us here. 'Let's head back inside.'

I nodded, and followed her back over to the vehicle, sweating and cursing as I tried to walk in the heavy suit. I felt fitter and in better shape than I had in a long time, thanks to the intensive programme of training the Authority were putting me through. They needed their

Pathfinders fit and healthy, but trying to walk around in the suit felt as if I was trying to wade through rapidly hardening mud.

The Excursion Vehicle – or EV for short – consisted of a pressurized steel cylinder with wheels like rugged balloons and a slit-like windscreen at the front. Once we had cycled through its airlock, Nadia barely paused to pull her helmet off before climbing into the driver's seat and leaning over a microphone built into the dashboard. I stood listening, my own helmet under the crook of one arm, as she spoke rapidly.

'Nadia Mirkowsky here, out on EV-6. I just received a priority alert and felt a couple of strong tremors. Can you give me any more information?'

She repeated this message twice more before a reply came. 'Miss Mirkowsky?' said a voice. 'There's a general evacuation alert being broadcast and your orders are to get back immediately.'

'Evacuation?' I echoed, more than a little alarmed, but Nadia abruptly put a hand up to quiet me.

'Anything else?' she asked. 'Last I heard, there was a dig team down inside the Retreat.'

The Retreat was the name the Icelanders had given to the subterranean stronghold in which they had hoped to survive the death of their world. 'I can't tell you their status,' came the reply, 'but the evacuation order still stands. All I know is, the seismometers are going off the scale, and anyone who's on excursion needs to get back here now. It looks like Hekla's going to blow sooner than expected.'

'Wait a minute,' she said. 'Why can't you tell me the status of the dig team?'

'Ma'am?' When the reply came, whoever was speaking had lowered his voice a little, as if he was trying not to be overheard. 'Comms Officer Levin here. From what I hear, there are three people still down inside the Retreat.'

'Who, exactly?' Nadia demanded. 'Are any of them Pathfinders?'

'At least one,' came the reply.

'Did anyone radio them? Or—'

'We did earlier, but they stopped responding to our calls. We don't know why. Plus, the below-ground relay's down,' Levin replied. 'Can't tell you what their status is, but the Commander's adamant that anyone who can, should prioritize coming back to the base. As for anyone down below . . . I'm sorry.'

Nadia slapped the dashboard hard with one gloved hand, cutting the connection. 'Fucking *asshole*,' she said. 'Commander Barnes, I mean.'

'Who?'

'The guy in charge of the Forward Base on this alternate,' she said by way of explanation.

She was facing away from me, but I could see her face reflected in the narrow windscreen before her. She was staring off into the darkness outside, her face pale and drawn.

'So what happens now?' I asked.

She leaned back in her chair and drummed her fingers on the dashboard. 'Can't leave them down there, Jerry.'

I looked out at the blackness and saw my own reflection staring back as well. 'You want to go down there,' I said, my bowels feeling as if they had turned to water. 'What do you think happened?'

'I have no idea,' she replied, looking distracted. She started the EV's engine and reached for the wheel, then paused and turned to look at me.

'I'm sorry,' she said. 'I . . . wasn't thinking. There's somebody down there who's very dear to me, Jerry. I can't leave them there, not if they're in some kind of trouble. I'd take you back first, but the moment I roll this EV back into the garage, no way is Barnes going to let me take it back out again.'

'Would Barnes really stop you? Even if it meant abandoning those people down there?'

She nodded. 'He probably thinks he's being a pragmatist,' she replied. 'But I don't leave our people behind, Jerry. You, me, and all the rest of the Pathfinders – we watch out for each other.'

I came to a sudden decision. 'Then let's go find them,' I said.

She turned her seat on its pivot until she was fully facing me. 'You need to understand this isn't something you have to do, Jerry.

You have a right to ask me to keep you safe from harm. And, just to be absolutely clear about this – I'm talking about disobeying a direct order. I don't know what kind of consequences that's going to have for either of us.'

I licked my lips. 'But if I ask you to take me back to the Forward Base and anything happens to those other people, it'd be my fault.'

'And if I take you down there and anything happened to *you* . . .'

'Then you'd know it was my decision to go,' I said firmly. 'We go down there.'

I couldn't read her expression as she studied me. 'Thank you,' she said at last. 'I know I'm asking a lot.'

I shook my head. 'Just promise me this kind of thing doesn't happen all the time.'

She chuckled and shook her head. 'It really, really doesn't. I swear.'

'In return,' I said, 'maybe you can tell me some things.'

'Sure,' she said guardedly. 'Mind if I drive while we talk?'

I nodded, and strapped myself into the passenger seat as Nadia swung back around and reached for the controls. I hoped to hell I wasn't about to get myself killed, barely a month after my miraculous rescue, but by the time that thought crossed my mind we were already rolling across the barren landscape at speed, and it was much too late to change my mind.

'Every time I ask Schultner who or what the Authority actually are, he just blanks me,' I said after a minute. Ernest Schultner gave me daily one-on-one briefings on everything I needed to know to survive as a Pathfinder. 'And, yes, I do remember you warning me that's what they'd do. But you or Yuichi or some of the others I've met so far must have figured out at least some things.'

'Nope.' She shook her head. 'Sorry to disappoint you. The Authority come from some other alternate that figured out how to travel between parallel universes, and they've ultimately got some kind of goal. But they're anything but willing to tell us what it is.'

'What about the stuff we're supposed to retrieve?' I asked. 'Can you work anything out from all of that?'

'Christ, no. There are machines, computers and a bunch of stuff that I can't make head or tail of. Sometimes we're sent to retrieve data – computer disks, hard drives, that kind of thing.'

'And always,' I noted, 'from parallels that underwent an extinction event. Have you ever been somewhere that *wasn't* like that? That hasn't been blown to smithereens, or had its atmosphere sucked away, or whatever?'

'Nope,' she replied.

'So none of you really knows anything?'

She chuckled, then reached to one side, patting my thigh with one hand. 'It's good to have you back, Jerry.'

I frowned. '"Back"?'

She blinked rapidly, then shook her head, smiling brightly. 'Jesus, listen to me. I've got cobwebs in the brain. Good to have you *here*, I meant.'

This is what I had learned from Ernest Schultner during my most recent mission briefing, when he sketched out the broad details by which this particular alternate had met its end.

Some years before, a brown dwarf star had entered this world's solar system. Over a period of several years, that ball of cold inert gas, not much smaller than Neptune, had crossed the ecliptic plane at a steep angle before becoming caught in the sun's gravity well. It had looped around the sun once and was then thrown back towards the outer reaches of the solar system.

On its way back out, this dwarf star – named Shiva by the astronomers tracking its progress – had passed close enough to Earth to yank it out of its normal orbit and send it slowly spiralling outwards, into a new orbit that lay much, much farther from the sun. They'd known almost from the moment Shiva showed up in their lenses just what was coming to them. And once it became public knowledge, anyone with a rudimentary grasp of orbital mechanics was able to come to the same conclusion: their world was coming to a terrible end.

When it finally happened, being literally dragged out of its regular orbit triggered unprecedented earthquakes right across the globe. Schultner had shown me recovered footage of vast tsunamis sweeping across continents, of terrible storms ravaging cities all over the planet. The few who lived through it got to enjoy the slow freeze that followed as the sun grew dimmer and more distant with every passing day.

Amongst these people were a few who had been preparing for survival almost as soon as Shiva was first detected on the extreme edge of the solar system. The Icelandic government in particular had thrown its every resource into digging deep subterranean shafts and caverns to shelter its populace indefinitely.

Once you knew a few salient facts about the geography and underlying topography of Iceland, the actions of that country's citizens made perfect sense. Their island home had certain properties that made it ideal for surviving even such a catastrophe: it straddled two continental plates and was dotted with a spectacular number of volcanoes, many of them active.

Like the Iceland of my own alternate, it had long since capitalized on this source of free geothermal energy to heat and power its homes. By the time Shiva loomed in their skies like the harbinger of death it was named after, most of the island's citizenry had already relocated into the deep artificial caverns – heated and powered by that same geothermal energy.

Unfortunately for them, however, survivors in other parts of the world – mostly military, and mostly in command either of deep underground bunkers or nuclear submarines – decided they wanted those caverns for themselves. Whatever it took. They sailed for Iceland even as the temperatures plummeted, armed with weapons of inconceivable destructive power.

The Icelanders had never stood a chance.

Nadia took us around the edge of the abyssal shaft, and before long we were rolling down the steep-angled road that looped around the edges of the shaft. Some of the mountains on the outskirts of

Reykjavik's ruins were, in fact, nothing more than mounds of ex-cavated dirt. On the way down we passed numerous abandoned vehicles that had been used during the excavation.

It took a full twenty minutes before we finally reached the bottom of the shaft and the first enormous door, designed to seal the city within from the harsh environment without. Someone had used nukes to blow through those doors – the Americans, perhaps, or the Russians, or possibly even some other faction within the multilateral navy whose ships were still moored in the frozen sea off the coast.

This hadn't worked out well for the invaders, or the people they were invading. From the presence of their tanks, armoured cars and other weapons of war, it was clear that this army of nations had suc-ceeded in taking the caverns from the native Icelanders, killing a substantial portion of their population in the process. Then, so far as anyone could tell, they had set about killing each other. In the process, they had done sufficient damage to the Retreat to ensure that no one was going to survive the big freeze.

We trundled on down the sloping floor of a long tunnel. The twin cones of light from our headlights were sharp edged in the vacuum. Soon the tunnel widened into an enormous cavern, its walls and roof invisible beyond the beams of light. I knew that the buildings and living spaces all through the vaults were filled with frozen corpses in their tens of thousands, and the thought of so many dead – and so many ghosts – made my skin prickle with horror.

I peered nervously into the darkness beyond the reach of the head-lights. 'So what is it particularly the Authority were looking for on this alternate?' I asked. 'Did they tell you?'

'Officially,' she said, 'all I know is that they're looking for scientific data of some kind.'

I looked at her. '"Officially"?'

She gave me a sly grin. 'I'll get to that. See, back when they started building their underground Retreat, the Icelanders on this alternate had the bright idea of inviting a bunch of really smart people from other parts of the world to come live in it with them. After Shiva showed up in their telescopes, a lot of people around the world decided to blame the scientists, as if they'd somehow caused it. Most of the very people who just might have been able to figure some way out of the mess they were all in wound up being hanged or burned alive on the grounds of universities.'

'Delightful.'

'Anyway, among these scientist refugees was a guy by name of Hilbert Lake, who had led a research team involved in some kind of really cutting-edge physics research. He and his team all upped and came to Iceland when they got the invite, except they ended up getting killed during the invasion.'

'Ernest Schultner never told me any of this during my last briefing,' I said.

'That's because I'm not supposed to know any of this.'

'So how . . . ?'

'Well,' she said in a faux-conspiratorial whisper, 'I heard something from Winnie, who heard it from a guy called Wallace.'

'Winnie? You mean Winifred Quaker?' Winifred was one of the Pathfinders I had met, although I was still to meet a few who were off on various long-term missions. They had been absent from the island base since before my arrival.

Nadia nodded, and it occurred to me that the headlights were now doing a better job of illuminating the cavern than they had just moments before. 'Wallace is another Pathfinder. It seems he was in the base compound back on Easter Island, helping them sort out some computer network problem. He overheard your man Ernest Schultner talking to Kip Mayer . . .'

'And Mayer is . . . ?'

'Second-in-Command to Mort Bramnik. Bramnik's the man in charge of the whole Easter Island Forward Base.' Another I hadn't yet encountered. 'Anyway,' she continued, 'from what Wallace overheard, it sounded like Lake and his team had been working on a prototype transfer stage.'

'You mean they were building something they could use to escape to a parallel universe?'

'Yep.'

I frowned. 'That's incredible,' I said. 'But the Authority already have transfer stages. They can already travel to parallel realities. Why would they need someone else's research?'

She shrugged. 'Just do me a favour and don't ask Schultner, or we're all in big trouble.'

'But—'

'Just remember what Yuichi and I explained back at the start – play your part, don't complain too much, and *especially* don't ask too many questions and one day we all get to retire to somewhere nice and safe.' She frowned. 'Is it just me, or is it getting brighter in here?'

After taking me on their grand tour of the multiverse, Nadia and Yuichi had ushered me into the Hotel du Mauna Loa, back on Easter Island – the place from which Yuichi had shot me with a tranquillizer dart a second time as I tried to evade capture. Here, they explained to me what retirement was.

The Hotel du Mauna Loa was a dilapidated hotel bar that functioned as a gathering point for the Pathfinders. It also catered to a few other survivors whom the Authority had contacted on other alternates, such as Tony Nuyakpuk. The Authority staff, by contrast, tended to keep clear of the place. I had a feeling, based on what I'd heard and seen, that they were under orders not to fraternize with us. Maybe their bosses were afraid they'd let something slip about the Authority after a couple of drinks.

On that particular day, however, the bar had been deserted, apart from one man who turned out to be Tony Nuyakpuk's cousin. Jim Nuyakpuk's job, it seemed, was to cook and clean as well as tend the bar – although it was clear from his conversation with the other two that he sometimes went on missions himself.

'We give the Authority ten years' service,' Yuichi explained as we sat down, his hands cradling an Irish coffee made for him by the Inuit barman. 'Then they let us go retire to some nice, safe alternate – some place just like where we all came from, but whole and unharmed.

That's the other reason we're as happy to do whatever they ask us as we are.'

'*Exactly* like where we came from?' I asked.

'I know what you're thinking,' Nadia had said. 'No, *nearly* the same, but not identical.' She cocked her head at me. 'You were married, right? Don't get your hopes up about finding her, if that's what you were thinking. Even if there was some version of your wife out there, chances are she's not the same person you knew. She might be married to someone else – if not to some other version of you – or have never met you. Or maybe that version of her got killed in a car crash, or her life worked out completely differently so she's a stranger.' She shook her head. 'When we retire, we don't literally go home – that's impossible. But some place that's hospitable, and close enough to being like home to fit, where you don't live in fear or have to risk your life on a daily basis.' She shrugged. 'That's where you get to go.'

'And how long have you got left before you retire?' I asked her.

'Four years,' she said, without hesitation.

I looked at Yuichi. 'Five,' he replied.

'And how many Pathfinders have retired so far?'

They glanced at each other. 'Well, none, actually,' said Yuichi. 'None of us has been working for the Authority long enough to actually retire.'

I looked ahead. It was, indeed, getting brighter. 'What's causing it?' I asked, with no little alarm.

By now we had covered most of the distance across the first vault. The ceiling rose up for perhaps fifteen metres, while all around us stood the empty ruins of buildings constructed within the vault. I had seen maps of the complex's many levels, and the sheer audacity of the project was breathtaking. They had had room enough down here for a hundred thousand people, nearly all of whom had worked in some capacity towards the construction of the Retreat. There were farms, breeding pens for animals, schools and houses and acres of laboratories. Here, refugee scientists had set up shop so they could help the Icelanders improve and expand their shelter deep beneath the frozen ground. Some of them had been working on creating genetically engineered microscopic flora to manufacture the oxygen they needed to breathe in bulk, down here in the light-less depths.

Nadia tapped with one gloved hand at a dashboard screen and it sprang to life, displaying the view to the rear of our EV. It showed a torrent of white fire gushing through a rent in the wall that hadn't been there just seconds before.

'Oh shit,' she said under her breath. 'Is that lava?'

I stared at the image, my lips numb even as the glow intensified. It was bright enough now that I could make out street signs as we passed them.

'How do we get back out?' I asked, staring in horror at the molten rock flooding across our escape route.

'We don't,' said Nadia, tight lipped and as white as a sheet. 'Not that way, at least.'

'But there are other exits,' I said. 'Aren't there?'

'Yeah, but it's going to take a while longer to reach them.'

'Just as long as we're not trapped down here.' The steel cage that had wrapped itself around my chest loosened slightly.

'Go take a look at the maps of the Retreat,' said Nadia, 'see which of those exits is nearest. You know where they're kept?'

'Sure.' I walked, stiff-legged with terror, through to the rear of the EV. Barnes, asshole or not, might have been right when he ordered Nadia not to come down here. I pulled open a drawer where printed maps of the entire Retreat were kept, then spread them out on a fold-down table next to the EV's tiny kitchenette, and tried not to think about the lava slowly filling up the whole vault.

'We found 'em!' Nadia practically screamed from up front, just a few minutes later. 'I got the others on the radio!'

By now, the vault was incandescently bright with lava. More and more of it came pouring in behind us, and showed absolutely no signs of abating. It had melted the frozen air that lay on every surface, filling the vault with dense clouds of gas and dust that pooled beneath the ceiling and reduced visibility to nearly zero. It took an effort to keep my focus as I studied the spread-out sheets.

I came back up beside her, but could see nothing through the windscreen – not even the far wall of the vault, although I knew we were rapidly approaching it.

'Where are they?' I asked, looking over at Nadia.

'In the next vault after this one,' Nadia replied. 'There's a connecting tunnel, if I remember the map. We should be able to just drive straight thr—Oh *shit*.'

Before I could ask her what the problem was, I looked back up and saw the fog had cleared sufficiently to reveal both the far wall and the connecting tunnel directly before us. The tunnel entrance, however, had become partly blocked by rubble – heavy girders from an adjacent construction project had collapsed across its entrance in a great pile. I knew immediately there was no way the EV was going to be able to get past such an obstruction.

'Is there enough space we can at least walk through?' I asked in desperation. Blocked or not, there were gaps through which I could see into the darkness of the next vault. Even if the EV couldn't get past the wreckage, it didn't mean we couldn't.

'I guess,' said Nadia, pressing a button next to the microphone. 'Rozalia, can you still hear me?'

'Loud and clear, sweetheart,' said a woman's voice. 'What the hell's going on back there? There's all that light and—'

'Hekla's erupting,' said Nadia. 'A lava flow's flooding the first vault.' She pulled to a halt as near the mess of collapsed girders as she dared. 'It looks like we're going to have to come through to your side on foot.'

'You shouldn't have come, Nads,' said the woman's voice. 'There were some real bad tremors down here and the EV went into a ditch and we've been stuck here ever since.'

'Anyone else with you?'

'Two Authority scientists I was escorting.'

'What about your towline?' asked Nadia. 'Did you try using that to get you out?'

'We tried. We got the winch running, but it got damaged when we crashed. It's not strong enough to pull us back out of the hole we're in.'

I could just make out a glint of silver in the next vault that might have been the other EV.

'Are they just on the other side of the tunnel?' I asked Nadia. 'I thought I could see them.'

'Yeah, they are. Why?'

'Maybe we can use our own towline, if it stretches that far. Our EV might be able to drag theirs back out of whatever hole it's stuck in.'

She gave me an appraising look. 'Smart boy,' she said approvingly, and leaned over the microphone. 'You hear any of that, Rozalia?'

'I did,' the other woman said, her voice crackling. 'Frankly, anything's worth a try. I can see you too, through on the other side. You're going to have to reverse your EV first, so you can pull once the line's attached.'

The ground shook, and I glanced at the rear-view screen in time to see a building collapse into the spreading pool of fire behind us.

Nadia tapped a button next to the microphone and leaned back.

'Do we have enough time?' I asked. 'That lava's not moving that fast, but it'll still catch up with us before long.'

'Well,' said Nadia, 'it's either this or we all try and walk out of here.'

Nadia reversed the EV until it was facing back the way it had come – and towards the approaching lava flow. The rear end, and the winch mounted there, she moved as close to the collapsed rubble and girders as she could.

There are, I think fewer sights more terrifying than what I saw, looking through that windscreen at the molten rock slowly oozing towards me. A thick dark crust was constantly forming on top of the flow before breaking open, as hotter rock pushed its way out. The first vault was wide enough to contain a lot of lava. But, even considering its slow accumulation, I doubted we had more than maybe ten or fifteen minutes before it swallowed our EV.

In the meantime, the three from the other EV made their way through the connecting corridor to join us, moving ponderously in their pressure suits, and helped Nadia unspool the cable from our rear-mounted winch. I followed them as they carried it back to their vehicle, and I gazed up at the concrete cap built into the roof of the connecting corridor.

Above that cap, made of high-density concrete and steel girders, was a vertical shaft, now filled with a couple of thousand tons of rubble and sand. It was a defensive measure, or so I had learned from flicking through Schultner's mission-briefing pack. The Icelanders had been aware of the threat of invasion by those less prepared for survival on a hostile Earth and, like the pharaohs of old, they'd filled their subterranean kingdom with booby traps. Explosive bolts in the concrete cap could blow it apart, and the steel girders that helped hold all that rock and sand were designed to give way once the bolts blew. In this way a vault could be sealed off, either keeping invaders outside, or trapping them on the inside. I saw two sets of ladders bolted to the wall on either side of the corridor, each leading up to one side of the cap. What a shame their front door hadn't been strong enough to withstand a tactical nuke.

The ground began to shake again. But instead of fading, the shaking grew stronger.

I helped attach the cable from our EV to the rear axle of the ditched vehicle. The cable was slightly bent where it went around and between fallen girders. The stricken EV's rear was angled upwards, its wheels hanging uselessly above the ground. The front chassis was invisible where it had slid into a huge crack in the vault's floor.

'Jerry!'

It was Nadia's voice, but I couldn't figure out which one of the suited figures around me was her. Then one of them came towards me and clapped me on the shoulder. 'I need you to drive forward while I operate the winch,' said Nadia. 'Think you can do it?'

I nodded inside my helmet, beads of sweat forming on my head at the thought of what I was going to have to do. I followed her back through to the first vault regardless, and was deeply alarmed to see the lava was now just metres away from the front of our own EV. The heat at such close proximity was astonishing.

Nadia headed for the winch, while I got back inside the vehicle. I didn't bother taking my helmet off, or cycling through the vehicle's tiny airlock. There wasn't the time. Instead I used an emergency override to evacuate all the air from inside in a few seconds, then climbed on board. I'd already been taught how to drive an EV, and I had the engine up and running in seconds.

'Okay,' said Nadia over the radio. 'Pull forward – but don't take any chances, Jerry. Don't hang around one second longer than you have to.'

I eased down on the accelerator and rolled the EV forwards as tentatively as I could manage.

The vehicle trundled a foot or so forward, and then the engine whined as the slack was taken up on the cable. My heart thudded at the sight of the fiery tide spreading towards me. How long before the lava reached the EV? One minute? Or less?

'Floor it,' Nadia yelled. 'She's moving, but she's still not out of that hole.'

'If I floor it,' I said through gritted teeth, 'I'll drive straight into the fucking lava.'

'No, you won't,' Nadia yelled, with what struck me as a remarkable lack of conviction.

I floored it and felt the rumble of the engine through the soles of my boots. The EV trembled around me and then, suddenly, slipped forward a couple of inches.

'That's it, Jerry!' Nadia yelled, sounding as if she was on the verge of hysteria. 'She's moving! Keep at it!'

I half-stood in the driver's seat, staring with clenched teeth through the windscreen at the lava. It was right in front of the EV now, and getting closer . . .

. . . Closer . . .

The EV surged forwards, and into the lava. Flames shot up around the windscreen as the tyres were instantly burned to a crisp.

Nadia was yelling something, but I wasn't paying attention. The floor shuddered beneath me, and the whole EV listed to one side. Flames were rushing up the front of the vehicle, and I saw the glass of the windscreen blacken and crack as I ran to the rear, where the airlock door was mounted.

I tried to open it, but it was stuck.

'Jesus Christ!' I screamed. 'I'm stuck in here! Nadia, get me out!'

'I'm trying!' she yelled back. 'Goddam son of a bitch . . .'

The airlock opened suddenly, and I fell out and on the ground. I looked around and saw a wall of lava come rolling towards me, barely metres away.

A pair of gloved hands grabbed hold of me and I stumbled to my feet. 'Run, you idiot!' she screamed. 'Just fucking run!'

I ran. We both did, regardless of how hard it was in the suits we wore. I glanced back in time to see the EV sinking into the lava, surrounded by great gouts of flame that rose towards the vault ceiling. When I heard – no, felt – the ground shudder beneath my feet with extraordinary violence, I at first thought something on board the EV had exploded.

Except that didn't make sense, I realized, as we ran towards the forest of girders between us and the next vault. There was nothing inside the EV that could possibly have triggered a ground shock of that nature.

I made the mistake of looking over my shoulder a second time as we made our way through the maze of girders blocking the tunnel. One entire wall of the first vault had come crumbling down, a veritable ocean of white-hot magma spilling through the rent and swamping almost the entire vault in seconds.

'Get on board!' I heard Rozalia yell. 'Nadia, are you there, sweet-heart?'

The second EV was out of its hole, and waiting ready to carry us away. The others had had the same thought, depressurizing the interior of their EV so they didn't need to waste too much time cycling everyone through one at a time. Gloved hands reached down and hauled us up and inside as the airlock door swung open, and by the time I was fully inside the vehicle it was already moving at a fair clip.

'What just happened back there?' a voice asked from up front. I looked over at the driver, a thin, dark-skinned woman, her helmet propped up on the dashboard before her, and recognized her voice as Rozalia's. 'That's the biggest tremor yet.'

'Just drive,' gasped Nadia. 'As fast as you can, and don't stop.'

I heard a hiss as the vehicle repressurized, the sound growing louder at first before quickly fading away. I pulled my helmet off, and the rest followed suit. The two Authority scientists, a man and woman, sat close together on the floor of the EV, clearly frightened out of their wits.

The EV bounced over the uneven floor of the vault with such force that I had to steady myself against one side. Nadia had made her way up front to take a seat next to Rozalia, who stared fixedly ahead as she steered. Nadia murmured something to her that I couldn't make out, then reached over to touch the other woman's hair in a way that implied a great deal of intimacy.

I got a look at the rear-view monitor on the dashboard and saw a veritable ocean of white-hot lava, pouring through the connecting tunnel and into the second vault behind us.

This time, the lava was moving much, much faster.

'If you're going to stay here,' said Rozalia, 'sit the hell down.'

I sat down against the wall just behind Nadia's seat. I could hear someone hyperventilating, letting out little panicked gasps. It took a moment to realize it was me.

Rozalia drove like a demon, but when I took another quick look at the rear-view monitor, I was far from sure we were going to escape alive. Not only was lava still spewing through from the first vault in a seemingly unending tide, but the vault around us was showing every sign of collapsing. I saw chunks of rock and dust come tumbling downwards from the roof.

We passed through a mercifully unblocked connecting tunnel into a third vault. The headlights picked out signs in Icelandic. A fountain of dust erupted somewhere to our right, signalling, I assumed, the collapse of some building or other.

'Straight ahead,' said Nadia. Her fingers stroked Rozalia's cheek. 'We're nearly there.'

'I can see it,' Rozalia muttered through gritted teeth. 'Almost there.'

I struggled upright again, so I could see what was happening. Rozalia had aimed for the mouth of another tunnel, wider and taller than the ones connecting the vaults together. We reached it after a few more minutes of driving, during which the shaking had still not shown any signs of abating. As we got closer I saw there was a slope, leading upwards, and I felt almost giddy with joy. We passed beneath an archway, the EV bouncing hard as it hit a sudden, sharp incline.

The incline got steeper, and I started to wonder if the tunnel would never end. Then I caught sight of a circle of stars directly ahead, and growing nearer by the second. Dust and debris fell all around us, small boulders and rocks falling from the rough-hewn ceiling and rolling down the steep incline towards us. Rozalia swerved around them with remarkable expertise. Then the circle of stars expanded, and we were back out on the surface, just a few miles from where I had first entered the Icelandic Retreat with Nadia.

I stared at the landscape around us, which had become completely transformed in just a few hours. In the distance, Hekla spewed dust and flames high into the airless sky, while rivers of fire, stark against the unending black night, spread all around us.

'Tell me again it won't be like this every time,' I said, gripping the back of the passenger seat.

'Oh, honey,' said Rozalia with a savage grin. 'Don't listen to *her*. That was just for starters.'

*

Thirty minutes later, we were back in the Reykjavik Forward Base for the first time since that morning. The base consisted of a single, large pressurized dome with a drive-in airlock garage, located in the centre of what had once been a park on the outskirts of Reykjavik.

Most of the interior of the dome was taken up by a single transfer stage. The rest of the place had already been stripped of all its equipment and supplies. By the time the five of us emerged from the garage, there were a few soldiers left, hurriedly wheeling the last remaining crates of equipment onto the stage. The rest of the staff had all gone.

'You're *alive*?' one of the soldiers exclaimed in shock.

'Don't look so surprised,' said Nadia, pulling off her helmet. 'What's happening? Has everyone else transferred back across?'

The soldier nodded. 'They have. We're the last to go. I . . . ought to give you a heads up. The Commander's pretty pissed at you people.'

'Barnes?' asked Nadia, and the man nodded. 'Why?'

'You disobeyed his orders,' the soldier replied.

'Who gives a shit?' Nadia barked. 'We saved a whole EV full of people, didn't we?'

Rozalia came up beside Nadia and took the woman's hand in her own. 'Now's not the time, Nads,' she said softly.

Nadia looked at her uncertainly.

A fresh tremor rolled under our feet, and I heard a bang from somewhere on the far side of the dome as something rolled off a shelf.

'We'd better get moving,' said the other of the two soldiers. 'Get up on the stage.'

We all hurried up the ramp and onto the stage. One of them remained behind just long enough to program the control rig before hurriedly scurrying back up to join us. When the air twisted around us and I felt an increasingly familiar momentary sense of weightlessness, I nearly wept.

FIVE

Back on the island, we found ourselves surrounded by chaos.

There were men – wearing civilian clothes, technician's jumpsuits and military fatigues – moving, sorting, cataloguing and loading what looked like hundreds of crates of every size and shape onto trucks parked haphazardly just outside the hangar doors. There was barely any room for myself and the others to squeeze past them all as we climbed back down from the transfer stage. We were all still wearing our spacesuits, helmets clutched in gloved hands.

Rozalia took Nadia and me by the arms and shouted over the din something I couldn't quite make out. The other two who had been with Rozalia, along with the two soldiers from the Forward Base, had disappeared into the throng. I had never even caught the names of the two scientists.

'You!' a voice shouted, loud enough to carry over even the tremendous noise. 'Stay right where you are!'

I looked around until I saw a red-faced man in uniform come storming towards us. He had a tag on his chest that read BARNES.

Here comes trouble, I thought, and steeled myself.

Barnes made straight for Nadia. 'You had a *direct order* to come back to base. What the hell were you—'

'I'm the Pathfinders' elected head,' Nadia interrupted him. 'Did you seriously think I was going to just *abandon* one of my own people down there? And I didn't just get her out – I got two of your people out as well.'

Barnes turned to stare at me, and in that moment I smelled his breath and knew he was drunk. He whipped back round to stare at Nadia, pointing his finger at her chest. 'Don't bullshit me,' he snarled. 'It was so you could rescue your *girlfriend*, wasn't it?'

Nadia stared back at him, having overcome her initial shock. 'I disobeyed your order,' she said, 'because you're an asshole and everyone knows it.'

'Where I come from,' said Barnes, 'we have *laws* about people like you. Do you hear—'

He never got to finish the sentence because Nadia had hauled back and landed a punch right on Barnes' nose. He stumbled backwards, one hand covering his nose and with a perplexed look on his face.

That was when I began to be really afraid of what kind of people the Authority might be. Most of the Authority types I had so far encountered, such as Ernest Schultner, were professional but distant. I felt that Barnes' stumbling, drunken behaviour had ripped the veneer away from that quietly professional surface, revealing something altogether more unpleasant.

Nobody, I noticed, made a move to help Barnes or to apprehend Nadia, even though the incident had been far from unnoticed.

Rozalia stepped up beside Nadia and grabbed her by the shoulder, quickly guiding her out through the open hangar doors. Nadia was still trembling with fury, but she let the other woman pull her along regardless.

I looked around, and then down at Barnes, who was struggling to stand. He fixed me with a look of psychotic anger, and I decided not to stick around. Besides, there were some things I really, really wanted to ask Nadia and Rozalia.

When I stepped out into the sunlight, it occurred to me there was nothing so beautiful as blue skies and clouds. The grass beneath my feet seemed like some kind of miracle after the hellish vistas I had just returned from. I looked around until I saw Nadia leaning against the outside wall of the hangar with a contrite look on her face while Rozalia lectured her.

'You're in a heap of trouble, you know that?' I heard Rozalia say as I approached. 'I mean, did you even *think* before you punched that son of a bitch?'

'I don't give a shit,' said Nadia tonelessly, as she stepped out of her spacesuit. Rozalia's already lay discarded to one side on the bright green grass. 'But did you ever doubt I'd come looking for you?'

Rozalia looked as if she was about to respond sharply, but then her features softened and she shook her head. 'Not for one moment, baby. Not for one single second.'

I cleared my throat and they looked around. 'I, uh, don't mean to interrupt . . .'

Rozalia grinned broadly and waved at me to come closer. Now that I wasn't either running for my life or trying to escape being burned or frozen alive, I had an opportunity to study her a little more closely. She had close-cropped hair with a touch of grey at the temples, and I could see a long, dimpled scar on one cheek. She also, I noted, walked with a very slight limp.

To my surprise, she pulled me into a hug. 'Thank you,' she said, 'for your help back there. Nadia's had a lot of good things to say about you, Jerry.' She leaned back again and extended a hand in a gesture of mock formality. 'And while we're at it, I'm Rozalia Ludke. Pleased to meet you.'

'You too,' I said, a little dazed. 'Exactly how much trouble are we in now?'

'A lot,' said Nadia, gloomily, then tipped her head forward.

'What the hell kind of people are running things around here?' I demanded. 'That man was stinking drunk. I wouldn't put him in charge of a fucking merry-go-round.'

'Believe me,' said Rozalia, 'he's not the worst I've encountered.'

I shook my head and began to climb out of my own suit. 'But doesn't it make you angry that you were sent all that way down there to retrieve data left by someone trying to build a transfer stage? Why, when the Authority already have the technology? It doesn't make any sense!'

'Jerry.' Rozalia said my name with a degree of firmness that shut me up. 'There isn't one of us that hasn't asked the same kind of question, time and time again, and none of us got any closer to an answer. If the Authority don't want to share information with us, there's not much we can do.'

I shook my head, feeling helpless. 'It's not fair.'

'Of course it isn't. Seeing everything you've ever known and loved die and fall apart isn't fair either. Or the fact that we survived while billions of others went to undeserved graves – and I'm betting you spent a lot of time wondering why it was you that got to live, when there were surely so many more deserving of life. But there's not a damn thing you can do to change it, same as any of us.'

'But if we *could* find out . . .' I dropped my unzipped suit next to Nadia and Rozalia's.

'There isn't,' she said, even more firmly. 'Don't do *anything* that'd give the Authority an excuse to put you the hell right back where you came from.'

'Sure,' I said, and looked back at the hangar entrance. I had thought soldiers might come storming out and arrest Nadia, but all I could see was the same hustle and bustle as when we had arrived. Perhaps Barnes was as ineffectual as he was drunk.

'About the transfer stages,' I said. 'Did any of you ever try to . . . ?'

'To what?' said Rozalia. 'Sneak in during the middle of the night and light off for some homely little alternate where they'll never find you?'

I reddened with embarrassment. 'That wasn't exactly what I was going to say.'

Rozalia gave me a knowing look. 'Wasn't it?'

'All right, fine,' I said, nettled. 'What's stopping you?'

'Well,' said Rozalia, 'disregarding the fact all the stages are guarded, you need to punch the right coordinates into the control rig, and the Authority keep those coordinates very much to themselves.'

'Okay,' I said, 'but what if you punched a random set of coordinates into the rig? Surely it would take you somewhere?'

'Don't *ever* do that,' Nadia warned.

'Why not?'

'Because the overwhelming probability is that you'd end up with a null sequence.'

'A what?'

'By its nature, the multiverse is full of parallel universes where the Earth never formed out of the cosmic dust, or where the universe itself evolved to have different laws of physics in its first moments of existence. Or maybe if you program a null sequence, you just wind up in some void between realities. The main thing is, the chances of winding up anywhere remotely hospitable to human life are infinitesimally small.'

'But maybe that's just what the Authority tell you. Maybe . . .'

'Hey.' Nadia waved a hand towards the hangar entrance. 'You want to test it out, be my guest. But nobody's volunteered yet.'

About then, I could sense the adrenalin start to fade, and it was obvious the other two were feeling the same way. Since it didn't look as if there were going to be any immediate repercussions for Nadia, the three of us piled into a jeep outside the barracks and drove back into town. I made my way inside my allotted home and fell asleep within seconds of putting my head down on the bed, still fully dressed. I dreamed of finding myself lost on frozen tundra and struggling to breathe as smoke choked my lungs.

I woke at dawn, when two men wearing neatly pressed dark suits broke into my bedroom and hauled me into the back of a jeep parked outside on the street. Nadia was already in the back of the jeep, looking tired and puffy eyed, and from the way she was leaning forward in her seat, I guessed she was wearing handcuffs. I was still trying to blink away the fatigue when they twisted my own arms behind my back and slapped the cuffs on before pushing me in next to her.

Before long, the jeep was bumping along the cracked and weed-infested road back to the base compound on the edge of town. Our route took us past the island's single, disused airstrip, and I saw the conning tower up ahead, the great dark bulk of the Rano Kau headland in the other direction.

'Nadia . . .'

She hadn't even looked at me since I had been pushed in next to her. 'Don't say it,' she muttered tonelessly under her breath. 'Don't say "I told you so" or, I swear, I'll knock *your* goddam lights out.'

'I just want to know what's going on,' I replied *sotto voce*. 'What about Rozalia? Have they . . . ?'

She finally wrenched her eyes around to look at me, and I saw she had been crying. 'Yeah, they got her and took her away on her own in another jeep.'

'But who are these guys?' I whispered. 'They don't look like soldiers . . .'

'They're not soldiers,' she whispered back. 'They're Patriot agents.'

'What the hell is a—'

One of the two men in front turned to stare at us. I closed my mouth again, and Nadia gave me a tiny shake of the head: *Not now*.

I gave up talking and fixed my gaze ahead. To my surprise, rather than heading straight on towards the base, our driver made a left and soon pulled up before a single-storey brick-and-wood building that looked like some kind of hunting lodge. It wasn't until I saw the multilingual sign outside that I realized it was, in fact, the island's former police station.

It didn't look like anything connected with law enforcement, at least from the outside. Overgrown grass and weeds partly hid the entrance, while overhanging palm trees swayed in the breeze. There was a second jeep parked outside, which I guessed must have been used to bring Rozalia.

Inside, one of the Patriot agents took Nadia into an office, while his associate led me through the back to a cell block.

'Shoes, belt,' he said, as he opened the barred door of a cell.

'You have to be fucking kidding,' I said, regarding him with a stunned expression. 'You think I might *kill* myself?'

'Now,' he repeated, glowering at me. I glanced at the holstered gun just visible beneath his open jacket and held my tongue.

He locked me in and I listened to him retreat down the corridor. The cell had a single barred window, and since I had nothing better to do, I sat and watched the clouds tracking across the sky before I gave up hoping they might let me out any time soon.

I lay back on the narrow bench bolted to the wall, until fatigue finally carried me back off into sleep.

It felt like midday when I woke some hours later to the sound of footsteps coming back. From what I could see out of the window, it was a fine and sunny day.

The cell door swung open, and someone new walked in. He was dressed the same as the two agents who'd picked up Nadia and I that morning, and he was accompanied by the agent who had earlier deprived me of my shoes and belt. The newcomer carried a small metal stool in one hand, which he placed in the centre of the cell, facing the bench on which I'd slept. He took a seat facing me. The other agent meanwhile stood by the cell door with a watchful expression, his hand never far from his holster.

'Mr Beche,' said the man on the stool. 'My name's Langward Greenbrooke and I represent an internal agency of the Authority that investigates various . . . irregularities, for want of a better word.' He spoke as if we were neighbours meeting for the first time over a garden fence. He reached out one hand. 'It's a pleasure to make your acquaintance.'

I leaned back, and fought the urge to shake his hand. 'I think,' I said as evenly as I could manage, 'you should tell me why I'm here.'

Greenbrooke gave an almost Gallic shrug, and leaned back on his stool. I wasn't fooled. He was acting friendly enough, but there was a hardness in his eyes that didn't reassure me.

He grinned widely and glanced around at his compatriot, still standing by the door, as if they were sharing a joke. 'I think you already know, Mr Beche,' he said, turning back to me and affecting an air of polite confusion.

'Is this about Barnes?'

Greenbrooke scratched at his cheek and rubbed one hand over his mouth as if about to broach a subject both difficult and embarrassing to him. 'Well, here's the thing, Mr Beche. I'll be honest with you. I hate to drag anyone out of bed first thing, but I really, really want to know why you and Miss Mirkowsky first countermanded a direct order and then, to top it all, *assaulted* the man who gave you that order.' Greenbrooke shook his head in wonder. 'Why did you do that?'

I licked my lips, tasting salt. 'There were people in trouble,' I said. 'And Nadia didn't want to leave them to die.'

Greenbrooke leaned forward. 'So you thought you'd endanger your own lives as well.'

I felt my face colour. 'That isn't how it was.'

'Do you mean you were involved in the decision to disobey an order?'

'What? That isn't what I said—'

'Wouldn't it also be accurate to say,' Greenbrooke interrupted me, 'that Nadia Mirkowsky allowed her ungodly and unnatural desire for Miss Ludke to override her duty?'

I struggled to control my temper. Greenbrooke was studying me closely, waiting to see how I would react. I glanced past him, seeing the other agent's hand creep incrementally closer to the butt of his gun, even as the blood sang in my ears.

'I think,' I said, as evenly as I could manage, 'that her sexual preferences don't really come into it at all.'

'Even worse,' Greenbrooke continued as if he hadn't even heard me, 'she assaulted a senior member of the Authority's staff. You could have apprehended her at the time, or gone to Commander Barnes' aid. Why didn't you?'

My temper finally won. 'Barnes,' I said through gritted teeth, 'was a fucking asshole.'

Greenbrooke leaned back again, with an expression of quiet triumph. 'On the contrary, Mr Beche, he was trying to do his job, which is organized according to a set of strict regulations that exist – let me assure you – for very good reasons. The fact you did nothing to stop her or defuse the situation makes you, in my eyes, equally responsible.'

'He was goading her!' I shouted, even though I knew I was being deliberately provoked. 'I haven't known Nadia long, but she's one of the bravest people I've ever met. She risked her neck to save three people's lives.'

'Or perhaps she's a thrill-seeker,' said Greenbrooke. 'Perhaps she sabotaged the EV that crashed in those vaults so that she would have the opportunity to make a daring rescue.'

I stood. 'That's it,' I said, raising both hands, palms forward as if to fend off any more questions. The agent guarding the cell door responded by immediately unholstering his pistol. For the moment, however, he kept it by his side. 'I'm not listening to any more of this.'

'Sit down, Mr Beche,' said Greenbrooke, looking up at me.

I stood where I was without moving, and Greenbrooke made a gesture without turning. The agent wielding the gun brought his weapon up and gestured with it for me to sit back down. My legs folded under me of their own accord, and I sat.

'There have been other, equally serious breaches in recent months, Mr Beche. You're new, so you likely won't be aware of most of those, but the fact remains you've been here barely a few weeks and your presence is already proving disruptive. You are aware, are you not, that we can put you right back where you came from just as easily as we found you?'

I reeled back, shocked by the threat. 'I just don't see what any of this has to do with—' I began to stammer.

I heard a sudden commotion from the direction of the cell block entrance. The second agent reholstered his gun, then stepped out into the corridor and walked out of sight. I could hear voices coming closer, sounding loud and angry as they echoed from the white-washed walls.

Greenbrooke stood from his stool just as two more men pushed past the other Patriot agent, who had tried ineffectually to stand in the way of the two newcomers. One of these was dressed in a pale grey suit and burgundy tie, and had the look and build of a retired boxer. He had broad, muscled shoulders and a stiff head of bristly grey hair that stood almost straight up from his scalp. The man accompanying him was smaller and slighter, with thin, pursed lips and almost translucent skin.

'. . . don't have the right to hold either of them, goddammit!' the one with the bristly grey hair was shouting. 'Get him the hell out of there,' he said, pointing towards me. 'He should never have been in here in the first damn place!'

'Commander Bramnik,' said Greenbrooke, 'we have the authority to carry out an investigation that—'

'I said *now*, Agent Greenbrooke,' Bramnik bellowed. 'I'm tired of you trying to override my command!'

This, I realized, must be Mort Bramnik – the man in charge of operations on the island. Two soldiers had also appeared outside the cell door, and as a result it was starting to get more than a little crowded.

Bramnik slammed one meaty finger into the palm of his other hand again and again, like a Roman senator plunging his dagger into an emperor's chest. 'There's no paperwork filed, no warrant issued, no reason for you or your men to be here *at all*. The way I see it,' he continued, his voice still escalating, 'you've just illegally detained two of my operatives in the course of performing their duty!'

'They *disobeyed orders*,' Greenbrooke peevishly insisted, 'and assaulted a base commander, no less. There are strict—'

'Actually, sir,' said the smaller man accompanying Bramnik, 'Miss Mirkowsky has a duty to ensure the safety of the Pathfinders under her command at all times, under the terms of the special mandate they operate by. Within the terms of that mandate, Commander Barnes has, in fact, contravened his own general orders. And as for the assault, well . . . the fact is the Commander has been charged with dereliction of duty on any number of occasions, and if this matter were to go any further, I don't have any doubt that those failings would be brought to light in a most unwelcome manner. Would I be correct, Agent Greenbrooke, in my understanding that Commander Barnes' father has strong personal and collegiate ties to yourself?'

Greenbrooke's face coloured, and he pressed his lips together in a thin line. In the meantime, Bramnik pulled a much-folded document from a jacket pocket and almost forcibly pushed it into the agent's hands.

'That,' said Bramnik, 'comes straight from the Special Department. I'll save you the trouble of reading it: you don't get to so much as take a shit around here unless I say you can. Do you understand?'

Greenbrooke unfolded the sheet of paper and quickly scanned the contents, before looking back up at Bramnik. 'I can have this over-turned,' he snarled.

'Knock yourself out,' said Bramnik. 'There are people right here on this island who owe Nadia Mirkowsky their lives, including members of the military detachment here. I don't think you'd make yourself very popular with them if you took this any further. You can go now.'

'This won't be the last you hear of this,' said Greenbrooke, trembling with anger. 'I've been taking a very special interest in some of those high-flying associates of yours, Commander Bramnik. *Particularly* the Senator. You've had a smooth ride until now, but change is coming. Do you understand me?'

Bramnik looked as if he was fairly close to slugging Greenbrooke himself. Instead, he turned to the two soldiers still waiting outside the cell door and gave them their orders.

'Escort Mr Beche out of here,' he said, 'and wait for me outside. Mr Beche,' he added, addressing me for the first time. 'You're free to go. But I'd like it if you would be so kind as to wait outside until I can have a word with you.'

I nodded and squeezed past them all, then followed the two soldiers back down the corridor while a tumult of voices rose in my wake.

'Goddammit,' I heard Greenbrooke yell, 'we need more men like Casey Vishnevsky. *Real* Americans.'

'He's Australian, you dumb piece of shit,' I heard Bramnik bellow in response. 'This project's still under my control – can't you get that through your thick goddam skull?'

The two soldiers escorting me came to a sudden halt just outside the entrance to the cell block, barring my way. I gave them a questioning look until one of them put a finger to his lips and nodded back the way we had come. It took me a moment to realize they wanted to hear what was said.

'So how many failed missions have you had?' I heard Greenbrooke shout in response. 'How many accidents? Keep going the way you are, this whole project's going to wind up in Patriot hands regardless, and the sooner the better, unless you start running a tighter ship and find some way to control your subversive elements!'

I caught the eye of one of the soldiers. 'Who *is* that guy?' I asked him, keeping my voice low. 'Greenbrooke, I mean.'

'Trouble,' the soldier replied. 'That's all you need to know.'

I heard a door slam, and the soldiers suddenly sprang back into action, briskly guiding me around a corner and into the police station's foyer.

Barely a second after I had sat down on a bench, Greenbrooke came charging out of the cell block, striding past without paying me the slightest heed. I watched as he continued straight out through the front entrance, his fellow Patriot agent hurrying to keep up.

Bramnik and his own companion were next to emerge, talking quietly with each other. 'You two wait for me outside,' Bramnik said to the two soldiers. They saluted and left. 'Kip, I'll be right out.'

Kip nodded and headed out into the sunshine. I remembered Nadia telling me Bramnik's second-in-command was named Kip Mayer.

'Some advice,' Bramnik said to me once we were alone. 'I like Nadia a lot. But she tends to be . . .' He waggled a hand in the air. '. . . a little *strong-willed* at times – put it that way.'

I nodded, unsure what to say.

Bramnik took a seat beside me on the bench, legs splayed and hands locked together before him. 'Just do us all a favour the next time anything like this happens while you're around, and see if you can talk her out of making a bad situation worse. That's all I ask.'

I looked round at him. 'Mind if I ask you something?'

'Shoot.'

'Has anyone – I mean, any of the Pathfinders – been sent back to where they came from for screwing up? Has that ever happened?'

A furrow formed between Bramnik's eyebrows. 'Did Greenbrooke make some kind of threat?'

'If you mean, did he offer to ship me straight back to my home parallel, then yes.'

Bramnik's expression hardened and he stared out of the door to where we could see the two Patriot agents getting into a jeep.

'I want you to understand something.' Bramnik's voice was taut with anger. 'What I said back there is true. The Patriots don't have any jurisdiction here. And we have *never* sent anyone "back where they came from".'

I nodded, relieved. 'What about Nadia and Rozalia? Aren't you going to let them out?'

'I already took care of that,' said Bramnik. He stood. 'What you and Miss Mirkowsky did yesterday was very brave, but it's not easy for me to protect you unless you're right here on the island. Anywhere else, and you're technically out of my jurisdiction. Got that?'

'Sure,' I said. 'I'll remember.'

Bramnik made for the door, beckoning to me to follow. We stepped outside, and I saw that Greenbrooke and his aide were gone. The two soldiers waited with Kip Mayer next to a parked BMW that looked like a well-preserved antique. I saw Yuichi waiting with them also, dressed in blue denim and scuffed cowboy boots, a bandana around his forehead.

'Hey, jailbird,' he said with a grin as I came up beside him. Bramnik meanwhile stepped over to Mayer, conferring quietly with him while the two soldiers got in the front of the BMW. 'I hear they let you out early for good behaviour.'

'What happened to Nadia and Rozalia?'

'They're over at the Hotel du Mauna Loa getting a late breakfast. Bramnik asked me to come fetch you.'

'Commander Bramnik,' I called past Yuichi's shoulder. 'Can I ask just one more question?'

Bramnik turned to look at me.

'Why is it,' I asked, 'you don't want us to know who the Authority are, or where they come from?'

Beside me, Yuichi had become completely still, as if he was holding his breath.

Bramnik's expression, as he gazed back, was as solid and unmoving as any of the statues dotting the island. 'We all deserve more answers than we can find, Mr Beche,' he said finally, then climbed in the rear of the BMW. I watched as they drove away.

'What the hell did that mean?' I asked Yuichi.

'Beats me,' he said, reaching up to adjust his bandana. 'Nice of them to offer us a lift back into town.'

'None of this,' I said, 'needed to happen.' I told him what Greenbrooke had said to me, about Nadia and Rozalia.

'Of course it didn't. The Authority folk are definitely on the conservative side when it comes to certain kinds of people. Like people of colour, atheists, women or lesbians. And Rosie in particular, God help her, ticks all four boxes.'

'They're like something out of a different era,' I said. 'Talking to them is like stepping into the past.'

'Or a different universe?' He batted me on the arm. 'C'mon. Beans and grits on the menu today.'

'How do you know?' I asked, as we made our way in the direction of the dilapidated runway and the town beyond.

'It's Saturday,' he replied. 'It's always beans and grits on a Saturday. Didn't you notice yet?'

SIX

We passed a tumbledown gas station, the harbour on our left, before making our way down a broad, palm-lined street that led past the Hotel Miranda. The Authority's civilian staff were housed here. Finally we reached the Hotel du Mauna Loa, which stood on a slight elevation in order to give long-gone tourists a better view of the ocean. Its front facade curved in a sinuous line, partly hidden behind bushes long grown wild and unkempt, and its lawns lush with tall grass and weeds.

A woman I hadn't seen before came down the hotel steps, wearing cut-off jeans and a baseball shirt. She had shoulder-length brown hair, and petite features that made me think of what Audrey Hepburn might have looked like – if she'd had to survive alone in the wilderness for ten years. I didn't have to be told she was another Pathfinder; I could see it just from the way she carried herself. Even so, there was a distracted look on her face, and she was almost upon us before she even realized we were there.

She came to a sudden halt and made a silent *Oh*, the way people do when they nearly collide with someone unexpectedly. Her eyes grew wide and round when they settled on me, and all the colour drained from her face.

'Hello, Chloe,' said Yuichi.

I watched her try and form words when she wasn't darting confused glances at me. 'I . . . hello,' she finally stuttered. 'I hadn't. . . I . . . excuse me.'

She fled past us with such haste she nearly broke into a run.

'What the hell was that about?' I asked.

'Maybe you should go on in first, get yourself something to eat,' said Yuichi, his eyes tracking the fleeing woman. 'I just remembered I need to talk to Chloe about something.'

'She's one of us, right? A Pathfinder?'

'Got it in one.' He raised his hand in a farewell gesture and hurried after Chloe, who was still retreating at speed. I stared after them both, wondering if I would ever understand the people here.

I made my way up the steps to the hotel entrance and found that the square of coloured card that had been stuck to the door since before my first arrival on the island had finally been replaced. Before, it had advertised *The Day the Earth Caught Fire*. Now somebody had stuck up a new card, which read:

!SHOWING ALL WEEK!
DESTROY ALL MONSTERS, 1968.
starring
AKIRA KUBO, JUN TAZAKI

Underneath was a crude sketch of a fire-breathing lizard surrounded by collapsing skyscrapers, while little stick figures fled in terror. I still hadn't found out who among the Pathfinders felt driven to share their deep and, to my mind, inexplicable love for disaster movies.

I stepped past the deserted front desk and made for the glass door to the left, beyond which I could hear the sound of tinny animal roars and overdubbed screaming. Near the glass door, pinned to the wall, were about two dozen photographs, all of the Statue of Liberty. It wasn't until you looked more closely that you realized they were not, in fact, pictures of the *same* Statue of Liberty. Some were half-drowned in ice, while others rose out of baking deserts. One lay on its side, its head separated from its body, while another was wreathed in jungle vines. Another Pathfinder's idea of a joke.

I could also smell the beans and grits Yuichi had mentioned, and I suddenly felt ravenous. I hadn't eaten since grabbing a snack in the EV a whole universe away.

I found the bar deserted. The monster movie was playing on a ceiling-mounted projector that threw the images onto a bare, cream-coloured wall. I paused for just long enough to see a man wearing a rubber monster costume manoeuvre his way past shoulder-high balsa wood skyscrapers. The scene cut away to Japanese and American actors in a room filled with fake computers, pretending to be thrown about as if by an earthquake.

The components of a still took up much of the top of the bar counter. Most of the liquor behind the bar had been brewed by Yuichi, who had set it up with the help of the Nuyakpuk cousins. A door to one side of the bar led into a room that had formerly been an office, and was now filled with vats of fermenting beer and wine. As well as all this, a couple of times a day either Tony or Jim Nuyakpuk dutifully fired up a portable gas stove to cook whatever was on the menu that day. I couldn't see either of the two cousins around, so I ladled some of the beans and grits into a cheap plastic bowl before grabbing some lukewarm coffee to go with it. It was there for the taking; it wasn't as if we had any use for money in a place like this, after all, nor a bank to keep it in. I'm pretty sure the Authority used cash wherever they came from, but for us at least, everything we needed was there for the taking.

I found Nadia sitting outside next to the pool, accessible through a sliding glass door. Another Pathfinder by the name of Selwyn Rudd was with her, his sailor's cap pulled tight over his fleshy, balding scalp. They nodded wordlessly as I sat with them, bowl in hand.

'My fellow jailbird,' said Nadia, raising a bottle of Yuichi's home brew as I pulled up a seat. Selwyn grunted something at me. 'Now you can tell us all about what life was like on the inside.'

'I heard what happened,' said Selwyn, his accent a deep Welsh rumble. 'Bit nasty, that.'

'Bramnik said he let you out,' I said to Nadia, and she nodded. I looked around. 'Where's Rozalia?'

'Went home to get some sleep,' Nadia replied. 'I've still got too much adrenalin in me.'

'That's the first time I've met Bramnik,' I said. 'You should know he had a huge argument with that guy Agent Greenbrooke right in front of me.'

'Really?' Nadia sat up a little more. 'That must have been a hell of a thing to see.'

I gave a quick rundown of what I'd heard and seen in between shovelling spoonfuls of beans and grits into my mouth, then nodded to the beer bottle clutched in her hand. 'Isn't it maybe just a little early for that?' I said, trying to make it sound like a joke.

'In your ass,' she said, draining the last dregs. 'I've been in three different alternates since breakfast yesterday, and my body clock insists it's Happy Hour.' She dropped the empty bottle back down with a thud. 'I make it beer o'clock, and screw you if you disagree.'

I put my hands up in surrender, then picked up my coffee. 'Now maybe someone can tell me what the hell a "Patriot agent" is, and why I never heard of them before.'

'They're not really called Patriots,' said Selwyn. He tapped a cigarette out of a crumpled pack and lit it, sucking hard until the tip glowed orange. 'That's just what I hear the soldier-boys at the base call them, and not necessarily in a complimentary way. They're like the equivalent of the FBI or CIA or something, back where the Authority all come from.'

'Yeah,' said Nadia. 'I think they're called something like the Department of Political Investigation. We've been seeing more of them around here lately.'

'Really?' I asked.

'Indeed.' Selwyn nodded. 'Greenbrooke – or the people he works for, at any rate – appear to have developed a special interest in how things are being run here.' He gave me a crooked smile. 'Whatever he said or did, don't take it personally. There isn't one of us hasn't had some kind of run-in with Greenbrooke or those other bastards.'

'The point is,' said Nadia, 'not only is Greenbrooke an asshole, he is the asshole by whom all other assholes are measured. Because, if there's one thing the Authority seems to excel at, it's grinding out officious little pricks like Langward Greenbrooke.' She shook her head. 'Jesus. Even that *name*. Some people, I swear, are screwed from birth.'

'I was stuck in that cell long enough that I really did start to wonder if they were ever going to let me out.'

Nadia shook her head. 'They can't touch you. However much we hate them, Mort Bramnik seems to hate them more.'

'Greenbrooke sounded as if he was threatening Bramnik,' I said. 'He said he'd been watching him, that he knew all about his high-flying friends. He also mentioned something about a senator. I don't know what he was talking about, but by the look on Bramnik's face, he was a long way from happy.'

The other two looked at me in surprise. 'I have no idea what that could've been about,' said Selwyn.

'Maybe Greenbrooke let slip something he shouldn't have,' suggested Nadia. 'All he did with me was bawl me out good and proper. He didn't even bother with Rozalia.' She shrugged. 'I just sat and waited for him to get a sore throat.'

'When I was on my way out,' I continued, 'I heard Greenbrooke and Bramnik arguing. Greenbrooke was yelling something about a Pathfinder named Casey Vishnevsky.'

'What exactly did he say?' asked Selwyn, leaning forward with keen interest.

'That they needed more men like Vishnevsky, because he's a "real American".'

They both laughed.

'He's Australian,' Nadia managed to gasp. 'Oh, Jesus. He really said that?'

'Bramnik made the exact same point,' I nodded. 'So what's the deal with this guy Vishnevsky?'

'Well, he's good,' said Nadia, a touch grudgingly. 'Probably the best Pathfinder out of all of us. Charming when he wants to be, but an opinionated right-wing asshole. Under different circumstances, he and Greenbrooke'd be bosom fucking buddies.'

'Really?'

'You can have a perfectly normal conversation with him,' said Selwyn, 'right up until the point where he starts to tell you why the abolition of slavery was the biggest mistake the US ever made, or why only people who fight in wars should be allowed to vote.'

'I would like,' said Nadia, 'to declare this an officially shitty day.' She leaned towards me, and patted me on the head. 'Jerry,' she said, 'I gotta write up my report on your training mission. Keep doing like you did back there, you're going to be the best of us before long.'

'Thanks,' I said. 'But right now all I can think of doing is going back home and getting some sleep.'

'Good idea,' said Selwyn. 'Better that than waste your time watching Casey make a fool of himself here tonight.'

I looked at him, confused. 'What do you mean?'

Nadia pressed a hand against her forehead. 'Fuck. I was going to tell you, but then that whole thing with Rozalia . . .'

'Ah.' Selwyn nodded. 'Perfectly understandable. The rest of the Pathfinders got back here while you were still in the clink, Jerry.'

'I think I met one of them already,' I said. 'A woman called Chloe?'

Nadia's expression froze in place. Selwyn folded one arm across his chest, and used his other hand to cover his mouth.

'What?' I demanded.

'Nothing,' said Nadia, suddenly smiling broadly. A look clearly passed between her and Selwyn. 'Of course. I remember now. Chloe was leaving just when you got here. Did she say anything to you?'

'Not really. Look, what am I missing here?'

'I don't know what you're talking about,' said Nadia. She turned to Selwyn. 'Casey's putting on some kind of show tonight, isn't he? You'll be along?'

Selwyn looked pained. 'You know I find the man morally repugnant at the best of times. Why on Earth give him yet another opportunity to be the centre of attention?'

'*Fi-i-ine*,' said Nadia, giving me a look. 'Just asking.'

'What kind of show?' I asked.

'I have no idea,' said Selwyn, airily, 'but given my previous experience of such affairs, I expect it to be of highly dubious morals.' He stood and bowed in the manner of a Renaissance gentleman. 'And with that, sir and good lady, I bid you a bloody good morning.'

I turned to Nadia once he was gone. 'I've been here a month, Nadia. But I still keep feeling like people are keeping something from me. Including you.'

'You're the new kid on the block,' she said, picking up her empty beer bottle and pretending to be engrossed in it. 'The rest of them are still just sounding you out, is all.' Her eyes flicked up to meet mine. 'You'll be here tonight, of course.'

'I don't know. It's been a hell of a day.'

She gave me a hard stare. 'You know I'm not going to let you get out of this, don't you?' She put the bottle back down. 'C'mon. You can walk me home. We're practically neighbours as it is.'

SEVEN

I woke later that evening with the smell of Alice's shampoo lingering in my memory, so familiar and evocative in that first moment of consciousness that I reached out to touch her hair. She wasn't there, of course. I had dug her grave myself, many years before. I touched the half-coin around my neck, then got the hell up before I had a chance to become any more morose.

I checked the time and saw it was about half six. I'd slept the entire afternoon away.

I'd just finished showering when I heard someone hammering at my front door. I went down and found Nadia standing there.

'Get some clothes on, will you?' she said, when I let her in. I still had a towel wrapped around my waist.

I gave her a disparaging look. 'I wasn't exactly expecting company at home.'

'Thought I'd come check on you in case you forgot about tonight,' she replied, squeezing past me and surveying the oriental wallpaper and gold-and-red striped furnishings of my living room. 'Nice,' she said drily. 'Doesn't it hurt your eyes, seeing this every day?'

'Surprisingly, you get used to it.'

Nadia shuddered. 'Well, I'm here to rescue you. Time to meet the rest of your neighbours, Jerry-boy.'

I wandered back through to the bedroom, pulling on a fresh T-shirt and a pair of cargo trousers left behind by the previous owner. When I came back through, I found Nadia standing by the bookshelf, flicking through one of my diaries.

'Hey. That's private.'

She looked at me in surprise as I swiped the notebook out of her hand and pushed it back into its place.

'Sorry,' she said. 'I didn't realize it was yours.'

I studied her. 'Did you read any of it?'

'Maybe a little.' She bit her lower lip. 'Sorry. Was I being intrusive?'

'It's . . .' I swallowed my anger. There was no real reason for me to be upset, after all. 'It's personal. Okay?'

'Okay,' she said. 'I get it. No touchey. Now let's go meet the rest of the crew.'

Someone had strung fairy lights around the entrance to the Hotel du Mauna Loa, and I could hear music mingling with the murmur of voices from the direction of the pool. The scent of barbecuing meat triggered a sudden, ravenous hunger in me.

I followed Nadia inside and saw Kip Mayer chatting with Yuichi and Randall Pimms, another Pathfinder, although I noted Mort Bramnik himself was not present. But then, I'd gained the distinct impression that he preferred to rule from a distance, so perhaps his presence was unlikely.

I saw more Pathfinders inside. Oskar Boche was propping up the bar, his enormous bull mastiff Lucky curled at his feet like Satan's own lapdog. To my surprise Selwyn Rudd was there, despite his earlier words. He was seated in a corner, deep in conversation with Winifred Quaker and Haden Brooks, who glanced my way with his strange, silver-flecked eyes. Lastly I saw Rozalia and Nadia by the bar, their hands touching and their heads close together as they talked quietly.

All of the Pathfinders, like me, were stationed here on the island between missions. While they waited to find out where the Authority would next send them, they spent their time at the Hotel du Mauna Loa. It wasn't, after all, as if there was anywhere else to go.

I recalled what I had learned about those Pathfinders I had met so far: Selwyn Rudd had been a military engineer on his alternate, until orbital nukes that weren't supposed to exist wiped out the rest of humanity. Winifred Quaker's parallel had, like my own, ended at the hands of a genocidal cult. I had heard rumours that Winifred had actually been a member of the cult responsible, and had tried and failed to stop them once she realized what they were intending. Yuichi's world had supposedly been razed clean by runaway nano-technology.

Despite his appearance and the drawling, slightly stoned way he spoke, Yuichi had been a figure of some note in the field of molecular physics. He had confided in me that he feared his own work had contributed significantly to the demise of his alternate. Randall Pimms I had barely spoken to yet, but he'd apparently survived a mass epidemic that compelled the infected to attack and kill the uninfected. Oskar Boche's home alternate suffered total environmental breakdown and mass starvation. Nadia and Rozalia had together survived a gamma-ray burst, a stellar detonation of a type that might also have been responsible for wiping out the dinosaurs, tens of millions of years before.

Haden's origin was by far the most inexplicable of our motley crew. He had been found on an alternate much like the one on which we made our home, in that there was no apparent or reasonable explanation for why everyone might have vanished almost overnight. He could offer no explanation for his having been left unharmed, nor for the strange silver flecks in his eyes that made his gaze subtly eerie.

As for me? I only survived the end of my world by doing a favour for an old college friend investigating an obscure cult.

Nadia waved me over. 'Look,' she said, nodding over at Selwyn, still chatting with Winifred. 'What a hypocrite. Now come on,' she added, standing and leading me away from Rozalia. 'I'll introduce you to Casey and Wallace.'

We approached two men just as they were in the act of dumping a cardboard box full of assorted equipment directly beneath the movie projector. As they stood back up, their faces were momentarily overlaid with images of B-movie actors in rubber costumes. The taller of the two wore a multi-pocketed vest over an open-necked shirt stretched tight over a muscular chest, grey hairs curling out from beneath the stretched buttons. His chin and cheeks were lightly bearded, and he wore a battered cowboy hat perched on top of a thick mane of greying hair. He also, I couldn't help but notice, had a gun somewhat conspicuously holstered to his right thigh.

His companion – shorter by a foot – had, by contrast, a round babyish face partly hidden behind a thick scraggly beard, and a black T-shirt displaying some obscure hacker in-joke. He said something briefly to his taller companion, then leaned down and began sorting through the box's contents, pulling out pieces of rods and things that looked like coloured lenses.

The hacker-type dude turned towards us as we approached, and quietly said something to his friend. The latter's shoulders tensed in the moment before he turned to greet us.

'Casey,' Nadia addressed the taller of the two. 'I want you to meet Jerry, our new recruit.'

'Mr Beche,' said Vishnevsky, extending his hand. 'I've been hearing about you.'

'And this is Wallace Deans,' Nadia continued, nodding to the shorter man, who wiped his hands on his trousers before taking his turn to shake my hand.

'Pleased to meet you,' said Wallace. I had the sense he was reluctant to speak to me, and he was clearly avoiding eye contact. His fleshy palm felt damp to the touch.

Wallace cleared his throat and turned to Nadia, at the same time reaching into one pocket and extracting an inhaler. He pressed it to his mouth and took a quick hit, then put it away again. 'If you don't mind,' he said, 'we're just a little busy at the moment.'

'I hear you boys are putting on some kind of show,' said Nadia, with forced levity.

'You could say that,' said Casey. He bent to lift out of the box some kind of spherical device, studded with numerous lenses of different sizes and colours, then he let go of it, gritting his teeth in pain.

'You okay?' I asked, as Casey reached around to clamp one hand against his lower spine.

'Sometimes I get a bad back,' he muttered. 'Wallace, hand me that thing, would you?'

Wallace picked the device back up and passed it to Casey. 'Back in a minute,' Wallace muttered, then disappeared in the direction of the bar.

'What is that?' I asked, nodding at the device in Casey's hand.

'This?' said Casey. 'Wait and see.' He grinned, though he was clearly still in pain.

Wallace returned moments later with an entire bottle of Yuichi's home-brewed whisky and a glass, both of which he set on a neighbouring table before pouring what struck me as a remarkably generous measure.

Nadia eyed the bottle. 'Didn't you get a warning about drinking too much, Wallace?'

'I won't keep it all to myself,' Wallace replied, draining the glass in one swift motion before as quickly refreshing it.

'Listen to the lady,' grunted Casey. Despite his evident discomfort, he was busy slotting together a number of metal brackets and rods until they formed a tripod. He reached up to the movie projector, slipping it out of the bracket holding it to the ceiling, and placed it on the floor beneath a table. He next fitted the multi-lensed device onto the apex of the tripod. He poked at it with a few stubby, calloused fingers, then frowned. 'Damn thing isn't working.'

'Jeez,' said Wallace. 'Just get out of the way before you break the thing again.'

I saw Wallace had already finished his second whisky. After seeing Nadia knocking back a beer first thing that morning, I was starting to wonder if I'd landed on the Island of Functional Alcoholics.

Wallace stepped forwards and expertly pressed different parts of the sphere until it glowed softly from somewhere deep inside. He stepped back, and made a number of curious gestures, in the manner of a medieval sorcerer in his laboratory summoning forth a demon.

I'd already guessed the device must itself be some kind of projector, but I found myself taking a startled step back when apparently solid spheres, rendered in primary colours, materialized in the air around us. They hung there in apparent defiance of gravity.

'One second,' said Wallace, making more gestures. The spheres suddenly shifted and morphed into a console floating weightlessly in the air before him.

I realized my mouth was hanging open and quickly closed it.

Wallace glanced our way. 'If I let Casey try and set all this up, he'd break it. Guaranteed.' He shook his head at Casey. 'Some people just shouldn't be allowed near anything remotely technical.'

Casey just shrugged, apparently unperturbed. 'So who's assigned to train Jerry, Nadia?'

'Me.' She grinned lopsidedly at me. 'Not that he needs any more training. Your baby wheels are coming off, kiddo. Officially, your next mission is your first real mission.'

'In what way does what I just went through not qualify as a "real" mission?'

She laughed. 'A point well made.'

'They training you hard?' asked Casey.

'Yeah. Why?'

'Because sometimes it helps in this job to be able to run really, really fast.'

'That does not,' I said, 'reassure me.'

'It wasn't meant to.' He nodded at the contraption mounted on its tripod. 'Hope you stick around for the show, Jerry. It's going to be a blast.'

He turned back to Wallace and they fell into conversation, as various colourful yet immaterial shapes bobbed in the air around us.

Nadia led me a little way away. 'Just so you know, your first official reconnaissance mission is a follow-up to a mapping expedition. Other Pathfinders spent a couple of months exploring and studying the alternate we'll be going to. Believe me, none of us would set foot in the place if we weren't sure it was perfectly safe.'

'That last time was—'

'A fluke,' she said. 'Understand?'

I nodded.

Selwyn came towards us, looking a little unsteady on his feet. 'Goddam you, Vishnevsky,' he roared at Casey. 'What you're doing is in bad taste, even by your usual standards. Don't you understand that?'

'Maybe you should relax,' said Casey, apparently unflustered. He seemed to have recovered from his back pain. 'Besides, I don't give a damn what you think.' He glanced around the bar. 'And I'm pretty sure no one else here does, either.'

Behind him, Wallace made some alteration to his virtual console, and a hyper-realistic, three-dimensional image of the Earth – looking solid enough to reach out and touch – materialized in the air above our heads. As Wallace made tiny adjustments, the globe first grew larger, then smaller. It was so sharp and clear, I could hardly imagine that gazing down at the real thing from orbit could have given me a better view.

'You're showing some kind of film?' I asked Wallace.

'"Film" isn't really the right word,' Wallace replied, with evident pride. 'What we've got here is a far more sophisticated technology than straightforward two-dimensional projection.'

Casey clapped Wallace on the shoulder. 'Couldn't have done any of this without my partner here,' he said. 'He keeps trying to tell me how all this junk works, and it's the best damn cure for insomnia I ever found.'

'Unfortunately,' said Wallace, 'Casey fails to appreciate the technical difficulties involved in hacking into heavily encrypted networks in order to obtain the kind of footage we're about to show.'

'Wallace used to work in network security,' added Nadia from beside me.

'We just got back from an alternate prior to its extinction event,' Wallace continued. He seemed to have lost his earlier reticence. 'That's what you're gonna see tonight. Back where we just came from,' said Wallace, his excitement palpable, 'there was absolutely *no* possibility of anyone surviving. It took more groundwork than you'd believe before we could even *begin* to hack into the networks.'

'Networks?' I echoed.

'Both orbital *and* ground-based military,' he said. 'And was it ever a challenge! Their satellite technology was at least a couple of years ahead of the curve compared to where I—'

'Wallace,' said Casey, 'let's save it for the damn show.' He looked around and saw people looking expectantly at the projection. 'I'd say about now is as good a time as any, since we're all here.'

Wallace nodded and turned back to his virtual console without another word. He stepped backwards, shooing the rest of us out of his way, and the console drifted after him, coming to a halt only when he did.

The holographic image of the Earth grew even larger, until it reached from the ceiling to the floor. Some trick of the technology now made it appear to be floating against starry blackness, obscuring even those people standing on the far side of the projection from me. I wondered if the technology to do all this came from the Authority's own parallel. Given they had invented the transfer stages, I felt sure they must be capable of any number of technological marvels.

Someone cut the music, and I saw a microphone had appeared in Casey's hand. He hoisted himself up on top of the bar, standing carefully until the top of his head brushed against the ceiling. He peered to either side of the projection until he could ascertain that he had the full attention of everyone present.

'You all hear me okay?' he asked, his voice booming across the bar. A last few stragglers wandered in from the pool as he spoke. 'All right, people. Now, me and Wallace only had a couple of hours to edit down what I'd estimate is maybe a couple of thousand hours of footage, but if you weren't there, it should still give you a pretty damn good idea just what we were dealing with on this latest trip.'

I leaned in towards Nadia. 'That woman I ran into earlier – Chloe. She's the only one who isn't here.'

'I wouldn't trouble yourself over it,' she said quietly, then determinedly turned away from me to watch the show.

The image of the Earth began to shrink again, stopping once the moon came into view. It was immediately clear that the moon was a great deal closer to its parent than it should be.

'Presenting our world-burster,' said Casey. 'What you're about to see, ladies and gentlemen, would have made generations of action-movie directors cream themselves.'

I had an unsettling realization that we were literally about to see the end of the world – or a world, at any rate. I had initially assumed that Wallace had used some software trick to make the moon and Earth appear to be so close to each other, but I now understood that what I was seeing was real, and it sent a dreadful chill through me.

Screeds of technical data appeared, floating in the air. None of it meant anything to me. Casey handed his microphone down to Wallace, who then began to describe in some considerable detail just how he had yanked data from a network of military satellites in order to gain most of the footage we were now watching.

'We're still working on the question of just how this particular extinction event came about,' said Wallace, 'but the most likely culprit is a high-energy physics experiment attempting to generate artificial gravitational waves. On a technical note, I—'

Casey reached down and grabbed the microphone back before Wallace could continue, and I heard a titter from someone in the audience.

'Right,' said Casey. '*However* the hell it happened, the results are startlingly clear. We stitched together all that orbital stuff with some ground-based surveillance footage to give you a pretty accurate depiction of just how things went down in the final hours.'

Wallace had returned his attention to his console. The image juddered and changed so that we all saw the Earth from low orbit. Clouds cast shadows over Asia Minor, far below. The moon, far larger than it should have been, hung huge above the curving horizon. I could tell from the exaggerated pace of the clouds that the footage had been sped up so that hours passed in minutes. I could have walked all the way around the projection if I had wanted, and Oskar in fact began to do precisely this, peering first at the Antarctic continent and then back at the approaching moon.

I could see what was coming, with dreadful inevitability.

'They knew they were going to die,' Casey continued, 'but someone down there still wanted to witness the whole damn thing for as long as they could.' He shrugged. 'Maybe the people in charge of their communications networks were crazy enough to think they could somehow survive. If not for them, we wouldn't have hardly any of this.'

A number of separate, two-dimensional moving images appeared, arranged in a ring around the Earth about level with the Antarctic. They showed what looked like ground-based views of the approaching moon. One in particular caught my attention. It appeared to have been filmed on a hand-held camera, its owner directing its lens towards the distorted face of the falling moon. Luna's craters and hills were entirely visible with the naked eye; indeed, the ancient satellite blocked out much of the sky as it rose over a savannah plain. As I watched, deep cracks appeared in its crust, growing wider and deeper with every passing second, like something out of a nightmare.

'How could they get this footage, if the guy was down on the ground while all this was happening?' I whispered to Nadia, but she just shook her head.

'Wallace's a wizard at this stuff,' she whispered back. 'That's all you need to know.'

I tore my gaze from the awful sight and moved my attention to another of the accompanying videos. This one showed a different view from orbit, and I watched an enormous shadow crawl across the face of the Earth.

I put one hand to my belly, feeling my insides twist. The things I had lived through back on my own alternate, as terrible as they were, barely compared to what I was witnessing. If some other version of me had lived on that world, he would have been under no illusions about his chances of survival.

'It took a month for their Moon to spiral all the way down from its usual orbit and towards the Earth,' said Casey, continuing his narration. 'We've got evidence there was some kind of attempt to build a ship at record speed, presumably to blast a few survivors off towards Mars, but I think they realized pretty soon that wasn't going to work.'

'Why not?' somebody shouted out. Someone else laughed, and I realized that many of those people around me, rather than being appalled, were in fact *enjoying* the spectacle.

'There's no way to create a long-term sustainable living environment under that kind of time limit,' Casey replied easily. 'They could have survived for a couple of years maybe, perhaps a little longer, but no more than that. I guess they decided they'd rather die quickly with the rest of humanity than face a long, slow death with no possibility of rescue.' He shrugged. 'Either that, or they killed each other fighting for a berth on the ship.'

'I'm not sure I can watch this,' I muttered to Nadia.

'Stick around,' she muttered. 'You need to get hardened to stuff like this, Jerry.'

'Now this mission,' Casey continued, 'was about collecting observational data for a change, instead of bloody artefact retrieval. Specifically, it was about. . .' He frowned and glanced over at Wallace. 'What the hell did they call it again?'

'"The interaction between two co-orbiting bodies following a quantum-phase trigger event",' Wallace replied.

'Yeah,' said Casey. 'That. Whatever the fuck *that* is.' That got him a few laughs from around the room.

I swallowed hard as the show continued. Whoever had been wielding the hand-held camera had somehow managed to keep a steady focus on the surface of the moon as it rushed towards them, the cracks in its surface growing yet wider. I couldn't imagine what kind of fortitude it took to just stand there and watch, instead of screaming and running.

I glanced back at the main projection, and saw there was something odd about the shape of both worlds. Their outlines were becoming distended where they were closest, as if they were being twisted out of shape.

Over the next minute the darkness separating the two worlds reduced to a narrow gap, then a sliver and, finally, nothing. The moon had by now become egg-shaped, with enormous fissures reaching around to its far side. Brilliant incandescent light flared where the two bodies met, and from that moment on they appeared to merge into each other, the moon sinking deep into the Earth's crust like a pebble dropped into wet mud. I saw lunar craters melting into molten slag before they, too, were sucked deep within the Earth's embrace.

Unbelievably, the view of the savannah continued. The moon had made contact with the ground at some point perhaps a thousand miles farther over the horizon from whoever was wielding the camera, and they now directed its gaze towards a great dark dome, tinted deep blue with distance, and sinking slowly downwards. A line of fire burned along the horizon, growing wider and taller. Great dust clouds at its base spread and darkened as they rushed towards the lens.

For whose benefit, I wondered, had they been recording all this? Or was it that witnessing the vehicle of their passing, from the other side of a camera lens, somehow made it seem less real?

Suddenly, all across the savannah, birds rose in great dark clouds, even as streaks of cirrus high in the atmosphere suddenly evaporated. The ground tilted, and fire shot upwards from distant black hills as magma was released from deep beneath the Earth's crust.

Dust rose in great clouds, obscuring the view, but not so much that I couldn't see the vast wall of superheated rock and lava sweeping over the hills and towards the camera . . .

The picture cut off. I drew a shuddering breath, realizing I'd been holding it in all this time. I had to force my hands, now damp with sweat, to unclench. I wiped them on my shirt, and tried to retrieve my scattered nerves.

Despite this I steeled myself, and continued to watch. If the rest of them could do it, so could I. As Nadia had said: I might well see far worse things than this.

All of the views of the merged Earth and moon were now from orbit. The planet's crust rippled like water, white-hot where the moon had collided with it, the colour fading to a deep burned orange farther around the globe. There were no longer any recognizable continents or oceans, only an endless ocean of fire as magma swallowed up the great landmasses.

And through it all Casey kept talking, narrating the whole damn thing, glancing occasionally at a piece of much-folded paper in one hand to remind himself of what he wanted to say.

I turned away, finally unable to bear any more. Casey's voice boomed in my ears like a particularly raucous, drunken angel sounding the final trumpet. And then I heard angry shouting, and turned back to see Selwyn, red-faced with fury, staring up at Casey with his hands balled into fists.

'Damn you, Vishnevsky! You have no respect for human life. You can't treat this as an entertainment!'

Casey said something I didn't catch. Selwyn responded by noisily pushing past the people nearest him, almost tripping over Oskar's enormous hound in the process.

I'd had enough too, but I wanted my exit to be rather more quiet and unobtrusive than Selwyn's. Perhaps, I thought, I could catch the little Welshman outside, and talk to him about what we had just seen. But as I quietly stepped towards the open patio door and made my way out past the pool, I could feel all of their eyes boring into my back regardless.

I quickened my pace, walking all the way around the side of the hotel until I was back at the front entrance. I breathed in deep, feeling as if my lungs were clogged with soot and ashes.

I couldn't see Selwyn Rudd anywhere, but then my attention was drawn towards a figure making its way along the road by the harbour. Whoever it was, it clearly wasn't Selwyn, particularly since it was coming towards the hotel, rather than away from it. It wasn't until the figure drew closer that I saw it was Chloe, the woman Yuichi had run off to speak to. It struck me in that moment, now that I could see her more clearly and she wasn't actively fleeing from my presence, that she was actually quite beautiful.

'Hi,' I said, stepping towards her. She appeared once again to be deep in contemplation. She looked up and saw me, slowly coming to a halt near the hotel steps. This time, at least, she didn't look as if she was going to run away, even though she regarded me with nearly as much trepidation as before.

I nodded towards the bar, Casey's amplified voice still booming noisily through the air. 'So how come you weren't in there with the rest of them?' I asked.

She shook her head. 'Because . . .' I waited as she searched for the right words. 'Because I knew Casey was just going to do his best to remind everyone he's an attention-seeking moron.'

'So you know what he's doing in there?'

'I was on that expedition with him,' she replied. Her whole body seemed tense with nervous energy. 'I've seen the footage already. Having to watch it first time around was bad enough.'

I glanced back towards the entrance at a sudden squeal of feedback, followed by a murmur of voices. Someone put on some music, and I guessed the show was finally over.

'I think they're done in there,' I said. I patted my pockets as if I was looking for a wallet, then looked up at her with a frown. 'I'd stand you a drink, but I'm a little short right now.'

That got a flicker of a smile, and I realized that her cheeks were damp with tears.

'Look,' I said carefully, 'I don't know if this makes any sense, but I have the weirdest feeling that we got off on the wrong foot somehow. So if there's anything at all I can do to—'

Suddenly her arms were around me, pulling my head down towards hers, her lips pushed against mine.

My nostrils filled with the scent of her; my senses were overwhelmed by the touch of her skin until I felt almost drunk on her. It had been so very, very long since I had held a woman in my arms, and I revelled in the smooth, soft sensuality of her body beneath the thin material of her shirt. I only gradually became aware that I was painfully erect.

Then, just as quickly, she was gone, running back into the night, vanished within seconds into the shadows of the nearby houses as she fled for the second time that day. I stared after her, speechless and bewildered and groggy and still full of the taste of her lips.

Some instinct made me turn to see Nadia standing on the steps behind me, with a look of terrible sadness on her face. I wondered how long she had been standing there, and how much she had seen.

'I don't understand what just happened,' I said, waving my hand after Chloe. 'Why did she—'

'I'm sorry, Jerry,' she said.

'Sorry? What for?' I demanded.

She opened her mouth, then seemed to change her mind about whatever she might have been about to say.

'Just go home,' she said instead, turning away.

'Wait.' I stepped closer. 'Why did she—'

'Go *home*,' Nadia repeated, much more forcefully this time.

I watched Nadia disappear back inside the hotel, feeling nearly as distressed as I had the day I found myself being tracked through woods by a retrieval team intent on rescuing me – whether I liked it or not.

EIGHT

A week later, and not long before midnight, I reported to the base compound outside town, and the hangar housing the transfer stages.

I'd had little in the way of free time in the month following my release from quarantine. When I wasn't undergoing weight-training and cardio in a gym, I was receiving constant check-ups and such a variety and quantity of shots that I eventually gave up asking what they were all for. One of my trainers, whose job was to teach me how to track both people and animals as well as evade them, claimed to be half-Navajo. I learned as best I could, and any remaining traces of fat in my body were soon replaced by lean, hard muscle.

You might wonder what a man who managed to survive alone on a desolate world for more than a decade might have to learn in terms of survival skills. But everything I had done to keep myself alive during those long, hard years had been learned through trial and error – with the emphasis on error. In my desperation to find more of the antidote Red Harvest had developed, and which kept me alive, I had taken such enormous risks that it pained me to remember them. The fact that I had survived at all had been as much down to luck as anything else.

My last week of training following Casey Vishnevsky's apocalyptic brand of show-and-tell, however, had more to do with logistics and operational procedures. I learned how to program a transfer stage control rig to get me back to the island in an emergency. I learned more about the 'null sequences' Nadia had warned me of, and how very dangerous inputting one could be. They showed me how to operate the specialized walkie-talkies used by the Pathfinders, and how to set up an impromptu communications network in case the main one failed. Finally I learned about the automated reconnaissance drones they used, and how they could be controlled through a computer built into the control rig itself. They could also be operated from remote machines that were essentially rugged laptops. There was more than enough to keep me too tired and worn out to do anything remotely resembling socializing, let alone have the leisure to wonder about that whole bizarre encounter with Chloe.

I had other things on my mind too. Earlier that week, while grabbing something to eat at the Hotel du Mauna Loa, I had learned from Nadia just how the whole Pathfinder project came into existence.

'Casey Vishnevsky was the first of us they retrieved,' she had explained over a bowl of broth, a bottle of beer by her side. 'They didn't go looking for him. They just found him, while they were exploring his alternate.'

'And he was the last man alive there?'

She chuckled and took a sip of her beer. 'Who knows? Maybe there were other people out there, but they didn't happen to find them. Are you certain there was no one left alive anywhere on your alternate?'

'No, of course not. There might have been, but . . .'

She nodded. 'No way of knowing. Anyway, they interviewed him, since he was a witness to the extinction event that did for his world. Once he understood they were trying to find something of value to them, he became a kind of native guide. I think he was worried that, if he didn't, they might leave him there. Anyway, that worked out so well that they took him along on a couple of expeditions to other post-extinction alternates, and he was so damn good at it they figured that if they were exploring those places, they might as well take a look and see if they could find anyone else who might be as useful as him.'

'And that's how they found you and Rozalia and all the rest?'

She nodded. 'Bingo. Same for all of us. I guess the kind of people who have the stamina and determination to survive, when everyone else around them is dead, also have some quality that makes them good at pathfinding.' She drank more of her beer and let out a loud burp. 'Not to mention,' she added, 'that we were all so fucking *delirious* at being saved, we'd have done just about literally anything in return for not having to stay where they found us one second longer.'

'It still doesn't explain . . .'

'Stop right there.' She gave me a slightly unfocused look, and I wondered how many beers she'd had before I arrived.

'You don't even know what I was going to say!'

'Yes, I do. You still want to know the ultimate purpose of all this, what we're looking for, *why* we're looking for it, what the Authority get out of it, and why these particular worlds.'

I shrugged. 'Well?'

'Focus on the reward,' she said, leaning towards me slightly. 'Stop asking questions none of us can answer and just do what you have to, so they let you retire. Nothing else matters.' She fixed me with a steady gaze. 'Understand? *Nothing else matters.*'

What I was slowly coming to understand was that I hadn't been far off the mark when I'd wondered if I was surrounded by functional alcoholics. The amount of booze the Pathfinders collectively went through was prodigious, as if by drinking themselves into oblivion they could avoid asking themselves the very same questions that still plagued me. When I found Oskar and Haden standing on one of the stages, along with Oskar's monstrous hound, Lucky, and a vehicle that looked like a cross between an SUV and a tank, I didn't fail to notice that Oskar's eyes were bloodshot. Haden seemed to be the exception to the rule in that I had never seen him drink alcohol.

'Got your shots?' asked a slightly green Oskar, as I joined him and Haden on the stage. I rubbed my arm where a medic had given me multiple injections the previous day and nodded. Oskar's bull mastiff came over to sniff at me before collapsing back at her master's feet in a sprawl. A technician sat next to the stage's control rig, looking bored.

'Sure I have,' I replied. 'Is that thing coming with us?' I asked, nodding at the dog.

Oskar just chuckled. 'Of course.'

Oskar was small and rail-thin, like a jockey, and wore a pair of mirror shades too big for his face. I had learned the hard way not to make jokes about the collection of fetishes he wore strung around his neck, and in which he put a worrying degree of faith. This evening he was wearing a rabbit's foot, a crucifix and a number of other less identifiable objects, strung on chains and leather twine. Then I remembered the half-coin hanging around my neck and wondered if I was really so different.

I nodded at the pimped-up SUV. 'Where the hell did that thing come from?'

Now I was closer to it, the car looked like some millionaire survivalist's weekend excursion vehicle. It had four enormous, rugged-looking wheels, along with a swept-back windscreen and mesh-covered headlights. The windows were small and high, while the chassis was covered over with some kind of armour plating. Small, directional klieg lights had been mounted above the windscreen.

Oskar pulled the door open on the driver's side, and I saw an interior of thick, creamy-coloured leather. Both the interior and the exterior were studded with reinforcing bolts. 'Front and rear night vision cameras,' Oskar explained with no small degree of pride. 'Tinted armoured glass throughout, oxygen survival kit, inbuilt fire-control system. There's even shielding against explosives built into the undercarriage.' He slapped the hard steel exterior. 'This baby's got everything.'

'What about the EVs?' I asked, referring to the excursion vehicles that were ubiquitous on every alternate I had so far visited.

'There's one there, but we won't be using it,' Haden explained, his eyes glinting silver. 'Not manoeuvrable enough, and too big as well. Plus, these things are a lot faster and nimbler.'

'Casey found a whole warehouse full of them in the same place we're going,' Oskar added. 'Any one of these babies would set you back a quarter of a million in anyone's money – this universe or any other.' He reached inside the truck and stroked the soft leather interior. 'Your drug warlord's preferred mode of travel. And bulletproof, of course.'

'Something's missing,' I said. 'Like maybe a turret.'

They both chuckled. Even Lucky let out a bark, her tail thumping at the stage.

God help me, but that dog really was a monster. I tried to imagine what it would be like, riding along with that thing sitting right behind my shoulder with its enormous jaws ready for action. I could easily picture it ripping my head off my shoulders and spitting it out of the window like a pistachio shell.

'You're really bringing the Hound of the Baskervilles along?' I asked nervously, nodding at Lucky.

Oskar stared at me in disbelief. 'You're kidding, right? Lucky's the reason I'm still alive. She's my biggest good-luck charm.'

'Yeah?'

'Lucky led Oskar to safety,' said Haden. 'Isn't that right?'

'You know the story about my alternate?' asked Oskar, hunkering down next to the beast and rubbing her belly.

'Environmental collapse, I heard.'

'Yeah. Lucky – well, Lucky's mother, anyway – was on her way to being someone's breakfast, lunch and dinner. I'd managed to get myself caught by some guys on my way to the coast, thinking maybe something in the ocean might still be alive and edible. They wanted to eat me too, right? Except they locked me up in this barn along with Lucky, and that damn hound not only chewed her way through the ropes holding her, but mine too.' He shook his head and chuckled. 'That's when I started believing in miracles.' He touched the crucifix hanging around his neck. 'I tell you, I know a sign when I see one. Once we got out, I managed to kill the one guy left to guard us, and me and Lucky made it out of there.'

'So did you make it to the ocean?' I asked. 'Was there anything to eat there?'

'Nope.' Oskar shook his head. 'It was as dead as everywhere else. But Lucky nosed out the entrance to some government hideout filled with enough food to last us both years and years. Like a lifetime's worth. That makes it twice the old girl pulled through for me.'

I frowned. 'Hang on. You're talking about two different dogs, right? Who found that hideout, Lucky or Lucky's mother?'

'They were both called Lucky,' Oskar explained.

I glanced at Haden, but he just shrugged.

'I didn't even know the old girl was carrying a litter until we reached the coast,' Oskar continued. 'Every one of them died except this girl here.' He scratched Lucky's head, and the dog pushed up against him hard enough that it made him stagger back. 'Hell of a girl,' he chuckled. 'The both of them.'

I stepped around to the open rear of the vehicle. The SUV was a four-seater, with plenty of rear storage. I threw my backpack in and slammed the door shut. 'So exactly what is it we're up against?' I asked them.

'Didn't Schultner brief you?' asked Haden.

I shook my head. 'Nope. Someone told me I'd be briefed on arrival.' I looked between them. 'Or has someone screwed up?'

'Oh, brother.' Oskar rolled his eyes. 'Yeah, sounds like it.'

'Better wait till we're on the other side,' said Haden, reaching for the front passenger door. 'Fact is, we're late to the party. Everyone else is there and waiting for us.'

I nodded at the SUV. 'So if we're driving around in this thing, does that mean there's a chance we'll run into trouble?'

'Hopefully it'll be a cakewalk,' said Haden. 'Long as nothing goes wrong, anyway.' He grinned to show he was kidding.

'*Shit*,' said Oskar. He had stopped with one hand on the driver's side door, a baleful look on his face. 'You had to *say* it, didn't you?'

'Say what?' asked Haden.

'You said something might go *wrong*.'

'I wasn't even talking to you,' said Haden, climbing in.

Oskar pressed his bunched fists to either side of his head. 'Just *shut up*, will you?'

'You've got your lucky card, right?' said Haden. He leaned out the window of the SUV and looked back at me. 'Better than plate armour any day.'

Oskar glared at the other man. 'Don't try and wind me up, you silver-eyed freak. I'm not in the mood.'

'Oskar used to be a professional gambler,' said Haden over his shoulder, as I got in the back of the SUV. I nearly got a mouthful of fur when Lucky leaped into the back next to me, and I began to wish I'd got in the front instead. Haden reached up as if to scratch his ear and slowly twirled one finger next to his ear. 'You should ask him some time about his lucky card. Ace of Spades, right?' he said, looking at Oskar.

'Shut the fuck up,' Oskar groused, and I wiped one hand across my mouth to hide my grin. Haden meanwhile leaned back out of the open window beside him, and gave the rig technician a thumbs-up. The technician nodded and put down the book he'd been reading, and within seconds the air began to flicker and shift around us. I closed my eyes and held my breath as gravity slipped away for an instant.

When I next opened my eyes, I found we had materialized in the open air. The SUV was at the centre of a portable transfer stage, which consisted of a dozen foot-high field-pillars arranged in a wide circle on scrubby grass. Beyond I saw woodlands and a motorway bridge arching over a lake, its far end collapsed. Farther away I made out a cluster of skyscrapers, a number of which looked to have been reduced to near-skeletons.

At first, the sudden shift from late evening to warm sunshine had sent my senses reeling, but I recovered quickly. From the position of the sun, I could see that it was morning. I knew by now that just because it happened to be evening in one alternate, it didn't mean it would be the same time in any other. And until I had a better idea of exactly where in the world we were, I had to also consider the strong likelihood that we were in an entirely different time zone from the one that Easter Island occupied.

So far, so post-apocalyptic. But what really caught my eye was a jarringly alien-looking structure that rose up higher than the sky-scrapers next to which it stood. The thing was *vast*. It looked like a patchwork egg, its outer surface a mottled canvas of grey, silver and brown. There was something tumbledown and rough-edged about it, as if it had been assembled from random found materials. Even from this distance, I could see what appeared to be enormous angled struts enmeshing and supporting the structure's lower half.

I looked around until I saw a second, apparently identical, struc-ture, rising above the treetops in the other direction, and separated from the first by a distance of maybe ten or fifteen kilometres.

Oskar carefully guided the SUV out between two of the field-pillars, then parked next to a full-sized EV and a second SUV. A standard-issue jeep stood nearby, along with a charging station used for powering and storing aerial surveillance drones. I also saw a tent crammed with crated supplies next to the charging station.

We got out and went to join Casey, Nadia and Winifred, who were studying a map spread out on a fold-down table. A couple of Major Howes' troops from the Easter Island compound stood gathered in a knot by the jeep, smoking and chatting. Casey wore the same floppy leather cowboy hat, and the same gun holster strapped to his thigh, as when I had first met him a week before.

'What are those things?' I asked, pointing to the nearest of the sky-scraper-sized eggs as we joined the others.

'Those are Hives,' said Casey. 'Now, apart from Jerry,' he contin-ued, looking around, 'most of you have already made multiple exploratory trips on this alternate. This time out, however, we're solely concerned with data retrieval before the bee-brains have a chance to demolish our target locations.'

'Just out of curiosity,' said Oskar, 'do we have any more idea yet whether the bee-brains are even aware of us?'

'Can't tell you,' Casey replied, and rapped the map with the knuckles of one hand. 'But remember, they're hostile with sufficient provocation.'

'Somebody,' I said, 'is going to have to tell me why we're here, and what the hell a bee-brain is.'

Casey's eyes narrowed. 'They briefed you, right?'

I shook my head. 'Schultner wasn't available. I was told I'd be briefed on arrival.'

Casey stared at me for a moment, then looked over at the soldiers loitering nearby. 'Hey,' he yelled. 'Was Arnold Wotzko expected to be here? Or Schultner, the other guy in charge of briefings?'

One of the soldiers dropped a cigarette stub and rubbed at it with his boot. 'Nope,' he said. 'Just us.'

Oskar gave me an *I-told-you-so* look, while Nadia just shook her head. 'Another fuck-up by our glorious leaders,' she muttered.

'So I was supposed to have been briefed by now?'

I saw Oskar reach inside his shirt and take a firm grip on one of the many fetishes he wore around his neck. 'It's a bad omen,' he moaned. 'We should head home before it's—'

'Shut *up*,' snapped Casey, stabbing one gloved finger at Oskar. 'I'm tired of your superstitious bullshit, Oskar. Nothing's going to go wrong.'

'For a change, I hope,' Nadia said under her breath.

Casey shot her a deadly look.

'Well, seriously,' said Nadia, looking at everyone else, 'am I the only one who double-checks every piece of equipment they give us?'

'Should we be *expecting* problems?' I asked, alarmed.

'Not outside of the usual snafus, no,' said Casey. 'And you can blame the Authority for all the substandard gear. There's only so much you can do with the tools you're given.'

'Those SUVs don't look too shoddy to me,' I said.

'Exactly,' said Casey. 'That's why we grabbed them when we found them. They're infinitely more reliable than the jeeps. Now *focus*,' he said, rapping his knuckles on the map once again. 'And Jerry, if you've got questions, feel free to ask them. You're assigned to Nadia's team, so maybe she can fill you in on anything I miss out once we're all under way.'

I looked at Nadia and she nodded. 'Okay,' I said to Casey. 'So where are we, exactly?'

'Just south of Sao Paolo, in this alternate's Brazil.' Casey nodded in the direction of the skyscrapers and the nearest Hive. 'The bridge leading over the reservoir and into town is wrecked, but the water's shallow enough to ford in the SUVs. Then we follow the road into the city centre.' He moved his fingers across the map. 'These red circles indicate the location of three properties belonging to a French research outfit called Retièn Biophysique. There's a research lab, and also a separate government-financed facility they used for long-term cryogenic storage. Lastly there's an office suite, making a total of three locations for them in this vicinity.'

I saw that the three circles were quite widely separated. Lines connected them to each other by what struck me as very indirect routes indeed.

'Now,' said Casey, 'we've already ripped the cryogenics facility apart, and we dug up a lot of stuff, but the other two places we've only scouted at a distance. That's mainly because they both sit more or less directly on the territorial borders between the two Hives that dominate the city. Bee-brains from either Hive have been fighting whenever they run into each other. If we wait too long, could be they'll wind up demolishing Retièn's labs and offices before we get a chance to look inside.'

'How certain are we that Retièn is responsible for the extinction event here?' asked Haden.

'Near as damn sure,' Casey replied. 'We're going in as two teams to do a quick reconnoitre and grab every piece of computer equipment or paperwork we can load in the cars before rendezvousing back here no later than nightfall.'

'What happened to the people here?' I asked, wondering yet again what possible use the Authority could have for such information.

'They were all infected by a highly modified variant of *Toxoplasma Gondii*,' explained Winifred.

I looked at her. 'And that is?'

'A parasitic agent that normally triggers suicidal behaviour in some mammalian species in its unaltered form, particularly rats and mice,' she explained. 'At heart, it reprogrammes mammalian behaviour via infection. Imagine being able to spray a whole advancing army with a gene-spliced variant so they all went crazy, or turned on each other. Or even better, it made them so terrified of the enemy that they put down their weapons and ran away.'

'And how does that connect to those things over there on the horizon?' I asked, nodding at the Hives.

'Somewhere down the line,' said Winifred, 'they got funding from the military to create genetic chimeras, through new gene recombination techniques they'd developed. It seems the original idea was to use genetically modified insects as a vector for delivering the parasite. Something went wrong, and a very unpleasant mutation got loose and interbred with the local bee populations. Then the bees infected people, and they in turn became active vectors for spreading the infection yet further. It took maybe a year for the entire globe to be subsumed. The people here are still alive, but . . . they aren't really people any more.' She shook her head wistfully. 'I'd kill for the opportunity to carry out a long-term study of the bee-brains. They're not merely infected. They're a kind of chimera themselves, almost a new species, in fact, born of a symbiotic relationship that reached its apotheosis in the night patrols.'

'You had shots, right?' said Casey, before I had a chance to ask Winifred what a 'night patrol' was.

'Sure,' I said, rubbing at the exposed skin of my arm as if I had already been stung. The sound of buzzing insects in the nearby woods now took on an ominous quality.

'Then you're safe from infection,' Casey continued. 'But you need to keep a serious fucking distance from the bee-brains in case they attack you. See this?'

I leaned forward, watching as he moved his finger along the zigzagging lines joining the target circles to each other. 'These are safe routes in and out of the city,' he explained, 'meaning there's a low probability of running into trouble so long as we all stick to them.' He looked around the others. 'Me and Nadia are taking charge of a team each. Jerry, Oskar, you're going for the labs with Nadia. Myself, Haden and Winnie are heading for the office complex.'

Nadia stepped around the table and put a hand on my shoulder. 'Stop looking so goddam worried. This is a low-risk operation. We've spent a lot of time figuring out how things work on this alternate. We'll have remote drones in the air the whole time we're out there.'

'Here,' said Casey, handing a copy of the map to Nadia. He next picked up a thick envelope and handed it to Oskar. 'Everyone check your weapons and gear, and get ready to move out in ten. Jerry, grab a rifle from the supplies tent.'

All this, I thought, just to retrieve what I imagined would amount to little more than some paper files and computer disks.

I stepped past the drone-charging station and pulled a rifle from a rack inside the supplies tent. I slung it over my shoulder by its strap, then followed Nadia and Oskar over to the second SUV, with Lucky darting ahead of us. I made sure to get in to the front passenger seat this time and felt the undercarriage sway slightly as the enormous hound climbed in the rear. It hung its massive head over my shoulder in exactly the way I'd worried it might, hitting me with a full blast of its sickly sweet breath.

Suddenly the dog whined and jumped back out again. Oskar tried to coax her back in, but to no avail. In the end he had no choice but to grab hold of the dog and literally lift her back inside the car, no mean feat given that the animal was nearly the same size as its owner. Nadia, clearly amused, watched Oskar struggle in the rear-view mirror.

'What the hell is wrong with that animal?' I grumbled, as Oskar climbed in next to the dog, pulling the door shut before it could stage another escape attempt.

'Beats me,' said Oskar, stroking Lucky's thick fur in an attempt to calm her down. 'She doesn't normally get like this.' He frowned at me. 'She ain't gonna bite you, if that's what you're worried about.'

'I'm not crazy about dogs,' I admitted.

'As long as you're not anything like Wallace Deans,' Oskar replied, 'you'll get along just fine.'

'What did Wallace do?' I asked.

Oskar had finally got the dog settled, although she whined and shifted as Nadia reached for the ignition. *Something* was making the animal nervous, but I was damned if I knew what it was.

'The murderous asshole tried to kill Lucky,' said Oskar.

'That's not quite how it was,' said Nadia.

'He tried to *run her over*,' said Oskar, his voice rising in protest.

Nadia leaned towards me as she pulled on her seatbelt. 'The drunken idiot got behind the wheel of a jeep after a night at the Mauna Loa and nearly hit Lucky.'

'I noticed he likes a drink,' I said, then stopped myself adding: *and so do the rest of you.*

Oskar laughed harshly. 'You think?'

Casey pulled ahead of us in the SUV we had first arrived in, waving out of the window to us with his battered leather hat.

'Wallace used to be a more-or-less functional alcoholic,' said Nadia, echoing my earlier thoughts as she sent the car bouncing over the grass. 'Although he's been getting less and less functional with each passing day.'

'So he's always been like that?' I asked.

'It only really got bad after his arrest,' said Oskar.

I looked at Nadia for explanation. 'Some of Greenbrooke's men caught him smuggling contraband from an alternate we'd been exploring,' Nadia explained, seeing my expression. 'They kind of went to town on him.'

I stared at her in surprise. 'Does that kind of thing happen a lot?'

'You mean contraband? More than you'd think. Alcohol, cigarettes – just the usual stuff. Anything that's an improvement on the shit the Authority supply us with.'

'And does Bramnik know this goes on?' I asked.

'Almost certainly,' said Nadia. 'Although he seems to prefer to turn a blind eye.'

'So who gets the contraband?' I asked. 'And what does Wallace get back?'

Nadia grinned lasciviously. 'Let's just say there's a couple of women among Bramnik's staff who don't mind granting certain *favours* in return for the right goods.'

'So Wallace was . . .'

'Yeah.' She nodded, then twisted around to regard Oskar. 'And not just Wallace.'

I glanced back at Oskar and saw the smirk vanish from his face. He peered out of the window as if he had developed a sudden deep fascination with our surroundings.

'What kind of items?' I asked.

'Whisky – certainly not the home-brew variety Yuichi comes up with,' she said. 'Cigars, some electronic goods. Stuff like that, all from alternates we've been exploring.'

'But surely they can get those things themselves back on the Authority's own alternate?' I asked.

'Apparently not, if the girls on Bramnik's staff are prepared to put out for it,' said Nadia. 'Makes you wonder just what it's like over on their own alternate, doesn't it?'

Nadia guided the vehicle down an incline below the ruined bridge, our passage raising a high plume of water as the SUV made its way across the shallow water. Then she steered up the other bank and back onto the road on the far side of the motorway bridge.

Up ahead, Casey gunned his engine, and his SUV shot forward, bouncing as it climbed onto a road. He put his arm out the window and gave us the finger. Beside me, I saw Nadia's mouth tighten, while Oskar giggled from the rear.

'Fucking asshole,' muttered Nadia.

Up ahead, the other SUV had almost vanished from sight. They were headed east, us to the west.

'This is the first I heard of any of this,' I said.

'Greenbrooke tried to force a crackdown. Bramnik got Wallace released in short order following his arrest, but by the time we got him back, it was clear that the Patriots had banged him up pretty good. Wallace claimed he'd been tortured.'

I stared at her, aghast. '*Tortured* him? For what, stealing a couple of bottles of booze?'

'Not quite.' Nadia shook her head. 'Some alternates we visit are more technologically developed than the ones most of us come from. That means there's all kinds of advanced technology just lying around, asking to be taken. That's what the Patriots accused him of trying to smuggle back to the island. To be honest, they're not entirely wrong in wanting to stamp on it. Sometimes you can't be sure what's safe to bring back, and what isn't. Depending on where you're going or where you've been, sometimes there's a strict quarantine procedure, and that covers more than just technology.' She glanced at me as she drove. 'As you know.'

'And he does this kind of thing a lot?'

'The man has sticky fingers,' Nadia replied. 'I don't know if it's kleptomania or the expression of some childhood trauma, but try not to leave anything lying around where he can grab it.'

'So whatever they did to him, it was bad enough to turn him into an alcoholic?'

She shrugged. 'He was on that road anyway. I think they just hurried him along a little bit.' She pulled up at an intersection. I saw a row of shops with apartments above, their windows smashed and open to the elements. The wind sighed around us.

Nadia handed me the map. 'Here. You're the navigator.'

'Sure.' I tried not to show how nervous I really was.

We drove on through deserted streets and across cracked and overgrown tarmac for another twenty minutes, while I told Nadia where to take each turn as we followed the strange, zigzagging routes through the city.

By now we were close enough to the first Hive that I could see just how rough edged and patchy looking its exterior really was. What on Earth, I wondered, lay within? Did people live in there? Or something else?

'These people,' I asked. 'The bee-brains. Do they still look like human beings?'

'Pretty much,' she said, looking distracted as she peered ahead, slowing a little as we reached another intersection. 'Okay, we're still where we're supposed to be. That's all well and good.'

I glanced at a street sign in Portuguese, then thought I saw something moving up at the next intersection. I told Nadia, and she pulled to a stop, before taking a pair of binoculars from the dashboard and peering ahead.

'Trouble?' asked Oskar.

'Probably not,' said Nadia. 'I don't see anything, so might just have been a lone . . . wait, no. I see them now. Hoo boy. A lot of them, too.'

I licked suddenly dry lips. 'What do we do? Take a different route?'

She shook her head. 'I don't think so. Long as we keep our distance, they're going to act like they don't even know we're here.' She put the binoculars back down. 'But we might have to wait a little while until they've passed through.'

'What are they doing?'

'Fixing that thing up,' she said, nodding through the windscreen at the Hive. 'It's built out of scraps of stuff from all over. You can see bee-brains hammering buildings apart all over the place. Best thing to do is wait until they're gone, like I said. Here,' she said, handing me the binoculars. 'Look and learn.'

I lifted them to my eyes and saw maybe a couple of dozen bedraggled-looking figures making their way across the intersection ahead. The majority were naked or wore rags that barely clung to their flesh. There were men and women of all ages, but no children. Every one of them was carrying something – bricks, or bits of rubble, and in some cases what looked to me like crude home-made tools. Any one of them could have glanced up and seen us immediately, less than a few dozen metres farther down the road. None of them did. They looked, I thought, like people walking in their sleep.

'Do they know what they're doing?' I asked. 'I mean, are they consciously aware?'

She shook her head. 'Not according to Winifred, no. She's the expert on this stuff.'

'They're not really human,' said Oskar from behind me. 'There's a reason they're called bee-brains. Don't get any ideas that you can communicate with them in any way. They can get pretty vicious at close enough range.'

A breeze stirred the air outside, and a few of the creatures came to a stumbling halt. One thickset fellow, his filthy face partly shrouded by a scraggly tangle of hair, looked up and towards us, then staggered in our direction a few paces before coming to a halt. His eyes were black, with hardly any white showing, every trace of humanity gone.

'Let me see that,' said Nadia, snatching the binoculars back. She stared silently ahead for several seconds. One or two other bee-brains had also come to a halt, swaying their heads as if they were sniffing at the air.

The breeze died down. All of a sudden they appeared to lose interest in us and began to shuffle off after the rest.

'Well,' said Nadia, lowering the glasses from her face, 'if that ain't a first. Did you see that, Oskar?'

'Yeah,' he said. 'It was almost like they were looking our way.'

'Could be coincidence,' she said. 'Them being completely brain dead and all.'

'They don't *look* that dangerous,' I said.

'There are three of us,' said Nadia, 'and a couple billion of them scattered all over this alternate. That means they win any fight by a knockout, even before they get in the ring.'

The last of the bee-brains moved out of sight. I felt my skin prickle at the thought of the people those strange, shambling figures had once been. I felt the irrational urge to breathe shallowly, as if it might protect me from a whole cornucopia of imagined airborne infections.

'Here we go,' said Nadia, putting the SUV into first gear. We trundled slowly forwards and across the now deserted intersection.

Nadia pulled a walkie-talkie out of the glove compartment and handed it back to Oskar. 'Check in with Casey and the rest,' she said. 'See about getting an update from base camp, see if the recon drones have spotted anything unusual. I don't like the way those bee-brains were acting.'

I studied the map while Nadia navigated us past a number of abandoned vehicles blocking the road, before we accelerated towards an on-ramp that linked to an elevated motorway. Soon, we rose above the dark waters of a river that cut through the heart of the city. She slowed as we approached a row of vehicles that looked to have been arranged in a deliberate barricade across the motorway, carefully edging the SUV between an overturned bus and the edge of the bridge. I caught sight again of the river below, which, according to the map spread across my knees, was called the Pinheiros.

'Hey,' said Oskar from behind me, jiggling the walkie-talkie. 'I've been trying to get through, but I can't.'

'Not at all?' asked Nadia.

'Nope.' He turned the walkie-talkie upside down and poked at its battery compartment. 'Don't think there's anything wrong with it. Maybe there's some kind of interference.'

'Christ,' muttered Nadia. 'Last thing we need is yet more problems.'

'Problems?' I asked. 'Why do you people never talk about anything but things going wrong?'

Nadia pursed her lips and didn't answer, which worried me even more.

Just past its apex, the elevated motorway was level with the upper floors of a multi-storey car park. Once we were past the blockade, I saw with a start that the building was crowded with thousands of figures milling around within.

I craned my neck to get a better look as we accelerated away from the barricade, seeing a mob of several dozen bee-brains working together to roll a single, huge lump of concrete and steel off the edge of a parapet. A car followed just moments later from the next storey up, and I watched as the rusted wreck went tumbling out of sight. Then the building was gone, lost in the distance behind us.

Nadia guided us towards an off-ramp leading down to the city on the far side of the river. I caught sight of hundreds more bee-brains forming a long, twisting column that wound through streets and across intersections. It looked as if its point of origin was the nearby Hive.

I felt sickened but also awed by everything I had so far witnessed. I trembled at the thought of all those people – former people, at any rate – crammed together inside that vast structure. I fought back a horrible image of being carried, kicking and screaming, deep within the Hive's vast maw . . .

I pressed one hand against the dashboard in front of me, tasting sour bile at the back of my throat. My heart thudded spasmodically inside my chest.

'You okay?' asked Nadia.

'I'm fine.'

She gave me a look as if she knew exactly what was going through my mind.

'I think we should take a vote,' she said suddenly. 'We're out of touch with the other team and we got unexpected attention from the locals. Do we keep going or not?'

'Turn back,' said Oskar without hesitation. 'I've been having a bad feeling about this trip right from the start.'

'Is that what you want to do?' I asked Nadia. 'Turn back?'

'I'm just saying that having your communications conk out on you is far from being a good thing. And I've never seen or heard of the bee-brains reacting like they just did.'

'I thought there was a risk of attack if we got too close to them. Wouldn't that explain it?'

'We weren't close enough to trigger a reaction,' she said, looking at me. 'At least, not based on previous experience.'

'Maybe it should be your decision,' I said. 'You're in charge, right?'

She nodded. 'I am. But that doesn't mean neither of you get a say in the matter. We're a democracy in here.'

'You still have the aerial reconnaissance?' I asked, meaning the drones.

'They're no use to us,' snapped Oskar. 'All the data in the world isn't any use unless we can talk to base to get that airborne intel. You see?'

'But *they* can still see where we are, using the drones, even if we can't talk to them, right?' I asked.

'That's still no—' Oskar began.

'I've got a better idea,' Nadia said suddenly, and quickly pulled up by the side of the motorway, just past the exit sign for the off-ramp. 'Oskar,' she said, pushing open the door on her side and climbing out, 'dig out the flares, will you?'

Oskar reached around into the rear compartment of the SUV, unzipping one of the numerous large canvas bags there. He rummaged around inside, then pulled out a flare pistol along with several flares of different colours. He pushed his door open and passed it all out to Nadia.

I got out as well, too full of nervous energy to sit in the car one moment longer than I had to. I stepped over to the rail at the side of the off-ramp and peered down at the conga line of former humanity snaking through distant streets. Even from a couple of kilometres distance, I could hear the massed shuffling of their feet.

I looked back, in the direction of the multi-storey car park. I could make out the distant echo of hundreds of crude tools hammering at its walls.

I turned back to see Nadia load a flare into the gun before aiming straight up and pulling the trigger. The flare shot high into the air, then exploded into a tiny white star, drifting in the wind before quickly fading.

'Remember your training?' Nadia asked, stepping back over to me.

'A white flare means our comms are down, but we're otherwise fine,' I replied.

'Very good.' She nodded. 'You *were* listening. Now all we have to do is wait and see if they send up an orange flare. If it's orange, we turn around and head on home. White means we keep going.'

'What do you think it'll be?' I asked.

'White,' she said immediately. 'I don't have any doubts about that, not unless something's seriously wrong.'

She glanced to the south, and I followed her gaze to see a second white flare rise above the dark green foliage, on the far side of the wrecked bridge and the reservoir.

Oskar snarled something I couldn't make out, and pulled his head back inside the car.

'Onwards, gentlemen,' said Nadia, and headed back to the SUV.

'What about Casey and the rest?' I asked, climbing back in. 'We haven't seen a flare from them, have we?'

'Unless we missed it,' said Nadia. Her shoulders rose and fell in a sigh. 'Or maybe it's just us who've got problems.'

NINE

We exited the motorway, and soon turned onto a broad highway that ran parallel to the nearby banks of the Pinheiros. I studied the map and saw we had already covered most of the distance to our destination.

'Okay,' said Nadia, glancing sideways at the map on my knees. 'We're almost there. Keep your eyes peeled, both of you.'

'This place we're going to,' I asked. 'Do we know what it looks like?'

Oskar reached into the envelope Casey had given him earlier, and pulled out some grainy-looking photographs before passing them over to me. 'Aerial drone reconnaissance,' he explained. 'See that white building, about two storeys high?' He leaned forward, reaching between the two front seats to tap at the picture.

I studied the photo, and then the map, comparing them. 'If I'm reading this right, then Retièn's labs are just seven or eight blocks from here, straight on ahead.'

'Slight problem,' said Nadia, nodding ahead. 'Look.'

I glanced through the windscreen, and saw that part of a building had collapsed across the street straight ahead of us, blocking the avenue.

'We're going to have to take a detour,' said Nadia, pulling once more to a halt. 'No way I can get past that. I'll hang a right, take a route down a side street, then come back onto this road.'

'I *really* don't like this,' said Oskar quietly.

Nadia's hands tapped out a staccato rhythm on the wheel. 'Me neither.'

For a second I thought she was going to turn back. She glanced sideways at me, fixing me with her gaze, and I knew she was trying to make up her mind. Then she started us forwards again, first taking a right into a side street, then a left at the next corner.

Up ahead, at the next intersection, I saw a number of bee-brains milling about in a loose mob like a sleepwalker's convention. Then I saw they were all carrying stuff out of the gutted shell of a shopping mall on the other side of the intersection. In their hands I saw pieces of broken furniture, desk ornaments, chairs, bricks, and pretty much anything that wasn't too big or unwieldy to either carry or drag after them. It was like stumbling across a fire sale in the midst of a zombie apocalypse.

'Oh hell,' said Nadia.

I had left the window open on my side, to alleviate the tropical heat. A cool breeze swept past us and towards the bee-brains. Almost immediately, a number of the creatures came to a halt, their heads swivelling around to regard us. I closed the window again, afraid they were about to come running at us.

'Nadia?' asked Oskar. 'Why the *fuck* are they looking at us?'

'I don't know.' She grabbed the map from my lap and studied it closely, her lips pale and bloodless.

More of the creatures appeared, stumbling to a halt before raising their chins apparently to sniff at the air. 'Why are they acting like that?' I asked. 'Is it because they can smell us? Is that what it is?'

'I don't know. All I know is, they follow scent paths laid down by patrol leaders,' said Oskar, without bothering to explain what a 'patrol leader' was. 'Those are the ones you *really* have to avoid.'

'I don't know why they're looking this way,' said Nadia, 'unless . . .'

She looked up, her eyes wide, and never finished her sentence. She slammed her foot down, reversing the SUV hard enough that its rear fishtailed wildly.

Oskar gasped and swore behind us, while Lucky let out a low, grumbling whine from somewhere deep inside her throat.

'Fuck this,' said Nadia, her voice high and tight and sharp. 'Check your guns. Both of you.'

'Are you expecting trouble?' I asked as calmly as I could.

'Something really, really doesn't feel right,' she muttered under her breath.

She hit the brake, spinning the wheel at the same time so that the car was spun through ninety degrees. Suddenly we were facing back the way we had come. I twisted around in my seat to look through the rear window behind Lucky, and saw some of the bee-brains take a few faltering steps after us. After a moment they began to run, their skinny, scarred legs pumping with furious motion.

'I fucking *told* you something was wrong,' Oskar yelled from behind me.

The SUVs tyres screeched as we emerged back onto the main avenue. I felt a deep shiver of shock at the sight of hundreds of bee-brains that had appeared from nowhere in just the last few minutes. It looked as if the conga line I had sighted earlier had moved to cut straight across our route back to the stage. Most carried or dragged pieces of junk, just like the bee-brains encountered moments before.

Nadia was forced to slow down to avoid a pile of twisted wreckage scattered across the road. Hundreds of bee-brains turned to watch us. I saw again how bruised and battered they all looked, how wrinkled and scarred.

They dropped what they were carrying, and started to walk, and then to run, straight at us.

'Fuck,' said Oskar in a high voice.

Nadia hit the accelerator once we were past the obstruction, aiming straight at a cluster of the creatures directly before us. I yelled and put a hand up before my face as we ploughed straight into them, the vehicle bumping and bouncing over their bodies. Hands reached out, sliding against the glass of the window nearest me, and I took a tight grip on my rifle. The thing that made it worse was that the creatures were entirely silent, like something out of a particularly unpleasant nightmare. Their mouths opened and closed, but no sound emerged.

I saw to my horror that thousands more were pouring into the street between us and the bridge over the river, sweeping towards us in a vast tide of flesh.

'I think,' said Nadia, her face shiny with perspiration and her voice trembling, 'we're going to have to call this one a wash. Oskar, fire off a red flare. Let the others know we're in trouble.'

'Seconded,' said Oskar, grabbing hold of the flare gun once more.

'But first,' she said, as if to herself, 'we're going to have to improvise a little.'

Nadia turned the wheel, sending us down another side street. There were bee-brains here, but not in such great numbers. The map was still spread out on my knees, and by the look of things we were now definitely outside the recommended routes. I reopened the window on my side and started to pick off the fastest and strongest of the bee-brains running towards us with my rifle.

Their heads snapped back in the moment before they went tumbling to the ground and I was suddenly very, very glad for all my recent marksmanship training. *They're not human*, I reminded myself, each time I looked into their blank and mindless eyes.

From behind me, Oskar cursed and muttered as he did the same thing from his side of the car.

'Conserve your ammunition,' said Nadia, 'in case we really, *really* need it. There's a lot more of them out there than we've got bullets.'

'Something's fucked up,' Oskar shouted, gripping the back of Nadia's seat with one hand and practically spitting his words in her ear. 'We should have been able to see all this with the drones. Why the hell did they send up a white flare, when they knew there were this many bee-brains waiting for us?'

'Shut up,' Nadia snarled over her shoulder. 'Soon as you've got a clear shot, fire that fucking flare.'

'It's *you*,' said Oskar, turning to me now. 'You've *jinxed* us all. Right from the beginning.'

'Are you out of your fucking mind?' I said.

'Oskar?' said Nadia, without looking around. 'I swear to God, you will shut the fuck up *right now* or I will make you walk the rest of the way back. You got that?'

She swerved to avoid a tight knot of bee-brains. I pulled the map back across my lap from where it had fallen and studied it with shaking hands, tracing my finger along the length of the Pinheiros. There were multiple bridges spanning it at different points. Some looked as if they were closer than the elevated motorway Nadia had taken us across, although they were certainly a long way away from any of the designated safe routes. If we could get to one of them, maybe we could make it to the other side of the river.

I told Nadia my idea. 'Sounds good,' she nodded.

'It's taking us off the safe routes,' said Oskar, his voice full of alarm.

'The safe routes, as you may have just noticed,' said Nadia, her voice terse, 'appear to be wildly inaccurate. So I don't think that's going to matter a great deal, do you?'

Nadia swung across the road, sending more bodies flying. I saw one of the creatures, her back broken and her mouth wide with pain, flailing as she struggled to pull herself upright on useless legs. Others crawled or moved weakly. Then they were gone behind us, Nadia slaloming the vehicle from side to side to catch more bee-brains as they lurched into our path. Every time we turned into a street too densely packed with bodies, both myself and Oskar picked off any that got too close until our ears sang from the thunder of bullets.

We swerved around yet another corner that was partly blocked by fallen masonry, but was miraculously devoid of bee-brains. I stared at the map, unable to figure out where the hell we were any more. Nadia slowed again to negotiate her way past the debris.

Lucky howled softly in my ear, so close that my neck was damp from her breath. I turned to try and reassure her just as something enormous fell out of the sky, slamming into the bonnet of the SUV and starring the windscreen's armoured glass.

Nadia sent us accelerating backwards at speed, to try to get out of range of whatever had collided with us, but she miscalculated; the SUV hit something that sent its rear bouncing high into the air fast and hard enough that the car came back down on its side. As the car rolled, I caught a momentary glimpse of an enormous chunk of masonry, not much smaller than the car itself, slowly rolling to a halt.

I wondered distantly where it had come from. My seatbelt was the only thing keeping me from collapsing on top of Nadia, who was now beneath me. I coughed and swallowed, tasting blood. I had bitten my tongue.

Lucky whimpered mournfully from behind me. When I turned to look, I saw she was half-standing on her owner, who was struggling to be free of his own seatbelt.

For a moment, I feared the worst; I had seen Nadia's head slam into the dashboard, and she wasn't moving. Then, without warning, she groaned and tried to sit up, her hand reaching for the wheel.

'Forget that,' I said, swallowing blood. 'We've got to get out of here.'

'Can't walk home,' she said thickly. She pressed the ignition, but nothing happened.

I tried to push open the door on my side, but it was jammed. The only way out, then, was through the open window next to me. I pulled myself up and out of the SUV, crouching on top of the door so I could take a look around. I glanced towards the huge chunk of masonry, and then moved my gaze up, until I saw nearly a dozen figures milling around on top of a neighbouring building.

Had the creatures been deliberately aiming at us, I wondered, when they pushed that huge chunk of concrete and rebar off the roof and on top of us? For creatures that were supposedly brain-dead, it struck me as pretty smart.

I leaned back in through the window. 'Get up here,' I shouted down at the others. 'We have to get the hell away from here before they overrun us.'

Oskar stood upright inside the SUV and managed to crawl out beside me before helping Lucky scramble up onto the side of the car. The hound dropped down onto the road with a low growl. I reached back inside and grabbed hold of Nadia's hand, ignoring the throbbing pain in my shoulders and back as I helped her climb out.

Oskar dropped down next to Lucky, and whistled sharply. Lucky responded by settling onto her haunches and regarding her master attentively. Under any other circumstances, I'd have been impressed.

'The car,' said Nadia, her voice scratchy. 'Need to get it upright.'

'The damn thing's trashed,' said Oskar, his voice terse. 'Besides, look over there.'

I followed the direction of his gaze, to where a number of bee-brains had come stumbling around the far corner of the street, attracted, perhaps, by the noise and commotion. I realized with a terrible sinking sensation that we had little choice but to abandon our vehicle.

Oskar rested his rifle on top of the SUV and began firing towards the bee-brains. Nadia, despite the blood on her forehead and what may have well been an incipient concussion, did the same – as did I, steadying my breathing before picking a target and pulling the trigger.

Bodies fell as the bullets slammed into the heads and chests of the approaching bee-brains. I hastily reloaded and started firing again.

A dark brown shape shot past me and towards the creatures. Oskar's hound leaped towards a bee-brain, her enormous jaws clamping around the creature's throat. The bee-brain collapsed to its knees, blood pumping from its neck. Lucky had already moved on to savage another of the creatures.

'Stop,' said Nadia, sounding breathless. More than a dozen bodies lay scattered. 'Let's get the hell out of here before any more come.'

'What about our supplies?' I asked, nodding at the SUV. 'Shouldn't we get them out of there?'

'No,' said Nadia. 'There isn't time.'

'I need just one thing,' said Oskar, half-pulling himself back inside the SUV before Nadia had a chance to protest. He resurfaced a moment later with a black canvas bag.

'Through there,' he said, slinging the bag over one shoulder and nodding towards a nearby vacant doorway.

'In there?' exclaimed Nadia. 'Are you crazy?'

'River's on the other side,' he said. 'No time to argue. Just follow me!'

He disappeared inside the doorway without another word, Lucky bounding after him. I looked at Nadia and she shrugged helplessly before following him.

I ran after them both, finding myself inside what must have been a very upmarket mall in its time. Discoloured posters advertising perfumes drooped from the walls, while glass-covered counters on all sides still contained rows of tiny, elegant-looking bottles.

Oskar came to a halt and unzipped the bag before extracting something flat and oblong. He fixed it to the wall just beside the entrance, then tapped at a digital readout affixed to it. Some kind of explosive, I realized.

'*Move*,' Oskar screamed, and ran deeper into the building, Lucky in his wake.

I didn't need any further persuasion. Nadia kept pace with me as we ran towards the sunlight coming through an open door on the far side of the mall. Oskar swerved behind an escalator and pulled Lucky down beside him, and both myself and Nadia moved to join him.

I had barely got behind cover when the air filled with a terrible thunder, the whole building shaking. Dense, choking dust filled the air, while what sounded like a couple of tons of glass came crashing down all around us.

I stood back up and peered through thick clouds of dust. All that remained of the entrance was a pile of rubble, blocking the bee-brains from following us.

Within seconds we emerged from the far side of the building and onto another street. I could see the banks of the Pinheiros, just past a row of warehouses parallel to it.

We ran, and kept running, until my lungs burned and my legs ached, but the thought of the creatures behind us was more than enough to keep me going regardless. It felt as if we'd run a hell of a long way before we began to slow down, but even then we kept walking at a brisk pace, darting wary glances at the shadows and street corners around us as we went.

I looked up and saw that the sun was well past its zenith. The plan, I recalled, had been to rendezvous with the others by nightfall at the latest.

Nadia finally came to a halt, bending over and putting her hands on her knees. Oskar collapsed to the ground beside her, rolling onto his back. I sank down onto a concrete bollard by the side of the road and looked around.

'I don't think anything's following us,' Nadia finally said, 'but it's going to be dark in a couple of hours.' She pushed her hair back from her face and looked at me. 'The bee-brains don't hang around after dark.'

'So we're safe.'

'Nope.' She shook her head. 'Once it's dark, we have to deal with the night patrol.'

'The what?' I said. Winifred had used the term earlier, but hadn't explained it.

Nadia shook her head, panting. 'All you need to know,' she said, 'is that however bad you think the bee-brains are, the night patrol is worse. Pray we don't run into one.'

'What now?' asked Oskar, finally sitting up.

'What else can we do but walk?' she replied with a shrug. 'The farther we get from the Hive, the better chance we have of surviving after dark.'

Oskar nodded up at the darkening sky. 'I've been keeping my eyes out for the recon drones,' he said. 'They should be looking for us, but I haven't seen a damn thing since before we ran into trouble.'

'Well, I guess it's stating the obvious to say something's gone very badly wrong,' said Nadia. 'C'mon,' she said, taking a weary step forwards. 'We walk, or we die.'

We were headed towards a second bridge beyond the one that had been our original destination, spanning the river some way off in the distance. 'That's one too many fuck-ups,' said Oskar. 'I've had it with this shit. No more fucking missions until they guarantee our safety.'

'I don't suppose you managed to keep hold of the flare gun?' asked Nadia.

'No,' said Oskar miserably. 'It fell under the vehicle when we crashed.'

*

We made steady progress over the next two hours, without further encounters. The Hive began to recede into the distance until I began to believe we had some chance of making it back across the city alive. Nadia called another halt just as the sun dipped closer to the horizon, the undersides of the clouds streaked with red.

Oskar shook his head. 'We can't afford to stop. We're too vulnerable as it is.'

'If we don't rest up, even just for a couple of minutes,' Nadia pointed out, 'we'll be too exhausted if we run into any more trouble.' She reached into a jacket pocket and pulled out a plastic bottle half-full of water, taking a sip from it before passing it to me. 'Easy with that,' she said. 'The rest is back in the SUV.'

The water tasted like sunlight as it flowed down my throat, and I had to fight the urge to drink it all down at once. I was ravenously hungry. I reluctantly passed the remaining water over to Oskar, and I watched him give most of his share to Lucky.

'Casey mentioned that the bee-brains stick to specific paths,' I said. 'They weren't supposed to be where we found them, were they?'

'That's what I said,' Oskar grumbled.

'I guess we're going to have to rethink what we know,' said Nadia.

'I think we were jinxed,' growled Oskar, giving me a foul look.

'I already told you to shut the hell up,' Nadia barked.

'Yeah, I remember,' he said, his tone sardonic. 'You said you were going to make me walk the rest of the way back.'

She glared at him, but didn't say anything more.

'Since we're here,' I said, 'maybe this would be a good time to tell me what the hell a "night patrol" is.'

Nadia regarded me through a fringe of hair that had fallen across her face. 'They're not quite the same as regular bee-brains,' she explained. 'They patrol the borders between different Hives, always after dark. Sometimes patrols from different Hives attack or kill each other. Also, unlike the regular bee-brains, they aren't restricted to scent-marked paths.' She regarded me darkly. 'That's what makes them particularly dangerous – they go wherever the hell they like.'

'So why are the Hives so antagonistic towards each other?'

'Mostly,' she said, 'they fight over resources.'

'If they do that, doesn't that imply there's some kind of intelligence at work?'

'You wouldn't be the first to ask that same question. Actual bees are pretty organized, but they don't have anything like human intelligence.'

'So you're saying . . .'

'It's an instinctive thing. No intelligence involved, or so Winifred tells me. She's the one who spent time studying the damn things. They caught one and took it apart, said they found that all the parts of the brain dealing with higher functions had essentially rotted away.' She shuddered visibly. 'Ask her for the gory details when we get back.'

'Anything else I should know?' I asked dryly.

'Lots,' Nadia replied, 'but I figure you're under enough stress already as it is.'

'You know,' I said, 'back when we were stuck in those vaults, running away from a lava flow, you told me it wasn't always going to be like this.'

Something in the look she gave me kept me from saying anything more.

TEN

We soon got moving again. I smoothed the map out as we walked, studying it as best as I could in the day's fading light, until I was pretty sure where we were. We were still walking parallel to the river, and well on our way to the bridge we had been aiming for. I figured we didn't have more than another twenty minutes of walking before we reached it, and the farther the Hive slipped behind us, the safer I felt.

Back when I had been stuck on my own alternate with no hope of rescue, I had learned fast to pay attention, never to let my mind drift so far that I would fail to notice the sound of wild dogs hunting me. The one time I had let my attention slip, when Yuichi and the others had hunted me across the fields and through the woods, I had come close to dying. So when I heard a faint buzzing, like that of insects, I was immediately aware of it. The sound came again, as if something had passed close by my ear.

I looked ahead of us, in the direction of the bridge, to where Lucky had run ahead. I saw that she had come to an absolute standstill just five or six metres in front of us, her body trembling with suppressed energy.

I came to a halt, and saw that Nadia and Oskar had both done the same. I felt suddenly, acutely aware of every shadow, every breeze, every sound around us.

Up ahead, the sun slipped down behind the ruins of an office building, and the darkness grew.

'Night patrol,' said Oskar, his voice low as he slipped his rifle from his shoulder.

Beside me, Nadia took the safety off her own weapon.

I looked around, but all I could see were the silhouettes of warehouses on either side of us.

'Hear anything?' asked Nadia. She spoke quietly, but her voice seemed to reverberate from the walls around us.

'Not a thing,' said Oskar. 'Not any more.'

'I definitely heard a buzzing,' said Nadia. 'Anyone else?'

'Me,' I said.

She glanced towards the river. 'If there's too many of them, head for the water and try and swim across.'

As if on cue, a figure emerged from the alley between two warehouses on our right. It was naked, with a sunken belly and a chest coated with thick grey hair. There was, I saw, something wrong with its head. Its skull was distended in such a way that the mouth was drawn wide in a terrifying, inhuman grimace.

'There should be more than one,' said Nadia, sounding surprisingly calm. 'Anyone see the rest?'

'Behind us,' I said, looking over my shoulder.

They had emerged from the shadows and alleyways in their dozens. Many, though not all, had the same strange, distended features as the one blocking our way ahead.

Oskar brought his rifle up and fired over Lucky's head, at the first creature we had seen. It staggered back as the bullets tore into its body, and it collapsed without a sound.

Then it did something I knew would give me nightmares for the rest of my life, assuming I lived long enough.

I saw the bee-brain's grimace grow wider and wider, until it gaped like a cavernous wound. Its head almost seemed to split apart like a piece of rotten fruit and, to my eternal horror, a dark cloud emerged from the depths of its gullet, streaming upwards before pooling in a buzzing mass above it.

A cloud of bees, I saw, the sound of their swarming filling the otherwise silent street. I fought back a rush of bile in the back of my throat, and understood that the bee-brains had been more than aptly named. I turned to see a number of the creatures blocking our retreat do the same, their mouths splitting open and clouds of bees emerging from deep in their throats.

'Run,' said Nadia. 'Go for the river!'

I obeyed her without hesitation, dashing towards the riverside warehouses and into a narrow alley separating two of them. I heard Nadia and Oskar running to catch up, but then Lucky bounded past us, beating us all to the water's edge.

I heard, rather than saw, Nadia stumble in the dark, and I stopped just long enough to haul her back upright while she cursed and hissed under her breath. From the way she was holding herself, it was clear she'd twisted her ankle at the very least. She grabbed hold of my arm and held on as we both ran the rest of the way to the dock, the river's water black under the rising moon. The far shore looked as if it was maybe thirty metres away, but at least it appeared to be deserted.

'How bad is it?' I asked Nadia. 'Can you swim?'

'Just get in the fucking water,' she said, hobbling back from me and stripping off her heavy jacket before discarding it on the ground. She limped past me towards the edge of the dock and threw herself into the water with a loud splash.

I could hear the buzzing of insects drawing nearer. I glanced back along the alley between warehouses, seeing the night patrol stumbling towards us, the wide black slashes of their mouths full of dreadful promise.

Oskar and Lucky were next into the water. I slung my rifle over my shoulder and stepped off the jetty. The water was far colder than I had anticipated, so much so that my chest started to cramp from the shock. I pushed hard towards the opposite shore regardless.

I heard Oskar shouting from somewhere close by, his voice full of panic. I came to a halt, kicking my legs to stay upright in the freezing water. I looked around until I saw him, barely visible in the moonlight, gesturing wildly towards the opposite shore.

It wasn't deserted any more. There were more bee-brains emerging from the shadows all along the far shore of the river. Instead of stopping at the water's edge, they kept coming, tumbling mindlessly into the cold and brackish water in their determination to catch us. I looked back the other way, and saw that the first patrol was doing the same, tumbling and sliding off the jetty and into the water. Above the rooftops, the bulk of the nearest Hive glittered in the night.

I remembered the map and realized that we were caught on the border between the two rival Hives. I wondered if I had the will or the courage to force myself to dive deep beneath the water and stay there until I drowned, rather than allow those things to catch me.

'Go towards the bridge!' I heard Nadia yell. 'Towards the bridge!'

Lucky was still powering towards the opposite shore. I saw her merge with the advancing bee-brains, her huge jaws gaping as she disappeared in a flurry of water and inhuman but vulnerable flesh.

I looked around until I saw Nadia and swam towards her. I could see she was struggling to make any progress, but she still tried to wave me away.

'Wrong way, Jerry!' she gasped.

'Not without you,' I shouted at her, grabbing her under one arm. 'Come on.'

She shook her head. 'I can't make it.'

Most of the night patrol simply sank to the bottom of the river, their limbs thrashing mindlessly, but the rest clearly retained enough muscle memory from their previous existence to be able to swim. I thought of ants bridging a stream by climbing on the bodies of their compatriots.

I led Nadia towards the centre of the river, keeping as far from either shore as I could as I aimed for the bridge. Oskar powered past the both of us as he, too, headed for the bridge.

There wasn't any sign of Lucky. I kicked hard at the water, seeing some of the stronger bee-brains were drawing uncomfortably close.

Something grabbed at my ankle from behind and I screamed, kicking wildly until I was free. Nadia slipped from my grasp as more hands reached up from beneath, dragging her beneath the surface.

I sucked in air and dived down to search for her, thrashing like a demon whenever I felt the hands of the creatures brush against me. I surfaced once more, gasping for air.

I couldn't find her.

Oskar had continued on, oblivious to what had happened. I saw him swim towards an abutment at the base of the bridge, far from either night patrol.

I dived down yet again, desperate to try and find Nadia, but it was impossible. I had no choice but to come up for air and follow after Oskar, who had managed to drag himself up onto the abutment. He stood on the concrete, shouting something incoherent towards me as I approached. Soon I felt the riverbed beneath my feet, and I waded towards him.

Suddenly, from out of nowhere, came the sound of rapid fire, and streaks of light flashed overhead. I looked up, seeing it was coming from on top of the bridge.

In the next moment, brilliant artificial light flooded the underside of the bridge, and I squeezed my eyes shut in the same moment that I felt a wave of intense heat sear one side of my body. When I was next able to look, the whole surface of the river was covered in flames, dozens of bodies writhing as they burned.

'They found us!' Oskar screamed. 'They found us!'

Light bloomed again as more napalm fire spread across the water. The wind carried the scent of burning meat towards me, and I leaned over and vomited.

Oskar grabbed hold of my arm and dragged me towards concrete steps that led up to the street level. I followed, seeing both the jeep and the other SUV, the light from its roof-mounted kliegs directed on to the river.

I looked back up at the bridge at the sound of rapid fire. Casey Vishnevsky was up on top, along with the soldiers I had seen back at base camp, all of them wielding rifles and picking off those few bee-brains that were still struggling to escape the blaze.

I reached up to touch the half-coin around my neck and discovered it was gone. I kneeled down, filled with a sudden, frantic despair, peering at the road beneath my feet in case I had lost it at just that moment. I must, I realized, have lost it in the river – most likely while diving to search for Nadia.

'Where the hell were you?' I yelled at Casey, my voice cracking.

'Do you know how long we were out there, trying to find our way back?'

'Something went wrong,' Casey yelled back over the din of gunfire, as he paused to reload. In the light of the flames, I saw how exhausted he looked, his face smudged with dirt.

Haden and Winifred, both carrying their own rifles, appeared from the direction of the SUV. 'We'll have the bee-brains swarming all over us if we don't get out of here now,' said Winifred. She looked over at Oskar, then back to me, the realization slowly dawning in her eyes. 'Nobody else?'

'No.' I shook my head, moisture pricking the corners of my eyes. 'Just us two.'

'Goddammit,' shouted Oskar, slumping to the ground. 'All these years!'

He sat with his head in his hands, his face streaked with tears. I knew he was thinking of Lucky just as much as Nadia, and I remembered my last sight of the hound as its jaws closed around the throat of an attacker. I felt suddenly ashamed of my panic over losing a mere pendant: it was nothing compared to his loss, or the death of Nadia, nothing more than a piece of cheap stamped metal.

I stepped over to Oskar and put my hand on his shoulder. 'I'm sorry about Lucky.'

'No!' He twisted away from me and sprang to his feet, his face twisted in fury. '*You're* the reason everything went wrong!'

I stared at him, too startled to be angry. 'Oskar, that doesn't make any sense.'

'Take it easy,' said Casey, who had by this time made his way down from the bridge to join us.

'No!' Oskar screamed. 'Don't you see? He's a *jinx*! A goddam jinx on us all!'

'Oskar—' I said, trying to appeal to him.

'You all know what happened to the first Jerry,' Oskar yelled at the others. 'They should never have brought him back, not with all his goddam bad luck. If not for him, Nadia and Lucky would still be alive!'

'"First" Jerry?' I asked. 'What the hell do you mean, the *first* Jerry?'

'Don't you get it?' Oskar said, his teeth bared in a snarl. 'You're not the real Jerry Beche. You're his replacement, after the first one died.'

Winifred came surging forward, slamming her fist into Oskar's gut. He collapsed back onto the ground like a deflating balloon.

'I'm sorry about Nadia,' said Winifred, her voice curt as she stepped back. 'Truly sorry. And I'm just as sorry about Lucky, Oskar. Really I am. But you've gone too far.'

'Just explain to me what the hell he's talking about,' I demanded, my voice trembling.

Casey sighed and shook his head. 'You already know there's nothing unique about any one of us,' he said, his voice calm and matter-of-fact. 'There's an infinity of possible timelines the stages can access, and that means an infinity of variations on each and every one of us. We always knew, in theory at least, that if one of us died, the Authority could just retrieve another version of us from a different, but essentially identical alternate.'

'No,' I mumbled, staring at him.

'You're a replacement,' wheezed Oskar from the ground nearby.

'I'm sorry,' said Casey, when I looked back at him. Winifred couldn't meet my eyes. 'I'm sorry you had to find out this way.'

'And the first Jerry?' I asked. My throat felt as if it was closing up, making it hard to get the words out. 'What happened to him?'

'He died, months before they retrieved you,' Casey explained. 'They brought you in to replace him, just to remind the rest of us how utterly fucking disposable the rest of us really are.'

'Casey,' said Winifred, a warning in her voice. Haden stood by her, his face expressionless as he listened.

'It's true, goddammit,' Casey snapped at her. 'He might as well know the truth.' He turned back to me. 'Any one of us can be replaced just as easily. Far as the Authority's concerned, we're an easily renewable resource, there for the taking, and we're all just so goddam grateful to work for the cocksuckers regardless.'

Haden finally stepped forward and spoke. 'Look, we're a long way from home, and this isn't exactly the time and place for a discussion.

Maybe we should get out of here to safety before any more of those creatures turn up?'

We rode the rest of the way to the transfer stage in silence. Oskar sat next to me in the back of the SUV, and we never spoke once.

Part of me kept wanting to believe I was the butt of a cruel joke. Casey and Winifred sat in the front and tried to fill the silence with conversation about everything that had happened since they had lost contact with us. I made the occasional grunt of acknowledgement, but I didn't feel at all like talking, and clearly neither did Oskar.

'First the drones went down,' Winifred said. 'That was the first real sign of trouble. Looked like some kind of software malfunction.'

Casey swore under his breath. 'Damn things are a waste of time, if you ask me, the number of times they break down.'

'Then our communications got scrambled,' Winifred continued. 'We've had equipment problems before, but this is the worst yet.'

'Shitty Authority gear yet again,' growled Casey. 'You couldn't ask for a clearer sign they really don't give a crap about us.'

'Why didn't any of you tell me before?' I asked.

Casey and Winifred exchanged a glance.

'We weren't supposed to say anything to you about it,' said Winifred, after a pause. 'Not a word.'

'Why not?'

'Because we were warned we'd lose our retirement privileges if we did,' said Oskar, speaking for the first time since Winifred had knocked him to the ground.

I forced myself to meet his eyes again. 'I meant what I said. I'm sorry about Lucky.'

His eyes dipped down, and I saw they were glistening with tears. 'Me too,' he said.

Casey and Winifred resumed their narration of events during our absence, and I listened without commenting. We had, they said, had the bad luck to get caught between two opposing night patrols from rival Hives, each intent on destroying the other.

I was only dimly aware of arriving back at the reservoir. Casey guided the SUV into the transfer stage, and I felt the familiar lurch that came with shifting from one alternate to another. I swallowed the nausea away as I had been taught as the hangar materialized around us.

Taught by Nadia, I suddenly recalled, and clenched my fists against my knees, feeling a sudden, overpowering surge of grief. The pain in my limbs, even the cold that had worked its way deep into my flesh and bones, made me feel as if I was experiencing it at a distance. Maybe I was going into shock.

Casey reversed the SUV down the transfer stage's ramp, to where a medical crew was waiting for us. One of the doctors I remembered from my time in quarantine came forward and tried to take my arm as I stepped out of the car, but I shook him off with sufficient force that he stumbled into one of his colleagues.

He yelled something after me, and I heard someone else call my name, but I wasn't listening. I headed straight for the wide open doors and the bright, clean sunlight that lay beyond.

Outside, I kept walking, making my way towards the barracks and the row of jeeps parked outside. I was tired, hungry and on the verge of absolute exhaustion, but the rage that burned within me drove me on.

I saw a couple of soldiers standing around next to the barracks, surrounded by the usual haze of cigarette smoke. Their conversation dropped away at my approach, and I knew what I must look like. My clothes had half-dried on my back, but I was covered in streaks of mud and filth. I didn't give a shit. I stepped past them, climbed into a jeep, grabbed its keys from the dashboard and put it into reverse hard enough I dented the front bumper of the vehicle parked behind it. I drove out through the compound gates and made for the first road that would take me out of town.

I made no conscious decision to take the road north. All I wanted to do was drive, and keep driving until I could drive no longer, however far or long that might be. I'd run rings around the damn island if I had to. At first I headed east, making my way onto the highway that ringed the coast, following it as it curved north past the runway until I had passed the ancient caldera of Rano Kau.

Soon I saw waves crashing against the shore on my right, the road rising and falling with the contours of the land. At one point I saw the wreck of a trawler beached close to the coast road, tipped over on one side and resting on pebbly sand, its hull broken in half and dark shadows within. It soon slid out of sight behind me, and I kept my foot pressed hard on the accelerator, relenting only on the sharper turns in the road. I narrowed my eyes as the wind whipped at my hair, and the engine built to an angry whine.

Much too soon, I ran out of island.

I came to a stop, staring out across the ocean beyond the island's northernmost point, listening to the quiet grumble of the engine. Then I reached down and turned it off.

I glanced inland, to where I could see a row of *moai* – enormous stone heads, built by the original islanders to revere their ancestors. Half a dozen were arranged on top of a massive stone plinth. This was the first time I'd seen them first hand, though I knew there were hundreds more scattered all across the island, their backs turned to the ocean as if refusing to acknowledge the world beyond the horizon.

On a whim, I made my way across the loamy soil to the row of *moai*. I soon saw that the statues were far larger than they appeared from the road. The tallest I estimated to be at least a dozen metres in height, while even the smallest towered above me. They looked, I thought, like toy soldiers abandoned by some gigantic child.

I came up to the great stone plinth and sank down with my back to it, staring out at the Pacific and feeling exhausted beyond imagining.

All I could think about was how long they had all been lying to me. What else, I wondered, had they been hiding?

I watched the clouds scud over the horizon for what must have been a good long while, a warm breeze blowing in from the ocean, because by the time I heard the sound of an approaching engine the sun had moved a fair distance across the sky. I sat up, seeing a lone figure on a motorbike sweeping along the coast road, before pulling up next to my parked jeep.

It was Yuichi. He looked all around until he saw me over by the statues, then started to make his way towards me on foot.

'I heard what happened,' he said, once he reached me. The wind had picked up. I noticed he had a bottle of home-brewed whisky in one hand. 'That's really shitty, especially about what happened to Nadia. That's just . . .' He looked lost for words for a moment. 'I'm sorry,' he said finally.

I nodded. 'What are you even doing here?'

He looked up at the statues, tipping his head back to stare along the length of the plinth, then back out to sea. 'Well, somebody had to,' he finally said with a shrug.

'Drew the short straw, huh?'

At least he had the good grace to laugh. He pulled the cap off the bottle, took a sip from it, grimaced and handed it down.

'I'm guessing that's not water,' I said.

'Newest batch,' he said. 'Try it.'

'Sure you should be driving and drinking?'

'I don't see any traffic cops, do you?'

I took the bottle and had a sip. The whisky burned my tongue, but I took a longer swig until I felt a pleasant numbness begin to seep through me. Then I handed it back to him.

'Just hang on to it for now,' said Yuichi.

I shrugged and set the bottle down on the grass beside me. 'I've got a question.'

'About?'

'Oskar said that the reason none of you ever told me the truth about who I really am, is because the Authority threatened to take away your retirement privileges if you did. Is that true? Does that mean they'd refuse to let Oskar ever retire?'

I watched him think it over, the wind catching his grey ponytail. 'I talked to the others,' he said at last. 'None of us are going to say how you found out, or who told you. Fact is, one way or the other, we'd have had to tell you the truth *eventually*. And we did warn Bramnik and the rest of them about that.' He smiled slightly. 'Nadia was especially vocal regarding how idiotic the whole thing was.'

Nadia. I saw her again in my mind's eye, sinking into the dark and freezing waters, as hands reached up to drag her down.

I looked up at him. 'Say I went marching up to Mort Bramnik and demanded I be allowed to go and live in some safe alternate without waiting ten years. What would happen?'

'It wouldn't be allowed,' he said.

'Then we're no better than prisoners, or indentured slaves at best.'

Yuichi looked pained. 'Come on,' he said. 'You know it's not that simple. Or even anywhere near that bad.'

I wondered what it must have been like for Yuichi and all the rest of them to see their friend – the first Jerry Beche – as good as come back to life, but with no memories of his time among them. I remembered the way Tony Nuyakpuk had looked at me the first time he saw me, and the time Nadia had said it was good to have me back, before quickly correcting herself. I especially remembered the numerous times I had walked into the Hotel du Mauna Loa and immediately felt as if I had been the subject of conversation until just a moment before.

'So, just to be clear,' I said, 'I'm from some alternate like the one the first Jerry Beche came from?'

'That's right.' Yuichi nodded.

'I have a lot of questions,' I said.

Yuichi nodded again. 'Of course you do. And we'll all try and answer them as best we can.'

'So what about Nadia?' I asked, my throat tight. 'Are they going to go retrieve some other version of her, from some other alternate, like they did me?'

'I don't know,' said Yuichi. 'I guess that's up to Bramnik and the rest of the Authority types to decide.'

I wondered what Rozalia might have to say about that.

'Back there,' I said, 'we couldn't even radio for help. All those

drones flying over that city might as well not even have been there.'
I took a long swig of Yuichi's whisky. 'All of it's an unmitigated, stinking, fucking mess – run, so far as I can tell, by idiots.'

'Yeah,' said Yuichi. He scuffed at the dirt underfoot with a boot. 'Still. Better than being stuck alone on some empty world, surrounded by death, with nothing to live for while you get older and nuttier. Right?'

I put my face in my hands and mumbled something.

'What you say?' asked Yuichi.

'I said you're a shithead,' I repeated, louder this time.

'For what?'

I looked back up, leaning my head against the cool ancient stone. 'For being right.'

He laughed.

I looked at him. 'At least tell me how he died.'

'The first Jerry? It was just a stupid accident. He was up high in the ruins of some building on an unexplored alternate when he lost his footing and fell.' He shrugged. 'It was just one of those cosmically stupid accidents.'

Yuichi reached a hand down to me. 'C'mon, man. I think it's time we got headed back into town, don't you?' His nose wrinkled. 'Seriously, dude. You need a shower.'

'Hey,' I said. 'Why didn't you just go find some other guy who could do this job, instead of me?'

'Why bother?' Yuichi replied. 'They'd have to go hunting that other guy down, figure out if he was crazy or not, whether or not he'd fit in with us or be able to work with other people, or if he might be psycho or paranoid or think he was being followed by black helicopters or any one of a dozen damn things. But another version of the same guy we know and trust, so similar you can't tell the difference? Someone like that's a whole lot more quantifiable – and a whole lot cheaper to retrieve and train if you know just where to find him, too.'

It started to rain. I shivered, feeling cold, and let him pull me upright before following him back down to the vehicles.

ELEVEN

I woke the next morning, with a pounding hangover, to the sound of someone walking around inside my house. I listened through a haze of pain to the clatter of pans in the kitchen, the inside of my mouth feeling as rough and dry as a lizard's scales.

I started to remember what had happened after I followed Yuichi back into town. I had kept hold of his home-brewed whisky, draining the rest of it as I followed behind his motorbike in my jeep. How the hell I ever made it back into town without smashing it beyond repair was beyond me. Mostly I remembered tumbling out of it before making my way inside the Hotel du Mauna Loa, where Wallace Deans sat alone, his table crammed with empty glasses. I recalled how he had watched in silence while I got behind the deserted bar and poked around for something else to drink.

I had stopped on my way back out, a half-bottle of some brown liquid cradled in my arms like a baby, looked over at Wallace and said, 'Fuck you.'

Wallace had just raised a glass in my direction. 'And fuck you too,' he responded with apparent relish, as I stumbled back out.

I came downstairs to find Rozalia sitting on a kitchen stool, about to work the plunger on my cafetière. From the look on her face when she turned to see me, I sensed I was not the only one who had drunk themselves to sleep.

'So,' she said, nodding around the room with a flick of her head. 'How are you settling into the new place?'

'It's okay. Still need to do a little more redecorating.'

'Previous owner's taste in home decor an issue?'

'Fake tigerskin rugs. Miniature Grecian statues on plinths. I hid it all in the back of a shed where I couldn't see it.' I stepped towards her. 'Rozalia . . .'

'Sit down,' she ordered, pushing the plunger on the cafetière all the way down. Her voice sounded raw and strained. 'You want eggs?'

I stared at her, unsure what to say or do.

'I said,' she repeated, anger edging into her voice, 'Do. You. Want. Eggs?'

I reached for a glass of water already sitting on the countertop and drained it. 'Sure,' I said, wiping my mouth before refilling the glass.

Rozalia nodded and pulled a pan from a hook, slamming it onto the hob with undue force before switching on the gas bottle beneath the hob. She broke six eggs against the side of the pan with the air of an executioner dispatching victims, then swirled them around the pan, staring at them as they sizzled. I got hold of a mug and filled it with coffee, shivering and coughing at the first sip as I took a seat. Clearly she liked it a lot stronger than I did.

Two minutes later, Rozalia dumped a plate of eggs in front of me. I was impressed. She'd managed to both undercook *and* burn them.

'You know,' I said, choosing my words as carefully as possible, 'I remember exactly what it's like to go through something like this. I mean, lose someone.'

Rozalia nodded. 'Your wife, Alice. I know what you're trying to do, Jerry. Don't. That's not why I'm here.'

'I know words don't help much, but—'

'I do *not want* your fucking sympathy!' she yelled.

I put both hands up in surrender.

The wild look faded from her eyes and she shovelled the remaining half-crisped, half-liquid eggs onto a second plate and sat down across from me, scooping the gooey mess into her mouth. I tried eating mine and quickly came to the conclusion I'd be better off sticking with the coffee. At least it was helping to burn away a little of the previous night's excess.

She finished her eggs, then pushed away the plate, and stared over at me. 'I don't think what happened last night was an accident.'

I tried to process the words, unsure if I'd heard her correctly. 'I got the impression there was some kind of equipment failure. Maybe—'

Her knuckles whitened where she gripped the edge of the counter top. I could see how hard she was fighting to hold herself together. 'No,' she said tightly. 'There are things you don't know, Jerry. Things no one else knows.'

'Maybe you didn't hear about it, but Oskar told me a few things about myself you'd all been keeping from me. If that's what you're—'

'No.' She shook her head. 'Not that. Nadia had . . . suspicions.'

'About what?'

Her shoulders rose and fell and her eyes met mine for the first time. 'About some of the circumstances around your predecessor's death.'

I put down my mug. 'You're talking about the other Jerry, right?' I realized my hands were trembling slightly, and not just because of the hangover. 'The one who was here before me.'

'It's important that everything I say stays between us.'

'Go on.'

She leaned forward, her expression intent. 'I want you to *swear*, Jerry. On your life.'

'Fine. I swear. Nothing goes beyond this kitchen.'

She nodded, apparently satisfied. 'That other you had been looking into something, just before he died. It's true that there have been accidents, equipment failures and software problems of all kinds, since before they brought you here. A few of them were nearly as bad as what happened to you last night, but rarely fatal.'

'What exactly do you mean, "looking into something"?'

'He had an idea that maybe some of those accidents weren't really accidents.'

I fought for understanding through the haze of hangover pain. 'Go on.'

'He had reasons,' she said carefully, 'to believe certain missions may have been deliberately sabotaged.'

'How could you know this? And what possible reason could anyone have to do something like that?'

'Good question. Anyway, a while back, he came to talk to Nadia about a specific incident that nearly got a lot of people killed.'

I licked my lips. 'What happened, exactly?'

'At the time, it had been arranged that Mort Bramnik was going to join some of us on an expedition to a recently opened alternate. Bramnik was intending to show some people from the Authority's own alternate around, and we were expected to talk to them as if we were nothing more than inter-dimensional fucking tourist guides. I don't know who these people were, but from the way Bramnik was acting towards them, not to mention the fact that they were getting the grand tour, it wasn't hard to guess they were important.'

She leaned back, turning her coffee mug in her hands. 'Something went wrong not long after we crossed over into the alternate, along with all the Authority tourists. We ran into something big and nasty that'd make you shit your pants in a second flat. Mort Bramnik himself nearly got killed as a result. Until that moment, we'd had every reason to believe we would be entirely safe, but the whole thing turned into a fuck-up of truly epic proportions.' She looked up at me. 'And until last night, that was the worst incident of all – even including the whole debacle in those vaults you saved me from. The only reason nobody got killed on that outing with the tourists was because Casey just about single-handedly saved our collective asses.'

'So what happened after that?' I asked.

'The Patriot agents started showing up, snooping around the island and generally getting in everyone's face. I think Bramnik's been under a lot of pressure because of that first bad incident. Over the past year, he's been away from the island with such frequency we started wondering if he'd ever come back, or who his replacement might be.'

'If he's screwing up so badly, maybe a replacement for him isn't such a bad idea,' I ventured.

'Except that Agent Greenbrooke would most likely be his replacement, the way things have been going around here. And if Greenbrooke wound up running things, there isn't one of us who'd be able to so much as take a shit without half a dozen Patriot agents taking photographs and writing extensive reports on the subversive nature of our bowel movements. Believe me, *nobody* wants Greenbrooke in charge.'

Having met the man, I could only agree. 'So Nadia had suspicions about my predecessor's death.' It still felt strange, saying the words.

She nodded. 'He had some reason for believing the mission with Bramnik might have been sabotaged, but he wanted to find proof before he started throwing accusations around. Except he went and got killed himself, not long after. Nadia figured that, in itself, was also more than a little suspicious, so she decided to see what else she could find out on her own.' She shrugged, her expression bleak. 'And now she's gone, too.'

I put my hands up in a stalling motion. 'Wait a minute. Why are you even telling me all of this?'

She frowned. 'Jerry – I mean the first Jerry – was a good friend of ours.' She looked down, and I saw she was trying hard to suppress tears. '*You* were. Seeing you alive like that, when you and Nadia both turned up in that EV, when I thought me and the others were goners for sure . . .' She hugged the coffee close to her. 'It was a shock, I'll tell you that, even though I already knew they'd retrieved you from your alternate, and that I'd have to meet you eventually.' Her eyes met mine. 'I'm also telling you all this because you saved my life, and you deserve to have someone tell you the truth for once.'

I thought for a moment. 'So did everyone else know Nadia was asking questions?'

Rozalia shook her head. 'She didn't announce it publicly, if that's what you mean. She just made a few careful, casual enquiries so as not to arouse suspicion.'

'But not careful enough, you think?'

Rozalia gave me a hopeless shrug. 'She also visited the alternate where the other Jerry died, I know that much. To be honest, I'm not clear on exactly who she might or might not have talked to.'

I got up and scraped my uneaten eggs into the bin before dropping both our dishes in the sink, just to give myself time to mull over everything I had just been told.

'I'm sorry about your loss,' I said, turning back to her, 'truly sorry. I liked Nadia a great deal. I'm not in the least surprised she and my predecessor were good friends, because you're clearly both good people. She made a real effort to make me feel welcome, even though it must have been like seeing a ghost. If there's *any* reason to think foul play was involved then, believe me, I'll be the first to want to know who's responsible.'

I drained the last of my coffee and dropped the mug in the sink along with the dishes before continuing. 'But none of this means anything unless you can prove there really was foul play involved. Just for a start, what possible motive could anyone have for wanting to sabotage any of the missions in the first place?'

'Well,' said Rozalia, a touch defensively, 'that's the reason your predecessor went looking to see if he could find any evidence.'

'Did he talk to you or Nadia? Is that how you know all this?'

Rozalia nodded. 'He spoke to Nadia, but not me. Unfortunately, she refused to share the full details of their conversation with me.'

'Why?'

'She was trying to protect me,' she replied, with undisguised bitterness.

'What from?'

'Everything,' she said. 'I loved that woman to bits, but at times she was like a damn mother hen.' She reached into a pocket and pulled out a crumpled packet of cigarettes. 'You mind?'

I shook my head – I wasn't a smoker, but the kitchen window was open next to where she sat. I waited as she lit up with a battered lighter, her breath faltering slightly as she let out the first rush of smoke.

'Like there was this one time I got sick,' she continued, waving away some of the smoke. 'This is before we were retrieved by the Authority, mind.'

'You survived together, the two of you, didn't you?'

Rozalia nodded. 'Nadia spent a lot of time and energy looking after me and keeping me alive back before our retrieval. Sometimes, if things got really bad, she'd keep it from me. She'd just . . . clam up rather than say anything. Maybe it's because I'm more than ten years younger than her; I don't know. But any time we had bad arguments then or since, it's because she'd kept something back from me. I didn't even know she'd *spoken* to Jerry until I came home and found them sitting there in our living room.' She laughed. 'I actually got worried they were having an affair or something, the way they were acting so secretively. But I made her tell me the truth in the end, and that's when I knew she was doing it again . . . protecting me, when I didn't need protecting.'

I reached up to touch a pendant that was no longer there, imagining what it might have been like if Alice had survived to stay by my side through the post-extinction years. Had she fallen ill, or been in danger of any kind, I might easily have been guilty of the same well-intentioned but overbearing care.

Rozalia got up and held the smoked butt of her cigarette under the tap before dropping it in the trash.

'You've been here for years,' I said, 'and I've barely arrived. You don't have any idea why either of them were so intent on keeping their concerns under their hats?'

She shrugged. 'Maybe they were afraid of the Patriots finding out. Everyone's scared to death of them, even the other Authority types. If they ever found out what your predecessor was up to, things might get worse for us.'

'How can you be so sure?' I asked her.

'Greenbrooke hates us,' she said, her voice low and venomous. 'He tortured Wallace. *He's* the reason all our missions have been getting longer, and also a lot more dangerous.' She met my eyes. 'And he *especially* hates me and Nadia. If I walked into Government House and tried to talk to Bramnik, I don't know what might happen. For all I know, the Patriots might be put in charge of an investigation, and then we'd *really* be fucked.'

'All right, so what now?' I said. 'I mean, I'm grateful you told me all this, but you're acting as if you think I'm going to pick up where the first Jerry left off.'

Her nostrils flared. 'Would that be so bad?'

I shook my head and chuckled. My comment hadn't been serious, but clearly she didn't see it that way. 'Rozalia . . . I think you're forgetting just how new here I am. I only just had my first real mission, and it was a complete disaster. And now . . . all this,' I said, waving my hand. 'I'm supposed to do what, exactly? Because I really don't have any idea.'

There was a wild look in her eyes. 'So you don't want to know. Is that what you're saying?'

'It's not that. It's just . . .' I sighed, collecting my thoughts. 'I'm not a detective. I honestly don't know what you expect me to actually *do*.'

Rozalia stood. 'You need,' she said, 'to talk to Chloe Wicks. She knows more about the other Jerry than anyone else on this island.'

'Chloe Wicks?' I repeated. 'I've barely even spoken to her, except the one time. How . . . ?'

Then I remembered the way she had kissed me so unexpectedly outside the entrance of the Hotel du Mauna Loa. Given what I now knew, the incident took on an entirely new and unexpected perspective.

'You were together for some time,' said Rozalia. 'Nadia told me she saw what happened between you and her when Casey was putting on his show.'

'It didn't make any sense,' I said. 'I guess it does now.'

I followed Rozalia to the front door, where she stood on the threshold. 'Does Chloe know anything about all this stuff you just told me?' I asked.

'Probably. Yes. I think so. Certainly Nadia spoke to her,' she said, 'after the first Jerry died. So? Are you going to talk to her?'

'I guess. But maybe you should come with me,' I said. 'It might be better if you were—'

Rozalia shook her head. 'I don't think so,' she said, forcing a smile. 'But don't wait too long.' Her hand brushed my arm as she turned away, and then she was gone, walking out through the gate and down the empty street.

I closed the door and leaned my forehead against it, feeling like the fragile foundations of my new life were about to slip out from under me.

TWELVE

Four hours later, after I had drunk enough coffee and water to take the edge off the lingering hangover, I was standing outside Chloe Wicks' home. It was a two-storey affair on the northern edge of town, its front yard filled with rusting chicken cages and overgrown grass and clearly untouched since the day its original owners vanished.

I knocked on the door several times, but got no response. I called out her name and waited, but nothing. Hell, for all I knew, she wasn't even on the island – away, perhaps, on some expedition to another alternate.

I tried the front door and found it was unlocked. I pushed it open slightly and called her name again, but still got no reply. I stepped inside anyway, finding myself within a small, cramped vestibule, a narrow staircase to one side leading to the upper floor. Through a door on my right I saw a kitchen, and the remains of vegetables on a chopping board, suggesting that perhaps she wasn't too far away. On my left I saw a living room, one wall lined with shelf after shelf of mouldering paperbacks. A framed photograph on a shelf drew my eye and when I stepped closer, I saw it was a picture of myself with my arm around Chloe.

The *other* Jerry, I corrected myself. Not me. I felt suddenly disoriented, and pressed my back against a wall until I could steady my breathing.

In truth, I had been expecting to find something like this, after what Rozalia had told me. Even so, the sight of this picture – it looked to have been taken in the bar of the Hotel du Mauna Loa –

sent a thrill of shock through my nerves. The two of them were laughing in the photograph, and now I looked closer, I could see other faces in the background – Casey, Nadia and Oskar.

Then I turned my attention to the books on the shelves, where I saw a dozen thick-bound notebooks placed close to the floor. I sank down onto a dusty couch, feeling all the strength go out of me. I clutched at my belly, feeling suddenly nauseous.

My diaries.

In my first years of solitude, when my primary concern had been survival, the idea of keeping a diary had seemed a deeply foolish one. And yet that simple act of writing entries as if I were describing events to Alice had somehow kept me sane – or relatively sane, at any rate. The routine of putting the words down, of describing the daily struggle to survive, kept me from cutting my own wrists. Later, when I wandered my alternate in a hopeless search for other survivors, I had managed to fill two thick books with crabbed writing and sketches. They had become so precious to me that I had, at times, risked my life in order to protect them.

And now I found myself staring at a dozen notebooks identical in appearance in every way to the ones that now sat in my own house, on the other side of town.

I reached down and pulled out the last of the notebooks on the right, assuming they were arranged, as my own were, in chrono-logical order. I expected to find mostly blank pages, since this was the last notebook in which I had written immediately prior to my own retrieval.

At that time, my entries had grown increasingly sporadic as the Alice in my thoughts took on a kind of reality of her own. Each day was becoming too much like every other, and the less I wrote, the more I struggled to find reasons to keep on living.

I had thought that I might start writing again, about the new life the Authority had gifted me with. But, in a way, a spell had been broken. I had barely written anything since a few short days after emerging from quarantine.

I opened my other self's last diary, but instead of finding the blank pages I had expected, I found them to be filled with tight, cramped handwriting identical to my own.

I flipped back to the beginning with shaking hands, finding the same sparse, barely descriptive passages I remembered making in the days immediately before my retrieval: a few brief words about necessary repairs to my home and observations about the weather.

I moved on to the newer, unfamiliar entries. I began to read, my heart racing in my chest.

It's been nearly a year since I first came here, I read, *and maybe it's time I started writing in this thing again*.

I slammed the notebook shut and threw it on the floor. That *other* Jerry had sat on this couch, slept under this roof, eaten in the kitchen I had seen through the door on the other side of the hallway.

I felt my skin crawl, literally *crawl*, the hairs on the backs of my arms bristling with terror.

'We lived here together,' said a voice from behind me. 'I guess you figured that out by now.'

I whirled around, to see Chloe Wicks standing at the entrance to her living room. She held a paper bag full of groceries from the commissary. I had not even heard her come in.

She put the bag down on the floor, then walked past me, dropping into a chair opposite the couch. 'I've been meaning to do something about them,' she said, nodding towards the notebooks. 'Stick them in the attic, maybe burn them. I hadn't really decided.'

'It must have been hard,' I managed to say, 'seeing me walking around the island, like . . .'

The words faltered in my mouth, and I let myself sink onto the couch. Despite everything, my mind at that moment was filled with the memory of that one, fleeting kiss before I knew anything about her.

'Like a ghost,' she said. 'I heard about what Oskar said to you. Winnie told me just now, down at the commissary.'

There was a moment's awkward silence. 'It's been hell, actually,' she said finally. 'You look like him, talk like him . . . but you're not him.' A perplexed look came over her face. 'I–I don't know. It's confusing.'

'There must be some differences,' I said.

I saw the flicker of a smile. 'Well, you're a couple of years younger than him, for a start. You're the same age he was when they retrieved him.'

'You almost make it sound like time travel,' I said.

'Weird physics, more like,' she said. 'It's how they can sometimes visit alternates before, as well as after, an extinction event. That's how Casey got that footage he was showing everyone that night we . . .'

I nodded. She didn't need to say which night. 'So I'm the same age he was, when he first arrived here?'

'Pretty much.'

I cleared my throat. 'I spoke to Rozalia this morning.'

Chloe stared at me, alarmed. 'Oh God. How is she doing?'

'Pretty much as you'd expect. She told me you might know a few things about the . . . the other Jerry.' I looked around again, at the diaries, the photograph. 'But I think I've got it pretty much figured out.'

'So you came here,' she said, 'to see if it was true.'

'There's another reason.' She looked at me, waiting. 'Rozalia came to see me because she thinks Nadia's death . . . well, she seems to think it might not have been an accident. That it might somehow have been connected to what happened to your Jerry.' I shrugged. 'She talked about him carrying out some kind of, I guess, investigation, for want of a better word. Does any of this mean anything to you?'

Instead of laughing at me or telling me I was crazy, she merely asked, 'Was that all she said?'

'Pretty much.'

Chloe's hands twisted together in her lap. 'I guess there's no reason not to tell you. Back when he was still alive, me and . . . and the other Jerry had a bad argument because he'd been disappearing for hours or even days at a time. I knew he must be taking trips to other alternates, because he was nowhere on the island. But if he was, they were clearly off the record, and that got me worried. Why would he be going on secret trips? And who was responsible for sending him on them?' She looked past me and out of the window. 'In the end, I was only able to get him to talk by threatening to tell the other Pathfinders he was up to something behind their backs.'

'And?'

'He confessed he'd been trying to find out about what was causing all the equipment failures and accidents.' Her eyes briefly met mine. 'He swore me to secrecy, said I couldn't tell anyone. Not even if something bad happened to him. *Especially* not then.' She shook her head. 'I could tell something had frightened him, and then . . . then he was gone.'

'And that's when Nadia came to talk to you?'

'Rozalia told you that?'

I nodded.

She sighed heavily. 'Goddam him. The other Jerry, I mean. I understand why he turned to Nadia – you know she used to be a cop?'

I looked at her, surprised. 'No, I didn't.'

'Well, it hurt that he felt he could share secrets with Nadia, but not me – even after I just about blackmailed him into telling me at least part of the truth.'

'Did you think about telling someone in charge about all this? Someone like Bramnik?'

She sighed and shook her head. 'No.'

'Why not?'

She picked at a loose cotton thread on her jeans. 'Where I came from was a bad place, Jerry. Things you probably took for granted, like free speech and being allowed to mind your own business, just didn't exist there. The last thing you'd ever want to do is trust *anyone* in authority. And people like Agent Greenbrooke remind me much too much of those days.'

'Surely Bramnik himself isn't that bad? He clearly despises the Patriots.'

'There are rumours the Patriots have spies among the civilian staff. Did Rozalia mention that?'

'She didn't. She did say, though, that Nadia was cautious about talking to Bramnik herself.'

'Well, now you know why. It pays to be careful who you speak to around here.'

'I'm worried about Rozalia,' I said. 'When she says she thinks Nadia's death is connected to all this, she's saying what happened last night wasn't an accident. But it doesn't make sense.'

'Why not?'

'Because I can't figure out how any saboteur could possibly have been able to pull off so many things all at once. They'd have to simultaneously shut down our communications, screw with the surveillance drones *and* lead the bee-brains towards us. Can you imagine someone arranging all that on their own? Because I can't.'

'So why does Rozalia think that?' asked Chloe.

I spread my hands. 'I guess she's grief stricken. It'd hardly be surprising.'

She eyed me sadly. 'Do you want my advice?' She shifted on the edge of her seat, her expression intent. 'Drop all of this. Forget about it. You met Greenbrooke, didn't you? I'm prepared to think he's not even the worst of the Authority. Don't make the same mistake your predecessor did. Don't draw their attention.'

She stood up then, and I could sense she wanted me to go. I had thought of asking her about the kiss, but I knew now that it had not been intended for me. It had been for him – my predecessor, the man in whose shadow I now walked.

I stopped at the open front door, hit by a sudden thought. 'After he died,' I asked, 'what did they do with him?'

'He's buried just outside of town,' she said, 'in a graveyard just past the runway—'

I ran out and into the unkempt garden. Rozalia's half-cooked eggs came surging up the back of my throat and onto the unmown grass.

'Oh God,' I heard Chloe say from somewhere behind me. 'I'm . . . I'm sorry. I should have thought, before I said anything. I just . . .'

I heard her rush back indoors, then come back out seconds later, shoving a wad of tissues into my hand. I wiped my mouth before pulling myself upright.

Somewhere within walking distance was a grave with my name on it. In that moment, I hated the Authority nearly as much as I had the people who'd wiped out everything I had ever known and loved on my own alternate. Bramnik and his ilk had brought me to this place without a moment's consideration either to the people I would be living among, or to how I might cope once I learned the truth, as I inevitably would.

'A favour,' I said. I tried to swallow some of the bad taste away. 'I'd like to borrow one of his diaries. The last one he kept, in particular.'

She glanced back inside the house. 'I . . . guess that's not a problem.'

It had occurred to me that if there might really be something suspicious about the first Jerry's death, and if he had continued writing in his diary after his retrieval, there might then be some clue in his diary entries – some hint of the truth, at least, if not an outright accusation.

Chloe went back inside, returning moments later with the notebook. I took it from her, holding it tentatively, as if it might burn me. I tucked it under my arm and stepped out past the gate, feeling dizzy, disconnected from my body. I wondered if I was in shock.

She followed me, stopping at the gate. 'You ought to know that I've asked for extra mission time – anything that'll take me away from the island for a while. I thought I'd had enough time to get over things, but I think maybe it's still too soon after all.' She looked at her house, then back at me. 'If you want to get hold of the other notebooks for any reason, feel free to just walk in and take them.'

'Maybe once you're back . . .'

'*If* I'm back,' she said, 'it'll be barely, if at all, for at least the foreseeable future.' She swallowed hard. 'Please don't take it the wrong way, but I'd rather you kept your distance for now.'

I watched her retreat, closing her door without looking back. I made my way home, feeling chilly despite the afternoon sunshine.

THIRTEEN

Seventy-two hours later I heard a knock at my front door and found Rozalia standing on my doorstep.

'Can I come in?'

'Sure,' I said, despite a whole welter of misgivings, and pulled the door wide.

She stepped past me and walked into my kitchen for the second time that week. I turned and followed, feeling irritable and tired from a lack of sleep. I'd been having some pretty bad nightmares the last couple of nights.

'I'll get straight to the point,' she said, turning to face me. 'I need your help. Are you scheduled to go on any missions any time soon?'

I scratched my head and yawned. 'Only the big one we're scheduled to take part in tomorrow morning,' I said. I had spent the best part of the last three days taking trips into Government House in the centre of town, to give recorded statements in Kip Mayer's office regarding the circumstances of Nadia's death.

Rozalia nodded. 'Great. I need you to go back with me to where Nadia died. Tonight. It'll be quick, I promise. In fact, we'll be finished in time for the morning's mission.'

I opened and closed my mouth a couple of times before I understood she really was asking what I thought she was. '*Tonight?*' I shook my head. 'Not a chance in hell. You heard me when I said I had a mission in the morning, didn't you? How long is this going to take, exactly?'

She stepped closer to me, a beseeching look on her face. 'Not long.

This is important, Jerry. There's no one else can show me just where . . . everything happened.'

I shook my head fervently. 'I don't ever want to run into one of those night patrols again.'

'You won't,' she said. 'It's late at night here, but it'll be morning over there. They'll all be back in their Hives.'

'Did the Authority actually give you permission to go back there?'

She looked furtive. 'Not exactly.'

I sighed and sank onto a kitchen stool. 'Explain "not exactly".'

'I bribed someone. A rig technician,' she blurted.

I shook my head. The idea of ever going back to that particular alternate filled me with a sense of crawling horror. 'No,' I said. 'Absolutely not. Why don't you ask Oskar instead?'

'Because I already know exactly what he'd say. Oskar doesn't give a damn about anyone but himself, and I don't know if I could even trust him to be discreet about my asking.'

'That's not true,' I said hotly. 'Well, he cared about that damn dog of his. And, besides, Nadia died in the water. If you're looking for her body, I have no idea what happened to it.'

I saw the look on her face and softened my voice. 'I'm sorry, I—'

She sank down onto a kitchen stool, her expression intent. 'It's all right,' she said, her voice filled with a determination that told me that nothing I said was going to make her change her mind. 'Anyway, it's not her body I'm looking for. I just want to see that SUV you abandoned.'

'Why?'

'I've seen some of the initial reports about what happened,' she explained. 'I also read some of the transcripts from the statements you've been giving Mayer over the last couple of days.'

I looked at her in surprise. 'They let you see those?'

'I wanted to know the exact circumstances around Nadia's death. I guess Kip took pity on me.' She shook her head. 'Not that there was any reason *not* to let me know, but there are parts of the overall story that frankly don't make sense to me.'

I shifted on my seat. 'Like?'

'Like the fact that the bee-brains attacked you the way they did.'

I remembered Nadia's own confusion on that exact point. 'They're supposed to be aggressive at close range, aren't they?'

'Yes, but the way they came after you is something I'd associate more with warfare between Hives.'

'It sounds like you know a lot about them,' I said.

'I worked with Winifred on the first mapping and observation expeditions,' she replied. 'We studied hundreds of hours of remote drone surveillance that show what happens when communities of bee-brains from rival Hives encounter each other. They always attack. There's good evidence they can tell friend from foe in the same way they know where to go around the city – by scent. Based on the transcripts, it seems to me that they were reacting to you as if you were from a rival Hive – which means far more aggressively than normal. Otherwise, their behaviour runs completely contrary to everything we've observed.'

I lifted my shoulders. 'All right, then. But that still doesn't explain why it happened the way it did.'

'I know.' She patted her backpack. 'But that's why I want in particular to take a look at that SUV you were driving, maybe even carry out some tests on it if it proves feasible. But I can't do that unless you guide me there.'

I rubbed at my face with my hands. 'Do you know how much you're asking?'

'I do,' she reassured me. 'I know this is a lot to ask, Jerry. Maybe even too much. I can't say I didn't have my doubts about how you'd react.' She leaned forward, putting a hand on my knee, her eyes searching mine. 'But if what happened to you and Nadia is anything like what happened to your predecessor – or what Nadia *thought* happened to him – then maybe there's some way to find the proof. Maybe somebody found a way to *make* those creatures attack you the way they did.'

I groaned out loud. 'And what about everything else that went wrong? The failing drones? The inoperative communications equipment? How are you going to explain all *that*?'

She leaned back and swallowed. 'I can't. But I have to try. I *have* to.' A note of defiance crept into her voice. 'Tell me honestly: do *you* believe that what happened was really just an accident?'

I shook my head wearily, cursing myself for a fool. 'I guess, if I were to be honest, I've been having my concerns. So many things went wrong, all at the same time.'

She nodded as if satisfied. 'Then the only way to be sure is to go there and see what we can find.'

I closed my eyes, suddenly regretting my good nature. 'If I do this, you will owe me forever. For the rest of time, Rozalia.'

'I'll pay you back for it somehow. We need to be at the hangar at midnight.'

I groaned. 'And it has to be tonight? Not tomorrow night, maybe?'

'Yes, it has to be tonight,' she said, bristling slightly. 'I already said this wasn't an official trip. Do you know how many bottles of purloined Chivas Regal I had to find to make this happen?'

'There'll be a guard at the stage. What about him?'

'I'm pretty sure the rig tech is splitting the booze with the guard.' She stood up. 'Meet me at half eleven, my place?'

'Sure. What the hell.'

She got up and, to my surprise, hugged me. 'Thank you, Jerry,' she whispered. 'This means a lot to me.'

'I know,' I replied, feeling guilty for my earlier recalcitrance.

I made the mistake of trying to catch at least some sleep before I had to go to meet Rozalia at eleven-thirty, and suffered the inevitable nightmares. Mostly they revolved around drowning, or of feeling sodden hands reach up from beneath to drag me down, and mouths that gaped too wide to be human. When I woke, I decided I'd tell Rozalia the deal was off. Then I changed my mind, then flip-flopped from one side to the other about a hundred times before I finally set out for Rozalia's on foot.

When I got there, I found her waiting by her front door with a pair of mountain bicycles and a heavy-looking rucksack. 'What are those for?' I asked, nodding at the bikes in confusion.

'A jeep would make too much noise,' she explained, 'and more than likely someone would see us driving up there and wonder why. This way is better.' She nodded at one of the two machines. 'You can have Nadia's.'

It took us twenty minutes to cycle to the main stage. When we got there, I saw a lone guard standing outside the warehouse doors, looking as jumpy as hell as we rolled up to him.

'Hey,' Rozalia said casually as she dismounted her bicycle and lifted her rucksack from her shoulders. 'Dom around?'

The guard glanced at the rucksack, which made a distinctive clinking sound as she took it off. 'Sure,' he said. 'Go right in.'

I wheeled both bicycles inside to the main stage while Rozalia carried the rucksack. I could hardly believe it had been this easy to get inside. I saw a small rotund man sitting smoking next to the control rig and guessed this must be Dom. He jumped slightly when he saw me enter beside Rozalia, and darted an accusing stare at her.

'What the hell?' he protested loudly. 'You didn't tell me you were bringing anyone else with you!'

'Here,' said Rozalia, dropping the rucksack at his feet. 'Take a look and stop complaining.'

She stepped back and watched as Dom kneeled by the bag with a wary look on his face, unzipping it to reveal half a dozen bottles of whisky.

'All yours,' said Rozalia.

Dom glared up at her. 'This had better not be any of that rotgut your friend Yuichi's been brewing,' he muttered.

'It's the real deal,' Rozalia insisted. 'Try some if you don't believe me.'

'Fine. I believe you,' the technician muttered, and nodded towards the stage. 'You got transport where you're going?'

'I checked the mission itinerary,' said Rozalia. 'There are vehicles over there we can use.'

Dom stepped towards the control rig and touched its keyboard.

In response, a screen lit up. 'I want to be clear about this,' he said, still glowering. 'You weren't here. I don't know *anything* about this.'

'All clear,' said Rozalia. 'And thanks.'

'Don't thank me,' he muttered. 'Just get the hell up on the stage so we can get this over with.'

A few minutes later I found myself staring at the ruined towers of Sao Paolo, off in the distance beyond parkland half-gone to jungle. I had hoped never to see them again.

Closer to hand sat the jeep and EV truck I remembered from last time, along with the SUV Casey had driven. A drone sat on its charging mount next to the equipment tent, humming quietly.

My gaze drifted towards the distant Hives, and I almost had to remind myself I wasn't trapped in one of my nightmares.

'Hey,' I said, nodding at the drone. 'Won't they pick us up driving into the city?'

Rozalia shook her head. 'Only if there's someone to watch the monitors,' she said. 'And, in case you hadn't noticed, we're alone.'

'Let's get this over with, then,' I said, heading for the SUV. Rozalia nodded, following in my wake. I found the map Casey had used to find his way along the city's safe routes, still neatly folded on the dashboard. I checked the rear seat and saw a pair of rifles there, along with enough boxes of ammunition to stage a coup in a small African nation.

I hoped Rozalia wasn't going to ask me if I'd spoken to Chloe yet. That was something I was a long way from being ready to talk about.

'Here,' I said, handing the map to Rozalia as she climbed into the front passenger seat next to me. 'Since you helped map this place out, you can navigate for me while I drive.'

Every inch of the road into Sao Paolo was burned into my brain. I drove across the shallow waters beneath the shattered bridge, then back up the incline, before guiding the car onto the road that led deeper into the city. Low one-storey suburban homes gave way to broad avenues lined with shops and businesses, and I saw the remains of the financial district off in the distance, once-glittering towers reduced to shattered, partially dismantled stubs.

Rozalia told me where to turn, and which avenues to follow, and where to go in order to best reduce our chances of running into any bee-brains. But in truth, I hardly needed her help, and I soon found my way back to the elevated motorway spanning the Pinheiros, and the blockade through which Nadia had carefully navigated the other SUV a lifetime before.

The whole way I kept having flashbacks, like a particularly bad case of déjà vu, to my last visit. My blood near as damn curdled when I once again saw swarms of bee-brains, still dismantling the multi-storey car park near the bridge. Most of the structure's upper floors had already been demolished; I couldn't imagine how the creatures managed to do so much, with nothing more than their bare hands and the crudest of tools – and neither did I want to know.

The building soon receded into the distance, and I banished it from my thoughts.

It wasn't long before we were making our way down the same avenue near where Oskar and Nadia and I had been forced to abandon the other SUV. I kept leaning forward to glance up at the rooftops, in case I saw more improvised missiles ready to be dropped on our heads. Instead the streets around us seemed quiet and deserted, and yet I knew from bitter experience how deceptive appearances could be.

'We're nearly there,' I said, nodding at the road ahead. 'See that pile of rubble scattered across the avenue? That's why we had to take a side route, to get past it.'

'Take it easy,' said Rozalia, looking at me with worry. 'You're shaking.'

'Am I?' I looked down at my hands where they gripped the wheel. They were, indeed, shaking, and quite badly too. 'Well, hell,' I said.

I turned into the same side street Nadia had taken us into, and saw the chunk of masonry that had landed right on top of us. I'd have recognized it anywhere, even without the presence of the other SUV, still lying tipped over nearby.

'We're here,' I said, the words like dull thunder in my mind.

'Good driving, Jerry.' Rozalia pushed open the door on her side, reaching at the same time into her jacket pocket and extracting a slim leather case. 'Come on. You can keep an eye out for trouble while I take a look at that car.'

I grabbed the two rifles out of the rear of the car and handed one to Rozalia. I scanned the streets and rooftops as I stepped out, but the only sound was that of the wind sighing between the buildings. Of course, after my last visit, I knew that didn't mean a damn thing.

I glanced towards Rozalia, seeing her unzip the leather case before lifting out a glass vial and a long thin metal instrument that glittered in the midday sun.

'What is that?' I asked.

'Sampling kit,' she said, dropping down on one knee next to the toppled-over SUV. I watched as she peered closely first at the vehicle's undercarriage, then at the tyres, wondering just what the hell she was looking for.

She reached out and touched something on the undercarriage with an extended finger, then brought it to her nose and sniffed. Next she took the metal instrument and started to scrape at something on the undercarriage. I moved a little closer, until I could see some sticky, mucus-like substance clinging to the metal instrument.

She got up again and handed me the vial. 'Hold this,' she said.

I took one last glance around, then shouldered my rifle and did as she asked. I watched as she pushed the metal tool inside the vial, depositing some of the sticky stuff inside before taking the vial back and carefully sealing it.

'So what is that stuff you found?'

'You remember we talked about how the bee-brains largely oper-ate on the basis of scent? Well,' she said, holding the vial up, 'if this is what I think it is, it just might be the proof we need that Nadia's death was no accident.'

I was still trying to process what she had just told me as we got back in the SUV. 'How sure of this are you?' I asked her. 'I mean, if this is true . . .'

'I'm far from sure,' she said.

'You think someone deliberately put that stuff on our SUV?'

She glanced sideways at me. 'In your official statement, you said you ran into a night patrol. Correct?'

'Sure.' I nodded. 'But that was after the SUV got totalled.'

'The night patrols are responsible for laying the scent-routes through the city.' She showed me the vial again. 'They do it by upchucking this stuff at different points, and the bee-brains follow after the scent of it like good little soldier ants.'

She chuckled when she saw me grimace. 'See,' she continued, 'in some ways the night patrols are the brains of the operation. If I'm right,' she said, before tucking the vial back inside its leather case, 'this stuff originated with a rival Hive, most likely the one that's on the other side of the city.'

'How the hell did you manage to figure all this out?' I asked.

'Deduction, my dear Watson,' she replied. 'I spent a lot of time on this alternate studying the bee-brains, and there had to be *some* reason they went so far out of their way to attack you the way they did. And this was the only logical answer.'

I reached for the ignition and got the engine started. 'If someone really did sabotage our vehicle,' I said, 'they couldn't have known we'd run into a night patrol. Is it possible they weren't necessarily trying to get us killed?'

She laughed scornfully. 'Are you kidding? They put you in a situation where you were guaranteed to come under attack by thousands of bee-brains the moment they caught the scent from your car – and, rest assured, they'd have had a very good idea just what your chances of survival were. I call that premeditated murder.'

'So what do we do now?' I asked, sitting and listening to the engine rumble. 'It sounds to me like you've got rock-solid evidence. Are you going to take it to Bramnik?'

She hesitated as I rolled the SUV back from the wreck of the other vehicle. 'Bramnik is absent from the island. *Again.*'

'Maybe Kip Mayer . . . ?'

'I need to run some tests first,' she said, her jaws clenched.

I couldn't understand her reticence. 'Surely you just found definitive evidence someone sabotaged our mission?'

'Not necessarily.'

I looked sideways at her, hardly believing what she had said. 'Oh, come *on* . . .'

'It's a question of knowing who to trust,' she said.

'So that's it?' I snapped. 'You dragged me all the way back to this shitty, dreadful place, and now you're just going to *sit* on what you found?'

'What we need to do,' she said, 'is bide our time. We need to build a strong case. That's what Nadia would have said. She understood these things. For all I know, if we go running to Bramnik or anyone else, they'll suggest *we* planted the scent-marker. Or maybe they'll make us quietly disappear, or set some other act of sabotage to disguise our sudden and unexpected deaths. Until we've got a better idea just what Nadia and your predecessor were on to, we watch, and we wait.'

'And if we don't ever find out?' I asked.

'You've got to have faith, Jerry,' she said, her voice tight, 'and faith is all I have left.'

We made it there and back with surprising speed, no more than a couple of hours either way. It came to me that, if not for the apparently engineered incident that cost Nadia her life, the mission with her and Oskar would probably have been entirely uneventful.

'Thank Christ you're done,' said Dom the rig technician, when we finally materialized back on the main hangar stage. 'Now get the hell out of here before anyone sees you.'

I stepped back outside, Rozalia by my side, and saw it was getting close to dawn. The same guard as before nodded to us with clear relief.

Rozalia turned and called back in to Dom. 'Thanks again.'

'This is a one-time deal,' he shouted back, jabbing a finger at the both of us. 'We clear on that? Never again.'

She nodded. 'As daylight.'

Twenty minutes later we had cycled back to my front door. Rozalia dismounted, then pulled me into a hug.

'Damn,' she said, regarding me with apparent affection. 'You know how easy it is to get the two of you confused? You and the other Jerry, that is.'

I didn't know what to say. 'I should get at least a couple of hours' sleep before we head back out,' I mumbled. 'Got that mission later, remember?'

She nodded. 'I'll see you and the others then.'

She got on her bicycle and set off, and I realized she'd forgotten about Nadia's bike. I wheeled it inside and glanced at my predecessor's diary, still sitting where I had left it on my living-room table, as yet untouched.

Something still held me back from opening it. Every time I thought about reading the rest of its contents, I found myself torn between unquenchable curiosity and overwhelming terror. I knew I *would* read it – eventually – but not yet.

Not yet. But eventually. That was one promise to myself I wasn't going to break.

Later that morning, I was back at the hangar, and considerably the worse for wear for lack of sleep. Dom was gone, replaced by another technician, and some other soldier had been posted to stand guard next to the hangar entrance.

'Hey,' Yuichi called to me from on top of a stage, tapping at his wrist when he saw me enter. 'You're making a habit of being late. The others already transferred across – we've been waiting for you.'

I yawned and made a dismissive gesture. 'Frankly, fuck them. All I care about is that wherever we're going, there's coffee.'

'Hah.' Yuichi shook his head. 'Unlikely.'

This time, we were tourist herding.

Not that Schultner had used that term during my most recent briefing, after apologizing for the screw-up that sent me unprepared into a new alternate. Instead, he said, we would be escorting a 'special investigations and assessment team' to an alternate in the hours immediately before it suffered an extinction event. I was also warned not to interact with the members of this team unless addressed directly by them.

When I next spoke to Yuichi and relayed what Schultner had said, he laughed and told me 'tourist herding' was a lot closer to the mark. In his experience, these 'special investigations and assessment teams' always turned out to be gaggles of VIPs from the Authority's home alternate, on what was essentially a sightseeing trip. Or touring the apocalypse, he said with a sneer.

I walked up the ramp to join Yuichi on the stage. Below, the rig tech punched at his keyboard until the air began to shimmer and twist around us.

'I can't imagine anyone wanting to visit some of these places for kicks,' I said, as the shimmer grew.

'Hey,' Yuichi shouted down at the rig tech just before the hangar faded from view. 'Which part of this alternate are we going, exactly?'

'Philadelphia,' the man shouted back, and then he was gone, in a blizzard of energy.

The bare walls of a deserted office shimmered into existence around us. Two Authority troopers were waiting just beyond the circle of field-pillars, along with someone manning a portable control rig. Exposed wiring stuck out of the walls or hung down from the ceiling, and the floor beneath our feet consisted of nothing more than bare dusty concrete. I had a feeling that the building either wasn't finished or construction had been abandoned.

Judging by what I could see of the neighbouring buildings visible through the windows all around us, we were on the upper floors of a skyscraper. I stepped towards a window and peered through the glass at the streets far below. I could see people – real, living people – in their hundreds. The sight filled me with a kind of emptiness that was almost too much to bear.

The two soldiers quickly guided me and Yuichi up a stairwell to the building's rooftop. I looked around, seeing Philadelphia's rooftops spread out in every direction. Another half dozen troopers stood at various points around the roof, studying the surrounding environment through long-range sights fixed to their rifles.

A loose crowd of people stood in the centre of the rooftop, none of whom I had ever seen before. Their attention was fixed on Kip Mayer, who was talking animatedly to them. I looked around until I spotted Casey, Winifred and Haden, standing away from everyone else.

I took another look at the people gathered around Kip Mayer. They looked entirely ordinary. The majority were men in their middle age, and all wore expensive-looking suits that nonetheless had that curiously old-fashioned look that marked them as citizens of the Authority. Some had the steel-grey hair and confident, upright posture I associated with seasoned politicians, or the CEOs of multi-national corporations.

A number of them, I noticed, were accompanied by women – either their wives or their mistresses, judging by how they were dressed, and the way they clung to the arms of the men. But what *really* took me aback was that there was also a small number of children among the group – some of them quite young. They were all well turned out in what looked to me like their Sunday best.

Yuichi had been right. They looked like nothing so much as tourists, albeit expensively and conservatively dressed ones.

I looked around, wondering at the nature of the apocalypse they had come to witness. I glanced up at the sky, and got my answer.

'What is that, an asteroid?' I asked Yuichi, pointing upwards, and he nodded.

I looked back at Mayer's audience. What kind of damn fools, I wondered, would actually bring their *children* to a place such as this? Or did the Authority have a surfeit of rich and jaded billionaires who thought nothing of witnessing the deaths of billions just for kicks?

'How long?' I asked. The asteroid was clearly visible, even with the naked eye, as a dark smudge near the noonday sun.

He shook his head. 'Not long. This is going to be short, sharp and sweet. It's due for impact any minute now.'

I felt my skin prickle, and wondered how Mayer's audience would feel if something went wrong with the transfer stage, leaving us stranded here.

'Just how big is it?'

'Twenty-five kilometres along its widest axis,' Yuichi replied. 'A real planet-buster.'

I shook my head, feeling fatigued from death and disasters, then followed Yuichi across the rooftop to join our fellow Pathfinders. I felt tense, wound-up; I'd hardly seen most of the others since storming off in a jeep just days before, but I needn't have worried. They all acted like nothing at all had happened – and for that I was grateful.

I nodded to them, exchanging greetings, then discreetly gestured towards the tourists. 'Anybody have any idea exactly who they are?'

'Vultures,' Casey muttered. 'That's about all you need to know.'

Winifred laughed. 'Maybe the Authority sent them here on a junket to find out where all their taxpayers' money is going.'

'But why the hell bring their *families*?' I asked. 'I mean, surely that's a hell of a risk?'

'Sure it is,' said Casey. 'But look at them. Why do you think they're really here, except for the fucking thrill of it all?'

The children were clearly excited, pointing up at the mountain falling towards them from out of the sky. Why they weren't pissing themselves with fear instead was beyond me. I couldn't hear what questions the adults were asking Mayer, but a few of them were taking turns peering upwards at the rock through a single pair of high-powered binoculars.

'Until now, when you said they were tourists, I really thought you must be kidding,' I said to Yuichi.

'In fairness, sometimes we end up babysitting teams of scientists collecting observational data,' said Yuichi. 'Something like this doesn't really happen so often.'

'You know what this is, right?' chuckled Casey. 'Bramnik's got Kip Mayer over there, leading a charm offensive on his behalf. Bramnik's so shit-scared he's going to lose his job to Greenbrooke, he's making sure his bosses hear all about what a really fine job he's been doing.'

I knew better now than just to ask outright what that job might actually be. That the Authority wanted to retrieve data related to transfer stage technology from an alternate Iceland made at least some kind of sense, but the thing I couldn't work out was what possible reason the Authority might have for wanting anything to do with how the bee-brain chimera had been developed. Even though Yuichi and others had warned me not to get too hung-up trying to figure out the ultimate purpose of all the missions the Authority sent us on, I couldn't let it go. Either I found out at least part of the truth, or I descended into the same incipient or full-blown alcoholism already afflicting many of my fellow Pathfinders.

'Maybe they'll put Mayer in charge,' Haden suggested. 'He's more or less running everything here as it is, Bramnik's away so much.'

Yuichi was about to say something else when Mayer beckoned us over. We joined him and the tourists, and Mayer got Casey to answer some of their questions while the rest of us hung back.

The Australian grinned toothily, and began to speak.

'I'll give him this,' I whispered to Yuichi. 'He's good. Maybe he should have been on TV.'

'He was,' Yuichi whispered back. 'He used to make wildlife documentaries back on his alternate.'

I listened as Casey told his audience all about the work we did, and about two other non-Pathfinder teams currently on stand-by in other parts of this alternate, ready to take measurements once the impact took place, following which they would escape via their own transfer stages. Casey was, indeed, an excellent raconteur, and I found even myself drawn in by his description of how we did our work.

After a few minutes of this, a soldier stepped over to Mayer and spoke quietly in his ear. 'That's it,' said Mayer, raising his hands until he had the undivided attention of everyone in his audience. 'Everyone get ready. Impact in just five minutes. If you'd care to follow me, I'll run through the safety procedures one more time . . .'

I watched as the tourists followed Mayer over to where two other soldiers were busily setting out folding deckchairs. The tourists all sat, facing east in the direction of the impact zone. The scene struck me as entirely surreal.

In the meantime, Casey had hauled a shoulder-mounted video camera out of a bag at his feet, before propping it on his shoulder. I watched as he fiddled with its controls, slowly sweeping the lens from one horizon to the other and frowning and mumbling to himself before making yet more minute adjustments to the camera settings.

From somewhere on the streets below us came the rattle of automatic gunfire and the screech of numerous cars accelerating hard. Then I heard screaming, the sound raw and ragged and echoing from the walls of the buildings around us.

This is wrong, I thought to myself.

'No,' Casey said quietly, and I saw he had stepped up beside me. 'This is life.'

I started, realizing with a shock that I must have spoken out loud. I glanced around at the other Pathfinders standing nearby, but none appeared to have overheard me. Or if they had, they weren't letting on.

'All this,' Casey continued, 'is what happens when you fail to have any kind of contingency plan for a fucking great asteroid coming straight at you. The people living on this alternate could have put the funding into watching the skies, to protecting themselves. But they didn't.'

I felt a long-suppressed anger bubbling up inside me. 'We should be helping these people, not treating their deaths like a sideshow.'

'Helping them?' Casey chuckled. 'And what about the next alternate after this one – will you save the people there? Or maybe the next one? Or did you miss the bit where someone explained to you that there's an *infinity* of possible timelines? Tell me, Jerry, which one would you pick?'

'Does that make it any less wrong?'

'And how would you go about warning them?' he continued, as if I hadn't said anything. 'By showing them a transfer stage? Maybe they'd confiscate it, or decide you were crazy and lock you up to eventually die with the rest of them. Or maybe they'd believe you and still not do a damn thing to help themselves.'

'We could at least save some of them—'

'And put them where? And how would you pick who you save, even assuming you could persuade the Authority to consider the idea? I get it, Jerry. You're the classic bleeding-heart liberal, not a realist. And I already told you – they could have saved themselves, but they didn't. Fucking idiots.'

I felt my face grow warm. 'You talk as if they deserve this.'

'Somewhere real close by this alternate, Jerry, I guarantee there are others just like it, except they actually exercised some forethought. I don't need to visit those alternates to tell you what they'd be doing right now – celebrating the fact they cheated death, instead of just waiting for it.'

'Then why the hell don't we go to those places instead? Doesn't it strike as you insanely morbid, the way we keep pitching up on all these post-apocalyptic realities?'

'Who cares why?' Casey grinned. 'Didn't it ever occur to you that getting to travel through the multiverse, to see all these different worlds, regardless of how they pitch up, is an incredible adventure?'

'You make me sick,' I said, turning away.

I saw Casey from out of the corner of my eye, regarding me sourly. 'Man, I'd forgotten what a pussy you were.'

I moved away from him, sick of the sound of his voice. 'You'll get used to stuff like this, Jerry,' he called softly from behind me. 'We all did. Even the old you managed, in the end.'

I needed to put some space between us, but there wasn't really anywhere to go on that rooftop, particularly given how crowded it was.

'Here it comes,' I heard someone shout.

It was as if the sun had dropped from out of the sky, trailing flames. The asteroid was now much too bright to see directly, and I instinctively averted my gaze. I looked instead over towards Mayer and his entourage, all of whom had put on dark glasses, so they could follow the asteroid's plummeting descent with relative ease.

I looked down at the concrete beneath my feet, seeing my shadow sweep in an arc as the asteroid roared through the atmosphere at tens of thousands of kilometres an hour. We were close enough to the impact zone that I could actually feel the heat on my face, even at a distance of a few hundred kilometres. The land directly beneath its path must surely be in flames.

And then, almost as soon as it had appeared, the asteroid was gone from sight. It was, I knew, busy burying itself deep in the Earth's crust, somewhere just off the East Coast of the USA. A wall of burning air would soon come rushing towards us at thousands of kilometres an hour, flattening everything in its path, and right behind that would be earthquakes of a kind never experienced by human beings in this alternate.

And then, finally, the ocean would come sweeping inland in a series of kilometre-high tsunamis, drowning the entire continent and delivering the final blow to anything left standing by the first wave of destruction.

I looked up again in time to see a black wall rising from beyond the horizon, rushing towards us at phenomenal speed. I felt a kind of primal terror I had never experienced, even when confronted by the night patrol. A gust swept across the roof, catching at people's hair; one of the children giggled nervously, and the building beneath our feet began to sway, gently.

My ears popped in the same instant that windows shattered all across Philadelphia. The building's swaying grew in intensity, and I heard a stifled scream.

'Everybody in place,' Mayer shouted, ushering the tourists back towards the stairwell. 'We've got a couple of minutes, tops, before the shockwave reaches Philly.'

They're cutting it too close, I thought. *Much too close*.

We followed after them, crowding down the narrow stairs to the lower floor, all of us clustering together at the centre of the transfer stage. There was barely enough room to fit all of us inside.

Most of the huge feature windows had been reduced to glittering rubble, but Casey was still filming, his teeth gritted in what was either a snarl or a happy grin as he swung the lens to and fro. I couldn't help but notice that a very few of our guests had a hungry, eager look about them, as if whatever appetite had brought them to this alternate had been insufficiently satisfied.

The rig technician made one final adjustment before joining the rest of us inside the circle of field-pillars. The wind had become much stronger, howling down Philly's broad avenues. I saw a deckchair go tumbling past a window as the air around us twisted.

I still had a clear view between two neighbouring buildings of the great black wall rushing towards us from over the horizon. In the very last moment before transition, I saw a distant tower shiver into dust just before it was swallowed up by the maelstrom. And then we were back in the hangar, back on Easter Island.

Someone laughed with clear relief, and I resisted the urge to fall to my knees and hug the floor of the stage.

'Did you *see* that?' I heard a woman's voice say, excited and urgent. 'When I saw that thing rushing towards us . . . ! I thought we were goners for sure!'

I followed the rest of the Pathfinders down the ramp. None of us said anything at first.

'That,' Winifred said finally, as we stepped outside the hangar, 'was fucking nightmare fuel.'

'It's reassuring to hear you feel the same way,' I said.

'It wasn't meant to be reassuring,' she said, and I watched her stalk off into the sunshine.

FOURTEEN

Somehow, the idea of reading my predecessor's last diary hardly seemed such a big deal any more, after everything I had just witnessed. So I followed the other Pathfinders to the Hotel du Mauna Loa for what I now understood to be a constant ritual: a drink to success and, most importantly, to survival. There was a toast to Nadia, and discussions concerning a much-delayed memorial service of some kind. Before long, a date was settled on, although all agreed to consult on the matter with Rozalia in case she had her own ideas.

I got home later that afternoon, tired and feeling less rattled after a few beers and something to eat. I slept for nearly twelve hours, into the next day, dreaming I was running away from an explosion that pulled me up off the ground and threw me high above the clouds, until I floated among the stars and the air froze in my lungs.

When I woke, I knew I could delay no longer. I picked up my predecessor's final diary and turned to the first entries, a cup of coffee by my side.

The first entries were as I remembered them: identical to my own. It was strange how quickly the memories came back of what now seemed another life, and I found myself remembering also how it had all started, and how I came to be alone in the world for so many years.

If it hadn't been for an old college friend, I might never have survived the end of the world.

Not long after graduation I had got myself hired by a research outfit named GreenTech based in San José, on the strength of my PhD thesis on experimental biogenetics. GreenTech liked the predictive computer models I'd developed to help in combating antiviral-resistant diseases. Then, over the course of my first year working for them, I gradually became aware that GreenTech had a number of research contracts with the US military.

Now, this was far from unusual, even in biotech, and the money that kind of work could bring in often made the difference between life and death for companies like GreenTech. I never had cause to think any more of it, until the day I got an email from Floyd Addison, an old friend from university, saying he was passing through town and asking me to meet him for lunch.

As it turned out, however, Floyd was doing anything but 'just passing through'.

We met at a diner a short walk from my work. I was still unused to the dry air and heat of California, after years of studying in Britain and dealing with its blustery rain and four-seasons-in-a-day weather. We talked about old friends, and about my recent wedding to Alice Crosby, and he apologized for not being able to make the wedding. We made small talk about buying vs renting, and the shocking rental prices in San José. I only realized that this was more than just an unexpected social call when he dropped a fat manila folder on the table between us.

'Have you ever heard of Red Harvest?' Floyd asked me, eyeing me speculatively.

'I don't think so.' I glanced uncertainly down at the folder and wondered what was going on. 'What is this?'

Floyd responded by pulling some photographs out of the folder. 'Know any of these people?'

I gave him an appraising look, then glanced through the photographs, feeling as if I'd just stumbled into some ridiculous spy movie. 'Sure,' I said warily. 'That's Marlon Keene, the other one is Herschel Nussbaum. They're colleagues at GreenTech.' I laughed uneasily. 'What are you these days, some kind of spook?'

'Red Harvest is a religious group,' said Floyd. His Oxford education had smoothed out the rougher edges of his Kentucky accent. 'A cult, by any other name, and one with strongly millennialist leanings.'

'What does that even mean?'

Floyd's eyebrows rose by a couple of millimetres. 'It means,' he said, 'that they'd really like to bring about the end of the world.'

'Oh, come *on*.' I could hardly believe I was hearing this. 'Marlon and Herschel are smart guys. They'd never get involved in crap like that.'

When I thought of Herschel, I thought of someone quiet and introspective and calmly intelligent. Marlon, like Floyd, was from the American South. He was the first in his family to go to university. When I thought of cults, I thought of glassy-eyed drones in matching jumpsuits, or wild-eyed Charles Manson types roaming the desert in pickup trucks looking for victims.

'Smart people are just as likely as anyone else to wind up in a cult,' Floyd insisted. 'And smart people aren't always that good at reading other people. Maybe they get lonely, or they lack certain social skills, or maybe they've got the kind of spiritual questions they don't think they can get the answers to from a church.' Floyd leaned back, tapping a finger against his coffee cup. 'After that, it's the proverbial long, slow slippery slide into believing the craziest shit. Intelligence has nothing to do with it.'

'What's going on, Floyd? Why are you even telling me this?'

'Were you aware GreenTech is about to be the subject of an external audit?'

I looked at him, stunned. 'I had no idea. How do you know?'

'I work for the government,' he said.

'Yeah,' I said. 'Somehow I'd figured that.'

'I know a lot of things about the work GreenTech does,' he continued. Then he rattled off a list of current projects, some of which I recognized, partly because my employers had required me and everyone else working at the facility to sign a number of frankly punitive non-disclosure agreements. Hearing those projects even named outside a lab environment made my heart freeze.

'Just to be clear,' I asked, only partly joking, '*which* government?'

He smirked, then pulled out his wallet and showed me his Central Intelligence ID.

'You were a maths major,' I said. 'How the hell does a maths major . . . ?'

'Codes and ciphers,' he replied. 'And that's all I'm saying on the subject.' He put his wallet away. 'Maybe if you help me out, I can shield you from the fallout that's going to come from that audit. Because, believe me, it's going to be a bitch.'

'I haven't done anything wrong,' I said, hating myself for whining.

'Dirt clings to the guilty and the innocent alike,' Floyd said. 'All I ask is that you keep an eye on Marlon and Herschel.' He scribbled some numbers on a napkin and pushed it over. 'And call me if you see or hear anything that strikes you as odd.'

Just before the audit came in, I managed to jump ship with Floyd's help, becoming an independent consultant. Things were tight for a little while, and Alice and I had to cancel our plans to buy our first house. In the end, we were priced out of San José anyway, so when a job came up back in the UK I grabbed it while I could.

In some ways, the move back across the Atlantic was easier for Alice than it was for me. English by birth, she had never been comfortable with the dry, hot Californian weather, whereas I, after too many years enduring rain and long, dark winters in our student days, had grown to love the West Coast weather.

Meanwhile, amidst all the furore around GreenTech, Marlon and Herschel quietly vanished without trace.

'We know they had help.' It was a different restaurant, this time on a rainy Saturday afternoon, in London. The people around us had Selfridges bags piled against their tables like sandbags around machine-gun nests. A thin grey drizzle carved tributaries through layers of dirt streaked across a street-facing window. I hadn't seen Floyd in two years.

'From who?' I asked. 'Red Harvest?'

'Who else?' Floyd gave me a look. 'Which brings me to why I'm here.'

'Ah.' I looked down at my steak tartare. 'No such thing as a free lunch, right?'

He smiled at that. 'Just before GreenTech's directors went before the board of inquiry, some gene cultures went missing.'

'You think Marlon and Herschel took them?'

The way he looked at me made me wonder if he'd had special training in how to make people feel there was nothing they could possibly hide. 'That's my belief, yes.'

'Why would they do that?'

'That's where you come in. Your calendar is free for the next five weeks. You're not due to take part in another consultation until at least March, and you won't even have to travel that far from home.'

How do you know all that? I almost asked him, then let it go. I had the same, unsettling feeling I'd had when Floyd had first remade my acquaintance.

I promised to make careful enquiries. I tracked down another former colleague from GreenTech, with Floyd's help. From him, I learned that the missing cultures had been ordered to be destroyed. Perhaps Marlon and Herschel had indeed done this, but Floyd clearly thought otherwise.

The third and last time I met with Floyd was in a pub we had often frequented, and which was still popular with other American students studying at Oxford. I had taken the train up, hoping this might be the last time Floyd required my services.

'Marlon and Herschel have set up a regular little home from home not far from here,' he told me. We were in a garden area at the rear of the pub, a wooden table and a half-finished shepherd's pie separating us. 'A farmhouse, set back from the road in the middle of a couple of acres.' He sipped at his latte. 'Nice place, too.'

'Last time I spoke to you, they'd disappeared off the face of the Earth.'

'We think they had prepared identities,' he replied. 'Ones they could just walk into when things got too hot.'

I laughed uneasily. 'This is all getting a bit James Bond for me.'

He regarded me stonily. 'This is all quite serious, Jerry.'

'And you really still think they're working on these . . . these cultures they stole?'

'They've been ordering lots of specialist equipment,' he explained, 'through shell companies. It took a great deal of work to trace them. That kind of thing takes an enormous amount of planning.'

'You're talking about Red Harvest again, aren't you?'

He raised his shoulders, then let them fall again. 'Red Harvest is wealthy,' he said. 'They've got a lot of rich members. Marlon and Herschel couldn't manage all this on their own. The question is, how far along are they with what they're planning?'

'What *are* they planning, Floyd?' I shook my head. 'You never made it clear.'

'We don't know.' He shrugged. 'But it's what we don't know that worries us.'

'That makes absolutely no sense.'

'Let me describe the equipment they've been ordering through those shell companies: incubation units; HEPA filters; lab equipment and sterilizing equipment; hazmat gear. What does that suggest to you, other than that they're growing bugs on behalf of their nut-job religion?'

'Look,' I said, 'GreenTech vetted *everyone*. There were psychological tests, batteries of them. If Marlon and Herschel really were that crazy, it would have shown up.'

'You can learn how to pass those tests,' he said, with such an air of authority I hesitated at pursuing it further.

'If you're so sure about all this,' I insisted, desperation edging into my voice, 'why don't you just go in there and arrest them?'

It was Floyd's turn to hesitate. 'There've been some fuck-ups. Technically, we don't yet have the necessary clearance or authority to be operating in the UK.' He glanced around in the most furtive manner possible. 'The thing is, time is running out, and I don't know if we can wait much longer.'

Then it dawned on me. 'You're not supposed to be here at all, are you?'

'I need to get in there,' he said, 'and see just what they're up to. But you're the expert in this kind of thing. I want you to come with me and take a look at whatever set-up they have running in there.'

'You mean . . . *break in*?'

'Why not?' he said, as if it were the most ordinary thing in the world.

The 'farmhouse' turned out to be a former hotel on a hillside on the outskirts of town, set back among concealing trees at the end of a long, private road. Officially, the farmhouse belonged to a local start-up looking to harvest graduates from the university. I listened to all this, and tried to ignore the small voice in the back of my head that kept wondering if this wasn't all some wild delusional fantasy Floyd had dreamed up. But then, if it hadn't been for his warning about the audit . . .

I listened to Floyd as we drove out to the farmhouse in his rented Land Rover. He spoke of a threat of biological Armageddon I could scarcely credit. He was right, of course, but by the time I knew that, it was too late, and Herschel and Marlon had already beaten and tortured him to death.

I didn't ask Floyd how he'd known the two men would be out, or how he'd got keys to get inside. I just assumed it was all spook stuff of some kind, but I still felt thoroughly scandalized when I saw just how easy it was for us to get inside the farmhouse.

My mind kept trying to find excuses for what we found in room after room. There were weapons, stockpiles of canned food and water filtration units. One room looked as if it had been converted into an engineering shop. Another had been turned into a miniature ward, filled with an impressive supply of medical equipment. It was like a paranoid's dream of what they'd need to survive the fall of civilization.

Even all that wasn't anything compared to what we found in the basement.

The basement was split into two long rooms, accessible only by a specially installed airlock system. HEPA filters hummed quietly, scraping the air clean. Most of the space was taken up by a number of temperature-controlled incubation units, and hazmat suits hung on racks next to crates and boxes of yet more supplies. A couple of computers had been set up in a corner on a desk, and there was sufficient lab equipment to grow bugs on a frankly industrial scale, even with just the two of them working in isolation.

I could no longer deny the obvious: whatever Herschel and Marlon were planning, it was big. Would whatever bugs they had developed be spread by blood, by skin or transmitted through the air? It was too early to tell, but my stomach roiled at finding that Floyd had been right in everything he had told me.

I don't know how Marlon or Herschel figured out we were there. Maybe they'd just forgotten something and come back to get it, but I remember clearly the sound of a gun's safety being taken off, and the ashen look on Floyd's face when Marlon appeared at the bottom of the stairs, his face twisted in an angry scowl.

Beside me, Floyd jerked forward, and then I was deafened by gunfire.

Floyd collapsed halfway to the stairwell, one knee a ruined mess.

I started to babble something, but then Marlon stepped forwards, knocking me to the floor before raising his gun above my head butt-first and bringing it crashing down, sending me spinning into darkness.

Things got hazy after that.

There are a variety of ways to get information out of people – drugs, torture, threats, even bribery. Marlon and Herschel opted for the first two. They kept me in one part of the basement, Floyd in the other. I was bound and gagged and handcuffed to a chair and shot full of something that sent me drifting off into a borderland between wakefulness and dreaming. Every now and then they took the gag off, and I mumbled answers to Herschel's questions, hardly aware of what I was saying. They did the same to Floyd, then started dunking me face-first into a bucket of water until I nearly passed out, before dragging me upright once more and demanding answers to questions that meant nothing to me.

Days passed in this way. I wondered what was happening back home, and what Alice might have told the police once she realized I was missing.

I started to get sick – more sick than I had ever felt in my whole life. I had trouble breathing, and sweat drenched my skin. I shivered as if I had been cast naked onto an ice floe and set adrift. My tongue swelled in my mouth and I began to hallucinate. At one point I watched as Herschel and Marlon argued about whether it was worth keeping me alive, then I slipped back into unconsciousness, wondering if I would die anyway before they finished bickering.

Then, the next morning, Marlon appeared beside me with a plastic ampoule filled with some kind of clear liquid and injected me with it. I rapidly got better; the fever subsided, and I began to breathe more easily and be able to keep food down.

The next day my interrogation resumed. What did I know about the Haven? Was there anyone inside Red Harvest who was working for us?

The questions went on, and on, the two men's anger only growing with each question I failed to answer adequately. Later that evening, I heard Floyd screaming from the next room as they tortured him, only for the sound to be abruptly cut off. I listened as his torturers bickered yet again, and I felt sure Floyd had died of his injuries.

Then it hit me. Sometime in the next few days, or maybe even sooner, I would be next. They had, after all, been unable to extract any information from me whatsoever.

Later that night I somehow got one arm free of the thick tape securing me to my chair. They had been feeding me sporadically at best, and by now I had lost so much weight I was able to wriggle free of my improvised restraints, although I nearly dislocated a shoulder in the process. I made my way through the doorway, noting that Floyd's body was gone. The airlock had been dismantled. I climbed the steps only to find the basement door locked.

I retreated into the shadows beneath the steps and waited a few hours, until I heard the jangle of keys. I had found a hammer lying on a workbench, and when Marlon came down the steps, I stepped out of the shadows, swinging it at his head.

He collapsed to the ground without a sound, his legs folding beneath him. I kept swinging the hammer, lost to blind fury and half-crazed from torture and the terror of my impending death. I recall little of what happened next, except that I found myself staring down at the pulped ruin of Marlon's head, unable at first to connect that terrible sight with the bloody hammer still gripped in one hand. Before that moment, I would never have believed I was capable of such awful violence.

I searched his body, finding a pistol tucked into his belt. I ran upstairs with the gun in my hand just as Herschel stepped in through the front door. He barely had time to look up and open his mouth before I shot him in the head, the contents of his skull spattering against the door behind him.

I found Herschel's mobile phone and tried to call Alice, but there was no signal. It was the same with the landline in the kitchen; when I picked it up, all I heard was a hiss of static, and not even a dialling tone.

Then I glanced up and saw a calendar with days crossed out hanging on the wall, and realized I had been held captive for very nearly a whole fortnight. I stared at the date, hardly able to believe it could have been so long, then searched around until I found some stale bread in a cupboard, stuffing it into my mouth until I retched and nearly passed out.

A little while later I made my way along the road on foot, through drizzling rain, until I reached the outskirts of Oxford. Everywhere I went I saw nothing but corpses, shrouded by great buzzing clouds of flies. I remembered the ampoule with which Marlon had injected me, and how I had recovered from a desperate and inexplicable illness in a matter of hours.

I wandered through the deserted streets, barely able to stand the smell of death and rot, before I made my way back to the farmhouse, high on its hill.

I searched the whole place, from top to bottom, until I found a plastic tray containing four ampoules identical to the one Marlon had used on me. If there was any chance whatsoever Alice was still alive, I knew I had to find her and inject her with it.

From a bedroom I grabbed a clean change of clothes that more or less fitted, and took the car keys from Herschel's still-cooling fingers. I had wondered if perhaps there had been others working here apart from Marlon and Herschel, but as I searched the house, I became convinced that they had been working here alone – although that did not preclude the possibility of other Red Harvest groups, in other parts of the world, working in similar secrecy.

I drove the car as far as I could before the sheer number of empty vehicles scattered across the roads forced me to abandon it for a motorbike with a full tank.

It took me another two days to reach London, during which I found no one alive. I had acquired a hunting-rifle from a sporting goods shop, having become concerned over the packs of increasingly feral dogs I was encountering. On my way through Ealing, I nearly came off my bike when someone, somewhere, started shooting at me, and I was forced to take a lengthy diversion before I could reach home. I don't know what happened to that person, but I strongly suspect they didn't survive much longer.

And then, at last, I arrived home, and looked down at Alice, her face strangely peaceful in death. I sat there by the side of our bed and wept until the sun rose above city streets that were silent for the first time in over a thousand years.

*

I buried Alice in our garden, the air full of the stink of putrefaction from the neighbouring houses. Then I left forever, making my way back to Oxford, and back to the basement where my new life had been born. There were computers there, and my hope was that they would contain information that might help me understand how Marlon and Herschel had carried out their act of genocide. If anyone else was alive out there in the rest of the world, they were going to need the antidote that had saved my own life.

But first, I wanted to see whether it might be possible to synthesize more than the pitiful four ampoules that remained in my possession.

It seemed strange to me that no one else came looking for Marlon or Herschel, although it soon became apparent to me, upon my return, that the two men had been preparing for a lengthy journey. Perhaps it had been their intention to leave the farmhouse forever. I slept in an empty property closer to town for a good while, maintaining a watchful eye to see if Red Harvest sent anyone to find out what had happened to the two cultists, but no one ever came. Why this should be remained a mystery, at least for the moment.

Eventually my fear subsided, and for a while, as I carried out my investigation into the antidote, the farmhouse became my home. I buried Floyd much as I had buried Alice, and simply discarded the bodies of the other two; as far as I was concerned, the feral dogs now wandering the countryside could have them.

There was a stockpile of fuel and a couple of portable diesel generators within the farmhouse sufficient to supply me with electricity for the foreseeable future. From the computers, I learned that the farmhouse was only one of a number of distribution points scattered around the globe, and that the Haven – Red Harvest's central base of operations – was located in Maine, on the east coast of the United States, near a town called Biddeford.

I watched the skies for contrails and scanned the radio waves for any sign of human life, but there was none. Even so, I could still not bring myself to believe what I would soon know to be true, that the human race was as good as extinct. I distracted myself with feverish work, and as I explored the information stored on the computers I slowly came to understand that the antidote I had been injected with was only of limited efficacy. Each dose was good for half a year at best. To stay alive beyond that would require further doses. Synthesizing it was out of the question – I lacked the necessary equipment, and all the indications seemed to be there were enormous, pre-prepared batches stored at the Biddeford Haven.

If I wanted to live any longer than the next several months, I would have no choice but to visit this Haven.

I began to prepare for a solo journey that would take me all the way across the Atlantic. I had sailed around Europe's coasts in my youth, so I searched moorings and harbours until I found a forty-foot yacht that needed minimal work to make it seaworthy.

I find it hard to remember my state of mind during all this. I know that I certainly contemplated suicide. The loneliness was dreadful beyond imagining. But such thoughts never came close to becoming actions. Something within me drove me to live at all costs. I simply would not, *could not*, allow myself to die.

Even so, time was passing all too quickly, and so I set sail barely three months after I had first stumbled out into the dawn of a new world, my shirt soaked in another man's blood.

I won't belabour the trials and terrors of that first ocean voyage. Suffice to say that, when I finally reached American soil, it was a thousand kilometres farther south than I had intended. Powerful storms had taken their toll on my yacht, and I sailed her as far north as I could before she finally ran aground in heavy squalls, still a hundred kilometres south of Biddeford. After I struggled to shore, I worked my way through a variety of vehicles in order to drive the rest of the way.

The Haven, when I finally reached it, proved to be a sprawling ranch with numerous outbuildings, all contained within a tall security fence with cameras posted around the perimeter. I walked the last six kilometres there, moving only at night, grasping a rifle in both hands. I holed up in the cabin of an abandoned truck until the morning, watching the compound through binoculars, but it was clear there were absolutely no signs of life or movement. In fact, the Haven appeared to be just as empty and deserted as anywhere else.

I waited until the next evening before cutting my way through the fence and sneaking up towards one of the buildings. When I looked inside and saw long-dead corpses, I knew death had not spared the cultists after all. I had my answer for why no one had ever come looking for Marlon or Herschel.

The carnage extended throughout the rest of the compound. The main building, a two-storey structure that looked as if it had started out as some rich man's summerhouse, had a makeshift barricade built across its front steps, while inside I found a cache of ampoules that seemed to have been deliberately smashed.

I explored further within, finding a dozen more corpses, their bony wrists secured with plastic ties. Judging by the tilt of their heads and the dark stains all around them, it was clear their throats had been cut.

After a while I figured out what had happened from bits and pieces of information: there had been a rebellion of some kind. The cult's leaders had used the supplies of antidote to control their followers, dispensing it only to those who were in their favour. Anyone who didn't toe the line, it seemed, simply died once the antidote stopped working. I found the evidence in the minutes of mob trials at which the former cult leaders had been found guilty of betraying their own stated principles, before undergoing immediate execution.

Beyond that, I can't say for certain just what had happened. But in the years that followed, I certainly speculated. I wondered if perhaps only an inner circle of the cult had known about the grand plan to wipe out humanity. And, once the deed had been irrevocably done, perhaps all they needed to do, to keep the rest of the cultists in line, was to threaten to withhold the antidote.

But their leaders were few, and their followers many. Once the promised paradise on Earth failed to materialize, that controlling minority – I felt increasingly certain – must have been faced with over-whelming opposition to their rule. And if those smashed ampoules were anything to judge by, those in charge must have been just as petty and venal as the billions they had sentenced to death. It looked as if they had destroyed the remaining supplies of the antidote rather than allow the rebels to seize it.

With the existing supplies of the antidote destroyed, how was I, then, to survive?

I found a place to sleep in a deserted dormitory within the com-pound, then spent the next several days looking for anything that might possibly help me survive longer than the next few months. Eventually I found a well-equipped laboratory, but most of the equip-ment had either been smashed to pieces or burned. This at least explained why the rebels had been unable to synthesize any more antidote themselves.

It took another week of searching, but finally I discovered an unharmed cache of the antidote. It was hidden in a crate at the back of a barn on the very edge of the property, along with lab workbooks detailing the requisite formulae to synthesize more.

I soon formulated a plan that would give me purpose in the coming years. First, I would search for other survivors, if they were out there. Somewhere in the world, there had to be secure facilities with people surviving on canned air, or in underground military com-plexes built to withstand nuclear or biological attack.

I was telling myself a lie, of course: one that gave me a reason to hold my grief and anger at bay, not to mention the dreadful guilt I felt at the thought that I could have found some way to escape sooner, to warn people of what was happening. Sometimes, the grief gave way to anger, and in my mind I called myself a coward.

Still the tenacious will to live that had spurred me this far refused to let go, and before long I was back on the road, making my way across the vastness of the North American continent. Over the next three years I criss-crossed from coast to coast, and found nothing but deserted ruins slowly reverting to nature. At some point I found another yacht and sailed it back across the ocean.

At times, especially in those first years, my sanity would teeter in the balance. I would have conversations with people I only realized later had never been there. Alice herself came sufficiently alive again, in my mind at least, that I became unable to distinguish reality fully from fantasy. Without the Authority's intervention, I might well have descended deep enough into my madness to have never been able to return to sanity.

Once I finally sat down and began to read that last diary, just those first few pages were enough to unleash a flood of memories. Even when I had actively been writing in my notebooks, I had rarely, if ever, reread my entries. Now, as I scanned the words, I found myself recalling things I had forgotten or suppressed for most of the last decade.

That was nothing, however, compared to what I found as I read past the point of that other Jerry's retrieval, and the details of his new-found life here on the island. Before long I had cause to wonder if I had ever really known myself at all.

Like me, he had been placed in quarantine as a precaution against the possibility he might still carry the EVE virus in his bloodstream. Only then had he been allowed to interact with the island's community of Pathfinders. I read on, his later diary entries becoming as sparse as my own had, although describing incidents and conversations that were entirely unfamiliar to me. I read of his first trips to other timelines, other parallel universes. His observations could so easily have been my own, except that he had never suffered the feeling that something was being kept back from him. But then again, neither had he discovered by accident that he was someone's replacement.

I gripped the pages harder as I read about his and Chloe's burgeoning romance, and his feelings of guilt when he thought about *his* Alice. He wrote of how his long-dead wife slowly ceased to be such a strong presence in his mind; never gone, but part of that other life he had left behind forever.

The time between entries grew and grew. First six months, then a year, as his new life became busier, and he found new demands on his time. But then came a sudden burst of activity within just the last twelve months – not really so long, I realized with a tingle, before my own retrieval.

His final entries detailed things that struck me as deeply humdrum: a few lines here and there recording picnics he and Chloe had taken on the island's north shore; a handful of observations about recent missions into the multiverse and sketches of some *moai*. And then, some bad fights with Chloe . . .

I stopped, flipping back a page and rereading the words. He had written of an occasion on which he had struck Chloe with such force he was afraid he might actually have killed her. He went on to describe a previously unrecorded incident when he had beaten her badly with his fists. The details were recorded impassively, with little in the way of emotion.

I felt as if something cold and greasy had clambered inside my belly and taken root there. What had started out as a diary had instead turned into a kind of confession of domestic violence that nauseated me. Their fights had been furious and, to me, incomprehensible. He begged forgiveness for his actions, but his words did not convince even me.

I put the diary down with trembling hands and stared out my window for a long time. I had never struck any woman in my life, nor could I imagine myself ever doing so.

It occurred to me that this might well be the reason for Chloe seeming so reticent in my presence. If I – if *he* – had been so dreadfully violent, I could hardly blame her for keeping her distance. But then she had reached out to kiss me just days before, and the memory left me sick with confusion.

I could no longer feel any kinship with the man who had written those words, and yet the fact remained that up until the point of his retrieval, I was absolutely identical in thought and history and deed to that other Jerry. How could I – how could *he* – really have changed so much, that he would commit such monstrous, unjustifiable acts?

I knew I needed to find Chloe and talk to her about this. I wanted more than anything to prove to her that I was different, that I could never be the same as that other me, pouring out his wounded regrets.

Assuming, of course, given what I now knew, she had any intention of talking to me ever again. And who could blame her if she didn't?

And yet . . . that kiss. It made little sense, even though the memory of it seemed to dominate my thoughts at times.

I remembered, then, what she had said – that she was taking as many missions as she could, to distance herself from the island – and, by implication, from me. No matter: as soon as she returned, for however long, I would go to her and talk with her about what I had read. Assuming, that is, she was willing to listen. Even so, I felt I needed some form of absolution, some way of distinguishing myself from the other me.

I wondered if she even knew he had written of these events in their life.

I put the diary down and found my jacket, a new and more immediate purpose on my mind. There was something I had to do before anything else: something I had to see with my own two eyes.

I stepped back outside, and went to visit my own grave.

FIFTEEN

Chloe had told me that the graveyard lay just beyond the runway of the island's single, derelict airport. I made my way there on foot, passing the police station where Greenbrooke had interrogated me and Nadia and Rozalia, and saw that same fractured moon hanging low in the sky. I wondered if the island had any boats capable of carrying me all the way to the Chilean coast a few thousand kilometres to the east, and what I might find there, and if any of the other Pathfinders had ever tried.

I kept on past the comms tower, stepping over discarded concrete blocks from some unfinished building project, tangled weeds underfoot and the crickets singing loud enough to drown out my thoughts. Eventually I came to a small plot of land surrounded by a low railing, within which stood a small clapboard building with a rusted iron cross mounted above its entrance.

The plot had perhaps a couple of dozen graves in all. The dedications on every headstone but one were written in Spanish. Most looked old, which meant my predecessor's was easy to find, since it was clearly much more recent than any of the rest.

I stared down at it for a while before turning away, feeling somehow weightless, as if I could drift away on the steady breeze coming in from the ocean. I knew that seeing your own grave was not necessarily a unique experience. People who went missing, returning long after they had been presumed deceased, would certainly have had that experience, as would those who successfully faked their own deaths.

Didn't everybody wonder what it would be like to attend their own funeral?

But I knew none of them had ever been faced with the knowledge that a body identical to their own lay within that grave.

I decided it was an overrated experience and returned home with every intention of getting seriously drunk.

The first time my doorbell rang, I had collapsed half off the couch in my living room. The second time it rang, I realized I wasn't hearing things. By the third time, I was hunched over the toilet bowl, vomiting up my breakfast and the half-bottle of home-made whisky I'd worked my way through following my return from the graveyard.

I finally made it to the door on the fourth attempt and found Yuichi standing there.

'You, uh . . . you don't look so good,' he said.

'What is it?' I croaked, crushing my eyes shut against the light.

'Something's up,' he said. 'Kip Mayer asked me to round up all the Pathfinders currently on the island and get us all to the Hotel du Mauna Loa by eight this evening. He's got something to say.'

I swallowed hard. 'About what?'

'I don't know,' he said. 'But I think it has to do with Nadia.'

It took me a long while to get ready after he left. I crawled back through to the toilet and crouched, shivering, over the bowl, feeling as if the flesh was about to slough off my bones. But nothing else came up, so I slowly peeled off my clothes and left them lying on the tiles before dragging myself inside the shower. It ran on a battery-powered pump that took a while to get going, and the water was always freezing cold for the first minute or so. I gasped as the icy stream hit me, then leaned my head back against the tiles once it heated up.

All I really wanted to do was crawl back into bed and stay there, but instead I dried myself off and found some fresh clothes before setting back out again.

*

'Dear God in Heaven,' said Randall Pimms when I finally walked into the bar, just before eight. 'It *lives*.'

I ignored him and grabbed hold of a stool, to keep myself upright as much as anything else. There was a faint singing in my ears, overlaying the grind and thud of blood flowing like tar through my veins.

'Get you anything?' asked Selwyn, one hand on my shoulder.

'Coffee,' I grunted.

'Good idea,' he replied, peering at my bloodshot eyes. 'Wait right there.'

I watched him ask Tony behind the bar for the coffee, then looked to see who else was there. Most, if not all, of the Pathfinders were present. Chloe, unsurprisingly, was not. The majority were outside on the patio, standing or sitting around the pool, a few empty bottles bobbing and floating in the murky water.

'Here.' Selwyn pushed a cup of hot black liquid into my hands. 'Strong as I could make it.'

I sipped at the coffee, feeling it burn its way down my throat. I was about to thank Selwyn when Kip Mayer walked in and the others started to trickle back inside from the patio.

'Mr Bramnik thought it best if you heard it from us first,' said Mayer, once everyone had found somewhere to stand or sit facing him. 'It looks as if the Patriots are going to be running their own, parallel investigation into the circumstances surrounding Nadia Mirkowsky's death. Langward Greenbrooke will be in charge of that investigation.'

The sounds of groans filled the air.

'This is bullshit,' said Casey, leaning against a pillar. 'They're taking advantage of a fucking tragedy for their own damn reasons.'

A chorus of voices rose in assent. I listened quietly, still nursing my coffee.

'Wait.' Mayer raised his hands over the tumult. 'All right. Okay, *shut up*.'

The noise finally abated, and Mayer continued. 'Now listen. Whether you like it or not, this is going to happen. It's going to mean some changes around here. There's also talk of a curfew—'

The level of noise rose abruptly once more. I glanced at Selwyn, red faced and shouting his anger almost as loudly as everyone else combined.

'—but it's not very likely things will get that far,' Mayer screamed over the din, '*as long as you all fucking cooperate*!'

'Casey is right,' said Rozalia, stepping forward and confronting Mayer with folded arms. 'I can't imagine anything more cynical and underhand than what Greenbrooke is doing. If I didn't like him before, I like him even less now.'

'Well,' said Mayer, 'if Mort Bramnik hadn't intervened personally, things would be a lot worse than they already are, believe me.' He looked around us all. 'There'd already be an island-wide lockdown and a permanent curfew, and not just for the duration of the investigation. My advice is, let the agents do their jobs, and then we can get back to normal faster.'

'And what if they decide they want to *talk* to us?' asked Casey, stepping up beside Rozalia. 'There isn't any one of us who doesn't know what those fucking assholes did to Wallace.' I glanced over, seeing Wallace sitting quietly in one corner, his face expressionless as he rolled a glass of whisky between his hands. 'Is that the kind of treatment we can expect?'

'We're going to monitor the entire process of the investigation,' said Mayer, before the level of noise could rise again. 'If any of you *do* get interviewed, I'll be in the room with you at all times. That's my promise.'

'What's going on, Kip?' Rozalia demanded. 'Why is Mort sending you down here to talk to us, instead of coming here himself?'

'Yeah,' said Casey. 'He's hardly been seen in weeks, but Greenbrooke seems to be around all the damn time. People are going to start wondering if Bramnik's *ever* coming back.'

'He's back home right now,' Mayer explained, 'on our own alternate, and taking care of business the same as always. Believe me, nothing's changed, and nothing is *going* to change.'

'Fuck this,' said Casey, stalking past Mayer and towards the door. He paused there and looked back at the rest of us. 'All this is total horse shit. There's some underhand stuff going on here they're not telling us about – some cloak-and-dagger crap back wherever the hell it is the Authority come from.' He pointed his finger at Mayer. 'So you listen to *me*. Any one of those sons of bitches comes anywhere near me, and I swear I'll kill them first.'

'If the Patriots want to talk to you, Casey,' said Mayer, his voice level, 'you're going to cooperate, just the same as the rest of us.'

Casey stared at him, then took a couple of lumbering steps back towards Mayer, towering over the smaller man. 'Tell you what,' said Casey. 'When you go running back to your bosses, make it clear there's only so far you can push us before we start to push back. Got that?'

'Damn right,' I heard someone say. It sounded like Randall.

Casey turned on his heel, pushing at the door on his way out with sufficient force that it slammed against the wall with a loud bang.

'He's right,' said Selwyn, getting up from his own seat. 'We're getting treated more and more like prisoners, Mr Mayer. For those that have been here the longest, our retirement dates have been pushed back so much we're starting to wonder if it's ever going to come, and that's not to mention the increased risks we're facing on every new mission. Asking us to submit to random interrogations and be happy about it is a step too far, I think.'

I watched as he left, somewhat less dramatically than Casey had. Yuichi soon followed suit, his expression sullen, although he clapped me on the shoulder as he passed me by.

Mayer looked around the rest of us. 'It's in your best interests to keep Casey in check while all this is going on,' he said. 'Believe me.'

He looked as if he was trying to think of something else to say, then simply shook his head and exited without another word.

I didn't see any reason to leave until I'd finished my coffee, and the few others remaining didn't look to be in a hurry to leave either. After a minute, people drifted outside to the pool area, and I heard the low murmur of conversation.

Rozalia slid onto the stool next to mine. 'So you're still not going to tell them what we found,' I asked her, 'even after everything Mayer just said?'

'I ran some tests,' she said. 'It's just what I thought it was.'

'You're not telling me anything the both of us don't already know.'

'We could get accused of faking the evidence. It's possible the SUV was scent-marked by a night patrol *after* the crash. And it's like you said: we *don't* have any explanation for how the drones and the communications could possibly have been screwed with. Who'd have the means to do all that, and somehow not get caught?'

'If it was up to me,' I said, 'I'd tell someone anyway.'

'Your predecessor had his reasons for not talking,' she replied. 'So did Nadia. Let's try not to wind up the same way before I can figure out how to nail whichever bastard turns out to be responsible for all this.'

'Rozalia . . .' I started to say.

She shook her head and put her hand on my arm. 'First things first. Did you talk to Chloe yet?'

The question I'd been dreading. 'I really, *really* don't want to talk about that.'

She frowned. 'It went that bad?'

'You know, it might have been better if you'd just told me the truth about her and me, before I went over there and embarrassed myself.'

She shook her head. 'Why? What did she say?'

I struggled to hold back my temper and stood. 'Rozalia . . . good luck with finding out the truth about Nadia.'

She stared at me. 'What are you talking about?'

'I don't want to be a part of this,' I said.

'What the hell?' she hissed, glancing towards the pool in case anyone was watching. 'You don't have any choice. Christ, your life might be in danger!'

'No, Rozalia, the *other* Jerry's life was in danger. But I'm not him, and up until a couple of days ago, every last one of you were happy to lie to me about who and what I was.'

Rozalia started to open her mouth, and I put up a hand to stop her. 'I haven't forgotten what I was told,' I said. 'I know that if you'd told me who I really was, things could've gone bad for you. But, Jesus . . . every one of you survived a fucking *apocalypse*, and all it takes to make you roll on your collective backs are a couple of suit-wearing nitwits with rulebooks wedged up their asses?' I bared my teeth and laughed. 'Tell me, Rozalia. If Oskar hadn't lost his rag, would I even know the truth yet?'

She stared at me in mute silence. 'I'm sorry,' she said. 'Maybe you're right. Maybe we should have been more—'

'But that's not the worst of it,' I interrupted. 'Because you forgot to mention that my previous incarnation was a total fucking asshole.'

Confusion spread across her face. 'What on Earth . . . ?'

'He hurt Chloe,' I said. 'And don't pretend you don't know. He beat her, badly. Apparently, that's the person I get to become after living here for a couple of years, doing a job that makes no sense, for people who won't tell me who they are. Well, fuck that.' I picked up my coffee and drained the last of it. 'Here's *my* plan. Soon as I can find some way to escape to some place where the Authority can't find me, I'm *gone*, do you understand? Even if it means risking a null sequence.'

My voice had risen. I backed away from her, ignoring the curious glances I was getting from out by the pool. 'And, unless you're crazy,' I added before departing, 'every last one of you'll find a way to do the exact same.'

Forty-eight hours later, I was back out on another mission, and still in a stinking foul mood.

I looked out and down, seeing rocky coastline half a kilometre below our plane, bordered by a beach that had been turned to fused glass by a thermonuclear detonation. The sun was invisible behind a dense layer of ash in the upper atmosphere that was still decades away from fully precipitating back into the soil.

When I had emerged from the transfer stage just outside this alternate's version of Phoenix, I had immediately been handed a heavy Arctic-style jacket, and been glad for it. It was freezing cold and would remain so, I was told, for many years yet.

Haden Brooks was in the pilot's seat, not that he seemed to be doing much piloting. In fact, I had the distinct impression that our aircraft was capable of taking off and landing at its destination without any human intervention whatsoever, although that didn't prevent him from summoning virtual controls that shimmered into existence around his hands. The plane also lacked anything that looked like an engine and could, he informed me, fly for up to a decade without once refuelling.

Even among as strange and disparate a group as the Pathfinders, Haden Brooks stood out. Apart from his silvered eyes, he was pale enough that he bordered on albino, although his thinning hair was dark and streaked with grey.

'You ever hear of the Toba eruption?' asked Haden.

I shook my head. 'Nope.'

'It happened about seventy thousand years ago, in all our shared histories,' he explained. We'd run out of things to say a while back, but clearly Haden was determined to make conversation. 'It was a hundred times more powerful than Krakatoa, and it nearly wiped out the human race at the time. All that were left were a few thousand survivors, from whom we're all descended.'

The aircraft bucked slightly as it hit turbulence and I gripped the side of my seat. I wasn't exactly afraid of flying, but from the outside the aircraft looked about as sturdy as a paper kite.

'So it was the same as the eruption that did for this alternate?'

'Pretty much.'

Our debriefing that morning had described how the magma chamber beneath this alternate's Yellowstone Park had erupted with enormous force, sending thousands of cubic kilometres of ash and sulphur into the atmosphere – much as it had on the alternate on which the Nuyakpuk cousins and their many Inuit relations had managed to survive.

On this alternate, however, a second blow had been dealt by nuclear missiles launched in the immediate aftermath of the eruption. Why they had been launched, and by whom, remained a mystery, but the added radioactive ash in the atmosphere had helped to extend and deepen the global winter to the point where we were pretty sure there were, indeed, no survivors, Inuit or otherwise.

I shook my head. 'The thing that gets me,' I said, 'is all those bunkers filled with bodies.' Several unearthed by previous exploration teams had found nothing but corpses dead from starvation, disease, radiation poisoning, suicide, or some combination of all of the above. This, I had learned, was typical, here or on any other alternate. 'What's the point of building a bunch of damn bunkers if everybody using them still winds up dead?'

'Bunkers, in my experience,' said Haden with a grin, 'are *hugely* overrated.'

'You're on a mission with Haden?' Yuichi had chuckled the day before, when I ran into him outside the commissary. 'Now *there's* a weird one.'

'Everybody's been saying that ever since I came out of quarantine, but nobody's bothered to explain it to me yet.'

'Really?' He looked surprised. 'Well, for one thing, nobody knows just what happened to the alternate they found him on. It's intact. There's no sign or evidence of violence, of unrest, of anything at all, really. It's like everyone just got up one day and disappeared.'

It occurred to me that much the same could be said for the island in whose empty homes we lived, but decided not to mention that. 'So what does he say happened?'

Yuichi shrugged. 'He ain't got much of an explanation himself, either,' he replied. 'Claims to have total amnesia. They worked him over with truth drugs, hypnosis, everything, so I hear.' He shook his head. 'Couldn't find nothing out. And then there's the . . . you know.' He glanced around before gesturing at his eyes.

'Are you sure he's not maybe just wearing contacts of some kind?'

'*Very* sure. He got worked over by the doctors at the base compound.'

I shook my head and chuckled. 'So maybe he's an alien.'

Yuichi looked alarmed. '*Don't* ever say that around Casey or Wallace. The pair of them are total conspiracy nuts. They love all that shit.'

'All right,' I said, 'what's your opinion of him?'

'Who cares? The universe is full of mysteries. I like it that way. Makes life more interesting, don't you think?'

'There we go,' said Haden, after some hours of flight. 'Destination in sight.'

I woke with a start, unaware I had fallen asleep. Brightly coloured controls hovered beneath Haden's fingertips, spun out of light. The aircraft had begun to angle downwards on its final approach.

I mumbled something and blinked sleep out of my eyes before looking out and down at Salt Lake City's empty streets. Our destination was the University of Utah's seismic research lab, from which we were required to retrieve data regarding the Yellowstone eruption.

'Don't you ever wonder what the point of all this is?' I asked. The plane dipped down more, and Haden leaned back, dismissing the controls. I tried not to show how nervous that made me.

He grinned. 'You sure are persistent, I'll give you that. Most of the rest of us gave up asking questions like that long ago.'

'Why do the Authority care about what happened here? Why do they even need to *know* any of this stuff?'

'Maybe they just want to avoid making the same mistakes these people did,' he said.

And yet, from the way he looked at me, I felt sure he felt the same dissatisfaction.

A day or so later I was back home, the useless data retrieved and our entirely pointless mission accomplished. I had kept waiting throughout for something to go wrong. It didn't, and I was again reminded just how much of an anomaly my first couple of missions had been, compared to most.

As soon as I got back, I walked into the Hotel du Mauna Loa to get something to eat and found the Godzilla movie had been changed for *No Blade of Grass*, directed by Cornel Wilde. I watched Nigel Davenport fleeing a motorbike gang across a desolate wasteland as I ate. Winifred and Selwyn were playing Go at a table, and I sipped at a tumbler of grapefruit juice, having lost my taste for alcohol.

Randall Pimms came stomping into the bar just as the film finished. He wore heavy boots, camouflage gear and a fur-trimmed parka, his face streaked with dirt.

'Jerry!' Randall cried, clapping me on the shoulder. Winifred flashed him a dirty look from across the room, annoyed to lose her concentration. 'I swear to God, I've been dreaming about beer for the last couple days. Fancy getting me one?'

'Sure,' I said, and filled a glass from one of the bottles of home-brew, while Randall hauled himself onto a stool beside my own. I handed the drink to him and watched him swallow most of it down in one go.

'Where've you been?' I asked, studying the parka. 'Somewhere cold?'

'Somewhere hot!' he exclaimed.

'Doesn't that make you a little overdressed?'

He shook his head. 'Nope. Most of the time we were down in sub-terranean caverns. *Damned* cold down there.'

He went on to tell me – and, soon enough, Winifred and Selwyn – about the alternate he had just returned from. Its sun had expanded, starting some time in the Middle Ages in our respective alternates. Much of the surface had been reduced to a lifeless desert beneath the parching heat, but a few tens of millions, despite having to rely on essentially medieval technology, had nonetheless dug deep into the Earth. He described cathedrals and palaces carved into the deep rock over long centuries, and entire cities on a scale to dwarf the Pyramids of Giza, dug deep beneath the earth – much as the Icelanders had done with their Retreat. But then, it seemed, the oceans had themselves turned to desert, and the people had all died, leaving only their cities as monuments to their struggle.

'It sounds utterly amazing,' I said, meaning it. I wondered if I might ever get to visit there. 'Who were you there with?'

'Oskar, Chloe, Wallace.'

Chloe. 'Did she come back at the same time as you?'

'Well, sure. I . . .'

'I have to go,' I said, standing and heading for the door.

I thought I heard Selwyn call after me, but I didn't stop.

I had to find her, and hope she was willing to tell me the truth about my predecessor.

Chloe was in front of her house when I got there just ten minutes later, a rucksack by the door. Like Randall, her clothes were caked with dirt, and she was in the process of pulling off a heavy parka. She did a literal double-take when she saw me, and I could see her mentally weighing the pros and cons of engaging with me. I was still breathing hard from running all the way across town.

I put up a hand. 'I'm not here to cause any trouble,' I said. 'But I need to talk to you about the diaries.'

'Jerry . . .'

'Look, all I want to know is how things got so bad between you that he would hit you. Because I want you to know, right now, that however much he looked like me or talked like me or anything else, I am absolutely, positively not that man.'

She stared at me, nonplussed. 'Who hit me?'

I looked back at her, equally confused. '*I* did. I mean the other Jerry did. He assaulted you, more than once.'

She laughed, which I hadn't expected. 'What the hell are you talking about?'

'The diaries,' I repeated. 'He wrote about what happened, when things got so bad he struck you with his fists. I just – I really need to talk to you about it, Chloe. If you don't want to talk to me, I understand. But I also need you to understand that there's no way I would ever, under any circumstances—'

'No bullshit?' she said, interrupting me and stepping closer. 'That's what he wrote? You're sure of this?'

'Yes. In the diary I took from here. I . . .' I halted, suddenly lost for words. 'Don't you . . . ?'

She came to stand on the other side of the gate from me. 'He never hit me,' she said carefully. 'Not once. And, frankly, if he'd ever tried something like that, I'd have taken the son of a bitch down, hard.' She shook her head. 'I don't know exactly what you read, but it sounds to me like you got it wrong.'

I felt my face grow red. *Could* I have got it wrong? Was it possible I could have so badly misunderstood the other Jerry's words? I didn't see how. He had been unsparing in his description of the pain he had inflicted.

'Can I come in for a moment?' I asked her.

'No,' she said, shaking her head. 'This is bullshit.'

I'd taken a seat in her living room while she got cleaned up, re-appearing after a few minutes in fresh jeans and a T-shirt, her hair damp and smelling faintly of shampoo.

'All right,' she said, perching on the arm of her couch and looking at me. 'Start from the beginning. What exactly did he write?'

'That you had some spectacularly bad fights. He wrote that he got wound up enough that one time he hit you hard enough that you were knocked out cold.'

'No,' she said, her voice brittle, a wounded look in her eyes. 'He would never have hit me, not in a million years. Sure, we argued sometimes. But never like what you're describing.'

'If you'd read his entries yourself,' I said, 'you'd have seen what he wrote.'

'And I already told you why I didn't. I was about ready to put them out of my sight by the time you got here.' Her voice softened. 'Look, maybe you're right and I should have read them. What else did he say?'

I spread my hands. 'Just domestic stuff. Picnics, up in the north of the island.'

'Picnics?' She laughed incredulously. '*What* picnics?'

I stood. 'Maybe,' I said, 'it's time we both took a look at that diary.'

She looked uncertain for a moment, then pulled on a pair of boots before following me out the door and back to my own house.

I spread the notebook open on the counter of my kitchen and watched as Chloe flipped back and forth through the pages. She scanned crude illustrations of statues that filled a few pages in the later entries, peering at the dense scribble surrounding them.

She looked up at me, her expression bleak. 'I swear on my life,' she said, 'none of this happened. Not any of it.'

'So he was lying?'

'All I'm saying is that none of this happened.' When she looked at me, I could see how much strain all this was causing her. 'What I don't understand is, why the hell would he make all this up?'

Something occurred to me. 'Just to be absolutely clear,' I asked her, pointing at one of the illustrations, 'you never visited the statues together either?'

'Well . . . maybe a couple of times, early on. Years ago, really, not long after we got to know each other for the first time. But not recently. And sure as hell not for a fucking *picnic*,' she snorted.

I tried to think of any reason why Chloe would be lying to me, but nothing would come to mind. Nor did I believe she was lying. I could see it in the lines of tension in her face, in the way she held herself. Her consternation and upset was palpably real. And yet, the seed of an idea was growing somewhere deep inside me.

I slid the notebook back towards me, spinning it around and flicking through the pages until I found one particular illustration. What possible reason could he have had for taking the considerable time and effort to sketch these statues, I wondered, if Chloe was telling the truth and they had never picnicked by them?

At the time the other Jerry had made these sketches, according to Rozalia, he would have been busy trying to figure out whether someone was carrying out acts of deliberate sabotage. Why, then, would he also suddenly decide to write so many apparently deliberate lies, knowing how much heartbreak they would cause the woman he loved, if ever she were to read them?

I tried to picture myself in his shoes, knowing what I now knew. How hard could it be, considering we were essentially identical? What would have driven *me* to construct such elaborate mistruths?

'I've got an idea,' I said, picking the notebook back up and tucking it under one arm. 'You up for a drive?'

She gave me a strange look. 'Where, exactly?'

'North,' I said, and patted the book under my arm. 'I'd like to take a look at the statues he drew.'

'Please don't tell me it's because you want to go on a fucking picnic,' she said, a warning in her voice.

I couldn't help laughing at that. 'Kind of, yeah.' She stared angrily at me and I put my hands up in surrender. 'Or at least,' I continued, 'that's what we can tell people we're doing if anyone asks where we're going.'

'But why?' she demanded. 'What the hell do you expect to find there?'

'It's just a hunch I have, okay? A feeling.'

She didn't look convinced. 'Look,' I explained, '*your* Jerry made up two stories, and I think they're connected in some way. The first is about all the fights you supposedly had, and the other is about a bunch of picnics that never happened. Not to mention that, prior to all this, he hadn't written anything in his diary for years. Now, since we can't exactly go back in time and *ask* him what he was up to, that means all we have left are those statues he was obsessed with drawing.'

'You think there's some reason for all that?'

'All I can think of,' I said, 'is to at least take a look at them. You never know, it might spark something.'

'I'll admit it sounds like a plan,' she said. 'But I'm too tired, Jerry. I haven't slept in at least a couple of days.'

'Chloe . . .'

She stepped towards the kitchen door, and when she turned to look back at me I could see she was fighting back tears. Her voice trembled when she spoke. 'Tomorrow, okay? I'm borderline halluci-nating, for God's sake. And then we can go on our pretend picnic.'

I watched her depart, thinking of how badly I wanted to go and see those statues at the first opportunity. I could have gone on my own, but something held me back. I needed Chloe to be there.

Those diary entries, after all, had been intended for her, and not me.

SIXTEEN

After she had gone, I sat in my kitchen, feeling frustrated and upset for quite some time. I didn't *want* to wait until tomorrow: I wanted to go right now. But I knew equally that I would never do so unless Chloe was also there. She had known my predecessor better than anyone else, after all. She might well have insights or ideas based on that knowledge that might help me make sense of the faked diary entries.

I decided I needed some kind of distraction until the next morning. Eventually I tossed the notebook down and headed back to the Hotel du Mauna Loa. But when I got there, the only other person present was Wallace Deans, squeezed into a chair in the corner. He was clearly deep into a binge, if the half-empty bottle of hooch by his arm was anything to judge by. He regarded me with me watery eyes, and I wondered just how long he had before his liver finally gave out.

'Maybe you should take it easy,' I said, nodding at the bottle.

'Go to hell,' he slurred at me, his head dipping down to regard the table.

I knew it wasn't really any of my business, but I pulled a chair up across from him anyway. 'I heard about what the Patriots did to you.'

Wallace let out a drunken snort. 'And you think *that's* what this is about?' he said, holding up his glass.

I leaned back and grimaced as a cloud of foul breath enveloped me. Now I was sitting across from him, I realized he smelled as if he hadn't washed or showered in weeks.

'Okay,' I said, doing my best to maintain an air of equanimity. 'So why all the drinking?'

He stared off past me for so long that I really began to think he'd forgotten I was even there. 'It doesn't matter,' he said quietly.

'Well, if you—'

'Fucking *Vishnevsky*,' he roared, slamming his glass down hard enough on the table to make me jump. 'Fuckin' *no good sonofabitch*.'

'What happened, Deans?' I heard a voice say from behind me. 'You and your boyfriend fall out?'

I twisted around to see Rozalia standing by the door. By the time I turned back, Wallace had already half-struggled out of his seat, a look of fury on his face. He stumbled and tried to grab hold of the table, and succeeded only in pulling it down with him as he collapsed on the floor.

I jumped up, pushing my chair back. The last thing I needed was Wallace throwing up all over my shoes.

'Jesus,' Rozalia muttered, gazing down at Wallace, who groaned as he tried, unsuccessfully, to sit back up. 'He stinks even worse than usual.'

I looked down at him uncertainly. I wanted to say something to Rozalia. I knew I had been too harsh on our last encounter, especially now I knew the truth about the diary entries, but she was acting as if nothing had happened.

'Maybe we should try and get him back home,' I suggested.

She gave me a look of horror. 'I don't even want to *touch* him while he's in that state.'

I looked down again at Wallace and, judging by the smell, suspected he had soiled himself. 'We can't just leave him like this.'

Rozalia gave a heavy sigh, and I could see from her expression that she was mentally resigning herself to Doing Something About Wallace. 'You know, I only came here to get something to eat,' she said. 'This isn't what I had in mind for how I was going to spend my evening.'

We managed to wrestle him more or less upright, but it proved harder than I thought it would be, particularly given his not inconsiderable girth. 'I thought they made all of us work out,' I gasped, standing up after we had got him in another chair. 'How the hell did he end up like this?'

'He's a genius at logistics and networking,' said Rozalia, her nose wrinkled in disgust. 'That kind of work doesn't require too much running around.'

'C'mon,' I said to Rozalia. 'Let's get this over with.'

Just as we reached down for Wallace, the door banged open and Casey walked in. 'What the hell's going on?' he demanded, seeing Wallace slumped between us.

'Your buddy's in a mess,' said Rozalia, standing upright again. 'He's going to wind up killing himself if he keeps drinking like this, you know that?'

Wallace made a snorting sound and his eyes flickered open. He waved one pudgy arm as if dismissing all of us.

'Yeah, well, it's none of your business anyway, is it?' said Casey. He gestured towards the door with his head. 'You leave him to me and I'll get him home.'

I bit back my words as Casey reached down and tried to get Wallace to stand up. 'C'mon, you sorry piece of crap,' he said. 'Get the hell *up*.'

'No,' Wallace mumbled, twisting away from Casey. 'All *your* fault.'

'We tried that already,' I said. 'There's no way he's going to be able to walk—'

'I already said, it's none of your goddam business,' Casey snapped, glaring at me. He bent down, wrapping one of Wallace's arms around his shoulder before trying to hoist him up and off the floor.

'Hey,' I said angrily. 'Don't talk to me like—'

Casey's face suddenly turned white, and he let go of Wallace, who slumped back down. It didn't take much to guess he'd put his back out again.

'*Fuck*,' Casey shouted, walking in circles and grimacing from the pain. 'Lousy stinking *bastard*.'

'Did you just mess your back up again?' said Rozalia, without a trace of sympathy.

Casey backed away towards the bar, grabbing hold of it with his other hand, and glared at us.

'You know,' I said to Casey, 'I was trying to help just now. You didn't need to be an asshole about it.'

'Don't bother trying to explain anything to him,' said Rozalia, her expression sour. 'Casey's all about looking out for number one. Isn't that right, Casey?'

'You want to help?' said Casey. 'Then just leave me the hell alone. *I'll* get Wallace home.'

'You're kidding,' I said, looking at him. '*Look* at you. You can barely stand upright. How long has your back been like this?'

'Fuck you,' Casey snapped. 'I can do my job better than the rest of you put together, this day or any other.'

I spread my hands and nodded at Wallace. 'Go right ahead.'

Casey just glared at me.

'Yeah, that's what I thought,' I said. I looked at Rozalia. 'We'll get him home.'

'Thanks for volunteering me for the job, asshole,' Rozalia muttered under her breath.

'And you should take it easy,' I said to Casey. I couldn't for the life of me figure out what his problem was, but when I stepped forward, taking hold of Wallace on one side while Rozalia took the other, he at least had the good grace not to say anything more.

But *damn*, Wallace was heavy.

'Maybe if we leave him in the street overnight the rain'll wash the smell away,' said Rozalia, once we finally had Wallace on his feet between us. I couldn't tell if she was kidding or not. Probably not.

Wallace swayed a little, but I felt confident he would stay upright so long as we remained on either side of him. We led him out through the front entrance and down the steps, Casey following after us the whole way and wincing with each step he took. Regardless, he appeared determined to accompany us the whole way.

Wallace belched mightily, and I struggled not to gag at the awful vapours emerging from the depths of his gullet.

'Leave me alone,' he slurred.

'C'mon, big boy,' said Rozalia, her voice strained from her exertion. 'We're going for a walk.'

In all, it took us nearly half an hour to guide Wallace back to his own place. Casey seemed to decide it was his job to take the lead, as if we actually needed him to guide us there. Soon he was barking orders, telling us which way to turn, and I started to realize why Nadia had had such a low opinion of him.

The interior of Wallace Deans' home resembled nothing so much as a dumping ground for domestic waste. The mess was, frankly, unbelievable.

'How the *hell* does anyone live like this?' I muttered through clenched teeth, once we had manoeuvred Wallace in through his front door. Even the air inside his home made the roof of my mouth itch. The furniture was nearly invisible beneath mounds of discarded clothing and pieces of dirt-stained machinery that sat on random oases of blackened carpet. I glanced through a doorway and saw that every kitchen surface was almost entirely hidden beneath half-gutted computers and other, less familiar pieces of junked technology.

I looked up, seeing a bundle of cables duct-taped to the ceiling. I followed it with my eyes, seeing that it terminated at a cramped table in one corner that supported at least four flat-screen monitors, arranged in haphazard fashion.

There was a constant faint but nonetheless discernible hum of electronics. I noticed that more cables ran across the floor, appearing to originate from several portable battery generators.

I looked at Rozalia, but she just shook her head, her mouth puckered up as if she'd eaten something bad.

By now, Wallace had recovered enough that he could just about put one foot in front of the other without immediately tipping over. We kept a tight grip on him anyway, and under Casey's droning guidance we guided him up a set of narrow steps and into his bedroom, where we found a mattress covered over with crumpled, greasy-looking sheets.

Wallace managed to get one knee up onto the mattress before tipping face-first onto it. After a moment he started to make a noise that sounded like an aeroplane's engine cutting out in the moments before it ploughs into the ground. The noise soon steadied, becoming more obviously the sound of a man snoring more loudly than I might otherwise have believed possible.

I looked over at Rozalia on the other side of the bed, and at Casey, who stood near the door. 'That's it,' I said, moving past Casey and towards the door. I had a sudden, desperate need for a shower. 'I've had more than enough for one night.'

'Not yet,' said Rozalia. 'Help me get him on his side. Last thing we need is him drowning in his own vomit.'

I suppressed a groan, and went back over, helping tip Wallace onto one side while Casey watched with an anxious expression whose meaning I couldn't begin to fathom. I noticed that Wallace had taped large sheets of black paper over the windows, and remembered it was much the same downstairs.

'What the hell is it with this place?' I gasped, stepping back from Wallace once more. 'How the hell can *anyone* live like this?'

'Thanks for all your help,' said Casey, with clear insincerity. 'I'll keep an eye on him now.'

'What is your fucking problem, exactly?' Rozalia snapped at him. From the look on her face, she'd clearly had enough.

Wallace stopped snoring. 'Imphhrrrerr,' he said.

'What did he say?' I asked.

'If we're lucky,' said Rozalia, 'that was a death rattle.'

Wallace's hand beat at the surface of the bed. '*Imphrurur,*' he said, with greater urgency.

'He wants his inhaler,' said Casey, somewhat testily.

'Oh.' Rozalia nodded in comprehension. 'Of course.'

Living in a shithole like this, I thought, it was hardly surprising he had trouble breathing. I looked over at Casey. 'Any idea where it is?'

He stared back at me in apparent outrage. 'How the fuck would *I* know?'

I gave up on asking him anything more, and looked around until

I saw a set of drawers by the side of the bed, half-buried beneath a mound of unwashed clothing. I opened them one by one until I found a shrink-wrapped inhaler. I reached in to get it, then noticed something gleaming dully at the back of the drawer. One half, I saw, of an I Ching coin.

I stared at it, frozen, one knee on the floor, my hand still on the drawer's handle.

It wasn't possible.

'Jerry?'

I glanced back at Rozalia and Casey, and felt a terrible tremor run through my muscles.

I looked again. The coin was still there. I wasn't imagining it.

I reached in and took hold of it. The scuffed and tarnished metal felt cool and hard against the palm of my hand. My head swam as I pushed the drawer shut. I had the inhaler in one hand, the coin in the other. I studied the latter in the sparse moonlight that somehow found its way past the sheets of card covering the windows.

It was identical in every respect to the half-coin I had worn around my neck for years in memory of my dead wife, and which I had lost in the river when Nadia died. How, then, could it possibly be here, in a drawer in Wallace Deans' home?

Assuming, I realized, that it was mine, and not the other Jerry's.

I pushed myself back upright, my legs feeling as if they were about to fold under me. I turned to look at Rozalia, and from her expression guessed my shock must be evident.

'What is it?' she asked, her voice full of worry.

I stood there, the half-coin in my open palm. I saw her eyes dip down to see it nestled there.

'I found his inhaler,' I said numbly.

I looked back down at Wallace and saw he had woken up again. I watched as his eyes moved from the set of drawers to my hand, working it out. He looked suddenly a great deal more sober than just a moment before.

I lowered my hand until he could clearly see the half-coin.

'Wallace,' I asked, forcing myself to remain calm, 'can you tell me where you got this?'

'I'm sorry,' he said, and leaned to one side before noisily throwing up on the floor close to my feet. I stepped back quickly, just avoiding the flow of liquid as it hit.

'*Fuck*,' shouted Rozalia, her face twisted up in disgust.

Casey's eyes were on the broken I Ching coin in my hand. His gaze moved up to meet mine, and he gave me a look I couldn't decipher.

'I'll get some tissues,' he said, his tone flat and emotionless, and stepped out of the room.

'Jerry,' said Rozalia, once Casey was gone, 'will you *please* tell me what's going on?'

Wallace made a moaning sound. I was just about to tell her when Casey returned, clutching an enormous wad of paper towels and carrying a bucket. He pushed past me, kneeling down carefully before making an attempt at cleaning the mess up.

I stared again at the half-coin grasped in my hand and tried to think how it could possibly have come into Wallace's possession. There had to be some rational explanation: something that would make perfect sense and chase away all the paranoid fantasies yelling for attention in the back of my head.

Maybe. But somehow I doubted it.

Casey stood back up. 'Maybe you should go now,' he said, his tone wooden. 'Thanks for your help and everything, but I think I'd better stick around and keep an eye on him.'

I glanced down at Wallace, who had drifted off into a more peaceful sleep, snoring more quietly this time.

'Does he still need his inhaler?' I asked, handing the shrink-wrapped device over to Casey.

'Mostly he just needs to dry out,' the other man replied. He nodded curtly to me. 'Thanks.'

There were so very many questions I wanted to ask Wallace, but I knew they would have to wait. Some instinct told me not to say anything while Casey was around.

Rozalia gave me one last, long questioning look before she followed me back outside.

We walked for maybe half a block before Rozalia stepped in front of me, a determined look on her face. 'Spill,' she said. 'What the *hell* just happened back there?'

I held the coin up so she could see it more clearly. Its Chinese characters glistened softly under the moonlight.

'Do you know what that is?' I asked. 'Did the other Jerry ever tell you the story about it?'

She opened her mouth and closed it. 'He always wore it around his neck.' She paused. 'I've seen you wearing it too, but I don't recall seeing it recently.'

I nodded. 'I lost this when I was in the river with Nadia. It was *gone*, Rozalia.'

'So how the hell did it get into Wallace Deans' . . . ?' Her eyes grew round and wide, and she stared at the coin as if seeing it for the first time. 'Oh.'

By some unconscious agreement, we followed the scent of brine and seaweed towards the harbour, a short walk from Wallace's home. 'All I know concerning my predecessor's death is that it was some kind of stupid accident,' I said. 'Except later, of course, Nadia started wondering if maybe it wasn't some stupid accident after all, but deliberate. There must have been at least some kind of investigation into what happened to the other Jerry when he died, right?'

She nodded. 'There was a short inquiry, yes.'

'So what do you know about the circumstances of his death? Was he alone, or was there anyone else with him at the time?'

'The way I heard it,' said Rozalia, 'he'd headed off to explore some ruins on an alternate, and climbed up high inside the remains of some building. He lost his footing and fell.'

'But there's always at least a two-man team, isn't there? So who was the other guy?'

'Haden,' she said. She nodded as if remembering something. 'He was first on the scene. But by the time he got there, well . . . your other self was already dead.'

'Could Haden have . . . ?'

She shook her head. 'I know what you're thinking, but no. They had a couple of wheeled drones with them at the time, and Haden was visible in the camera of one of them when your predecessor died. He was nowhere near Jerry and didn't manage to get to him for some minutes. By the time he did, it was too late.'

'Wallace Deans is supposed to be some kind of computer wizard,' I said. 'Given what I just found in his house, isn't it at least possible he had something to do with it?'

She nodded. 'It's possible, in theory at least. As a matter of fact, I was on that expedition along with Wallace as well – but we were both back at the staging area, maybe a hundred kilometres from where your predecessor was when he had his fatal fall. I'd say that puts Wallace in the clear.' She frowned. 'Or at least, I think it does.'

'Nadia told me once that Wallace has a reputation for sticky fingers.'

Rozalia chuckled. 'Yeah. The man's a full-blooded kleptomaniac, which gives credence to the idea he maybe stole it from your predecessor.'

'Except it still doesn't explain how the hell the damn thing wound up in his bedroom drawer, if he was a hundred kilometres away. Could Wallace have stolen the coin from the other Jerry's body after they brought it back?'

Rozalia glanced back towards Wallace's place. 'I guess it's possible. But if you want to be sure one way or the other, your only real course of action is just to go back there and ask him while you have the chance.'

'No.' I shook my head.

'Why not?'

I glanced at her.

'Because of Casey?' she asked.

'He started acting weird from the moment he walked into the bar. Didn't you notice how he was trying to get rid of us the whole time?'

'Under any other circumstances, I'd have said that was just Casey being an asshole. He's antediluvian enough to think looking weak in front of a woman is about the worst thing that could happen to him. He's always strutting around with that damn gun strapped to his leg like he's the fucking Lone Ranger.'

I'm sorry, Wallace had said. He might just have been apologizing for nearly throwing up on my shoes, but I felt sure it was because of the coin he'd seen in my hand. *Sorry for what?*

I came to a decision. 'I'm going to tell you something,' I said to Rozalia.

She listened while I detailed everything I had learned about my predecessor's final diary entries, and why I was beginning to suspect they had been deliberately fabricated.

'I'll have to be honest,' Rozalia said drily once I'd finished, 'Chloe's not the kind of girl who'd ever put up with that kind of shit. Anyone who did try something like that, I guarantee they'd find themselves relieved of their balls in a second flat.'

'There has to be some reason,' I said, 'for him to have fabricated those entries.' I pounded one fist into the other. 'It's a message of some kind, and it has to do with those statues, I'm *sure* of it.'

'Well?' asked Rozalia, leaning against the sea wall by the harbour and studying me, 'what's stopping you?'

'I tried to get Chloe to go and take a look at them with me, but she was insistent about getting some rest. She's just back from a mission and, to be fair, she was asleep on her feet.'

Rozalia shook her head. 'Don't get me wrong,' she said, 'but why's it so important to have her along?'

'My predecessor didn't write those entries and draw those pictures for my benefit. He did them for Chloe's, and he must have believed she could work something out from clues he left. Unless she comes with me, I can't be sure I can work out whatever it is he intended.'

'Well,' said Rozalia, looking around the deserted harbour. 'The night's still young. I knew him, though certainly not as well as Chloe. How about I go out there with you and we can take a look ourselves first? And if we don't find anything, we head out again in the morning with Chloe.'

'That,' I said, with feverish excitement, 'sounds like a damn good idea.'

SEVENTEEN

Not long after I had got home and grabbed up the notebook and stuffed it in a satchel, I saw headlights pull up outside. I slung the satchel over my shoulders and stepped back outside to find Rozalia waiting there for me behind the wheel of an open-top jeep. To my surprise, Chloe was sitting behind her.

'I hate you,' Chloe said tonelessly, as I climbed in the front beside Rozalia.

I stared over my shoulder at her in bafflement. 'What the hell did I do?'

She glared at me. 'Not you. Queen Bitch there in the driver's seat.'

'Now, now,' said Rozalia.

'I need to *sleep*,' Chloe moaned.

'So sleep,' said Rozalia testily. 'I'm the one who's driving.'

'Maybe Chloe's right,' I said. 'She needs to get some rest. You and me can handle this just fine.'

Rozalia gave me a withering look. 'The sooner we get out there and try and figure this out,' she said, 'the more chance I have of working out whether there's any connection with what happened to Nadia. And I'm not waiting one damn minute more than I absolutely have to. So *I* say we're going now. Got that?'

Chloe stared at her blearily, then let her head sink back against her seat until she stared up at the stars.

'Here,' said Rozalia, grabbing a plastic tin from the dashboard and handing it back to Chloe, who stared dully at it in her hand.

'What is this?' she asked.

'Mother's little helper,' said Rozalia with a grin. 'Couple of those and you'll be scaling mountains in no time.'

Chloe shook her head wearily, shaking a couple of the amphetamine tablets into her palm and dry-swallowing them. I pulled the notebook back out of my satchel, riffling through the pages until I found the entry I wanted.

'Did you tell Chloe about what just happened at Wallace's place?' I asked Rozalia.

'She told me,' Chloe muttered from behind me. 'And I know all about the half-coin you and the other Jerry always wore. He'd never walk out of the house without it.'

'You sound like you resented it,' I said.

She nodded. 'I did. But I couldn't blame him either.' She sighed. 'We compromised, and he just carried it in his pocket.'

I smoothed down the notebook pages, then passed it back to Chloe. 'Look at the drawing,' I said.

The picture covered the top half of two pages and showed a row of Easter Island statues – the very same ones, in fact, that I had happened upon during my earlier trip north. My predecessor had seen fit to depict one of the central *moai* clutching a handbag.

'The entry's about one of those picnics that never happened,' I explained. 'Now turn to the next page.'

Chloe dutifully turned the page, which featured another large illustration, again taking up half the page. This time the illustration was of that same central statue, but this time minus the handbag.

Chloe looked up at me, befuddled and exhausted, from the rear seat. 'What about it?'

'What is it about that statue,' I asked, 'that he's so determined to draw your attention to it?'

She gave me a look. 'Are you sure you're not reading too much into all this?'

'I know how his mind worked,' I said, 'because we have the *same* mind. Why *that* statue? Why draw it at all, or even make up any of these entries?'

Chloe passed the notebook back to me and I looked at Rozalia.

'Aren't you worried someone might ask where we're going at this time of night?'

She shrugged and started the engine. 'I figure we can just tell them we're going on a picnic.'

We reached our destination a little under half an hour later, the wind sharp and cool against our faces. The statues were easy to spot, being silhouetted by moonlight that made the whole scene somehow eerie and primordial. Rozalia cut the engine, and I looked back at Chloe.

'Coming?' I asked her.

'Sure,' she said, climbing out. 'Not that I have one damn idea what's so special about these statues.'

Rozalia was next out of the jeep, then myself. The three of us made our way in silence across the grass towards the row of statues. I had forgotten just how huge the things were. Once again I extracted the notebook from my satchel and opened it as we drew closer to the statues.

'So what exactly do you think we're looking for here?' asked Rozalia, staring up at the towering forms.

'No bloody idea,' I replied, then stepped up close to the stone platform supporting the statues. Rozalia watched me with a perplexed expression.

I trailed my hand along the edge of the Cyclopean platform as I walked along its length, until I came to a point where a few sea-rounded boulders had been pushed up against its side. On a whim, I hoisted myself up on top of them and found that with a little work I could just about get a handhold on the platform's upper surface.

It took a few tries, but I finally managed to hoist myself up on top of the platform. I leaned against the foot of one of the statues, breathing hard from my effort. Even though I knew these *moai* had stood here for centuries, surviving hurricanes and storms and gales, some part of me couldn't shake the conviction that I might end up toppling them over like dominoes, were I to lean against them too hard.

I got back up and carefully made my way along the platform to the statue illustrated in the diary. Rozalia kept pace with me on the ground, and I waved down at her. She waved back half-heartedly, and with a look that implied she thought I should be locked up. Chloe had been staring out to sea, lost in her own thoughts, but then she turned round to look up at me.

'See anything?' she called up.

I leaned back, staring up the height of the statue until I felt a twinge of vertigo. 'Not a damn thing,' I called back down. Suddenly I felt ridiculous; I had no idea what I was doing or what I was looking for. For all I knew, I was just wasting time.

I was just about to give up and climb back down again when I thought I saw something, wedged into a crevice between the foot of the statue and the platform on which it stood.

'Are you coming down yet?' Rozalia called up.

'Hang on,' I said, lowering myself on to my hands and knees by the bottom of the statue.

The moonlight was just bright enough that I could see that something had indeed been pushed into a crevice at the base of one of the statues. It looked as if it had been wrapped in something wrinkled and shiny. I wriggled my fingers into the crack, just catching the edge of the package. It felt slippery, like plastic. I tried to get a grip on it, but succeeded only in pushing it deeper into the crevice.

'Damn it,' I said, then looked back down at the two women. 'Have either of you got something I can use to prise something out of here? I think I see something wedged in there, but I can't reach it.'

'What is it?' Chloe called up.

'I'm not sure yet.'

'Hang on,' said Rozalia. I glanced down and saw she was holding up a penknife. 'Will this do?'

'Sure,' I called down. 'Better than nothing.'

Rozalia tossed it up, and I caught it in my cupped hands.

'Thanks.' I turned back to the crevice, pushing the thin blade inside the crevice, working it in slowly until its tip caught the edge of the package.

It took a lot more work and time than I would have preferred. I swore and struggled until, finally, I was able to shift the concealed package from side to side, slowly sliding it closer and closer. Eventually, I could get enough of a grip on it to pull it out altogether. I found myself holding something wrapped in oilskins and secured with plastic twine, and felt a burst of savage triumph.

At last, perhaps, I could have some answers.

Two minutes later I was back on the ground. I knelt by the platform for shelter against the wind and used Rozalia's knife to slice through the twine before unwrapping what proved to be a single large sheet of oilskin containing a few dozen pages ripped from a notebook, and covered in handwriting I instantly recognized as my own.

'How did you *know*?' Chloe exclaimed, staring at the pages in my hand. The wind pulled at my hair, and I felt a few small spits of rain land on my face. I had a feeling a storm was on its way.

I pressed the pages against my chest before they had a chance to blow away. 'We should get out of here before it really starts pelting down,' I said.

Rozalia and Chloe looked at each other, then both nodded. 'Agreed.'

Thunder rolled across the landscape as we climbed back inside the jeep, and it soon began to rain heavily. There was more thunder, closer this time, and preceded by a flash.

'I don't want to drive all the way back south through this,' said Rozalia, reaching hurriedly for the ignition as the rain came down. 'There's a fisherman's hut just half a mile from here. We can wait the storm out there and take a look at whatever the hell it is you found.'

The 'hut' turned out to be slightly more substantial than the name suggested. It was big enough to hold a cot bed and a small wood-burning stove, beside which someone had left a pile of ready-chopped wood. There was even a small basin, a plastic canister full of water sitting next to it.

'How did you know about this place?' I asked Rozalia. She was busy brushing the rainwater out of her hair.

'Came this way a couple of times with Nadia,' she explained.

'Romantic getaway?' I asked.

She grinned. 'Guilty as charged. It's kind of cosy, if you don't mind cobwebs.' I watched as she pushed some of the chopped wood inside the stove, before setting it alight with the help of a box of firelighters sitting on a nearby shelf.

I had shoved the oilskin-wrapped papers inside my satchel along with the notebook as we drove for shelter. I lifted the bundle back out, carrying it over to a small wooden table in one corner. Lastly I took off my soaked jacket, hanging it on a nail.

Outside, the rain began to come down in earnest, hammering at the roof.

'Still here,' said Rozalia, pulling a cardboard box out from beneath the basin. She lifted a can of instant coffee out of the box, and then a small saucepan and a couple of tin mugs. 'How's that fire going?' she asked, looking over at Chloe.

'Swell,' said Chloe, hunkered down by the stove and peering intently at the flames. 'Is that coffee?'

'Sure is.' Rozalia looked over at me. 'How about you, Jerry? You like your coffee black, I seem to recall.'

'Unless you've got a cow stashed somewhere around here, I figure I don't really have a choice.'

Rozalia tipped some of the water in the canister into the saucepan and placed it on top of the stove. 'I guess you don't. So how about telling us just what it is we've got?'

I caught Chloe's eye. 'Want to take a look through this with me?'

'Sort of yes, and sort of hell no,' she muttered, and shook her head. 'I still don't feel ready for all this.'

'Sure.' I nodded. 'I understand.' I looked at Rozalia, but she just gave me a shrug.

My predecessor had done a good job of wrapping up the pages so that they were watertight. I leafed through them, then started reading. I barely even noticed when Rozalia put a mug of hot coffee down next to me some minutes later.

'So, don't keep us in suspense any longer,' she said.

I put the pages down and looked at her. 'I'm not sure you're going to believe this.'

'Try me.'

I looked at her, and then at Chloe, still squatting by the stove, and held up a page. 'According to this, my predecessor was carrying out his investigation on Mort Bramnik's behalf, and at his specific request.'

Both women's jaws flopped open. '*What?*' exclaimed Rozalia.

'Specifically, Bramnik charged him to try and find out if all the equipment failures and other problems might indeed be sabotage. But he was required to carry out his investigation under the strictest secrecy.' I put the page down heavily. 'It's all here,' I said, waving my hand across the rest of the oilskin's contents.

'A secret investigation?' asked Chloe. 'Why?'

'And why go to the effort of hiding all this stuff under a statue?' asked Rozalia.

'He wrote a letter to Chloe,' I said, picking another page up and holding it out towards her. 'Here.'

Chloe stared at the sheet of paper in my hand, then got up and took it from me and started to read.

Rozalia looked between us. 'So? What does it say?'

'He hid all this because he was trying to protect Chloe,' I explained. 'He was afraid to tell her the truth about his investigation, in case the Patriots found out about it. He thought if that happened, they'd interrogate her the way they did Wallace. He wrote up everything he knew because he was convinced something might happen to him, and he left clues in his diary that would lead her to the statues if that day ever came.'

Chloe looked pale and dazed. 'I can't believe I've been so stupid,' she said, staring at the words. 'If I'd just read that damn diary, I could have figured all of this out by now.'

'There's no point beating yourself up,' said Rozalia. 'You'd have got round to it eventually.'

'Maybe.'

'Okay,' I said. 'Listen to this.' I began to read from some of the rest of the pages.

If you're reading this, it began, *it means something's happened to me. You know there've been a lot of problems recently, what with Mort Bramnik and some other people nearly getting themselves killed when a mission went wrong. Just after that Bramnik himself came to me in confidence and asked if I'd take a look into all these incidents that have been piling up.*

'Why me?' I asked him, and he said it was because he trusted me the most out of all the Pathfinders.

I'll admit I was wary, particularly when he said he wanted to do it in strict secrecy. He was sure, he said, that what happened to him out on that alternate we had visited was no accident.

I looked up at Rozalia. 'You told me how the other Jerry got killed,' I said. 'But exactly what happened on the expedition Bramnik was part of?'

She shuddered. 'To be honest, I've tried quite hard to forget it.'

'It was that bad?'

'They were hunted,' said Chloe, 'by werewolves.'

Rozalia twisted around to look at her. 'Do *not*,' she said, 'use that word.'

'Well, I saw the drone footage from that mission,' said Chloe, 'and that's what they looked like to *me*.'

'So what were they, then?' I asked Rozalia.

'Lab-bred mutants that bust out of some military lab,' Rozalia explained. 'Isn't that always the way? We called them Howlers. Imagine something the size of a bear, but ten times as smart, and fast as all hell. I once saw one rip open an abandoned truck like it was made of confetti.' She rubbed her hands together. 'The humans on their alternate were mostly wiped out after a nuclear war. There were survivors, but after the Howlers broke out of whatever lab they were invented in, they bred fast and got busy hunting the survivors down to the very last person alive.'

'Nice,' I said. 'But why did Bramnik decide to visit somewhere with so much potential for danger?'

'I spent a lot of time studying the Howlers,' said Rozalia. 'They hunt by night and hole up during the day. As long as we were out of there by dark, we should have been fine. That time, however, things were different, and I could never figure out why.'

Doesn't that sound familiar, I thought, thinking of the bee-brains. 'So the expedition was attacked by Howlers?'

She nodded. 'We made a run for a building we'd already scouted out that had previously been fortified, presumably by someone making their last stand against the things. We were shooting the creatures down the whole way. That's what I remember: Casey, with his shotgun, taking them down calm as anything, one after the other, as they came running towards us.' She wrapped her arms around her shoulders as if suddenly cold. 'But we had to get back through the transfer stage before dusk, or none of us would ever have made it out. Casey managed to trap the Howlers in a basement for long enough to give the rest of us a chance to make a dash for a 'copter waiting to lift us back to the staging area. I really hate to say it, but if it wasn't for Casey . . .'

I looked down at the pages spread out on the oilskin. 'It sounds like a standard screw-up, from the description at least.'

'There was an investigation,' said Chloe drily. 'There's *always* an investigation.'

'And?'

She gave me a thumbs-down gesture. 'And zilch. They just blamed us for not doing a good enough job of keeping Bramnik and his guests safe. Which is bullshit, based on what I heard from Rozalia and the others.'

Chloe nodded at the papers in my lap. 'What else does it say?'

I picked up the next page. 'Says here he – I mean, the other Jerry – had a hard time talking to anyone about any of the incidents or asking any kind of questions without giving the game away. Instead he tried to learn how some of the equipment worked by talking to members of the Authority's technical and civilian staff. That way, maybe he could figure out just what it was that kept going wrong.'

'Makes sense,' said Rozalia. 'Once you get some of those technical guys talking, you can't shut them up. Getting them to *not* talk would be harder.'

I looked at her. 'I thought there were rules about none of them communicating with us?'

'Sure,' Rozalia agreed. 'If it's something important, like where they're all from, or anything like that. But how a field radio works or how you repair a drone isn't nearly so much of a problem.'

'Listen to this,' I said, and read aloud:

There was just too much going wrong, said Bramnik, for it not to be some kind of sabotage. But then, who could be responsible?

It seemed to him that the only way that any such sabotage could be carried out was by someone with unrestricted access to a transfer stage; someone able to come and go across the multiverse any time they pleased. But according to Bramnik, none of the Authority's civilian staff was allowed near a stage unless they were going somewhere. And all the rig technicians are strictly vetted by Major Howes, who, as you know, recently took charge of the military detachment at the compound.

Bramnik went on to tell me that, apart from himself, the rig technicians and a very few other high-ranking individuals, the transfer coordinates for the various alternates are kept a closely guarded secret. Despite this, he wanted somebody he trusted to take a look around the Howler alternate and see if there was any evidence that would contradict the official investigation. And he knew I had prior experience on that alternate; I'd helped Rozalia and Winifred collect their data on the Howlers, after all.

So by prior arrangement I sneaked out late one night while you were still asleep and found Bramnik waiting for me at the main transfer stage. Nobody else was around; just me and him. Bramnik himself worked the control rig and sent me over. I was to return at a pre-arranged time when he would, again, be the only one around.

I'll cut a long story short, Chloe. While I was over on that alternate,

I found hard evidence that someone had set a trap for Bramnik and the rest of our party. Someone had programmed a couple of the robots to gather up brushwood and anything else that might burn and dumped it in the mouth of a nearby Howler den, before setting it on fire and smoking them out in the middle of the day. I found one of the robots stuck in a ditch where it had fallen, and raided its memory for the evidence.

Bramnik was particular that I should retrieve anything I could from the site of the evacuation, and that made me wonder if he'd lost something valuable. But by the time I had a look around, the whole place had been swept clean – as if someone had beaten me there.

When I got back to the island and told him what I'd found, Bramnik turned kind of grey, as if he'd aged a couple of decades there and then. He told me he'd be in touch soon; he was going to have to go back to his home alternate for a couple of weeks, and in the meantime I should try and find out anything else I could.

Here's something I learned during that last conversation with Bramnik: he believes the Patriots really are trying to take over operations on Easter Island. That's the main reason he keeps getting called away as much as he does – he's in deep shit on whatever alternate they all come from. He explained that he's under investigation himself back there – for what, he didn't specify – and Agent Greenbrooke himself is involved in that investigation in some senior capacity.

After I got home, I spent a couple of days thinking about what I had learned. Who knew as much about the Howlers, for instance, as me or Rozalia or Winifred, both of whom I trusted implicitly? Who had the field experience on that alternate, that they would know just how those animals might react were you to smoke them out in the middle of the day?

That's when I decided to start keeping an eye on Casey.

I looked up at the other two. Rozalia had her hand to her mouth. 'Don't stop now, for pity's sake,' she said.

I cleared my throat and kept going.

I realized that Casey had a habit of being around whenever things went wrong. During the last few weeks I made sure to keep close tabs on him, even volunteering for the same missions. As closely as I watched him, I saw and heard nothing to raise my suspicions and started to think I was chasing down the wrong alley.

Then, one day, while I was back on the island and walking across town from Nadia and Rozalia's place, I saw Wallace and Casey heading off for one of those fishing trips they always seem to be taking together up along the coast. I was feeling frustrated and concerned by the fact that Bramnik still had not yet returned, and I found myself following them from a distance. They were making their way on foot out past the suburbs, carrying rods and fishing tackle and the whole damn works. It was getting dark, so I knew I'd be able to keep a reasonable distance without too much risk of them figuring out they were being followed.

They were making their way towards a wharf on the east coast, just north of the base compound, when they suddenly came to a stop, looking around like they wanted to make certain nobody was watching them. I made sure to hide somewhere I could still keep an eye on them, and I saw them stow every last bit of their fishing gear in a rowing boat moored at the wharf before doubling back into town. I followed them the whole way back and saw them slip inside one of the abandoned houses.

'Does he say which one?' Rozalia asked me. I lifted the page up and showed her a small map that my predecessor had drawn in one corner of the page before continuing my narration.

I got close enough that I could hear the pair of them talking and moving around inside. At one point I heard a window rattle. I tried to take a peek inside, but it looked as if Wallace had covered all the windows up with the same black card that he puts on his own windows. I stayed hidden there around the back of the house until close to dawn, until Wallace finally emerged – but there was no sign of Casey.

As soon as Wallace was out of sight I made my way inside the house. I didn't feel worried about running into Casey because by now I had a pretty good idea what I was going to find. And there it was, down in the basement: a set of field-pillars – in other words, a portable transfer stage.

EIGHTEEN

'Well, shit,' said Rozalia, clearly stunned. 'Didn't see that one coming.'

I looked between the two of them. 'Why? Is it that hard to get hold of a portable stage?'

Rozalia let out a stifled laugh. 'Hell, yes. You can't just walk in and grab a bunch of field-pillars and something to run them with. All the equipment's kept under lock and key, and guarded to boot.'

'I want to hear the rest of what he wrote,' said Chloe. She looked scared and lost in a way that made me want to wrap her up in my arms. I took a swallow of my coffee, which had turned lukewarm, before continuing:

The whole time I was thinking, Who had the power or the resources to give Casey and Wallace a private transfer stage? It had to be someone from inside the Authority itself, and whoever they were, they'd done it without Bramnik's knowledge or consent.

By now I felt little doubt that the two men would prove to be involved somehow with what had happened in the Howler alternate. With their own transfer stage to take them there any time they wanted, they'd have had numerous opportunities to interfere with on-site equipment in between the scheduled trips.

Well, I was damned if I was going to sit on all this until Bramnik finally decided to get the hell back to the island. I decided to confront one or both of them – and since Casey wasn't anywhere around, that meant it had to be Wallace.

I didn't wait a moment longer. I headed straight round to Wallace's and hammered on his door until he let me in. From the smell of his breath he'd started drinking from the moment he got in the door. When he saw the look on my face I think he guessed why I was there; he tried to slam the door shut, but I forced my way in and threw him into a chair before demanding he give me the answers I wanted.

I thought I'd have a hard time getting him to talk, but once I told him what I knew already, he just caved there and then and told me everything. It was like pulling the plug out of a dam; I couldn't have stopped him talking if I'd tried.

Do you remember Wallace was 'interrogated' by the Patriots a while back for thieving alternate technology? That's when his drinking got serious. I guess it's no surprise that he'd been harbouring a great deal of resentment over that whole episode.

That, he explained, was when he decided to get even.

Now, Wallace is a smart guy. There's no doubt about that. He's hellishly good with computers, and a lot of the time he winds up getting put in charge of mission logistics and other stuff like programming our reconnaissance drones. Because of that, he explained, the Authority frequently gave him access to otherwise restricted computers inside the base compound. By then he had already figured out that some parts of their computer network were heavily encrypted. To a guy like Wallace, that's a challenge, not a barrier.

He eventually worked out that to get inside those restricted sectors, he'd need access to a special kind of alphanumeric key. One time when he was up at the base, he learned by accident that this key got changed once every week. Wallace knew that, if he could get hold of an up-to-date key, maybe he'd be able to find something among all those restricted files that he could use to hurt the Patriots, and Greenbrooke in particular.

He bided his time and took care to cover his tracks when he explored the unsecured parts of the network. He came across a text file somebody had left in the wrong place that proved to be a set of security guidelines. From this he learned that every six months a new set of keys was generated in advance, printed up into three separate physical documents and distributed to three high-ranking members of the Authority's staff; one went to Mort Bramnik, one to Major Howes and the last to the Patriots – meaning, in this case, Agent Greenbrooke.

The guidelines further stated that these three printed documents also contained the complete set of transfer coordinates known to the Authority. Naturally, Wallace assumed that this included the coordinates for those alternates we can all expect to one day retire to if we choose. The guidelines went on to say that Bramnik kept his copy of the document on him at all times, in a locked briefcase, carried either by himself or his deputy assistant Kip Mayer.

Once Wallace got this far, he knew that, without access to the various codes and keys contained in those printouts, he couldn't get hold of the kind of information he was hoping to find. It niggled and worried at him for weeks afterwards, until eventually he wound up blabbing his frustration to Casey while they were fishing and drinking down by the harbour.

This was when Wallace learned that Casey had a secret of his own. He was covertly working for the Patriots, just like I'm now secretly working for Mort Bramnik.

Casey explained that just a few months before, Greenbrooke had approached him about carrying out some kind of work for the Patriots. Greenbrooke tried to get Casey on side by saying how much Casey's outlook and philosophy reflected his own. You know how Casey's a big fan of Ayn Rand? Well, Greenbrooke apparently presented Casey with – get this – a signed copy of Atlas Shrugged, from the Authority's own alternate. In return for working clandestinely for the Patriots, Greenbrooke told Casey, he would be handsomely rewarded. Not only with early retirement to the alternate of his choosing, but also with enough material wealth sourced from other extinct alternates to set him up for life, wherever he wound up.

Casey bit. The nature of all this clandestine activity? Nothing less than sabotage. Greenbrooke explained he wanted to hurt both Bramnik and his civilian administration, which Casey himself, after all, had never been afraid to criticize at length. If enough things went wrong, Greenbrooke suggested, the Patriots would be able to make a case for taking over operations on the island. In order for Casey to carry out his work, they would provide him with a portable transfer stage that he could use to make his own trips – but with a limited set of coordinates.

In one respect, I think Greenbrooke judged Casey correctly; they shared the same love for tradition, for the military, for rugged individualism.

But in other respects, Greenbrooke got Casey all wrong. Greenbrooke forgot that a man like Casey never likes having to kowtow to anyone else, whatever their similarities otherwise. More than that, Wallace explained to me, Casey smelled a rat. He figured that, instead of letting him retire, Greenbrooke was more likely to order his men to put a bullet in the back of Casey's head and dump his body in the sea. That's what Casey would have done had the roles been reversed.

Your next question might be, Why did Casey tell all of this to Wallace?

After Wallace told him everything he knew about the security keys and the transfer coordinates, Casey had a brainwave. He knew that a mission was coming up in which Mort Bramnik, along with other high-ranking types visiting from the Authority, were due to get a tour of the island and of a recently opened alternate. And since Bramnik carried a copy of this high-security document everywhere with him, maybe there could be an opportunity to steal it – at this point, Bramnik just wasn't around that much, having to deal with politics 'back home'. Then, with the private transfer stage provided by Greenbrooke, Casey and Wallace would be able to make their own escape without waiting for the Authority's permission. They even talked about sharing that information with the rest of us, in case we also felt like lighting out.

So Casey and Wallace started planning a supreme act of sabotage – one that had nothing to do with Greenbrooke's plans for taking over the Pathfinder project. Their plan was to disrupt the mission enough that Bramnik, along with everyone else, would be forced to evacuate back to the island at short notice. Somewhere in the chaos, Casey would try and find an opportunity to separate Bramnik from his briefcase.

Their plan worked, although Casey wasn't able to get his hands on the briefcase at the time. Instead he returned to the Howler alternate a day or two later and hunted around until he found the abandoned case. He brought it back and gave it to Wallace who, when he next returned to the base compound to make use of the computers there, was able to gain root access to otherwise secure networks. There, he could find out which specific coordinates related to which alternates.

By the time Wallace told me all this, some hours had passed, and it was well into the early hours of the morning. I could see a hint of dawn light gleaming through a narrow gap between the window frame and the sheet of black card covering it.

I asked Wallace the next, obvious, question: if he and Casey had the means to leave forever, why hadn't they done so already?

At about this time Wallace started to lose his nerve and didn't want to talk any more, however much I promised him I'd help protect him from Casey and also from the Patriots. He was never a strong-willed man. I knew most of what he'd done had been at Casey's instigation. But I could tell he was still holding something back – something that clearly terrified him.

When I pushed, the poor bastard actually started crying. Finally, he told me Casey had a new goal: he wanted to find a way to destroy the Authority. Literally to obliterate them, wipe them out of existence. Why, I didn't know, but it seemed to have something to do with whatever Wallace found after he wormed his way inside all those encrypted files.

The idea that Casey wanted to do any such thing sent a chill through me, precisely because it was plausible, whatever the motivation. We've all seen any number of alternates where human life was extinguished by a staggering variety of extinction events. With your own private transfer stage, and access to enough of those worlds, you'd have no trouble tracking down something you could use to wipe out some other alternate. Including that of the Authority, should you happen to have access to their transfer coordinates.

By this point I was angry and frightened enough myself that I went over and slapped Wallace hard across the face, demanding he tell me the truth. He kept repeating again and again that Casey wanted revenge, but the stupid bastard kept refusing to tell me why.

If I'd just had more time, I know I could have got the truth out of him. But that's when I heard someone hammering on Wallace's front door, and Casey yelling my name. I near as damn jumped out of my skin.

My guess is that Casey had returned through the transfer stage hidden *in the abandoned house and came looking for Wallace. He must have heard me shouting at Wallace when I lost my temper, or maybe he'd been listening in by the window for longer than that. Either way, the front door slammed open a second later, and Casey came charging in on us, gun drawn.*

He told me to get out. I stood my ground and asked him why the hell I should. Casey was all keyed up, eyes filled with rage, and I wondered if he'd really shoot me as he was threatening to do. But if he did, someone would hear it, and there would be too many questions were I suddenly to disappear right there on the island. I could see from Casey's face that he knew it as well as I did.

I gave Wallace one last look before I walked past Casey and back out of the house. I think, now that I've had time to consider it, than Wallace is frightened of Casey. Perhaps even more frightened of him than of the Patriots. Maybe if I'd had more time I could have persuaded Wallace to turn against him, to stop whatever it is he's planning. But I knew all I needed to do was bide my time until Bramnik got back from the Authority and I could set the facts out for him. In the meantime, there would, I felt sure, be other opportunities to speak with Wallace, to try to persuade him to my side.

Eventually the date came when Bramnik had told me he'd back, except he never appeared. I made up an excuse to go and ask for him at the base compound and, as is often the case, I got nothing like a straight answer. Plus ça change, *right?*

So I figured I could wait if Bramnik was late getting back. Except he didn't show up the next day, or the next. And at the time of writing, it's been weeks, and still no word of when he's getting back.

Worse, I haven't seen sight or sound of either Casey or Wallace in all that time. The morning after confronting Wallace, I asked around and discovered that both he and Casey had been volunteered at short notice for a long-term mission.

I went looking for Casey's portable transfer stage with an eye to packing it up, but they had been there already. It was gone, disappeared from that house.

I thought, then, about calling a meeting with the other Pathfinders to tell them what I knew. But at the same time I knew now that we would be going up against the Patriots. If they could make all this happen right under Bramnik's nose, who knew what might happen to us if the Patriots decided we were a serious threat to them? Particularly when the man supposedly in charge of us was constantly absent from the island. Or maybe Greenbrooke had recruited moles other than Casey.

It was only yesterday that I finally realized that I had not in fact been nearly paranoid enough. Someone had been in our home, Chloe. They'd done a good job of hiding it, but I could tell. A couple of things weren't quite where I'd left them. Some of my diaries weren't in the right order; that's when I knew that the Patriots were watching me, that Casey had told them I was a threat.

I came so close to telling you what I know, Chloe. But I couldn't take the risk. It's been so long now that I don't know if Bramnik's ever coming back, and who the hell knows who might end up in charge around here? The idea of Greenbrooke running things makes me break out in a sweat.

Yes, I thought about talking to Kip Mayer, except he hardly steps out of his office apart from trips back to the Authority, and every time he does that it's a Patriot agent behind the wheel of the jeep. I took a chance anyway and went to the compound and asked to speak to Mayer, and as soon as she saw me the woman manning the desk got up and disappeared. I waited around for a minute or two, until a Patriot agent came out through the same door and asked me what I wanted.

That's when I knew that Greenbrooke was just waiting for some excuse to get rid of me. I decided the best thing I could do was to find some mission that would take me away from everything for a good long while in the hope that this all blows over, or Bramnik comes back, whichever comes first. I know they're watching me, and that means they're watching you too. The farther away I am from you, the safer you are.

If you're reading this, Chloe, you know that I love you. I never really felt alive until I came to this place and found you. This, I realize now, is my home.

Now maybe you understand why I had to go to such elaborate lengths to hide these pages. I still don't know what Wallace might have been about to tell me that night, but if Casey really means to hurt the Authority, it's going to be just as bad for us as it is for them.

If anything happens to me, and you find this, the rest is up to you and the others. Maybe I should have told you anyway; I don't know. But I couldn't ever bear the thought of you being hurt by them.

I put the last page down. Chloe was twisted around in her seat, staring towards the window and the ocean beyond. She glanced towards me, and hurriedly wiped at her eyes with one sleeve.

For the first time in my life, I understood what it meant when people said they'd had the wind knocked out of them. I felt like a deflated balloon, limp and empty, my mind reeling. The three of us just sat there for a good minute before I finally found the gumption to say anything.

'Okay,' I said, 'I guess that's it. We'll take all this to Bramnik and he can figure the rest of this whole mess out. I don't think we'll need to worry about the Patriots once the dust settles.' I glanced towards the window and caught a glimpse of the moon shining dully through the storm clouds. 'What time is it, anyway?'

'Not much past midnight,' said Rozalia. She blinked tiredly. The window rattled fiercely, gusting rain against the panes.

'I don't think that storm's in any hurry to be gone,' she said.

'We can wait it out,' I said. 'My mind's whirling as it is.' I nodded towards the stove. 'Is there any coffee left?'

'You can have it,' said Chloe. 'I think those pills are starting to wear off already. I'm going to try and sleep for a little while.'

She pulled herself to her feet and lay down on the narrow cot, her coat pulled up around her shoulders, much as she'd had it on the drive up. She closed her eyes, and within moments seemed to have slipped off into a deep sleep, her shoulders rising and falling with a steady rhythm.

Rozalia glanced at her, then back at me. 'Hell of a lot for anyone to take in,' she said quietly, and moved in closer to me. 'So Casey wanted revenge. Any ideas why?'

'Beats me,' I said. 'Maybe we should go and ask Wallace ourselves.' I got up and poured myself some more coffee.

'Sounds like a good idea,' said Rozalia. 'Much as I hate to admit it, I'm starting to feel some sympathy for Bramnik, if Greenbrooke's gunning for him this hard.'

'Listen,' I said. 'I'm sorry about taking my frustration out on you after Kip Mayer talked to us all at the Mauna Loa.' I'd been more than a little upset over the revelations of domestic violence in my predecessor's diary and had taken it out on Rozalia, believing the entries to be true.

She shook her head. 'And more than a little hungover, maybe?'

'Yeah.' I scratched my chin, suddenly embarrassed. 'That, too.'

Her shoulders rose and fell in a sigh. 'You know, you weren't entirely wrong in what you said. No apologies are necessary. You were right – we *should* have ignored the pencil-necks and just told you the damn truth at the start. I know I'm not the only one who regrets playing along with them.'

'I'm sorry, anyway,' I said. 'I lost my temper.'

'So would anyone, with the same information at hand.' She cocked her head to one side and gave me a quizzical smile. 'So we're good, right?'

I nodded and sipped at the warm liquid, my own head buzzing from fatigue and caffeine. 'We're good,' I said.

'Then there's one other thing I want to be clear about,' she said. 'I've got my own reasons for wanting to find Casey's secret transfer stage. With Nadia gone, there's no damn reason for me to stick around here any more, because that girl was the one thing that made life here bearable for me. If Casey's really got hold of all of our retirement coordinates, then I'm out of here, the moment I have them. Are we clear on that too?'

'We are,' I said.

She nodded and I settled back in my chair, fatigue numbing my senses. I figured it wouldn't hurt if I closed my eyes, just for one . . .

*

'Hey.'

I came to with a start. Chloe stood over me, her coat still wrapped around her shoulders like a blanket.

I blinked and looked around, realizing I must have fallen asleep without being aware of it. Early morning light seeped in through the window, and I saw the storm had passed.

I sat forward, feeling stiff and tired and sore. 'Rozalia?' I asked, looking around. 'Where . . . ?'

'She just left to go fishing.' I gave her a look and she laughed. 'Seriously. There's hooks and tackle and everything here.'

I glanced at the stove. 'Maybe we should get that fired back up.'

'Already done,' said Chloe. 'Can't you feel the heat?'

She took hold of my hand and pulled me upright, leading me over towards the stove. I passed my hands over the top of the stove, feeling the delicious warmth soak into my skin. I heard the *pop* of wood burning.

'Now come on,' she said, pulling me back in the direction of the cot. 'I don't know how long we have before Rozalia gets back.'

'What are you . . . ?'

'The thing we've both been thinking about from the first moment we saw each other,' she said, her voice low. She looked suddenly uncertain. 'Unless I've been reading you wrong . . . ?'

'No,' I said, my voice thick. 'No, you haven't.' First that inexplicable kiss, then the photograph in her home, of the other Jerry with his arm around her. Chloe had never been far from my thoughts, and I realized I had been fooling myself by thinking this moment was anything other than inevitable.

I glanced towards the door. 'But what if Rozalia walks in?'

Chloe shook her head. 'She won't.'

Something in the way she said this made me certain that Rozalia's sudden absence had been arranged, and that she would be careful not to return from her fishing trip too quickly. It was strange: I had known Chloe for only a short while, but she had known me – the *other* me – for years.

I moved in close to her and pressed my lips to hers, filled with a sudden and urgent hunger. I could feel my erection straining hard against my jeans even as she reached for my belt buckle. I slid my hands around the curve of her breasts beneath her thin T-shirt, then down to her hips, which pressed into me. She let out a small gasp, then ground her hips against mine.

Less than a minute later we fell, still struggling out of our clothes, onto the cot. She was right: I'd been thinking about such a moment for a long time. I finally wriggled free of my jeans, but Chloe pressed both hands against my chest, holding me back, even as I reached down to slide my fingers between her thighs. I felt her shudder in response.

Then, finally, she relented, her hands sliding around my back. Rozalia could have walked in at that moment and I wouldn't have given a damn. But we were alone, and would be for some time, and I soon slid deep inside her warmth, her fingers kneading at my flesh as I pushed deeper and deeper inside her.

It's hardly surprising I came as quickly as I did, given how very long it had been. I felt a surge of emotion that threatened to over-whelm me, but she kept stroking and massaging my back, kissing my neck and chest, whispering something to me I couldn't make out. Then she held me tight, her hips still moving against mine, her body rigid in the moment before she gave out a single small cry. Then she relaxed beneath me, her chest rising and falling from her exertions.

'Jerry,' she said, and I saw her cheeks were damp again.

'Well, lookee here,' said Rozalia with a grin, when she came stamp-ing back into the hut more than an hour later.

We had both got dressed again, and I had stoked up the flames and was already onto my second pot of coffee. Rozalia was carrying a line and rod, a couple of fat bream hanging from hooks. Her expres-sion told me she was under no illusions about what had taken place during her absence.

'Say,' she said, holding her catch up high, 'either of you gutted a fish before?'

*

I took the wheel of the jeep an hour later, my belly full of fish and coffee. The morning light was thin, and the day's warmth had not yet arrived, and so I kept my jacket buttoned up to the neck. As we made our way back along the coast road, I caught sight of the beached trawler I'd seen on my first trip to the statues.

'Christ,' said Chloe, sitting beside me in the front passenger seat. She was staring off in the direction of the trawler herself. I glanced to the side and saw she was pressing the heels of both hands against her eyes. 'I think I'm hallucinating from sheer fatigue.'

'You need to get some proper rest,' I said, squeezing her hand as I drove.

'I was thinking,' said Rozalia from behind us, 'about what must have happened after Casey chased your predecessor out of Wallace's place. Casey must have put the fear of God into Wallace.'

'I was thinking that too,' I said. 'Wallace, according to my predecessor, was terrified of Casey.'

'God damn,' said Rozalia. 'They must have killed Nadia. I'm sure of it. They must have known she had suspicions about the other Jerry's death. They *must* have.'

'What about the Patriots themselves?' I suggested. 'One of their own agents could have sabotaged the SUV that I was in with her and Oskar . . .'

Rozalia shot me an angry look. 'You really believe that after what you've just read? Who the hell else would Greenbrooke have got to do his dirty work but Wallace and Casey? Who else but those two would have known enough about how the bee-brains work to sabotage the SUV the way they did?' She started to weep. 'And when I think of all the times I saw them in the Hotel du Mauna Loa, acting like nothing was wrong, taking me for a fool because I didn't know what they'd done . . .'

'I guess you ought to know,' I said to Chloe. 'Rozalia and I took a trip back to the alternate where Nadia died. We no longer have any doubt that her death was anything but an accident.' I filled her in on the details, her hand to her mouth the whole time.

'We need to find Casey's transfer stage,' Chloe said quietly, once I had finished. 'He can't have taken it far. The island's only so big, and there are only so many places to hide something like that.'

'Hey,' said Rozalia from behind us, a touch of alarm in her voice. 'Look.'

The black bulk of Rano Kau rose up ahead on the island's southernmost tip, the road curving to the west as it followed the coast towards town. I had been so deep in my own thoughts that I had failed to notice the thick pall of smoke rising above the rooftops and carried seawards by the wind.

'It looks like it's coming from somewhere near Wallace's place,' said Chloe, her voice tight.

She was right. I gripped the wheel hard and again remembered the look on Casey's face when we had stood together in Wallace's bedroom, his eyes on the half-coin in my open hand. In that moment I felt sure he had acted decisively in order to keep us from interfering with the plans Wallace had tried to warn my predecessor about.

NINETEEN

There wasn't much left of Wallace's house. It must have been a hell of a blaze, I thought, breathing shallowly to avoid taking in too much smoke.

I pulled the jeep up across the street from where Wallace's place had been. The air was thick with ash, and I had the feeling that the rain had probably done most of the work of putting out the flames.

On the way through town, we had narrowly avoided crashing into a jeep full of Patriot agents speeding down a narrow road, and had seen other agents wandering in and out of vacant houses. Fortunately, in the chaos none had thought to stop us and ask where we'd been all night.

I saw most of the other Pathfinders gathered in a loose knot farther down the street. They were watching as two of Major Howes' troops half-heartedly poked through the still-smouldering remains. A few of them glanced our way and muttered among themselves. I also noted the presence of three Patriot agents standing by another jeep parked next to Wallace's front gate, caught up in what looked like an intense conversation. That was fine by me, because it meant they weren't paying us much attention.

It didn't look to me as if Wallace could possibly have got out alive, particularly given how very inebriated he had been the last time I saw him. I could see how the palm trees lining the street nearest were themselves blackened from the blaze. Faint wisps of smoke still rose from their singed leaves.

I looked around at the houses next to Wallace's – all of them built from wood and brick. It struck me that, if not for the late-night storm, half the town could easily have gone up in flames. I wondered whether that might in fact have been Casey's intention, and realized any remaining doubts regarding whether he was responsible for the fire had fled.

As I watched, one of the soldiers stepped out through the gate and went to confer with the Patriot agents. Where was Mayer, I wondered? Or any other of the Authority's civilian staff? Shouldn't they be here?

Or were the Patriots now in charge?

'We were away for just one night,' said Chloe, 'and now . . .'

'Casey did this,' snarled Rozalia from the back seat. 'I guess he got tired of waiting for Wallace to find someone else to confess to. Well, fuck it. He got what he deserved.'

'Nobody deserves that,' I said, staring at the smouldering walls and the collapsed roof.

She leaned forward, putting her mouth close to my ear. 'I have no doubt now that Wallace had a hand in murdering Nadia. There's every reason to believe he also helped to murder the first Jerry. That's almost like he murdered *you*. Or did you forget?'

'We should try and find Mayer,' I said, trying to change the subject. 'We can show him what we found. He can help protect us from the Patriots once we've explained everything.'

'Maybe we should find out just what happened here before we do anything at all,' said Chloe. She nodded towards the other Pathfinders. 'One of the others might have seen Casey around.'

'Yeah,' said Rozalia, her voice full of venom. 'The more of us out looking for that son of a bitch, the sooner we can kill him.'

From the sound of her voice, I had little doubt that Rozalia would try and kill Casey at the first opportunity.

Winifred Quaker stepped away from the other Pathfinders and came towards us. 'Oh, thank God you're here,' she said, her thin arms wrapped around her chest as if to ward off cold, even though it was showing every sign of being a warm day. 'Yuichi and Selwyn went around to your houses to see if you were there, and when they couldn't find you we started to get worried that something might have happened to you.'

'What exactly *did* happen?' I asked.

She looked over at the charred ruins of the house and shook her head. 'I guess it's not hard to figure out, really. I woke up when I smelled the smoke. It's everywhere, you know? It'll be weeks before the stink is gone. You should have seen the flames.'

'Hell of a way to die,' I muttered, thinking of the lava licking its way towards me, down in the deep vaults of a dead world.

She darted a look at me. 'I'm sorry, I didn't explain properly. Wallace is still alive.'

'He is?' I exclaimed, getting out of the jeep and stepping closer to her. I still had my satchel slung over one shoulder, my oilskin-wrapped treasure within. 'Where is he?'

'They took him to the base compound, to the hospital there,' she said. Chloe and Rozalia had joined me beside the jeep. 'Selwyn and Randall were the first on the scene, and they managed to fight their way inside to him. They've both got a couple of minor burns, but nothing serious. Wallace, though . . .' She shook her head.

'Go on,' Chloe prompted.

'He's alive,' said Winifred. 'But I don't know if he's going to stay that way for long. I think he inhaled too much smoke.'

Selwyn was next to join us, his face dirty with ash. I saw that he had heavy bandages wrapped around one arm. 'Hey,' he said. 'I figured I'd better warn you now you're here. Kip Mayer's been arrested.' He inclined his head towards the Patriot agents. 'By *them*.'

Rozalia grabbed his arm. '*What?*'

'I heard about it from Yuichi just now. He saw Mayer being bundled into a jeep by a couple of Patriot types, back in town, outside the Authority's offices there. They drove off towards the base, so they've probably got him locked up there, unless they've already taken him back to the Authority's own alternate.'

'What do you mean "bundled", exactly?' I asked.

'I mean that Mayer was in handcuffs, so Yuichi said.'

'But why?' I asked. 'What possible reason could they—'

'They don't need a reason,' Rozalia said, her voice full of a terrible finality. 'They'll just make up some damn excuse. And with us stuck here, and no way to talk to anyone else in the Authority except through them, they'll be free to take control of the transfer stages and consolidate their power over the island and all the alternates it gives access to.'

Selwyn stared at Rozalia with his mouth open.

'Anything else we need to know?' I asked him, to forestall the inevitable flood of questions.

'I-I heard that they interrogated Wallace, up at the base hospital.' He thought for a moment. 'It seems kind of weird they'd put Kip in chains like that, right after they finished talking to Wallace.'

'So Wallace can still talk?' asked Chloe.

Selwyn made a face. 'Just about. Right after me and Randall got him out of that inferno he was babbling something, but nothing that made any sense. We got him in a jeep and drove him up to the hospital and raised seven shades of bloody hell until they all woke up and helped get him inside. We stuck around long enough to see him get wired up with tubes and monitors and all kinds of stuff, but then the Patriots turned up and threw us out on our arses.' He shuddered. 'I don't even want to imagine how much pain Wallace must be in, the state he was in when we got him there. I really thought we'd carried a corpse out of there at first, he was so badly burned.'

I stepped up close to Selwyn. 'What did Wallace say, exactly?'

Selwyn looked at me with a troubled expression. 'I already told you, nothing that made any sense to me—'

'Just tell me, dammit!'

'Take it easy,' said Chloe, putting her hand on my arm.

'I don't know,' said Selwyn. 'He was babbling about Casey and people dying.' He peered at me. 'Why? You know something I don't?'

'We saw Patriots searching through houses all across town on our way here,' Chloe said to me, her voice full of alarm. 'I can't think of any reason why, unless Wallace told them about the secret transfer stage.'

Or they're looking for Casey. But wherever Casey was, I felt sure, his transfer stage would be also. And if the Patriots found either him or the stage before we did, then any hope we had of obtaining it for our own use would be gone forever.

I glanced surreptitiously towards the knot of Patriot agents still standing nearby and wondered if any of Greenbrooke's men had the skill to hunt down a Pathfinder with years of experience in traversing multiple hostile environments. Assuming, that is, Casey hadn't already fled to some other alternate, using whatever transfer coordinates he had filched from Bramnik's stolen briefcase. And if Rozalia was right about the Patriots wanting to take control of the island, we had to move fast.

To be back on some world so close to my own I could hardly tell the difference . . . it was so near that I could almost taste it.

But as soon as the thought passed through my head, I felt a spasm of guilt. Wallace had told my predecessor that Casey was planning some act of genocide against the Authority. It was a threat, I now knew, that he might well be capable of carrying out. Could I really flee to some other world, and leave the billions who presumably lived on the Authority's alternate to die at Casey's hands?

I pressed the heel of one hand against my forehead, feeling the blood throb through my skull. Telling any of this to the Patriots would be tantamount to suicide, that much was clear – assuming they even listened to us. And that left only myself, and my fellow Pathfinders, to do what had to be done and find Casey first.

Both Winifred and Selwyn were regarding us with suspicion. 'What's been going on with you three, exactly?' Winifred demanded. 'What's all this about a secret transfer stage?'

'It's a long story,' Rozalia replied. 'And we're going to tell you and everyone else about it first real chance we get.'

I took a deep, steadying breath. 'Selwyn, do you think there's any way we'd be able to get back inside the base hospital to talk to Wallace ourselves? Are the Patriots likely to have him under guard or anything like that?'

Selwyn rubbed at his jaw. 'I don't know,' he said. 'Greenbrooke's got pretty much every last one of his agents running all over town. If there is anyone guarding him, I'm guessing that it'll more than likely be just the one guy. But I'd better warn you, I'm not exaggerating when I say how bad Wallace is. I'm not placing any bets on him surviving the morning.'

I nodded and put my hand on Selwyn's shoulder. 'How many Pathfinders are on the island just now?' I asked him. 'How many of us are away on missions?'

He thought for a moment. 'I checked the schedule the other day, and as far as I know we're all on the island.' He frowned. 'Except I also went looking for Haden and Casey after the fire, and I still haven't been able to find either of them. If you happen to see them . . .'

'I'll be keeping an eye out for both of them,' I promised, although I had no idea what might have happened to Haden. 'I want you to get together everyone you can find and get them to meet us later this morning at the Hotel du Mauna Loa. It's about eight right now, so let's say midday at the latest. Will you do that? We have something to tell you all, but I'd rather not do it with *them* around,' I added, casting a significant glance in the direction of the Patriots.

Selwyn flicked his eyes towards the agents, then back at me. 'Sure,' he said carefully, looking as if he had a million questions. 'I'll do that.'

Selwyn walked back over to join the others. Winifred made to follow him, then paused, fixing me with a steady eye. 'Whatever's going on,' she said, 'I hope for your sakes you know what you're doing.'

So do I, I thought, as she turned and walked away.

The more I thought about it, the more certain I was that Casey had tried not only to kill Wallace, but also to make Wallace's death appear to be an accident. No one would have been surprised by someone like Wallace accidentally setting themselves on fire, especially given the depth of his alcoholism.

It struck me that none of this would ever have happened if I hadn't stumbled across that coin in Wallace's drawer. Casey, of course, had understood the significance of that broken piece of metal just as well as I now did, given all that I had learned about him from my predecessor's carefully concealed evidence. Everything since then had been like a line of dominoes toppling over. A series of unavoidable events, ultimately forcing Casey to make what struck me as a sudden, desperate gambit – before we had a chance to confront Wallace and wrest the truth from him.

'I hate to say it,' said Rozalia, a brittle edge to her voice, 'even though I'm going to choke the life out of the murderous son of a bitch the moment I find him, there's a part of me wonders if what Casey's planning for the Authority is such a bad idea.'

At first I thought I had misheard her. 'What are you talking about?'

She turned to face me. 'Don't pretend you don't know. Wallace told your predecessor that Casey's going to try and find some way to destroy the Authority. I hate to be the one to say it, but if he can do that, it'd solve a hell of a lot of problems for the rest of us.'

I stared at her in disbelief. 'You want to just stand by and let Casey commit *genocide*?'

'No, I'm not saying that,' she said, her voice taking on a defensive edge. 'I'm just saying that *if* it came to that, we'd still be safe here on the island, with full access to the transfer stages. And I'm willing to bet that, if push came to shove, Major Howes and his soldiers would side with us against any Patriots still here on this alternate with us. We'd be able to take our time finding somewhere safe to go, without worrying about the Authority trying to stop us.'

A part of me that I didn't like saw the appeal in what she was saying, and yet the flaws were immediately evident. 'Do you seriously think either Howes or his men would be grateful to us for standing by while Casey murdered their entire world and everyone they had ever known?'

Rozalia clenched her jaw. 'I didn't say we'd stand by and let him do it.'

'No,' I said. 'But maybe you'd prefer not to try *too* hard?'

Rozalia's nostrils flared in anger, and she looked away. I didn't have to be a genius to work out she was still hurting badly over Nadia, and to see how much it was affecting her thinking.

'Look,' I said, 'we don't know if Casey can pull something like this off – even assuming he's really planning to do any such thing. We can't be sure Wallace wasn't lying to my predecessor.'

'And if he *can* pull it off?' asked Chloe, looking between us.

'Well, then we'd better find him first.'

Chloe's eyes grew suddenly wide. 'The stage,' she hissed excitedly at the both of us. 'I think I know where it might be!'

'You do?'

She grabbed hold of both Rozalia and me, pulling us close. 'Don't you remember when we passed the beached trawler on the coast road, on the way back into town this morning?'

'Sure.' I nodded. I remembered the rusting trawler, stranded on the beach and tipped over on its side.

'I thought I saw something,' she said. 'I was so tired I thought I was just imagining it. But I swear I saw something moving down there, inside the hull.'

'Inside it? Can you even get inside there?' I asked.

'You can walk right in,' she said. 'The hull broke in half when it was beached. You could easily hide a small portable stage in there if you wanted.'

'You know,' Rozalia said slowly, 'it's not as if there are a lot of places to hide something like that on an island this size, and that trawler's about as far away from town as you can get, while still being within reach.'

'Look,' I said, nodding towards the Patriot agents.

Rozalia and Chloe turned in time to see the three men get back in their jeep and drive away. The soldiers, meanwhile, continued to search the burned ruins. I wondered if Howes was still in charge of them, or if they were now entirely under Greenbrooke's command.

'We need to talk to Wallace,' I said, 'and find out what we can from him, if he's lucid enough.' *Assuming he's even still alive – and assuming we can get past any guards.*

'In that case,' said Rozalia, 'I think you should speak to him, Jerry. I'll go check out the trawler.'

I shook my head. 'Not on your own,' I said. 'It's too much of a risk. I'll come with you.'

She put her hand on my wrist. 'I appreciate that, but this is personal, Jerry. And . . . don't take it the wrong way, but you haven't been at this job long enough. You're good, but you're still new, and I can track him a lot better if I go on my own.'

'She's right,' said Chloe. 'You and me can go and talk to Wallace, if it's at all possible. Rozalia can handle things on her own just fine.'

I looked back at Rozalia. 'If Casey's there . . .'

'Well, even if he is, he won't know *I'm* there.' Rozalia's mouth spread wide in a rictus-like grin that sent shivers through me. 'Not until he feels my knife against his throat, anyway.' She nodded towards our jeep. 'Mind if I take that? It's a lot farther to the trawler than it is to the hospital.'

'Sure,' I said, and Rozalia moved towards the jeep. Chloe reached out a hand and stopped her.

'I need more of those pills,' she said. 'I can't afford to feel tired. Not while all this is happening.'

Rozalia hesitated a moment, then took the plastic tin out of the pocket where she'd stashed it and dropped it in Chloe's hand. 'Don't overdo it,' she warned.

I watched her drive off, and felt Chloe's hand slip into mine.

'C'mon,' she said. 'Let's go and see Wallace.'

TWENTY

The stink of ashes followed us all the way across town. Not far from the Hotel du Mauna Loa stood Government House – a grand name for a small, nondescript office building that had been the island's former seat of government. Bramnik and Mayer used it as a base, and it was also the location of the commissary, where the Pathfinders got their regular rations of basic household supplies. As at the base compound, a line of jeeps were kept outside, fuelled and ready for the taking.

Every now and then, as we walked, another jeep packed with Patriots would go racing past us, and at one point we observed a couple of agents using a handheld battering ram to smash down the front door of a house. I wondered if they'd do the same to my place, and felt queasy at the thought of them picking through my stuff.

When we got to Government House, I was less than surprised to discover that everything on four wheels had already been appropriated. I was beginning to think we were going to have to walk the whole way to the medical facility.

'Over there,' said Chloe, pointing towards a pair of ramshackle bicycles with half-rusted chains leaning against a wall. I laughed at the sight of them, remembering when I had pedalled through the night with Rozalia not so very long ago.

'Better than nothing,' I said, starting forward.

We cycled the rest of the way to the base compound, the bicycles rattling and squeaking so loudly I fully expected one or both of them to crumble beneath us. My satchel, weighed down by the oilskin-wrapped package within, banged against my knees the whole way.

I had been half-afraid we might find Major Howes' troops gone once we reached the compound, replaced by whey-faced Patriot agents in dark suits. I was relieved to see instead a single ordinary trooper standing guard at the compound entrance, and he waved us through without question. We left our bikes leaning against the wall of the barracks before making for the hospital building.

Inside, we found two nurses and a single doctor I vaguely recognized from my brief incarceration there. Once we explained we wanted to visit Wallace, they looked less than delighted. The doctor, in particular, looked as if he wanted to spit.

'I don't know what your friend did to piss off those agents so badly,' said a nurse, her voice full of outrage, 'but that's no way to treat a man in that state, whatever they think he's done.'

I looked at Chloe, then back at the nurse. 'What did they do to him?'

The doctor replied instead, his mouth set in a thin, angry line. 'All you need to know is, right after they went in to talk to him, he started screaming. What do you want with him, exactly?'

They were being far more voluble than Authority civilian staff usually were in the presence of Pathfinders. Whatever Greenbrooke's men had done to Wallace must have been pretty bad, to make them open up like this.

'We just want to talk to him,' said Chloe quickly. 'That's all, I swear. He's our . . . friend.'

'You could try,' said the doctor. 'But he's under guard now. I doubt they'd let you.'

'Let us at least try,' I said.

The doctor shrugged to say he had no objection. 'To be honest, I'm not sure how lucid he'll be,' he warned us, as we headed for the stairwell leading up to the wards on the upper floor. 'He's been slipping in and out of consciousness.'

*

There was just a single guard outside the hospital's second-floor ward. I pulled my head back around the corner before he saw me and leaned towards Chloe. 'Any ideas?' I whispered.

She looked around. So did I. Between the stairwell doors and the corridor leading to the ward was a small nook containing a desk, a chair and an ageing computer. There were also a set of steel lockers beside the desk, their doors unlocked and open.

I had an idea and stepped quietly over to the lockers, looking through them until I found a couple of white coats hanging on hooks.

'Could it get any better?' I whispered to Chloe, pulling one of them on before handing another to her.

I gently placed the satchel on the chair behind the desk, then tip-toed over to the stairwell doors, pulling them open and letting them bang shut again. Then we walked past the desk and around the corner, and I snatched up a clipboard lying there, tucking it under one arm. I was hoping the Patriot agent left to guard Wallace wouldn't know who we really were.

'I need to check the patient,' I said, indicating the ward entrance with the clipboard. 'The saline solution needs swapping out.'

Until we appeared, the guard had been sitting slumped in his chair, staring at the floor and obviously bored out of his mind. 'What happened to the other doctor?' he asked, regarding us with mild suspicion. 'Wasn't there some other guy on duty?'

'He got called away,' I said. 'One of your men got himself hurt back in town. Something to do with that fire earlier?' I gestured impatiently at the door. 'If you don't mind? I'm sure you'd prefer Mr Deans didn't die while you were supposed to be keeping an eye on him.'

The guard sat up a little. 'Yeah, sure,' he said, waving us past. 'Go ahead.'

'I can't believe that worked,' Chloe whispered as the ward doors banged shut behind us. She was about to say something else when she saw just how bad a state Wallace was in.

He was, as I had expected, the ward's sole occupant. Neither myself nor Chloe, I think, really understood the measure of Selwyn's warning about what we would find until the moment we finally set eyes on him. A morphine drip fed into one of his arms, while an intravenous tube ran from his nose and into a wheeled ventilator that looked like an antique from a medical museum. His breath was torn and ragged and horribly laboured, and those parts of his flesh that weren't wrapped in thick layers of gauze had the appearance of charred wood.

It was a dreadful, nauseating sight, and like Selwyn I found it difficult to imagine how much pain Wallace must be in, even with the morphine. It took an effort of will to take hold of a plastic chair and pull it up next to where he lay. Chloe hung back slightly, her face chalk-white with horror.

At first I thought Wallace was unconscious. His eyes were half-lidded, and the only sign of life lay in the steady rise and fall of his chest. But as I took my seat, the chair's plastic legs scraped against the linoleum, his eyes flickered open, and he swallowed with what I suspected was considerable effort.

'Hurts,' he said.

I tried to find adequate words, but couldn't. 'I'm sorry.'

'S'okay.' He coughed and grimaced. 'Thanks. For coming.'

I reached out to put a hand on his arm, then thought better of it. 'Is there anything I can do?'

He swallowed again. 'No.'

'Wallace,' said Chloe, 'did Casey do this to you?'

Wallace gave the tiniest, almost imperceptible nod. 'He was angry. After you left.' He swallowed again.

'If this is too hard for you . . .'

'No.' It was clear that talking took a considerable effort, and he paused often, but he appeared determined to speak. 'Casey made me use the . . . the remote robot. To push Jerry. Found the coin next to his body.' He licked his lips. 'It must have fallen . . . fallen out of his pocket. Used the robot to pick it up and bring it back. Couldn't tell you why.'

I remembered that Chloe had told me how the other Jerry kept the half-coin in his pocket instead of round his neck. I felt something icy take a hold of me, as I realized Wallace was describing how he had murdered my predecessor.

'Just to be clear,' I said. 'You took control of one of the robots and you sent it towards him when he wasn't looking, then used it to push him to his death.'

Chloe suddenly moved from my side. I heard the sound of her shoes scraping on the linoleum as she hurried back out of the ward, the door banging loudly as she slammed through it. I kept my eyes on Wallace the whole time.

'Casey's idea,' he mumbled.

But you still delivered the death-blow, I thought. 'Is it true that Casey was working for the Patriots the whole time?'

Wallace nodded. 'Threatened to. Hand me over. To them. When I said. Didn't want to. Hurt anyone.' He swallowed again and made a gulping noise, and I realized he was crying.

'You told the other Jerry that Casey wanted revenge against the Authority for some reason.' I took care not to rush my words; Wallace's eyelids were fluttering as if he was slipping in and out of consciousness.

'Hacked. Into networks. Found out truth. About retirement.'

'You mean our retiring to safe alternates?' I asked, leaning forward.

He nodded. 'Lies,' he said. 'Can't send us home. They don't know how to.' He coughed. 'The whole time. Bramnik. Mayer. All of them lying.'

I stayed for a while longer to try and get as much as I could out of Wallace until he finally slipped into what might have been deep sleep, or might equally have been a coma. I stared down at his prone form for some time, mulling over everything he had told me, before I finally went to find Chloe. I only stopped when the guard came in, his face twisted into a suspicious scowl, and asked me what the hell was taking so long.

I didn't argue. I walked past him, pausing only once I was out of the guard's sight to take off the white coat and dump both it and the clipboard under the desk and out of sight. I retrieved my satchel and made my way downstairs, where I discovered from one of the nurses that Chloe was waiting for me outside.

I stepped into the warm evening air and looked around until I saw her sitting against the wall, arms folded around her knees in a way that made her look much younger than she really was. Her right foot twitched rapidly from the effect of all the amphetamines she'd been taking.

'Know what the doctor told me?' she asked when she saw me. 'Those bastards turned off Wallace's morphine drip to get him to talk. He said he was surprised we didn't hear the screaming the whole way across the island.'

'We've still got an hour or so before we meet the others at the Mauna Loa,' I said. 'I'd prefer to walk back, if you don't mind.'

She stood and followed me towards the compound gates, and on towards town. 'So?' she asked. 'What else did Wallace say?'

My head was still spinning with the revelation about retirement. 'I'll tell you,' I said, 'but you're not going to like it. Not one little bit.'

She listened as I talked, and soon fell into a deep silence. A number of jeeps roared past us, headed back to the base and packed full of more Patriot agents than I'd ever seen at once. Choking dust rose in their wake, and I felt a terrible sense of foreboding.

When we finally walked into the Hotel du Mauna Loa, we found Yuichi attending to his still, while Randall, Oskar, Winifred and Selwyn sat together around a table near the movie projector. For once, there wasn't a film showing, nor were either of the Nuyakpuk cousins there. Chloe made her way over to the bar and sat near Yuichi, her expression bleak.

There was, I noticed, still no sign of Haden. But that didn't worry me as much as the fact that neither was there any sign of Rozalia. It had been a couple of hours since she had set out to investigate the wrecked trawler, and I felt sure she should have been back long before now.

'So?' demanded Oskar, leaning back in his seat and peering over at me. 'The island's going to hell, and you've got the inside scoop, or so I hear.'

I looked around the room. 'I guess you've all heard about Kip Mayer,' I said. Heads nodded. 'I think the fact they've arrested him is a pretty strong indication that the Patriots are trying to take over the running of operations on the island.'

Randall, sitting beside Selwyn, shook his head and chuckled. 'You think we couldn't figure *that* out? Sounds like you don't have any more idea what's going on than any of the rest of us.'

I glared at him. 'I know more than you think.'

'I saw the three of you pull up outside Wallace's this morning,' said Yuichi. 'You and Chloe and Roz. We all did. Selwyn and Randall tried to find you after Wallace's house burned down and none of you was home. So where were you all night?'

I dropped my satchel on a table and lifted out the oilskin-wrapped package. 'Looking for this,' I replied, unfolding the package and lifting out the bundled pages within.

I held the sheaf of paper up so they could all see it. 'This was written by the man I replaced,' I told them. 'The first Jerry Beche.' I saw the uncertain looks on their faces. 'He hid it well, for reasons I'll explain.'

I stepped over to Yuichi and dropped the untidy pile of paper on his lap. He stared down at it all with a puzzled expression.

'Read it,' I said, then turned to the others. 'You all should. It'll tell you exactly what's been going on around here right under your noses, since before I was even retrieved.'

'What does it say?' asked Winifred, peering anxiously towards Yuichi, who was flicking curiously through the pages.

'Mort Bramnik got my predecessor to carry out a secret investigation, on his behalf, into the incident that nearly got him and a lot of other people, including some of you, killed by Howlers. Bramnik had reason to suspect someone had deliberately sabotaged the mission.'

I paused for a moment, letting all of this sink in. 'What he found is that Casey's been leading a double life. He's been carrying out acts of sabotage, on behalf of Langward Greenbrooke, and all in order to discredit Bramnik. In return, Greenbrooke was offering him early retirement with some hefty benefits.'

'But what's the point of all this?' asked Selwyn, looking both shocked and befuddled.

'If the Patriots could make Bramnik's administration look incompetent enough, they'd have an excuse to put Greenbrooke or someone like him in charge of everything we do,' I explained. 'According to what my predecessor wrote, the Patriots even gave Casey his own portable transfer stage, so he could carry out his acts of petty sabotage at will, and without interference.'

'This is *insane*,' Oskar practically bellowed. 'You can't expect us all to believe Casey would ever—'

I raised a hand to stop him. 'Just hear me out, okay? Casey was playing his own game, counter to the Patriots, the whole time. He recruited Wallace, who wanted revenge against the Patriots, and they concocted that whole incident with the Howlers just so they could get their hands on a complete set of transfer coordinates. Including the ones for our retirement alternates. Greenbrooke had no idea what Casey was really up to, with all the resources he'd been given.'

'And all this that you're telling us,' asked Selwyn, 'is in those pages?' He nodded towards Yuichi, who was now deeply engrossed in my predecessor's account.

'Most, but not all. I just got back from the base hospital where Chloe and I managed to talk to Wallace. He was just about lucid enough to fill in a lot of the missing details. *Including* the fact that the fire this morning wasn't an accident either. It looks like Casey tried to get rid of Wallace because he was becoming a liability.'

'You can't expect us to take your word for all this!' Randall shouted.

'I already explained you don't need to take my word for it.' I went over and picked up some of the pages Yuichi had finished reading and handed them to Randall. 'Read it. That's all I'm asking. The first Jerry realized that the Patriots were keeping close tabs on him after he'd confronted both Wallace and Casey. He was afraid that if he told any of you about any of this, they'd torture Chloe like they did Wallace, or worse. He waited for Bramnik to come back from the Authority so he could tell him what he found, except Jerry died before he ever got the chance.'

'Are you suggesting,' asked Selwyn, his expression increasingly troubled, 'he was *murdered*?'

'Not only murdered,' I said, 'but Wallace confessed his involvement to me just this morning.' I gave him a quick summary of what Wallace had described.

'Suddenly I don't feel so bad for Wallace any more,' Yuichi mumbled quietly.

'And he was happy just to tell you all of this?' asked Oskar.

'I think he's been labouring under enormous guilt,' I said. 'Not to mention he was out of his mind from pain and morphine. I think he wanted to confess – before, well, before it was too late for him.' I looked around them all. 'Casey pressured him into doing things he might never have done otherwise, and I'm certain that's the real reason he drank as heavily as he did. What the Patriots did to him is only a small part of it.'

'What about Nadia?' asked Selwyn. 'Jesus Christ, they didn't have something to do with that as well, did they?'

'As a matter of fact, they did.' I looked at Oskar. 'Rozalia believed that someone deliberately smeared some kind of gunk on our transport to make any bee-brains we encountered think we were from a rival Hive, so they'd attack us. Well, I just learned from Wallace that Casey did exactly that, sabotaging the SUV while Wallace himself made sure our communications and drones failed just when we needed them. They worked hard to make the whole thing look like an accident. It wasn't a jinx, Oskar – it was deliberate.'

'So where's Casey now?' asked Winifred.

'I don't know. Last night, before we found all this out, me and Rozalia helped Wallace home after we found him rolling drunk. Casey came along uninvited. He hung around after we left, and nobody's seen him since.'

'Look,' said Selwyn, leaning forward, his expression intent. 'I'm not calling you a liar, but you're going to need some pretty fucking incontrovertible proof that Casey really had a hand in all of this, regardless of what your predecessor claimed.'

'Hey,' said Yuichi, shaking the pages in his hand. 'I'd call *this* pretty fucking incontrovertible.'

I reached into a pocket and took out the half-coin I had discovered in Wallace's bedside drawer, holding it up as I explained its significance, and how I had come to find it where I had. I watched their expressions grow dark as I detailed the sequence of events that had led us to explore the island's northernmost tip, and what we had found there.

'Chloe can corroborate most of this,' I said, returning the coin to my pocket. 'Rozalia can vouch for the rest.'

'Bullshit!' shouted Randall, standing up and looking about ready to launch himself at me. 'You're making all of this up. You're . . .'

'Shut *up*!' Chloe screamed.

I turned to look at her. She had stood back up from her stool after sitting quietly all this time, a wild look in her eyes. 'You haven't even told them the really important thing,' she spat, then pushed in front of me until she was facing the others. '*There is no retirement*,' she yelled. 'Wallace hacked into the Authority's computers and found out the truth. There's no going home, or some place better. They were lying to us all these years, and now Casey's going to take his revenge on the Authority for that lie by doing his damnedest to kill their whole damn world.'

Randall's mouth opened and closed a number of times before he finally sat back down, looking shell-shocked. The rest stared at Chloe with open mouths. I noted with interest that Winifred Quaker, by contrast, was as poker-faced and calm as ever.

'So, fine,' said Selwyn, looking harried. 'So Casey wants to screw the Authority for screwing with us. Why not just let him?'

'You mean apart from the fact it'd be genocide?' I said. 'We depend on the Authority for *everything*. Medical supplies, food, drink . . . all of that, in case you hadn't noticed, comes from that commissary around the corner. And that only gets restocked from the Authority's own home alternate. So, unless you fancy trying to farm this damn island, or subsisting entirely on Yuichi's home-brew, I'd suggest we're pretty seriously fucking reliant on them for just about everything. *Especially* now we know there's no such thing as retirement.'

'Chloe,' said Yuichi, 'you said Casey wanted "revenge". How's he going to go about getting it, exactly?'

'We think he's searching for something he can carry over to the Authority that'll wipe them out,' I said. 'Some super-weapon from one of the explored alternates, maybe.'

'Wait a second,' said Selwyn. 'Why would the Authority lie to us in the first place? They built the transfer stages. If they can find the alternates where all of us come from, why not ones we can retire to? What's stopping them, exactly?'

'Because they *didn't* build them,' I explained. 'They didn't even invent them. They just found them.'

'No,' said Randall, shaking his head. 'No, no, no.'

Wallace had told me all of it in his halting, careful words before the guard had interrupted us. 'They just stumbled across an abandoned stage in a jungle on their own alternate. They don't even really understand how the damn things work, which is why they can't program them with their own destinations. As a matter of fact, every coordinate they have, including the ones they used to find and retrieve us, they found right here, on this island, when that first stage led them here.'

I looked around them all before continuing. 'I took a trip with Nadia to an alternate Iceland with no sun, and she told me that the Authority wanted to find research connected to a prototype transfer stage someone there had tried to build. I asked her, at the time, what possible reason the Authority could have for wanting to find that research, when they already had transfer stages. Well, now we know. They wanted it because they were hoping it could tell them how their *own* stages worked.'

'Then . . . where did the transfer stages come from, if not the Authority?' asked Oskar. 'And how did Wallace find all this out?'

'Wallace and Casey set up that Howler so they could engineer the theft of a briefcase containing access keys to a bunch of encrypted files on the Authority's hard drives. Wallace subsequently learned that when the Authority first came here, they found the main transfer stages just as they are, along with a bunch of computers and stuff apparently deliberately smashed to pieces. I can't tell you why whoever built the stages smashed their own stuff – maybe they were afraid of something, or maybe it was something else, something we can't even imagine. The evidence points to them at least being human. But the one thing I *can* tell you for definite is that every transfer coordinate the Authority possess came from a single computer that wasn't smashed thoroughly enough.'

'I helped pull Wallace out of that fire,' said Selwyn. 'Isn't it at least possible all this is some wild confabulation on his part? I mean, doesn't it seem likely he hallucinated at least some of this because he was in so much pain and—'

'Oh, for God's sake,' Winifred snapped at him. 'It's all true, every last word. I can tell you that for a fact.'

It was my turn to stare open-mouthed as Winifred looked around at us with something approaching pity.

'How . . . ?' I asked.

'Me and Wallace had a thing going,' she said. 'For a little while, anyway.'

I tried to picture Wallace and Winifred in some kind of a romantic relationship, but it was like trying to fit together two pieces from different puzzles. Wallace was smart, and a motormouth, while Winifred by contrast was buttoned-up, her face seemingly permanently set in a disapproving scowl. I could think of no more unlikely couple.

'Well,' Chloe muttered. 'You sure as hell kept *that* under your hats.'

'I ended it because of his drinking,' Winifred explained, 'although we remained on good terms. I always thought his alcoholism was because of his ordeal with the Patriots too, but then he told me something that made me think otherwise.'

I dropped into a seat and listened as she continued. 'I knew he still liked me even after that,' she said. 'He'd drop little hints from time to time that he knew something I didn't, but I never paid attention to any of it. Then I found him in here, drinking alone, as he was starting to do more and more. He started telling me this long, rambling story about how he'd discovered everything we'd been told about retirement wasn't true.'

Randall stared at her, his eyes practically bugging out of his head. 'Why didn't you *tell* us!'

'Why? Don't you think the life we have here is infinitely better than what we had before our retrieval?' She looked around, her arms folded like a teacher confronting an unruly classroom. 'You're all so focused on going home. Well, I've got news for you: even if you could, you probably wouldn't like it as much as you think you would. You've all changed too much to ever go back.'

Her words made me think of another conversation I'd had, when I'd wondered if it was still possible to find some other version of Alice, somewhere out there in the multiverse. Randall, however, was having none of it. 'Oh come on!' he exclaimed. 'That's ridiculous!'

'Is it?' She turned to him. 'Think of all those stories of traumatized soldiers coming back home after years away fighting in far-off lands, trying to fit into their old lives and surrounded by people with no idea of what they've been through. People like that always either wound up dead, in jail or re-enlisting.' She arched an eyebrow, fixing Randall firmly with her gaze. 'Every one of us lived through the end of a world, and that puts us in the same boat. Whoever you were before that is gone. Trying to slip back into your old lives would be like trying to wear a dead man's shoes. Sooner or later, you'd go crazy or run away or worse. Whether you like it or not, Randall, we just don't belong in such places any more.'

Altogether, this was by far the longest speech I had ever heard Winifred utter. 'So where *do* we belong?' I asked, curious for her answer.

'Why, right here, of course.' She looked around again, and seemed to relent a little. 'Look, I knew how upset you'd all get if I'd told you any of this, plus I thought it unlikely you'd ever believe me anyway, so I chose *not* to. We've already got better lives than we could possibly hope for just by being here. Telling you what Wallace told me would have been . . . cruel, I think. And unnecessary, to boot.'

'Would you go home, if you could?' I asked her.

'I thought you understood,' she said, looking puzzled. 'I already am.'

Just then, I heard a sound like a cough, coming from somewhere far off. The sound repeated at regular intervals for some seconds, then cut off as abruptly as it had begun.

Yuichi turned to stare towards the entrance. 'Who the hell's shooting out there?'

Oskar went the other way, through the sliding glass doors next to the pool. From its far side, he had a clear line of sight along the side of the building, past the low fence that shielded the pool from prying eyes.

I heard what sounded like another rattle of gunfire, and then the sound of a car, accelerating into the distance.

'Maybe it's Casey,' said Chloe, alarmed. 'Maybe the Patriots finally caught up with him.'

'If they have,' Yuichi muttered, 'that's one whole lot of shooting to catch just one man.'

'Wait,' said Randall. 'I thought he was *working* for the Patriots.'

'Weren't you listening?' Yuichi hissed. 'He double-crossed them!'

'One of us should go and take a closer look,' Oskar called back in to us. 'See what's going on.'

'Maybe,' Randall shouted back, 'we should stay the hell right where we are until the shooting *stops*.'

'Hear, hear,' cried Selwyn. 'We're safe in here, whatever the hell's going on out there.'

I had my doubts about that, but said nothing.

'Rozalia's out there somewhere,' Chloe said to me. 'She was supposed to be back by now.'

'And Haden,' said Selwyn, overhearing her. 'Where did Rozalia go, exactly?'

'To look for the portable transfer stage the Patriots gave to Casey,' I replied. 'That's why the Patriots are tearing the whole town apart. They're desperate to find it. They interrogated Wallace before we got a chance to talk to him and, given the state he was in, I think he must have told them pretty much everything – including Casey's plans for revenge against the Authority.'

'But if the Patriots find that stage first,' said Randall, 'and catch Casey, we won't have to do a damn thing!'

Yuichi regarded him with amusement. 'Jesus, dude. Sometimes I seriously wonder about you, you know? You think those morons are going to be able to track a guy like Casey, when they've barely got any mission experience of their own?' He pointed a thumb at me and Chloe. 'It's like they said. Our best hope for survival is finding him ourselves, because the Patriots sure as hell never will. We need to find Casey's stage first.'

I felt full of nervous energy. 'We need weapons,' I said. 'Not just for going after Casey; but in case whoever's out there decides to start shooting at us next.'

Selwyn shook his head. 'You'd need access to the base armoury, and it's not like Major Howes is going to just hand us the keys.'

'Hey!' Oskar shouted from where he still stood by the pool. 'Speak of the fucking devil!'

I went out to where Oskar was standing and saw Howes himself coming towards us, one arm flung around Rozalia's shoulder. His uniform was dark with blood as he limped along beside her, a pistol hanging from one hand.

'Christ in hell,' yelled Randall, leaping up as we helped them inside. 'What in God's name is going *on* around here?'

Oskar had taken Howes' other side, and together he and Rozalia lowered the Major into a chair.

'It's not as bad as it looks,' Rozalia gasped, straightening up again. There were scratches and bruises on her face. 'Although it could be that he's lost some blood.'

Howes' hands trembled as he tried to shift into a more comfortable position. 'Any alcohol around here?' he asked.

'If you're thinking about cleaning that wound,' said Oskar, 'I don't think we've got anything pure enough for—'

'To *drink*, goddammit.'

Yuichi came forward and handed him a bottle of his home-brew. Howes swallowed some of it, then grimaced. I heard him say something under his breath that sounded like a curse. 'It's a miracle you don't all go blind from drinking this stuff,' he wheezed, and Yuichi regarded him darkly.

Rozalia had slumped into another chair. 'What the hell happened to you?' I asked her.

'It was right there, where Chloe thought it was,' she said. She looked as if she'd been pushed to the edge of endurance. 'Casey hid the stage behind some tarpaulins, inside the part of the hull of the trawler where you can walk right in. You'd never see it, not unless you stepped right up to it. He's even got it up on a platform to keep it out of the water when the tide comes in.'

'Was there any sign of him?' asked Oskar. 'Or do you think he's transferred over to some other alternate?'

She shook her head and looked at me. 'I thought about running whatever coordinates he'd last run, and maybe transferring across in case he'd done just that. Unfortunately, I ran into a little trouble before I had a chance.'

'I told you it was a bad idea going there on your own,' I said.

She gave me a dark look. 'I heard noise from up on the coast road while I was poking around,' she continued. 'I stuck my head out and a jeep full of fucking Patriots had pulled up next to my own transport. I didn't want them coming anywhere near the wreck, and they hadn't seen me, so I sneaked back along the shore a ways, then climbed up onto another part of the road just a short distance from them. Then I stuck my head out of some bushes like I'd gone there to take a leak.'

'And then?' I asked.

'Well, it worked, because they didn't go near the wreck, but the cocksuckers went and arrested me instead.' She touched her face.

'They weren't friendly about it either. They drove me back to the base and locked me in a room there, until they could figure out if I'd been up to anything, I guess.'

'This was when?'

'Couple of hours ago.' She nodded towards Howes. 'When everything started to kick off, I had a ringside seat in the window of the room they put me in. The Patriots all turned up en masse and said they were taking charge.'

I looked at Howes.

'I guess it doesn't hurt to tell you,' said the Major, regarding me wearily. 'I refused. They were asking for unrestricted access to the main stage, without authorization or orders, and actually seemed to expect me to keep Kip Mayer locked up when my primary job's to protect him.'

'So Greenbrooke backed down?' asked Oskar.

Howes shook his head. 'Greenbrooke wasn't there. His agents drew their weapons and ordered my men through to the main stage, then locked me in my own office. I'm guessing they sent my men back home so they wouldn't have to worry about dealing with them here.'

I realized all this must have occurred after Chloe and I had left the hospital, when jeeps full of Patriots had driven past us on their way to the compound.

'So how did the two of you get out of there?' asked Yuichi.

'Stupid bastards didn't think I might have a spare key for my office, so, as soon as I was out, I waited until the coast was clear and sprang Miss Ludke,' he said, nodding at Rozalia. 'I needed some backup, and had a feeling that, if they'd locked her up, it might mean she had a better idea what was going on than I did.'

'You couldn't get Mayer out?' I asked.

'No,' he said heavily. 'They took him somewhere else, but I need to go back and get him. I don't even know if he's still on the island. But whatever we do, we have to do it quickly. We just ran into a pair of agents, but we managed to kill them. The others will have heard the shooting.'

'I told the Major everything I knew on the way here,' said Rozalia.

Beside her, Howes made a face as if he wanted to spit. 'Not that I'm having an easy time believing it.'

I gathered up my predecessor's notes and handed them to the Major. 'If you want proof,' I said, 'I've got a fat chunk of it right here.'

Howes regarded the bundle of pages wearily. 'Maybe later. In the meantime, we have a job to do, and that's stopping your friend carrying out this threat of his to commit genocide, assuming it's real. Miss Ludke was very clear about the consequences if we fail.'

'And then what?' said Selwyn, coming to stand directly before the Major. 'Everything goes back to the way it was, with us running around like rats in a cage until we drop dead? Because I just got told there's no retirement plan for any of us, and never has been.'

'And who told you that?' asked Howes, with surprising equanimity.

'What the hell are you talking about?' asked Rozalia. Chloe pulled her to one side and quickly told her what we had learned from Wallace.

'So you admit it's true,' said Randall, coming to stand by Selwyn's side and glaring at the Major.

Howes looked around us all and sighed. 'I guess I do.'

'Then there's one thing that doesn't make sense to me,' Randall continued, nodding over at me. 'How could you retrieve Jerry more than once, if you only ever had the one set of coordinates for his alternate? How come you can find more than one alternate with a version of Jerry on it, but you can't find somewhere that's safe for us to retire?'

Howes shook his head. 'Alternates with minute variations in their histories are bundled together in "braids". The first time you program a coordinate into a rig, it grabs one particular strand – an alternate – out of that braid of highly similar universes. The Mr Beche standing over there we found by picking a different strand from the same braid that the first Mr Beche came from.' He looked around us. 'Each one of you comes from a braid containing a multitude of alternates just like your own, with only very minor variations. To find one where your world *didn't* end, so the theory goes, would require us to find an entirely separate braid, and that's what the scientists can't work out how to do. Now, we can't waste any more—'

'One moment,' said Oskar. 'I get the how. It doesn't tell us *why* you'd lie about retirement.'

I could see Howes' patience was wearing thin, but he clearly understood that we needed answers. 'They were sure they were on the verge of figuring out how to program the stages right at the start,' said Howes. 'I guess they thought wrong, because they're still trying. I'm sorry you were lied to, but I swear it had nothing to do with me.'

'Enough of this,' I said. 'He's right. We need to act *now*.'

'We've got maybe one gun between all of us,' said Yuichi, pointing at Howes' pistol. 'That's hardly enough to do anything.'

'There's an armoury in the basement of Government House,' said Howes. 'It's got an electronic lock. You'll need the entry key, or you won't get inside.' He rattled off a short sequence of numbers. Yuichi went behind the bar and found a pen, quickly writing the key out on the back of his hand.

'That's it, then,' said Yuichi. 'We'll grab some guns and go find Casey, wherever he's headed.'

'Wait a minute,' said Howes, raising a hand. 'Someone's going to have to try and find Kip Mayer and spring him, if he's still here.'

'Why?' I asked.

'Rozalia told me you had proof that the Patriots recruited Casey, right?' I nodded. 'Well,' Howes continued, 'you're going to need Mayer to get that evidence to the right people. And since my own men aren't around, that means you're going to have to take Mayer, as well as that evidence, back to the Authority yourselves.'

TWENTY-ONE

'Where is everybody?' asked Yuichi, looking around the reception area of Government House when we walked in some twenty minutes later.

There was no sign of the half-dozen men and women who normally staffed the building where Bramnik and Mayer usually kept their offices. Doors stood open around us, and I saw signs of disarray that suggested a scuffle. The Patriots had undoubtedly been here.

'I'm guessing they're holed up in their rooms in the Hotel Miranda,' I said. 'Or they were ordered to stay there.' The Miranda had been appropriated by the Authority to house their staff.

'Yeah. I guess.' Yuichi looked around. 'Which way from here?'

'Down there,' said Rozalia, pointing towards a door. 'Howes said the armoury was in the basement.'

We had split into two teams. Four of us – myself, Yuichi, Oskar and Rozalia – were going after Casey. The others – Winifred, Randall, Chloe and Selwyn – were going to return to the base with Howes to try and release Mayer. Then, if all went well, they'd either cross over to the Authority's alternate via the main stage or, if they couldn't get to it, hightail it to the wrecked trawler and make use of Casey's stage.

First, our team was going to grab whatever weapons we could, so we'd at least be able to defend ourselves.

I tried to ignore the churning in my belly every time I thought of Chloe walking into danger. She was smart and capable, and her presence here on the island told me everything I needed to know about just how much shit she could take and still walk out smiling. Even so, I had to work hard not to show my dismay when she decided to take part in Mayer's rescue operation.

'I know what you're thinking,' she had said, leaning in close to me. 'And I know you're not that guy.'

'What guy?' I had asked, the smell of her hair intoxicating me.

'You know,' she said. 'The overprotective guy.'

'I'm not that guy. I *know* you can handle yourself.'

'Yeah. I *hear* that. But that's not what your face is saying.'

Even so, she had leaned up and kissed me, ignoring the snickers and muttered comments before I headed for the armoury with the others.

Yuichi led the way, and we followed him down a narrow staircase to a low-ceilinged basement half-filled with cardboard boxes and discarded computers. Yuichi stepped towards a steel door at the far end, punching the sequence of numbers scrawled on his hand into a number pad mounted on the wall.

I heard a soft beep, followed by a clunk, and the door swung open to reveal a rack of assault rifles and a considerable number of small black snub-nosed pistols.

Yuichi grabbed a rifle, stuffing two of the pistols into the pockets of his trousers, before kneeling to scoop up an armful of boxed ammunition from a tray on the floor.

'Me next,' said Oskar, stepping eagerly forward, while Rozalia and I waited our turn.

We exited Government House as cautiously as we had entered it. The preferred option by far was to avoid any confrontation whatsoever. According to Howes, there were at most a few dozen Patriot agents on the entire island; even so, the chances were high that they'd be better armed than us, and able to call on reinforcements.

The more I thought about it, and about all the things that could or probably would go wrong, the more I didn't want to think about any of it at all. I looked at the grim faces of my compatriots and decided they were all thinking the same thing.

'All right,' said Yuichi, looking around us. 'I guess we're good to go.'

We headed back up to the reception area, and I opened a large canvas gardening sack that Yuichi had dug out of a closet in the Mauna Loa. I waited as everyone put their rifles and ammunition inside the sack, until Oskar came before me, his arms full of deadly weaponry.

'This is fucking *madness*,' he exclaimed. 'If we run into any Pat—'

'If we run into any Patriots,' I interrupted him, 'I'd much prefer to look like a confused and concerned Pathfinder desperately trying to find out what's going on, instead of a heavily armed maniac.' I shook the bag, and the rifles inside clanked against each other. 'These guns are just as a last resort,' I reminded him, 'so hurry the hell up. We don't have all day.'

Oskar shook his head in exasperation, and dropped a rifle and a couple of boxes of ammo into the sack. 'But I can keep this, right?' he asked, opening his jacket to indicate a pistol lodged in his waistband.

'I guess. Just make sure it's well out of sight.' I glanced at the others. 'Same goes for the rest of you.'

We stepped back out onto the street, but there was no sound or sign of movement. I hauled the sack over one shoulder, struggling under the weight, and wondered if maybe Oskar didn't have a point after all. More than likely any Patriot agents who decided to treat us with suspicion would want a look inside the bag.

I felt my stomach sink half a block later at the sound of an approaching engine. I looked sideways at Yuichi, seeing his alarm. Rozalia was walking up ahead of us, and she paused at the corner before looking back and mouthing *Patriots* at us.

Oskar hurried up behind me, grabbing hold of the rear of the sack. Together we carried it over to a dense patch of weeds growing around a tree which provided the perfect concealment.

A jeep drove past, slowing when the two Patriot agents inside it saw us. Both of them were conspicuously armed.

'Hey,' said one of them as he climbed out of the jeep. 'Why are you out during the curfew?'

'What curfew?' asked Rozalia, sounding genuinely puzzled.

'You're supposed to be inside,' said the other agent, stepping out of the jeep to join his buddy.

I stepped forward, putting myself between them and the patch of weeds. 'Nobody's heard anything about a curfew,' I said truthfully. I tried to look scared and confused; it wasn't hard. 'We just went to Government House to try and find out what's going on, but there's nobody there.'

'You need to go home,' said the second Patriot, his rifle held pointing to the ground, but angled so he could bring it back up in a moment. 'And stay there.'

'Absolutely,' said Rozalia, nodding intently. 'We'll do that right away.'

'You can't tell us what's going on?' asked Oskar, with more than a touch of belligerence. 'The way I see it, you people owe us an explanation. Or do you just drive around with those big guns of yours for fun?'

I fought down the urge to turn and scream at him to shut up. If he screwed this up for us, the chances were that people were going to get killed.

The Patriot's expression hardened, and I saw his hands tighten around his rifle. 'Get the hell out of here,' he snarled. 'And if I see any of you out in the streets again, you go in a goddam cell and stay there until someone maybe feels like letting you out. Do you understand me?'

'Absolutely,' I said, smiling and nodding as obsequiously as I could. 'No problem, sir.' I gave him a cheery wave which, in retrospect, might have been overkill.

The two agents glanced at each other and shook their heads, then got back in their jeep and drove off. Once they were out of sight I sat hard on the ground, my legs feeling like jelly.

'We could have taken them on,' Oskar grumbled. 'We had the guns. What the hell were you doing, kowtowing to them like some damn—'

'Shut the fuck up,' Rozalia snapped. 'You nearly got us all killed.'

'I *said* we could have taken them,' said Oskar, visibly bristling. 'There's four of us, we're carrying enough guns and ammunition to—'

Yuichi stepped up to Oskar and punched him hard in the gut. Oskar doubled over immediately, staggering back before he slumped to the ground, struggling to draw breath.

'Don't *ever* do something that fucking stupid again, man,' Yuichi shouted. 'Or you can go the fuck home and sweat it out there while the rest of us get on with this. *Your* choice.'

Oskar glared balefully at him. I sighed and pushed myself upright, then went over to help him back up. However right Yuichi was, the fact remained that we needed all the help we could get.

'We're all under a lot of strain,' I told him, after he let me help him up. 'I understand you're spoiling for a fight. But that's just what we've got to avoid until we find Casey. Okay?'

Oskar scowled at me, and I wondered if I'd made a mistake, and he was in fact an even bigger asshole than I thought.

'Fine,' he said at length, to my considerable relief. He stabbed a finger towards Yuichi. 'But if you ever – *ever* – pull a stunt like that again, I won't need a gun to rip your fucking head from your shoulders.'

Yuichi gave him a look as if to say he was welcome to try. All the laid-back hippie attitude seemed to have faded in an instant, replaced by something much harder.

Rozalia started hauling the sack of rifles back out of the weeds. 'How about you all stop showing each other your dicks and give me a hand,' she suggested, 'before they change their mind and come back to use us for target practice.'

*

Ten minutes later we were back at the Hotel du Mauna Loa. Randall was keeping watch from the main entrance, and he pulled the door all the way open as we came towards him.

Rozalia dropped the sack on the floor and started passing out the rifles and ammunition. I saw that Randall had been busy, cutting away part of Howes' uniform and wrapping his wounded shoulder in gauze sourced from the bar's first-aid kit.

'We all ready to go?' I asked, looking around.

People nodded, and I turned to Howes. 'Are you sure you're up to this? You lost some blood on the way here, and nobody'd blame you for sitting this out.'

'I'll be fine,' he replied.

'What exactly *are* you planning to do when you get there?' Yuichi asked the Major.

Howes' mouth curled up on one side. 'I'm going to surrender.'

I wondered if I had misheard him. 'Excuse me?'

'I'm going to walk up to whoever's in charge of the base, surrender, and tell them any damn pack of lies I can come up with to keep them all occupied long enough for your friends to sneak in and, with luck, spring Kip Mayer.'

I remembered to close my mouth. 'And that's actually going to work?'

'I don't know,' Howes replied. 'But if they're as dumb as I think they are, the Patriots are all going to be too busy following orders – either looking for Vishnevsky, or guarding the transfer stages. I don't think they're expecting anyone to try and rescue Mayer, especially not if they're sure he can't get off the island any other way.'

'Sounds dangerous,' I hazarded.

'Yeah,' he said. 'That's why you've all got guns.'

I nodded, embarrassed.

Howes stood carefully. He was steady on his feet despite his injury. 'Anyone with a desperate need to take a shit, do it now,' he announced. 'Otherwise, I think it's time we got moving.'

TWENTY-TWO

I'd been trying hard to think of some way we could maybe drive up to the shipwreck without running into any more trouble, but I kept coming up blank, particularly since everything with four wheels had been appropriated by the Patriots. That seemed to leave the four of us little choice but to walk the whole damn way across the island and take our chances, regardless of how long it took, or the danger of being spotted by another Patriot patrol. I explained my concerns to Rozalia as we all hustled back out of the Mauna Loa.

'Why don't we just go by boat?' she suggested, once Howes and the others had slipped off in the direction of the compound.

I came to a halt, wondering how I could have been so dumb as not to think of anything so obvious. We were on an island, after all, and our destination was just a few kilometres up the coast. It wasn't even as if I lacked sailing experience of my own.

Yuichi and Oskar became excited at the prospect.

'Sounds great,' I said, 'but where the hell are we going to find a working boat?' All I'd seen were a few dilapidated rowing boats down by the harbour that looked as if they'd disintegrate the moment they hit the water.

'There's an old Chilean Navy Coast Guard station at the harbour's edge,' Rozalia explained. 'There's a search-and-rescue dinghy in there that's easily big enough for all of us, and it's in good condition as well. There's also a slipway leading straight into the water, and nobody'll be able to see us while we're working inside the station.'

'Shit, yes,' said Yuichi. 'You were fixing that boat up with Nadia, said you were going to take some of us out in it some time.'

'Well, it looks like this is the time,' she said.

Rozalia, it turned out, was something of a sailing enthusiast, having grown up on the Florida coast. We kept our eyes open for trouble, but we reached the lifeboat station without incident.

It proved to be a dilapidated wooden structure, with a sloping concrete slipway leading straight into the sea. We followed her inside, where I saw a twelve-foot orange and grey dinghy with an outboard motor and a pennant reading ARMADE DE CHILE. Rozalia regarded it with undisguised pride.

'I hate boats,' Oskar grumbled. 'Unless you're fishing or actually going somewhere, what's the fucking point?'

I watched Rozalia check the outboard motor. 'Aren't we going to attract the wrong kind of attention with all the noise from the engine?'

'I figure the best thing is not to use it at first,' she said, looking back at me. 'We'll start out with the oars, then turn the engine on once we're far enough from the shore that we won't be heard.' She chuckled. 'I'll bet you anything it's never occurred to those assholes to even look out to sea.'

Oskar looked horrified. 'Did you say we were going to *row* there?'

'Part of the way.' Rozalia nodded at two pairs of long wooden oars mounted on racks. 'The water today doesn't look too choppy, so we'll have a relatively easy time of it.' She looked at us. 'So who's going to help me get them down?'

Oskar and Yuichi stepped forward and helped get the oars down. I leaned my rifle against a wall, then made my way down towards the prow, near where the slipway led down to the water's edge. The dinghy looked to have been kept in good condition.

We all followed Rozalia's directions, gathering around either side of the dinghy, before pushing and dragging it down towards the waves. I was panting slightly from the effort by the time it hit the water. Rozalia raced after it down the slipway, then threw herself forward and inside the dinghy, letting out a whoop as she pulled herself the rest of the way in.

The rest of us followed suit, splashing and cursing as we grabbed hold of the lip of the dinghy before it got away from us. I managed to throw myself forward and inside before clambering onto one of its hard wooden benches. Rozalia lifted one of the oars up, expertly sliding it into a rowlock before dipping its blade into the water.

I did the same, along with Yuichi and Oskar but, it must be said, with considerably less grace than Rozalia. Soon, however, all four oars were fitted to their rowlocks, and we sat facing back towards the harbour, the dinghy falling and rising beneath us with the tide. I could see no sign of movement beyond the harbour wall. The farther we got, the less likely we were to be seen.

'All ready?' asked Rozalia, looking around and clearly struggling to hide the fact she was having the time of her life. 'Then let's go.'

I had multiple opportunities over the next half-hour to regret my initial enthusiasm. My back ached, my butt was in agony from sitting on that hard wooden bench, and I had incipient blisters on the palms of my hands. But at least I kept my discomfort to myself, unlike Oskar, who cursed and muttered the whole damn way, until I had serious thoughts of tossing him overboard.

After a while, though, I got into the rhythm of the rowing and the steady beat of the oarblades as they rose and dipped, rose and dipped. Every now and then a particularly large wave lifted us up high, before sending us crashing back down with enough force to give me butterflies in my stomach.

Rozalia, by contrast, was in her element. She was sweating, but looked happy for the first time since Nadia's demise.

'Okay,' Rozalia finally gasped, pulling her oar back in after what felt like a century of rowing. 'Stop.'

Oskar let out a long groan, dragging his oar across his lap before reaching up to wipe the sweat from his neck and face.

'How far out are we?' I asked, staring back towards the harbour. It didn't look like we'd covered that much distance.

'Farther than you think,' she replied. 'Wind's blowing out to sea. The noise from the outboard won't carry back to shore so much.'

She made her way to the rearmost bench to fiddle with the outboard engine until it let out a muted roar, its blades cutting into the ocean waters. We began to pick up speed, cutting with ease through the water. Rozalia peered ahead, one hand on the tiller, slowly swinging the dinghy around until we were sailing parallel to the coast. First we would sail around the northern tip of the island, and then make our way along the east coast.

The sun tracked its way across the sky towards late afternoon. I started to feel tired, the constant rocking motion lulling me. It had been a long, hard couple of days, with barely a moment to rest. Rozalia's hand remained steady on the tiller, her eyes fixed either directly ahead or on the coast.

The harbour passed out of sight once we had rounded the sea cliffs that formed one slope of Rano Kau. I felt myself relax a little; we were out of sight of any unwanted observers.

'If they haven't seen us by now,' Rozalia murmured, as if reading my thoughts, 'they never will.'

'I wonder how the others are doing,' said Yuichi. But no one answered him.

Rano Kau itself soon slipped to rearwards, and sooner than I'd anticipated Rozalia began to guide the dinghy in towards the rocky cove and the wrecked trawler. I saw it from the sea for the first time, its upper deck leaning towards us, streaked and pitted with rust.

Up above on the headland lay the coast road where Rozalia had been arrested. Should another patrol have chosen that moment to drive by, they would have had little difficulty in seeing us. That was unavoidable, and so we had to work fast.

Rozalia cut the engine a few metres from the water's edge, jumping out and into the shallow water, taking hold of a short rope attached to the prow of the dinghy in order to pull it farther up the beach.

'Give me a hand,' she yelled. 'We're going to need to get this thing out of sight.'

Soon we were all splashing about, hauling on the rope until the dinghy slid up and on to the sand. We decided to hide it directly behind the wreck itself, on the seaward site, where it couldn't be seen from land. I kept glancing towards the coast road, expecting to see approaching headlights, but there was nothing.

'Okay,' said Oskar, checking his rifle before snapping it shut and nodding to the rent in the trawler's hull. 'Let's go see what's in there.'

We followed in his wake, our feet leaving shallow impressions in the sand.

The bottom of the hull had been torn nearly in half, and gaped like a set of open jaws. I wondered under what circumstances the ship had gained such a deep and mortal wound, and if it had had anything to do with whatever cataclysm swept away the island's original inhabitants. The tear was easily wide and tall enough to walk right inside, just as Rozalia had said.

I ducked down slightly as I followed Oskar into the dim interior of the beached craft and saw grey tarpaulins hanging from a cord strung from one end of the wreck to the other, like a washing line. Oskar tugged at a tarpaulin, and it fell onto the sand, revealing a tiny transfer stage.

The stage had been crammed into the available space on top of a crude platform, constructed from yet more tarpaulins, stretched across a rough wooden framework about three metres across. Most probably Casey and Wallace had scavenged the wood for the platform from one of the town's many abandoned houses. I pressed my hand against it, and found to my surprise that it was a great deal sturdier than it appeared. I saw one of the rugged laptops normally used to control the portable stages sitting to one side of a field-pillar, connected to it via a cable. Yuichi stepped towards the laptop and tapped at its keyboard; the screen sprang to life in response.

'Well?' I asked. 'Does it show the last programmed coordinates?'

Yuichi looked at me, his expression strained. 'I don't know why, Jerry, but he's gone back to where Nadia got killed.'

I closed my eyes and listened to the sudden, terrified pounding of my heart.

Because the stage by necessity was so small, we had to transfer across to the bee-brain alternate in pairs, rather than all at once.

I went first, along with Yuichi, both of us with our weapons levelled in case we found Casey waiting on the other side. But once the shimmer of transition faded, I saw we were all alone.

In fact, everything looked just the same as it had the last time I had been here with Rozalia, except that it was now just before dawn, if I remembered the time-deviation between this alternate and the island's.

I stepped out of the stage's perimeter and saw a drone drop slowly out of the sky and settle onto its charging station. A light on its undercarriage switched from green to red as its central rotor fell silent.

The air smelled damp, moisture beading the grass. It must have rained sometime in the last couple of hours. The air shimmered around the stage as Rozalia and Oskar next arrived from the island. I continued to keep my rifle at the ready, wary of any surprises. The SUV I had last ridden into the city with Rozalia was still there, along with the EV truck.

'Casey was here no more than a few hours ago,' said Rozalia, stepping away from the transfer stage and towards the SUV. 'Look.'

She pointed at a square of dry grass next to the SUV, barely visible in the dim light of dawn. The jeep had been parked there and had kept the patch of grass dry from the rain. Casey had obviously driven it into the city and not yet returned.

She stepped back, peering into the distance. 'Guess it's not much of a leap to assume he's gone north, into the city.' She looked at me. 'Not really anywhere else he could be going.'

Yuichi headed for the SUV. 'Well, at least we can take this—'

'Hang on,' I said, stopping him with a hand on his shoulder. 'I want to take a look at it first. Rozalia?'

She nodded, and together we crawled in and around the SUV for a solid twenty minutes, while Oskar and Yuichi watched in apparent bafflement. I couldn't find a trace or scent of anything, and neither could Rozalia.

'Mind telling us just what you're looking for?' asked Yuichi after a couple of minutes of this. 'You worried he might have planted a bomb on it or something?'

'Not a bomb,' said Rozalia. 'Worse.'

'Remember what I told you back at the Mauna Loa?' I said. 'Casey smeared stuff onto our SUV so the bee-brains attacked us. '

'Bile, to be precise,' said Rozalia, peering at the back of a wheel and running her fingers along the rim.

Oskar blanched. 'You were serious about that?'

She nodded.

'So, did you find anything?' asked Yuichi, when we finally gave up our search.

'It's clean, as far as I can tell,' said Rozalia.

'Maybe we should take the EV instead,' said Oskar.

'Nope.' Rozalia shook her head. 'We'd need to check it too, and there's a lot more of it to search.'

'How are we even going to find him?' asked Yuichi. 'I don't remember anyone telling me just how we were going to do that.'

I looked over at Rozalia. 'Well,' I said, 'the first time I came here it was because we were looking for labs with samples of whatever genetically engineered bug triggered the extinction event on this alternate. And since, according to Wallace, Casey's looking for some way to wipe out the Authority, he could only be heading for those same labs.'

'Makes sense to me,' said Rozalia, nodding.

'We all got shots to keep us safe while we're here,' said Oskar, 'so there's obviously an antidote already in existence . . .'

Rozalia shook her head. 'Except we only have enough for ourselves, and there'd never be enough time to manufacture and distribute in enough quantity to make any difference to the Authority.'

'Then what's the point of even being here, if it might be too late?' Oskar went on. 'Or is there any way of figuring out if he's already gone and done the deed?'

Yuichi stepped over to the control rig for the transfer stage and tapped at its keyboard. 'Looks like he's been back and forth between here and the island a good few times over the last couple of days. I don't see any other programmed destinations, or any place that might be the Authority.' He glanced over at us. 'If he hasn't been there yet, then my guess is ,whatever he's got planned, he hasn't done it yet.'

'So we go looking for him at Retièn's gene labs,' I said.

Oskar nodded his agreement. 'It's just about the only place Casey could be, assuming there's something there he can use to wipe out the Authority. And Casey has been on missions here more than anyone else, if I think back.'

I looked back across at the ruined, collapsing city and the ramshackle Hives rising above its skyline, and shuddered.

'You know,' said Oskar, rubbing at his chin, 'it just hit me that maybe we don't have to go chasing after Casey at all.'

'How do you mean?' asked Yuichi.

Oskar pointed to the stage. 'That's the only way in and out of this alternate, right? If Casey wants to go anywhere – the Authority, the island or anywhere else – he's going to have to come back here, surely? So maybe all we need to do is sit tight right here and wait for him to show up.'

'He's got a point,' said Yuichi, looking at me and Rozalia. 'We'd have a hell of a welcoming party set up for when he *did* show up.'

'I don't see any problem with that,' said Rozalia, nodding towards the supplies tent. 'We've got food and water to keep us going for a while, not to mention that we're a good safe distance from the Hives.'

'What about the night patrols?' I asked. 'Could they come this way?'

'It's possible, but not very likely this far from either Hive,' she said. 'Besides, we're way out in the open here and we'd see them coming from a long way off. And even if they did, we could transfer back across to the island in a pinch.'

I felt myself begin to relax for the first time in a long while. Maybe things were going to work out okay after all, and Casey had painted himself into a corner, trapped on this world with no way past four heavily armed Pathfinders.

Yuichi shrugged, unslinging his rifle before walking inside the supplies tent. He returned moments later with an armful of cans.

'If anyone fancies cooking some of this up,' he said, 'I'll take first watch.'

'Hey,' said Rozalia, not long after. 'Incoming.'

Yuichi and Oskar had gathered up some loose wood and made a campfire. It was getting gradually lighter as daybreak approached. At that moment, I had been close to dozing off. Yuichi was sitting quietly nearby, looking contemplative, while Oskar stood on the roof of the EV, scanning the horizon with a pair of binoculars.

I sat next to the monitoring screen for the drones, which showed an aerial heat-map of the city and the Hives. If Casey was travelling back towards us from the city, the drone currently in the air would pick him up, and we'd have at least some warning that he was on his way. So far, it had found nothing apart from the seemingly random movements of night patrols. A second drone sat in its charging slot nearby.

I glanced up, following the direction of Rozalia's gaze, to see the dark speck of the second drone dropping towards the charging station.

'Does one of those things stay up all the time?' I asked her.

'Pretty much.'

I turned to look at Yuichi, who had spoken.

'They run on automatic, twenty-four hours a day, long as you keep the station's batteries topped up.'

The drone dropped low enough that I could hear the lawnmower buzz of its rotor. Once it was in place, the other drone, now recharged, would lift up and take over surveillance.

The buzz increased rapidly in pitch, the speck moving faster against the dawn sky. I frowned; it was coming in awfully fast . . .

I rolled to one side, thinking the drone was plummeting straight towards me. Instead of slowing down, it had picked up speed, giving a high-pitched whine as it executed a kamikaze dive into the transfer stage's control rig. The sound of the impact rolled across the grass and the reservoir beyond, echoing faintly.

Oskar scrambled down from the roof of the EV, his mouth open in shock, and dashed over to peer down at what was left of the rig.

'It's smashed to pieces,' he moaned, reaching up to grab at his head. 'Oh, Jesus. *Jesus*. We're fucking *stranded*.'

I stared, dry mouthed, at the smashed pieces of machinery lying scattered all across the clearing.

Oskar walked stiff-legged back over to the EV and vomited noisily next to one of its wheels.

'This can't be happening,' Rozalia mumbled. 'It can't be.'

I looked at Yuichi. 'There must be some way we can get back,' I said.

He stared helplessly at the ruins. 'I don't think so, Jerry,' he said quietly. 'I really don't.'

I went over to kneel by the smashed rig, pushing my hand through the bits and pieces of shredded component. 'Maybe there's still some way we could try to fix it . . .'

'No, Jerry,' Yuichi repeated. '*Look* at it, for fuck's sake. It's completely trashed.'

I tried to make sense of what had just happened, to quell the dreadful awareness that we might very well be lost on this alternate forever.

'Could it have been an accident?' I asked, looking around at him in panic. 'Some failure in the drone's programming, maybe, or . . . ?'

'No,' said Rozalia, her voice taut. 'You saw what happened. It didn't just crash – it *aimed* itself at the control rig.' She turned to look at the second drone, still sitting on its charging mount. 'It's got to be Casey. Somehow he programmed the drone to do that. He knew we'd try to find him. Nothing else makes sense.'

We'd walked into a trap, I thought numbly. Like blind men stumbling into the mouth of a lion.

Oskar staggered back over from the SUV, wiping his mouth before grabbing hold of his rifle from where he had dropped it. He lifted it to his shoulder and fired at the surviving drone, still parked on its charging station. The drone tilted backwards, then slid off its mount before falling to the hard-packed soil. A small trickle of greasy smoke rose from a bullet hole in its ventilator grille.

I heard a click, and Yuichi stepped forward. He had taken the safety off his own rifle and now had it aimed straight at Oskar's belly. There was a look in his eyes I had never seen before.

'You idiot,' Yuichi seethed. 'You stupid, asinine, trigger-happy, moronic fucking *idiot.*'

Oskar stared back at him in fright and confusion.

'Yuichi, don't,' I said.

'I could have reprogrammed that drone from here,' Yuichi continued, ignoring me. 'I could have rebooted it, cleared out its memory, then sent it back up to search that whole damn city for Casey. But no. *You* had to fucking destroy it.'

'Yuichi. Stop. Please.'

It was Rozalia this time. She had lifted her own rifle to her shoulder, and aimed it at Yuichi.

'We can't do this,' she continued, and I could tell she was fighting to keep her voice steady. 'We're all in this together. Trying to kill each other isn't going to help us figure a way out of this mess.'

'For all we know, Casey could have been watching us through the damn thing's cameras the whole damn time we've been here!' Oskar screamed. He threw his rifle to the ground and fell to his knees, and

I saw that he was weeping. 'Don't you understand?' he wailed, tumbling to his knees. 'We're dead. *Dead!*'

'Is it possible?' I asked. 'Could he have been watching us from somewhere else in the city?'

'I don't know,' Rozalia said quietly. 'The drones broadcast their data back to us, so I guess it'd be possible to rig up some kind of portable control unit. Except Casey doesn't have the brains or the know-how to do any such thing.'

'But if anyone could, Wallace could,' said Yuichi.

'What does it matter any more?' Oskar shouted hoarsely. 'There's no point looking for Casey any more, not if we can't get home, not without—'

They all ducked as I fired my rifle into the air. I was wasting a bullet, but I didn't care. I'd had enough. Oskar tripped on something underfoot as he scrambled backwards from me.

'You're not thinking straight,' I shouted. 'None of you is. Why the *hell* would Casey strand himself here along with us? Does that sound to you like something he'd do?'

I brought my rifle back down, pointing it at the ground.

'Jerry,' said Yuichi, 'did you *see* what just happened?'

'I did. But do you really believe Casey doesn't have some other way out of here?'

'What are you talking about?' demanded Rozalia.

'Use your brains,' I said. 'There has to be more than one transfer stage around here. With access to every transfer coordinate the Authority has, who's to say Casey can't scrounge up a second portable transfer stage from somewhere, as a backup in case someone tracked him down the same way we just did? That way, if someone discovered his secret stage back on the island while he was on some alternate, he wouldn't necessarily get trapped there – he'd always have a way out. What makes more sense to you – Casey dooming himself with the rest of us, or him figuring out some way to strand only *us*?'

Oskar gaped open-mouthed at me. Yuichi chuckled and shook his head, then walked away to the edge of the clearing, his back to the rest of us.

'Maybe he made a mistake,' Rozalia said slowly.

'How do you mean?' I asked.

'Maybe,' she said, 'he's overplayed his hand. He didn't need to attack us.'

'God *damn*,' said Yuichi, turning back towards us. 'You're right. If he'd just left us alone – assuming we're not completely insane, and he really *does* have another stage out there somewhere – he could have got on with his job while we just sat here waiting forever for him to turn up.'

I pointed towards the city. 'He's panicking,' I said, suddenly sure beyond a doubt that I was right. 'Otherwise, he'd never have done something this stupid. He's trying to slow us down, and that means we still have a chance of stopping him.'

'Then we need to find that other stage as well,' said Oskar, his voice low and full of venom, 'because if we don't we'll be stuck in this shit-hole alternate for the rest of our very short lives.'

When Rozalia's eyes met mine they were full of bleak anger. 'Agreed,' she said. 'And then we kill the fucking son of a bitch.'

'Yes.' I nodded, and saw the others were doing the same. 'And then we kill him.'

TWENTY-THREE

Yuichi rooted around inside the supply tent until he located the laminated maps of the city, then spread them out for us on the fold-down table. Once again, I found myself studying a map of Sao Paolo, a tangle of blue and rēd lines sketched over it with marker pens indicating the last-known safe routes. My eyes followed the length of the Pinheiros as it cut diagonally north to south through the city. A circle around several city blocks in the north-west indicated the location of Retièn's laboratories.

'Same procedure as before,' said Rozalia. 'We stick to the safe routes as much as possible. It's a long time until nightfall, which is to our advantage since we won't have to deal with any night patrols.'

'It's settled, then,' said Yuichi. 'We head for the labs. The other stage has to be there.'

Oskar peered at him. 'And if it isn't?'

'Then we figure something else out,' Yuichi spat at him from between gritted teeth.

'Hey.' Oskar put his hands up in mock surrender. 'I was just—'

'No, please,' Yuichi barked. 'Feel free to share your brilliant and incisive insights. But in the meantime, how about we just go fucking look and see what we find?'

I looked away so Oskar couldn't see me smirk.

We were soon off, all four of us crammed into the bile-free SUV. I gripped the wheel hard as I guided us once more beneath the ruined bridge, across the shallow waters and back up onto the road on the other side. I soon threw caution to the wind, taking my foot off the accelerator only when I was absolutely forced to.

'Careful,' Yuichi shouted, bracing himself against the ceiling with one hand as we hit a particularly nasty bump. 'I don't think I could deal with the irony if you wind up trashing the car before we get there.'

I didn't reply, my eyes fixed straight ahead as I picked out routes around wrecked cars and rubble. I'd come this way enough times now that I pretty much knew it off by heart.

I slowed only once I reached the elevated motorway over the Pinheiros so I could navigate my way past the blockade of cars. As I eased past the obstruction, I couldn't help but glance towards the high-rise car park, only to find that it was now almost entirely demolished.

I caught a glimpse of a line of bee-brains, straggling along a street far below. What if, I wondered, Nadia hadn't simply drowned as I had assumed? What if the bee-brains had taken her alive? Would they have made her into one of them? I suddenly imagined Nadia among their number, and ground my teeth until my jaws ached. As soon as we were past the blockade, I floored the accelerator again.

'Slow down,' said Rozalia as we came back down from the motorway. 'We don't know if Casey has any other surprises waiting for us.'

'Sure.' Even so, it took an effort of will to make myself ease off on the pedal.

A few minutes later we reached the avenue leading towards Retièn, and by then I had little choice but to slow down anyway. The whole length of the road was just as crowded with ruined vehicles and rubble as I remembered.

'Hey,' Rozalia said suddenly, her voice tense. She was in the rear, leaning over the side of my seat and pointing ahead. 'Did anyone see something?'

'Like what?' I asked, leaning my head back slightly without taking my eyes off the road. 'Bee-brains?'

'I don't know,' she said. I could hear puzzlement in her voice. 'I don't think so. Or at least, it didn't look like it.'

'I didn't see anything,' said Yuichi from beside me.

Rozalia blew air through her nose. 'Well, it was moving too fast to be a bee-brain, anyway.'

'Some kind of animal?' Oskar ventured.

Rozalia laughed hollowly. 'See, I would have agreed with you, except there isn't anything with four legs in a ten-mile radius of any Hive. The bee-brains'd just kill them for food.'

'Aren't they infected by the virus?' I asked.

'Animals?' Rozalia shook her head. 'No, it's human specific, far as we know.'

'Then what did you see?' I asked.

She shook her head irritably. 'I don't know. Besides, it's not like we have any choice except to keep going.'

She was right, of course. My hands grew damp where they grasped the wheel. As I steered, I had been studying not only the way ahead, but also possible avenues of retreat. I could see the part-collapsed building up ahead that had forced Nadia into an unexpected detour, and thereby sealed her fate. I knew I had no choice but to make precisely the same detour, in order to reach our destination, and had to fight down a mounting sense of dread. But when I turned the corner, there were no milling crowds of bee-brains ready to launch themselves at us: only empty, deserted streets and the wreck of the SUV we had been forced to abandon.

Maybe the bee-brains are all late risers, I thought to myself, forcing myself to relax a little to reduce the painful tension in my chest.

And then, incredibly, I heard what sounded like a dog barking.

'Did anybody else hear that?' Rozalia demanded, her hand nearly crushing my shoulder. 'Did you?'

'I think we all heard it,' Yuichi said drily. 'Guess *something's* managed to stay alive around here after all, despite the bee-brains.'

I glanced at Oskar in the rear-view mirror; he had a strange look on his face. Small beads of sweat had formed on his forehead. I kept on going, taking the next left to get us back onto the main avenue, after which we could head straight for Retièn.

'Goddammit,' Oskar croaked from behind me. 'Goddammit, stop the car!'

I glanced at the rear-view mirror again in time to see him clawing for the door handle.

'Fuck, Oskar,' I shouted, 'what are you . . . ?'

'Look,' said Rozalia, pointing ahead.

I looked, but I couldn't believe it. It was Oskar's dog, Lucky, straight up ahead at the next intersection, her belly to the ground and her tail wagging furiously. She leaped up and barked again, then started to bound down the length of the street towards us.

Oskar slammed the door open and jumped out almost before I had pulled to a halt. Rozalia followed him, climbing out of the car and starting towards the dog.

'Well, goddam,' said Yuichi, shaking his head in wonder as he got out as well. 'Looks like his hound didn't drown after all.'

I jumped out. Oskar had stopped in front of the SUV, a look of boundless joy on his face. Lucky came dashing across the intersection and straight towards her owner. The brilliant morning sunlight made it hard to see her clearly at first.

Too late, I saw the thick belt of explosives wrapped around the dog's midriff.

'Oskar!' I screamed. 'Run!'

He turned to look at me, his expression faltering at the sound of my voice.

After that, everything appeared to happen in slow motion, with the grim inevitability of a nightmare playing out to the very end.

I dropped my rifle and ran, just as Lucky came bounding up to Oskar. Something picked me up and carried me through the air before slamming me back down again. My ears filled with a muted roar that seemed to go on forever; intense, painful heat bathed my legs, and I cried out, afraid I was on fire.

I tried to crawl away, gasping and choking on the thick dust that now filled the air, and tried to push myself up on my elbows. My hands were raw and bleeding, and there was a pain deep in my chest that gave me pause.

But I was alive.

I looked around, hearing a sound like rain pattering down. A hand, neatly severed at the wrist and wearing a signet ring I recognized as Oskar's, hit the tarmac close by. Bits of metal and ground concrete fell all around.

I finally staggered back upright once more and gaped at what was left of our SUV. Its windows were shattered, the front crumpled and stained with red gore. There wasn't much left of either Oskar or Lucky that was remotely recognizable.

Lucky. I like to think Oskar might have appreciated the irony.

I limped back towards the SUV and found Rozalia lying face down some metres away, her legs and arms sprawled out around her. She wasn't moving.

'Jerry.'

I looked around and saw Yuichi, who'd dragged himself over to the side of a building, propping himself up against the wall. One of his legs was twisted in a way that was deeply unnatural, the blue denim of his jeans dark with blood.

I hurried over to Rozalia. At first I was terribly afraid she might be dead, but as I kneeled by her she suddenly shifted and coughed, and I felt a wash of desperate relief. I took hold of her shoulders, helping her onto her side just as carefully as I could.

Her eyes flickered open, and she stared up at me. 'Casey,' she whispered.

'It's me, Jerry. Casey's not here. I don't know where he is.'

'Oskar . . . ?'

I shook my head. 'Can you move? Get up?'

She licked her lips. 'Think so. Maybe.'

I got an arm around her shoulder and helped her up, pausing only once when she yelped with pain. She leaned heavily on me as I helped her over towards Yuichi, seating her beside him.

Finally, I collapsed onto the pavement, worn-out and aching.

'You know what this means, right, Jerry?' said Yuichi. 'Neither of us are going anywhere fast. You need to go and find Casey.'

I shook my head. 'I need to get you somewhere safe first.'

Rozalia shook her head. 'Listen to him. Casey must have been watching when he hit the detonator. He could be getting ready to pick us off with a rifle and a sniper sight. There *is* nowhere safe you can take us.'

'I—'

'No, Jerry,' she gritted. 'Get the *fuck* out of sight now, while you can. If there's another stage around here somewhere, find it first and then come back for us.'

I glanced at the windows and rooftops around us. Casey must have been hiding somewhere up high and watching us, I figured. I knew Rozalia was right, but I still felt that I would be committing some terrible betrayal by simply leaving them both here like this, entirely vulnerable should any bee-brains happen upon them.

I pulled myself back up and hunted around until I had gathered all but one of our rifles. Where the last might have gone, I had no idea. Presumably the force of the explosion had flung it somewhere far away, and the air was still too thick with dust for me to be able to see where it might have landed. Of the three left, one was clearly too badly damaged to be operational, so I discarded it. I checked over the two remaining rifles, then pulled one over my shoulder by its strap before handing the other to Rozalia.

'I'll be back,' I said to them both.

Yuichi nodded tightly. 'Good luck, Jerry.'

I ran for cover, trying to ignore the very real possibility that this might be the last time I'd see them alive.

I kept one eye on the surrounding buildings as I hurried along to the next intersection, keeping to the sides of buildings and the shelter of doorways. Some instinct, however, made me sure that Casey wasn't anywhere nearby any more.

I figured that Lucky must have escaped from the river and got lost in Sao Paolo's streets until Casey came across her on one of his secret visits. In the brief moment I'd seen her, she looked to be in good condition, as if someone had been looking after her. I'd have admitted to a certain grudging admiration for Casey's strategy if I wasn't so intent on blowing his fucking head off at the first opportunity.

I reached the corner of the next block and pulled myself into the recessed doorway of a bank, then stuck my head out to take a look around. The front entrance of Retièn was just across the road from where I crouched, a dozen metres away on the far side of an intersection. The building housing the labs was a blocky concrete affair, and its empty shattered windows offered no end of opportunities for Casey to take potshots at me if he was hiding in there somewhere. Nonetheless, I had to find some way inside.

A truck lay on its side across the middle of the intersection, partly blocking my view of the entrance to the labs. It angled across the road towards a children's play park bordered by a waist-high concrete wall. The wall was perhaps six or seven metres in length, and at the far end stood the gutted remains of a taxi. I sketched out a route in my mind, took a deep breath, and made my move.

First I scuttled towards the truck, dropping down behind it and waiting. Nothing happened. I stayed there for another minute, sucking up my courage, before running towards the low wall, pulling myself over it and flattening myself to the ground.

Still no sound or sign of any kind of reaction.

I started to crawl on my hands and knees to where the concrete wall terminated. I peered around the corner towards the taxi, then ran towards it, dropping down to take advantage of what meagre shelter it offered.

Maybe this wouldn't be as hard as I thought. Directly neighbouring the labs was a garage, the skeleton of a car still mounted on a part-raised hydraulic platform. A narrow alleyway between the garage and the labs led to the next block down. Perhaps if I headed down that way, I could enter the labs from the rear and circle around behind Casey . . .

I ran towards the alley, then came to a halt, looking around.

Still nothing. I steadied my breath and began to make my way down to the far end.

I felt something press against my ankle and heard a *click*. I looked down, too late, to see a tripwire had been stretched across the alley.

Then the strangest thing happened: I saw myself die – and also escape death – not just once, but multiple times.

I saw how the detonation neatly separated my legs from my upper torso, like taking a piece of soft toffee and twisting it in half.

I saw the silver wire tense against my ankle, heard the same *click*, the crude, home-made mine somehow failing to detonate.

I saw myself take an entirely different route, never encountering the tripwire.

I saw sunlight glinting from the tripwire, making me hesitate just at the last moment.

I saw all of these, superimposed on each other, somehow happening, yet not happening, all at once.

Then I was somewhere else – somewhere that was neither *here* nor *there*. It was as if I had suddenly found myself in a darkened cinema, the alleyway reduced to a kind of projection, with me standing outside the universe and looking in.

A myriad possible outcomes merged and broke apart, until it became impossible to distinguish one from another.

'Hello, Jerry,' said a voice, and I crashed back into the real world to find Haden Brooks crouched against the wall beside me, his eyes flashing silver in the sun.

TWENTY-FOUR

I looked down again at the tripwire, almost invisible in the sunlight, just inches from my foot. One more step . . .

And yet I could clearly remember walking straight into it. I had heard the *click*, felt the heat and thunder of the detonation as it tore me apart . . .

Or had I? It was getting hard to remember, like trying to hold on to the memory of a dream.

I shuffled slowly back from the tripwire, my nerves singing with imagined pain.

'What the hell did you just do?' I demanded, my fear morphing into fury. 'And where the hell did you . . .'

'I interfered,' he said. 'I wasn't supposed to.'

'You . . . interfered?' I stared down again at the wire, then back up at Haden. 'Nobody could find you,' I said. 'You disappeared. I thought maybe the Patriots locked you in a cell, or you ran away once the fighting started . . .'

He shook his head. 'None of the above.'

'Haden,' I said, 'how can you even *be* here?'

'You still have time,' he said. 'Here.' His hand pressed something into mine. I looked down and saw an envelope crumpled into my palm.

I looked back up at him. 'What the *hell*?'

'You won't see me again,' he said, reaching out to squeeze my shoulder, a warm grin on his face. 'It's been good, Jerry,' he said, taking a step back.

'Haden, wait. I . . .'

I blinked and looked around. My position had changed. I was once again standing with my foot just inches from the tripwire.

I stepped back again, darting my head around wildly. There was no sign of Haden.

It was as if the whole universe had suffered some glitch and reset itself; as if Haden had never really been there.

And yet, when I looked down at my open hand, the envelope was still grasped in it.

I squatted down on my haunches back at the mouth of the alley and pulled the envelope open with trembling hands. Inside I found a single sheet of paper with nine names scrawled in neat, cursive handwriting: Chloe, Randall, Selwyn, Winifred, Yuichi, Rozalia, Oskar, Wallace and, finally, my own. Below each, Haden had written out a series of numbers and letters that were clearly transfer coordinates.

I swallowed, my mouth suddenly desperately dry. My mind kept trying to reject everything that had happened in just the last minute or two. I had a hard time accepting even the reality of the envelope. Somehow I managed to slide the sheet back inside the envelope before pushing it deep into a pocket where I was sure it would not be lost.

I stepped carefully over the tripwire, with no lack of trepidation, and continued on my way down the length of the alley. When I came to the next street, I looked around and saw a rear entrance to the laboratories. I hustled up some steps to the frame of a smashed-in door and stepped through to a foyer, my rifle at the ready.

Now I knew just what to look out for, I had no trouble spotting a second tripwire. I moved with extreme caution, stepping over the wire and continuing deeper into the building.

I found myself surrounded by empty doorways. I swung my rifle from side to side, half expecting Casey to come charging out of one of them with guns blazing. I was met only by silence. I saw the mouth of a corridor, extending deep within the building, most of its length lost in darkness.

I heard a rattling sound from the other side of the foyer and twisted around, bringing my rifle to bear. An empty beer can rolled across the floor before bumping into a wall and coming to a stop.

Too late, I realized my mistake.

I turned. Casey emerged from the shadows, bringing the butt of his rifle crashing down on my head. The foyer tumbled around me, darkness limning the edges of my vision.

'Too fucking easy, mate,' I heard Casey say, before the darkness swallowed me up.

'C'mon. Get up.'

A hand slapped my cheek. Something warm and liquid hit my face and I spluttered, rolling forward and onto my knees, the taste of brackish water on my lips. I blinked my eyes open, my head feeling as if it had been stuffed with old rags, and quickly discovered that my hands were cuffed together in front of me.

I was lying on the floor in a windowless room, most probably a basement. Buckets and mops stood in one corner next to stacks of dusty office supplies. A water bowl sat on the floor, along with a folded blanket on which Lucky must have slept. An unlit furnace stood in another corner, along with a portable battery-powered generator that hummed quietly to itself. A cord emerged from a tangle of wires at the rear of the generator, reaching up to a single caged light bulb suspended from a ceiling hook. Wooden steps led up the side of the far wall to a door, while just beneath the steps stood a portable video camera mounted on a tripod, its lens pointing towards me.

I was far from surprised to see that most of the basement floor was taken up by a circle of field-pillars. The usual laptop sat next to the portable transfer stage, its screensaver morphing into abstract shapes.

But none of this drew my attention as much as the steel cage placed in the precise centre of the stage. The cage was just large enough to contain the crumpled form of a man, curled up in a foetal position and nearly invisible beneath the hordes of bees that otherwise filled the cage. Their angry, muted buzzing seemed to fill the room. It wasn't until I looked closer and saw the glass lining the inside of the cage that I understood why the bees couldn't escape. As for the figure within, it looked as if it might be a member of a night patrol – one of the creatures that had killed Nadia.

Casey appeared from somewhere behind me and stepped towards the cage, a rifle held loosely in one hand. He carefully tapped at the bars of the cage with the rifle's barrel, and the creature within jerked in response. Its head lifted in the exact same manner as a disturbed sleeper.

I just barely caught a glimpse of dead eyes and an open mouth through the maelstrom of swarming insects. Horror gripped me as yet more bees came surging out of the depths of the creature's throat. I turned away from the sight, feeling sick to my stomach.

Casey stepped back over to stand before me. 'You,' he said, 'are a massive fucking pain in the arse.'

'Go to hell,' I managed to rasp.

Casey just chuckled, and raised his free hand. 'How many fingers am I holding up?'

'What?'

'I want to know if you're concussed or not.'

'Why don't you go fuck yourse—'

He stepped forward, kicking me hard enough in the gut to drive the wind out of me. I scrabbled back against the wall as best I could.

'How. Many. Fingers?'

I lifted my cuffed hands with the middle finger of each raised.

Casey laughed. 'Very droll. And your name?'

I opened my mouth to voice another complaint, then realized there was no point. 'Jerry Beche,' I said with a sigh.

'Good.' He turned, making his way over to the video camera beneath the steps. 'There's not much point to the conversation we're going to have if you're not in full possession of your faculties.' I watched as he leaned down to peer through its lens at me, then made some kind of adjustment.

'Casey . . . whatever you're planning, and I have a pretty good idea what it is, you need to stop. Wallace told us everything.'

He looked up at me, and I saw a flash of anger. 'Knew I should have just put a bullet through the silly fucker's head, instead of wasting time with matches.' He leaned back down, peering through the camera once more and made a final adjustment. 'So what exactly did he tell you?'

'That you're going to try and wipe out the Authority because they lied to us about retirement.'

'And you think that's the only reason? You can't think of a whole list of them yourself, even after being among us for as short a time as you have?'

'Casey . . .'

'I hear you, I hear you. What do you think I'm going to do: walk over there, uncuff you and beg your forgiveness? Fuck that.' He stood back, as if satisfied. 'Thing is, Jerry, I'm really not sure why you *want* me to stop.'

'Because you're out of your fucking mind, that's why. You killed Nadia, you killed the other Jerry, and if Wallace isn't dead yet from his injuries, he will be soon enough.'

'Wow.' He put his hands on his hips. 'You really *have* figured it all out, haven't you?'

'There's not much we don't know, Casey. You were working for the Patriots and you betrayed them. Everyone else knows where we are, and whatever happens to me, they're going to come after you even harder.'

He shook his head in apparent disbelief. 'I sincerely doubt that. The crazy thing is, you should be thanking me. You ever think about that? If it wasn't for me, you'd never have been rescued – did that ever cross your mind?' he tapped at his chest. 'If I hadn't been forced to prevent the *first* Jerry from screwing everything up, you – and by *you*, I mean the person sitting right there, in front of me – would still be rotting away on some dead alternate. If it wasn't for me, you'd never have had a chance at a new life with the rest of us.'

I gaped at him. 'So basically,' I said, 'we're supposed to be *grateful* for you murdering anyone who gets in your way?'

'Goddammit, Jerry,' he shouted. 'Don't you understand that the

Authority don't give a shit about any of us? And yet here you are, treating me like *I'm* the bad guy here. What the hell would *you* have done?'

'I don't know,' I admitted, and glanced towards the cage. 'One thing I'm sure of, though, is that if you go ahead with this, you're putting all of our lives in jeopardy, yours included.'

'How the hell do you figure that out?'

'What's left if you wipe out the Authority? Nothing but that island, and nowhere to go from there but a bunch of extinct alternates.'

'But at least we'll be free,' Casey replied with unexpected fervour, 'instead of being worked until we drop, or something kills us on some under-equipped mission. We're little better than slaves, except you're all so fucking grateful for your chains.'

'Why are you filming all this, Casey? So you can justify yourself to the rest of them?'

His expression soured, and I knew I had guessed right. 'Here's another question right back at you. Why is it that the Authority are so hell-bent on getting us to recover the kind of information or weapons that could be used to destroy whole worlds? Like those damn bee-brains. Didn't you ever wonder what possible reason they could have, even to come to this goddam alternate?'

'Fine,' I admitted after a moment. 'I don't know. I wish I did.'

'Yeah. Ever notice there's a *lot* you don't know?' he growled. 'Maybe you should ask *him*,' and he nodded towards the cage.

I frowned, watching as he lifted the camera from its tripod and carried it towards the cage, pressing its lens close up against the bars, aiming it at the figure within, still obscured by the thousands of bees crawling all over it.

'C'mon, Jerry,' Casey chided me. 'Don't you recognize who it is? Get a little closer. Take a look.'

I stared at him, terrified of what he might be planning to do. Moving cautiously, I pushed myself up onto my knees and shuffled a few inches closer to the cage, my bound hands before me.

Casey gave the bars of the cage a good hard kick, and I saw the figure within flinch, then sit up. Its head twisted from side to side, coming closer to the glass, and I finally got a good look at who it was.

Greenbrooke.

'What did you . . . how . . .' I stammered.

'I kidnapped him, I think is the word you're looking for,' said Casey, stepping back over to the tripod and replacing the camera on its mount.

I remembered seeing all those Patriot agents, roaming the island, and how I had assumed they were looking only for Casey's hidden transfer stage. Maybe, I thought, they hadn't just been looking for the stage. Maybe they'd been trying to find Greenbrooke as well.

'Don't feel pity for him,' said Casey. 'He told me what I needed to know, and then I stuck him in there. He'll be a walking plague vector when I send him over to the Authority's alternate, him and those bees.' He cocked his head at me. 'Don't you want to know just what he told me?'

I stared down at my feet, too frightened to meet Casey's eyes.

Casey shrugged when I didn't answer, and continued regardless. 'Turns out there was a nuclear war where the Authority came from,' he said. 'All the way back in their Eighties. Not some two-minute affair, either; seems it dragged on for some decades, long into the Nineties, with the US fighting Soviet detachments all over South America. Seems like democracy took a distinct step back during all this. Want to know why they call themselves "the Authority"? It's short for "Provisional Civil Authority for the Emergency".'

He walked across the basement, staring back in at Greenbrooke for a moment before continuing. 'Over there, the CIA was replaced by the Patriots, the nearest thing their America ever had to the Gestapo. Then all of a sudden,' he said, turning back to look at me and waving one hand as if it were holding a magic wand, 'they stumble across this abandoned transfer stage, somewhere in the Bolivian jungle when they're supposed to be hunting Cuban troops.'

I looked back up at him. 'I know half of this already,' I said. 'Wallace told me, so you can shut the hell up.'

'So did he mention the way the original stage-builders abandoned their bases, destroying all their computers and most of their records before disappearing?' I nodded. 'The only reason I can see why they'd have done any such thing,' he continued, 'is because they were afraid of something – something they encountered while they were exploring all those alternate realities themselves. At first I thought maybe that's why the Authority wanted to find such terrible weapons – because they were afraid they might run into whatever it is that scared the stage-builders so bad.' He shook his head sadly. 'But the real reason, it turns out, is hardly so noble. No, the reason Greenbrooke and his Patriot cronies pushed as hard as they did for the Pathfinder project to focus on weapons acquisition was so they could beat the Soviets in their own alternate into submission.'

'You're certain of this?'

'I wish I wasn't, but I am. You see, Jerry, the Authority are what you get when you let people like Greenbrooke run things. Bleak, austere and absolutely devoid of hope or freedom.' He shook his head. 'I've been to their world, just briefly. You should see it: endless black skies, people scurrying from door to door to avoid the freezing cold, streets full of empty, barren shops. From what I saw, I'm guessing there must have been a hell of a big die-off once the nukes started to fly. Fact is, they're already dead, or will be soon, anyway. You can see it in their faces; it's a real privilege for some of them to be assigned to our island, did you know that? Warm skies, clean air, sunshine.'

'If the Authority's alternate is so cold,' I said, 'the bees'll just die, won't they?'

He shook his head. 'These aren't your regular garden-issue insects,' he said. 'Remember – they were designed as a weapon. The only way you can take those things out is with a flamethrower. Cold doesn't matter to them.' He nodded at Greenbrooke. 'And even if it does, they're quite good at finding somewhere nice and warm to live, wouldn't you say?' He stabbed at his chest with one thumb. 'Now listen to me. We're the victims. The people running the Authority are the same kind of people who decimated our own alternates. Didn't you dream of finding those people and killing them? Well, I've got a chance to do just that, and I'm not giving it up.'

I regarded him bleakly. 'And what happens to the rest of us?'

Casey turned on his heel without answering me and went to kneel by the laptop controlling the transfer stage. The screensaver vanished, to be replaced by the control interface. One after the other, the status lights on the field-pillars blinked into life as they came online.

That was when I knew it was too late, and he was on his way to the Authority with Greenbrooke.

'For Christ's sake, Casey!' I yelled in desperation. 'The Authority'll kill all the rest of us once they know what you've done! Don't you understand that?'

He glanced over and gave me a sunny smile. 'Not if you show them the recording I'm making just now. That's your alibi, right there. It proves I'm responsible for everything, and not any of you. I'll happily take the blame right on the goddam chin, but they'd have to catch me first.' He smiled broadly. 'See? I'm not such a bad guy after all.'

I opened my mouth to try once more and beg him to stop, even knowing it was useless. I'd seen madness like this before, in Herschel and Marlon, before they murdered my own world. And I was going to have to watch it happen all over again.

I wondered if I had the strength to rush him, to throw myself at him and knock him over, smash the laptop or damage one of the field-pillars, maybe. But I knew he would most likely shoot me dead first, rather than risk my further interference. But then again, maybe that was preferable to sitting by and watching another world die when I had at least some kind of chance of stopping him.

Something made me look up at the top of the basement steps and I saw Rozalia, crouched down in the open doorway. She was looking down at me, a finger raised to her mouth. She looked shockingly pale, sweat making her hair cling to her face. It must have taken an enormous effort to follow me here, as badly wounded as she was. I wondered how she had avoided getting caught by the tripwires. Or had Haden been there to help her as well?

She sank back into the shadows, and I saw her raise her rifle, aiming it straight at Casey's head. But I could see she was struggling to hold the rifle steady. If she managed to hit him, it'd be a miracle.

I glanced back over at Casey and saw him staring at me. He stood up quickly and stared up at the steps.

He saw Rozalia, her weapon wavering in her hands. He moved fast, reaching for his rifle and bringing it to bear on her.

There wasn't time to think.

I stumbled upright and ran towards Casey. He fired at Rozalia just as I threw both wrists around his head, pulling the chain of the cuffs taut around his throat. I heard Rozalia cry out, and I dragged Casey across the basement and towards the cage in the middle of the transfer stage. I fought a sudden dizziness, the blood thundering in my ears.

Casey must have sensed my sudden weakness, for he slammed one elbow backwards into my chest. I slumped, but it only increased the pressure on his throat. He reached up in desperation to try and wriggle free, and I again pulled as hard as I could.

I glanced quickly towards Rozalia, seeing that she had tumbled down the steps and now lay bleeding on the dusty concrete. Her rifle lay nearby. I knew I didn't have the strength to fight Casey for much longer.

By now, the air above the transfer stage had begun to shiver and twist. I had no more than seconds before it carried Greenbrooke and the cargo of bees back to the Authority.

I realized that Casey was growing weaker. He was on his knees now, still struggling to be free, and I let myself fall to one side, pulling him after me. I looked over at Rozalia, and saw she had managed once more to get a hold of her rifle and was struggling to aim it.

Casey took advantage of my distraction, reaching back to dig his fingers into my eyes. I screamed and twisted away, and he took the advantage, surging back to his feet just as a loud explosion filled the confined space. Casey staggered and fell within the transfer stage's perimeter, blood pouring down his leg.

The air around him shimmered like a summer heat haze and I knew I was out of time. Even badly wounded, Casey would still be able to open the cage once he crossed over to the Authority.

In an instant, I knew what I had to do.

I scrambled over to the laptop controlling the stage. The screen showed a countdown with just seconds to go, and a set of transfer coordinates flashing red. I had been taught, during my last week of training, how to program a transfer stage control rig to get me back to the island in an emergency. I quickly tapped an icon, then reset the coordinates to a null sequence.

I turned in time to see Casey crawling towards the transfer stage's perimeter, stark terror etched on his face. He knew what I had done. Then he vanished, sent spinning into some unimaginable void along with Greenbrooke and the cage of bees. The space encircled by the field-pillars was as silent and empty as if nothing and no one had ever been there.

'Jerry.'

I went over to kneel by Rozalia. I could see she was struggling to breathe.

'Just hang on there,' I said, feeling helpless. 'I can recalibrate the stage, jump us all the way back to the island. There are doctors there . . .'

'Stop trying to be a fucking hero,' she gasped. 'Go get Yuichi. He's right where you left him.'

'Of course.' I glanced back towards the stage. How long would it take me to power it up again? How many minutes? Too many, I realized.

'I wanted Casey to pay for what he did to Nadia. And to you. Do you understand?' Her hand reached out, taking hold of my own. 'You're a good man, Jerry Beche.'

'Yeah, and we can talk about that when you're feeling better. How the hell did you even get past those tripwires?'

She smiled faintly. 'By paying attention,' she whispered.

Her eyes closed and I felt her grow slack in my arms.

'No,' I said. 'Come on. Wake up. Rozalia. *Wake the fuck up*. I . . .'

And then I looked down, at the blood still spreading across the floor, and knew it was already much too late.

I got back up and hunted around until I found a key, sitting on a dusty shelf, that fitted the cuffs. I programmed some adjustments to the transfer stage's settings, then paused, seeing Casey's video camera still mounted on its tripod.

I picked the camera up and turned it this way and that until I found a slot with a memory card. I popped the card out and pocketed it, then made my way up the stairs and out into the late afternoon sunshine. Off in the distance, I saw a trailing line of bee-brains. They didn't look as if they were headed my way, but I wasn't taking any chances. I started to run back to where I'd left Yuichi.

I found him right where I had left him. His head was slumped to one side, his jaw slack, his eyes closed as if in death.

I felt the bottom fall out of my stomach, thinking I had lost another friend. But then his eyes opened, and he squinted up at me.

'I guess she found you,' he said. 'You catch Casey?'

I knelt down beside him and helped him to stand. 'We caught him,' I said.

'And Rozalia?' he asked haltingly. 'I heard shooting.'

I shook my head and said nothing. Yuichi just nodded, looking suddenly old.

'Come on, you goddam hippie,' I muttered, doing my best to take his weight. 'Time to get the hell out of here.'

TWENTY-FIVE

Yuichi gazed down at Rozalia's body with a look of infinite sadness when I manoeuvred him down the steps of the basement some minutes later. The stage was powered up and ready to take us home. All I had to do was punch in a last command.

'We'll come back and get her, I promise,' I said, just before the basement faded from view.

'Yeah,' Yuichi muttered, looking lost. 'No one gets left behind, right?'

I felt the familiar seesaw during the moment of transition, and then we were back inside the shipwrecked trawler. My heart swelled inside my chest when I saw Chloe standing framed in the moonlight, just beyond the rent in the hull. She came forwards and I held her tightly, feeling tears run down my cheeks. I had never been so glad to see someone alive.

Finally I let go of her, and she helped me guide Yuichi back outside, to where Randall, Winifred and Selwyn were waiting for us. Kip Mayer sat on a rock nearby, looking dishevelled and forlorn, his suit streaked with dirt. As we emerged from the hull he stared at us as if we were ghosts.

Selwyn grabbed hold of me by both arms. 'Casey?'

'Dead,' I replied. I looked over at Mayer. 'The Authority's safe. We stopped him just in time.'

'We were going to go through and look for you, but we couldn't make the connection,' said Selwyn. 'We were afraid something terrible had happened.'

I glanced at Mayer, and suddenly decided I didn't want him to know about the second secret transfer stage. 'There was a glitch, that's all,' I told Selwyn, extemporizing quickly.

Selwyn peered into my eyes, looking for something. 'And Rozalia? Oskar?'

I met his gaze as steadily as I could. 'They didn't make it.'

Selwyn took a step back and nodded grimly. 'I'm sorry to hear that.'

I walked over to Mayer, who sat staring off into space. I saw he had my predecessor's last testament gripped in one hand, as if he'd just been reading it.

'You people shouldn't have lied to us about retirement,' I said, nodding at the crumpled pages. 'None of this would have happened otherwise. As far as I'm concerned, that makes you people nearly as much to blame as Casey.'

He gazed at me hopelessly, then looked away again. The moonlight revealed bruises on his face, and I wondered if he'd received them during his brief incarceration at the hands of the Patriots.

'There isn't time for this, Jerry,' said Winifred, coming towards me. 'We need to get going.'

I turned to look at her. 'Where to?'

'The Authority,' she replied. 'Remember what Howes said back at the Mauna Loa? We have to take the evidence back through to the Authority ourselves, along with Kip.'

I nodded as it came back to me. 'What happened at the base?' I asked her. 'It all went okay?'

She nodded. 'Pretty much the way Howes said it would. They took him prisoner, and that gave us the opportunity to get Kip out while their backs were turned. We can't hang around. They might have seen our headlights.'

Selwyn stepped towards Mayer. 'Mr Mayer? If you'd care to program the stage with the appropriate coordinates, we'd be delighted.'

Mayer nodded. 'You'll need to leave your weapons,' he said.

We all looked at each other. 'If you go through armed,' said Mayer, 'the people on the other side will shoot first, trust me. Just leave them somewhere out of sight here.'

We did as he said, not without some trepidation, then waited as he programmed the stage for the Authority. He and Yuichi were the first to climb onto the tiny stage, followed some minutes later by Winifred and Randall, then Selwyn on his own and, lastly, myself and Chloe, gripping each other's hands as the light swarmed around us.

Men in dark suits were waiting for us when we arrived at our destination, all of them conspicuously armed. I felt a brief moment of terror, thinking perhaps we had misjudged Mayer and inadvertently walked straight into a trap. But when I saw the other surviving Pathfinders standing unguarded nearby I decided we were safe.

Two of the men – agents? Soldiers? I had no idea – guided us out from the circle of field-pillars, then led us towards the other Pathfinders. I saw Mayer standing in a far corner of the room, tapping at the notes in his hand and speaking animatedly to another man.

'Do you think they all share the same tailor to keep the bills down?' muttered Selwyn, leaning in close to me as he regarded the armed men all around us.

I looked about, seeing that the stage occupied one end of a long, high-ceilinged room with peeling wallpaper. It looked like a ballroom that had seen far better days. Rows of ancient-looking computers sat on desks pushed up against one wall, their screens shrouded with plastic dust covers. I heard the muffled honk of traffic from beyond heavily curtained windows, and shivered. It was freezing cold.

Tall doors opened and yet more men in the same dark suits entered. One of them stepped towards Mayer.

'I need a situation report,' he said, before glancing towards us and frowning. 'What are they doing here? Are they cleared?'

Mayer shook his head. 'No, but there wasn't any choice. I had to bring them with me.'

'They shouldn't be here,' the other man insisted. 'There are strict quarantine laws, you know that.'

'I need to show you something first,' said Mayer, pressing the pages into his hands.

'Kip . . .'

'I'm serious,' Mayer insisted. He glanced towards us again. 'They can wait while we talk, okay? Then, if you're still not happy about it, we can send them back over. But only if you insist.'

Mayer's companion regarded us for what felt like a long time.

'All right,' the man said with a sigh. 'But make this quick.'

'That, sir,' said Mayer, 'is not something I can guarantee,'

Mayer disappeared in the company of this other man, and the rest of us were led away down a corridor beyond the tall doors. A wheeled stretcher appeared, along with a nurse, and Yuichi was hoisted up and onto it by Randall and Selwyn, who had been helping him along thus far. I watched as they trundled him away, trying to ignore my misgivings at being separated in this way in this cold and bleak place.

They led the rest of us along a corridor and past a dust-specked window, through which I caught sight of a city's streets.

'We're in Washington,' Winifred said from behind my shoulder as we walked on, almost whispering the words. 'I'd know the place anywhere.'

We came to a small room, devoid of either windows or any furniture apart from some rickety wooden chairs. They locked the door when they exited, and I sat there, tense, hoping it didn't mean we were prisoners.

Randall tried to make small talk, but gave up after a couple of minutes. No one was in the mood for anything more than waiting for whatever came next.

An hour passed before the door next opened, and two of the men who had brought us to the room entered, one of them pushing a trolley loaded with food. They left the door unlocked behind them as they handed out paper cups of oily coffee and thin, moist sandwiches that tasted of grease and fat and little else.

Before they departed once more, one of the two men turned to me. 'We need to talk to you, sir.' He indicated the door with his head.

I regarded him warily. 'About what?'

'Why just him?' asked Chloe.

'Relax, lady,' the man said. 'We're not Patriot agents. We just want you to tell us everything that happened, Mr Beche, all in your own words. We'll be recording it. That okay by you?'

'Sure,' I said, aware that saying "no" almost certainly wasn't an option. I stood carefully, then looked around at the others. 'I'll see you in a bit.'

'Famous last words,' said Selwyn with a faltering smile.

I wondered how Yuichi was doing, wherever he was.

I followed the man out while his companion took charge of the now-empty trolley, locking the door behind us.

'Is that really necessary?' I asked.

'Orders,' said the first man with a shrug. 'They see you wandering around, people might ask questions. And we might have difficulty answering them.'

This time I was led upstairs. They took me into a room with a table, two chairs, a microphone and a large mirror on one wall that I assumed was one-way. My predecessor's pages were sitting on the table, arranged in a neat pile. According to the calendar on the wall, it was some time in August.

One of my guards closed the door, the other taking one seat before gesturing to me to take the other. 'Relax, pal,' he said. 'My name's Louie. Just tell me everything that happened, right from the beginning. Can you do that for me?'

I swallowed away the dryness in my mouth. 'Sure,' I said. And then I started talking. But I was careful to omit any mention of Haden, and more than once I reached into my pocket to confirm that the envelope he had given me was, indeed, still there. Then my fingers touched the memory card from Casey's camera. I hesitated a moment before lifting it out and handing it over to them, explaining what it was and how it had come into my hands.

*

I answered questions for another couple of hours after that. By the time they took me back downstairs and unlocked the door again, most of the others had curled up where they could to try and get some sleep. Chloe opened her eyes and blinked as they brought me in.

'What happened?' she murmured.

'It's just like they said,' I told her. 'They asked me questions and I told them everything I knew that happened.'

I sank onto the vacant chair beside her, and she laid her head on my lap before closing her eyes again. Within seconds she was asleep. I leaned my own head back and closed my eyes, and it wasn't long before I had joined her.

I woke to the sound of the door unlocking. This time it was Mayer, in a fresh suit, and accompanied by Louie and the other guard. The others woke, grumbling and stretching.

'Sorry that took so long,' said Mayer.

'They kept us locked up like prisoners,' I said.

'I'm sorry about that,' he said. 'They just weren't taking any chances.' He gestured to the empty corridor behind him. 'I need you all up and ready, because we're going for a ride.'

We shuffled after him and the two guards. They led us down an echoing stairwell that terminated in an underground car park. Light from the street above filtered down a steep access ramp. It was bitingly cold and felt like late December or early January back home. I remembered the date on the calendar and wondered if perhaps it hadn't been changed in a long while. I also couldn't help but notice that the air smelled of burning wood, as if there was a fire nearby.

Apart from two old and dusty-looking limousines that had to be at least thirty years old, the car park was empty. Louie guided us all towards one of the limousines, before pulling open the rear door and gesturing to us to get in.

I paused by the door, my teeth chattering from the cold, and looked over at Mayer.

'Go on,' said Mayer. 'I'll be in the other car, right behind you.'

'What about Yuichi?' I demanded. 'Where did they take him?'

'He's in there,' said Mayer. 'Just get in.'

I dipped my head and peered into the darkened interior of the limousine and saw a grinning Yuichi, his leg wrapped up in heavy bandages, a pair of crutches by his side.

'Don't look so surprised,' he said. 'Just get the hell in before you let all the warm air out.'

We piled in around him, laughing and chattering and suddenly I felt that everything was going to be all right after all. We got comfortable on two dark leather couches facing each other across the rear compartment while Louie got in behind the wheel, the back of his head visible through a thick sheet of glass separating him from us. It wasn't long before we were underway, driving up the ramp and onto a broad avenue streaked with slushy snow.

The Washington skies were cloudy and dark, with little hint of sunshine. Everything looked grey and miserable. Even so, I marvelled at the sight of a city with people filling its streets; no one smiled, however, and no one looked remotely happy. It might just have been down to the lousy weather, but I had not failed to notice that the clothes they all wore were dark and threadbare.

'You notice something?' Randall muttered. 'I hardly see any other cars.'

'Me neither,' said Chloe, glancing out of the window.

There were indeed few, if any, other motorized vehicles. Most people seemed to travel on foot, although I saw one or two hardy souls pedalling past on rickety bicycles. Most of the shop windows were as empty as Casey had described them, and I saw little in the way of advertising. At one point we skirted a park denuded of trees, their low, black stumps stretching across the unweeded grass. I had already noticed the many trails of dark smoke rising from roofs and into the sky, and realized with a shock that people here burned wood for heat.

This, then, was the Authority.

At one point we passed several army trucks parked by the side of the road, along with a couple of limousines that looked more or less identical to our own. Men wearing suits with a similar cut to those worn by the Patriot agents were kneeling in a row in the slushy snow, their hands on top of their heads, while uniformed soldiers stood watch over them. A body lay sprawled face-up in a gutter, a dark stain across the white of its shirt.

We drove on out into the suburbs, which were hardly more joyful than the city; eventually we pulled up before a set of broad iron gates that swung open at our approach. Louie guided the limousine down a long driveway that terminated before a building that might have been a private mansion, or might equally have been an embassy. The second limousine, carrying Mayer, drove on around the other side of the building and out of sight.

After that, Louie ushered us through a marble-clad entrance flanked by stone angels, then guided us into a room that was clearly someone's private office. A mahogany desk stood before a set of French windows, while wood crackled and popped in a fireplace. Louie left us alone, and we stood waiting for a few minutes until a second door opened.

Mort Bramnik stepped through, accompanied by the same man who had argued with Kip Mayer just after we had crossed over to the Authority.

'Senator,' said Bramnik, clasping one of the man's hands in both of his own. 'Thank you. I'll take it from here.'

The Senator nodded to us, then left.

'Now will you *please* tell us what the goddam hell is going on?' Winifred demanded.

Bramnik took a seat behind the desk and spread his hands on the varnished wood. 'I've been talking with Kip,' he said. 'He told me everything you told him, as well as showing me your predecessor's written evidence, Mr Beche. It's quite a story.'

'Wallace Deans can tell you the rest,' I said.

'I'm afraid he died a few hours ago,' said Bramnik.

I let that sink in. There were so few of us left now.

'And Howes?' I asked. 'Is there any news about him?'

Bramnik nodded. 'He's fine. We sent a number of detachments back to the island just after you arrived, in order to place the Patriot agents under arrest. A lot's been happening since you came here.'

'What's going on with them?' asked Chloe. 'The Patriots, I mean. Are you going through some kind of a civil war, or is that just how you people do business?'

Bramnik shook his head. 'Let's just say there are elements in our government that believe strongly in one way of thinking, and others that feel strongly in the opposite direction. As it happens, the group to which I belong managed to win the day. And that's all that matters.' He gazed around at us all. 'It's been hard work, keeping your presence here a secret.'

I nodded past him, to the snowy gardens visible through a window behind the desk. 'It's the middle of August,' I said. 'It's getting bad, right? How long do you have, before the extinction event really kicks in?'

'What are you talking about?' asked Chloe.

'When they interviewed me,' I said, 'there was a calendar on the wall. It said it was August.' I turned back to Bramnik. 'Snow and freezing skies in the middle of summer? That's a hell of a pickle you people are in.'

Bramnik leaned back in his chair. 'You have no idea.'

'So what's the reason for bringing us to this place?' I asked, indicating the office around us.

'Because you deserve explanations.' He looked around the others as well. 'All of you. I've barely had time to scan the documents your predecessor left behind, Mr Beche, but his discoveries and his insights are going to be invaluable to us.'

'Who is "us", exactly?' asked Winifred.

'I said there are groups struggling for influence within our government, and they have different ideas on how to handle our . . . current difficulties.'

'What's your approach?' I asked.

'I, and others like me,' said Bramnik, 'believe that working openly towards a common goal is the only way to ensure our survival, as a species as much as a civilization. The Patriots had different ideas. For a long time now, Greenbrooke and his agency were in the ascendant here. They had growing influence over policy, and they wanted nothing more than to . . . neutralize our mutual enemies. Myself and the Senator feel our best chance at long-term survival is by working with them.'

'You're talking about the Russians,' I said.

'We've got an ice age coming,' said Bramnik. 'The global temperature's dipped too low, for too long. We have maybe ten years to figure something out, and we're not ruling out some kind of a mass evacuation, if we can ever get enough transfer stages running – and find somewhere safe enough to point them at. We thought the alternate you've all been living on might be such a place, but when we investigated the mainland . . . well, let's just say there's a reason we stick to that island. But wherever we end up going, assuming we can find such a place, and assuming evacuating the entire population of an alternate is even remotely feasible, we won't be able to do it without the help of the Soviets.'

'You need somewhere with an intact infrastructure,' I suggested. 'Somewhere that's lost its population, but is safe to repopulate.'

'That's just one possible option among a thousand,' said Bramnik, 'I'm not even joking when I say I'd be hanged if they knew how much I've told you. As far as you or anyone else is concerned, you were never here.'

'I want to thank you,' I said, 'for telling us the truth.'

'No,' said Bramnik, 'thank *you*. I saw the video you handed over, of Casey's confession. We know now exactly what he was planning. Without your help, things would clearly have been infinitely worse for all of us.'

'So what next?' demanded Randall. 'We just keep doing what we've always done?'

'Why not?' asked Bramnik. 'The deal you've got is a hell of a lot better than any of the people you saw on the drive over here have. And, compared to most other places on this alternate, they're the lucky ones. Look – things will be different, Mr Pimms, I guarantee you. Better equipment, better backup, much more transparency and no more weapons retrieval. But we still need data, or anything, really, that can help us figure out how to program safe destinations into the transfer stages. Maybe then you'll be able to retire, and we'll be able to find some place safe for our people – but in the meantime, I'd count your blessings.'

The door opened and the guard named Louie entered. It was time for us to leave.

I was glad, to be honest. I'd been delaying telling the others about Haden for much too long.

TWENTY-SIX

We were driven back across town to the underground garage, from where Louie ushered us back upstairs to the transfer stage. I had the feeling it wasn't the main stage, though. It was hidden away in a building that was clearly decrepit and, so far as I could tell, deserted. I felt sure there would be others, perhaps tucked away in military bases.

We watched the ballroom fade from view and found ourselves back in the main hangar by the base.

For the first time, there was no rig technician on duty to greet us. Instead, there were unfamiliar men in military uniforms, all of them armed, although from the way they acted, it was clear they had been expecting us.

We looked around at each other, then made our way unchallenged out into the morning of a new day. We didn't have to look too hard to find evidence of fighting: there were bloodstains on the concrete just outside the hangar entrance and bullet holes in the doors.

I motioned to the others to gather around me once we were far away enough from the hangar we wouldn't be overheard, and pulled the envelope out of my pocket.

'What is that?' asked Chloe.

'Haden gave this to me,' I said, and for the first time told them about my encounter with him outside Retièn.

'That's impossible,' said Randall, some minutes later. He looked shaken; they all did.

'Explain this, then,' I said, taking the scrap of paper back from Yuichi, who had been staring obsessively at his name and the transfer coordinates beneath it for some minutes.

'I don't know,' he muttered, his eyes darting away from mine. 'You invented it, maybe.'

'Oh, for fuck's sake,' said Selwyn, regarding him with disgust. 'What is it with you?'

'But if it's real,' said Randall, 'then . . .' He shook his head and lapsed into silence.

'I've got a theory,' I said. 'Or at least, something that makes some kind of sense.' I paused before continuing. 'Maybe Haden's a stage-builder.'

They all looked at each other. 'You're serious?' asked Winifred.

'Well, either he's that,' said Yuichi, 'or he really *is* an alien with those damn eyes of his . . .'

'Or it's a cruel joke,' said Chloe. 'We'll never know until we actually try and use some of those coordinates, will we?'

'Question is,' I asked, 'who goes first?'

'I will,' said Randall, his jaw set. 'If those coordinates can really take me home . . . then I want to *go* home.'

'Randall,' said Winifred, 'remember what I said back at the Mauna Loa, about how you can never really go home . . .'

'Oh, shut the hell up,' Randall snapped. Winifred glared at him, and he reddened.

'Look, I'm sorry,' Randall continued, 'but all I've ever wanted to do is to find my way to some place like the world I was living in before everything fell to shit. I don't care if I've changed, or it's changed, or it's completely different or their tacos taste funny, or whatever.' He bared his teeth. 'I want to find myself some little town, with ordinary people walking around the streets, with hardware stores and farms and ice-cream parlours and beer on tap, with absolutely zero fucking prospect of asteroids falling on it or military germ-warfare turning everyone into monsters. I want some place with cable sports and pretty girls serving you whisky and country and western dances every Friday night. I want, more than *anything*,' he continued, clenching his fists, 'to live somewhere where every day is exactly the same as every other and I am gloriously, joyously bored out of my fucking skull.'

'Amen,' said Selwyn, quietly.

No one really seemed to have anything to say to that.

'Well, if we're going to try out those coordinates,' I said eventually, 'we probably shouldn't wait around.'

Chloe glanced back at the hangar. 'I don't think they're going to let us just walk in there and use the stage,' she said. 'But you're not talking about that, are you?'

'You think maybe they haven't done anything yet about the stage hidden in the trawler?' suggested Yuichi.

I shook my head. 'I think they've got too much on their hands to worry about it just yet. But it won't stay there forever, not now Mayer and the rest know about it.'

'Then that's it,' said Randall. 'We drive back out there again and use Haden's coordinates.'

I glanced to one side, seeing Winifred's tight-lipped expression. 'I know you don't want to hear this,' she said, 'but we still don't know where those coordinates really lead, or what Haden's motives really are.'

'I don't care,' said Randall. 'I'm prepared to take that chance.'

'What do you think, Jerry?' Yuichi asked me. 'It was you he gave them to, after all.'

I thought for a moment. 'I'm convinced he was trying to help us.' I looked around the rest of them. 'Anyone else apart from Randall and Selwyn want to test these out?'

'Consider me undecided,' said Yuichi, 'for the same reasons as Winifred. That's not to say I wouldn't want to take a look, at least, if I thought the coordinates would really work.'

'Randall,' I said, 'are you really willing to be a guinea pig on this one?'

He nodded tightly. 'I am.'

They all looked at me as if it was my decision. I looked at Chloe, who hadn't replied, and thought about how badly I'd wanted to find somewhere like home not so very long ago. But now I had the chance, I found myself far from sure I wanted to take it.

'I guess we go, then.'

Government House had a few bullet holes studded around its entrance that hadn't been there before. Soldiers stood guard outside the building for the first time since my retrieval. They eyed us watchfully as we commandeered a couple of jeeps from the pool, but made no move to stop us, and soon we were driving back up along the coast road.

The beached trawler was just as we'd left it. We went inside and started the power-up sequence while I pulled out the envelope and read the appropriate coordinates out to Randall. I watched as he programmed them into the laptop himself.

Randall looked around us all, and I could see how terrified he was, and how determined. 'Well, here goes nothing,' he said, stepping inside the ring on its rickety wood and canvas support. I saw the perspiration on his skin, his fear written in the lines on his face. 'I'll take a look around, see what I can see and report back. I won't be long.'

We had set the stage to automatically bring him back after five minutes, since there was no way of knowing if there was a transfer stage on the other side. As long as he made sure to stand exactly where he'd been when he arrived, he'd be able to return. If we tried to maintain the connection any longer than that, the power drain would quickly become exponential.

The air shimmered, and when it faded, Randall was gone. I wondered what he was seeing, or if we had just sent him to an unimaginable death. Yuichi hobbled back outside on his crutches to smoke; Winifred went with him. I sat down on the sand with my back against the rusting hull and was still staring towards the stage when Randall reappeared right on time five minutes later. Despite my certainty that everything would be all right, I still felt a powerful rush of relief.

It hit me that all through the hunt for Casey, I had not thought about Alice once.

Winifred crowded in through the rent in the hull with Yuichi. 'What did you see?' she asked Randall excitedly.

'I was in an old abandoned hotel,' he said, grinning more broadly and looking more happy than I had ever seen him. 'I had just enough time to stick my head outside and take a look, and . . .' he trailed off, shaking his head.

'C'mon,' urged Yuichi. His cigarette, forgotten, burned its way down towards his knuckles.

Randall spread his hands and grinned. 'Just . . . people. I don't know where I was, exactly. There was a coffee shop on the other side of the road. It *looked* like Albuquerque, where I'm from. Everything just looked . . . normal.'

Selwyn stepped over to the laptop and picked up the scrap of paper Randall had left lying there. 'Me next,' he said, tears trembling in the corners of his eyes.

We all agreed to take turns, even Winifred. But first we argued, and made arrangements, even in some cases made farewells. Randall wasn't coming back. Neither was Selwyn, once he realized his destination was his hometown of Cardiff. After confirming where the coordinates would take him, he came back just long enough to say goodbye, and then he was gone forever. Winifred went and looked and came back, and so did Yuichi. So far, all the coordinates functioned perfectly.

By now, there were just four of us left. Me and Chloe and Winifred and Yuichi.

'I guess it's good to know I could go there if I really wanted to,' said Winifred. 'That's enough for me.'

'You're staying,' I said.

'I already told you.' For the first time, I saw her smile, really smile, and it made her look like an entirely different person. 'Does that seem crazy?'

'I think you explained yourself well enough before,' I said. I looked over at Yuichi. 'Well?'

He gave me a scornful look. 'C'mon, Jerry. Give up my chance to be a wasteland warrior?'

I grinned, glad not to lose him.

'That still leaves you two,' said Winifred, studying Chloe and me.

'I'll go with Jerry,' she said. 'Nothing could induce me to go to any place like where I came from, pre-or post-extinction.' She looked at me uncertainly. 'If . . . that's okay with you?'

I could sense the fear in her voice. She was thinking about Alice, of course, and whether some other version of her might be found at the coordinates Haden had given me.

'I'm going,' I said. 'But not just for five minutes.'

Chloe swallowed. 'You're . . . you're not coming back?'

I turned and put both hands on her shoulders. 'You don't understand. I am. But I just want a little more than five minutes to look around. Are you okay with that?'

She gazed into my eyes, and I thought she had never looked so beautiful as in that moment. 'Sure.' She nodded, then smiled uncertainly. 'Okay.'

I looked up at the other two. 'An hour,' I said. 'That's all.'

Yuichi regarded me sceptically. 'You're sure? We'll need to shut the link down, then reopen it again after an hour. I wouldn't advise wandering too far in the meantime.'

I knew he was worried that the soldiers might come and take the stage away before we had time to get back. 'I'll be careful,' I reassured him. 'In the meantime, we're probably going to have to think up some kind of story to explain Randall and Selwyn's disappearance.'

Yuichi laughed. 'Hell, yeah. Good point. Now *that's* going to take some explaining.'

Chloe took my hand. 'I'm ready,' she said. 'Are you?'

'I'm ready.'

TWENTY-SEVEN

We materialized in the attic of an empty house, surrounded by furniture hidden beneath dust sheets. I found a screwdriver lying in a corner of the attic and used it to quickly scratch a cross where we had appeared, then checked the time on my watch. We'd have to be back at this exact spot in precisely one hour.

I led Chloe downstairs and out onto a quiet street lined with trees. I could hear the honking of traffic a block away. I felt as if I was in a dream, afraid I might wake up. The only thing anchoring me back to reality was the sensation of Chloe's hand in mine.

We were in London, in the suburbs, not far from where I had once lived with Alice. We started to walk. I saw vans and buses and people leading ordinary lives, shopping and chattering and doing ordinary things I had forgotten how to do. I drank it all in until I felt numb from sensory overload.

'This way,' I said, my voice shaking. I kept having to wipe the tears from my eyes.

'Where are we going?' Chloe asked me.

I looked at her, suddenly unable to speak.

'You think I don't get it,' she said, her voice tight with emotion. 'But I do.' She reached up to touch my face. 'So hurry up and get your goddam closure, already.'

I nodded and we walked on. I led her to a sandstone building on a quiet street. I stared at the buzzers next to the front entrance, but I kept my distance rather than read the names there.

'This was where we lived,' I said. I didn't need to tell her I meant myself and Alice. Was there another Alice here, another Jerry? Could this reality be that close to the one I had come from? Or was it just different enough that it lacked a doppelgänger, an alternative version of me?

I turned and looked up and down the busy streets, Chloe watching me intently the whole time. I had seen these same avenues filled with nothing but corpses, the air choked with clouds of buzzing flies. Since then I had literally seen worlds colliding, entire cities of people transformed into mindless, insect-like armies.

I had learned, above all, the enormous fragility of life. I had learned that everything I once believed to be permanent and solid and immutable could change in an instant and be wiped out forever without warning.

I looked at the people passing us on the street, imagined them dying, or partying their last days away as the moon slid out of the sky before crashing down on their heads.

'Come on,' I said to Chloe, taking a tighter grasp on her hand and turning back the way we had come. 'Let's go home.'

All you can do is find some place to call home, and hope for the best.

A few days later, I found myself facing Bramnik from across his desk. Outside, rain thumped against the window of his office in Government House. A tropical storm had hit the island, it being that time of year. He looked older, more tired, despite his full reinstatement as head of the Pathfinder project.

'And that's all you can tell me?' he said. 'That they're gone?'

'We searched for them,' I said. 'Haden, Selwyn and Randall. They're nowhere on the island.'

'But where could they . . . ?'

I stared towards the window, trying my damnedest to look grief stricken. I'd practised that morning, in my mirror, and thought I'd been pretty good at it. Maybe in another life I'd have been an actor.

'We searched for them everywhere,' I said. 'But then I remembered something I heard Selwyn and Randall saying, when it looked as if the Patriots were going to take over.' I sighed heavily. 'They said they'd rather take their chances with a null sequence.'

Bramnik regarded me with horror. I began to think he might really believe me.

'I'll admit,' I said, 'we used the transfer stage Casey had mounted in the trawler to travel to a bunch of known alternates, but there was no sign any of them had travelled to those places.' I raised my hands in my lap and let them fall again. 'Out of all of us, they were the ones most dissatisfied with the way things were. Randall talked more than anyone, I think, about how desperate he was to retire.'

'You think they killed themselves? Because they found out they couldn't retire?'

I gave a heavy shrug. 'It crossed my mind. Who knows? But I'm not so sure it was suicide. I think they decided it was worth the risk, to see where each of them might end up. After all, nobody really knows where you go when you program a null sequence. All we know is that nobody ever comes back – and with nobody to report back, there's no way of knowing what's on the other side.'

Bramnik shook his head. 'It just seems incredible that they would do such a thing.'

I shrugged helplessly. 'I can't ever be certain what they did, or why. All I'm saying is I can't think of anything else that makes any kind of sense. Either way, they're gone – all three of them.'

After Selwyn and Randall departed forever, Winifred and I had decided to make one final trip to the bee-brain alternate. The decision to do so, to say the least, had not been made lightly. We had transferred across to the basement from where Casey had vanished into an unknowable void, and collected the field-pillars. We carried them outside, carefully avoiding the tripwires, and loaded them into Casey's jeep, once we figured out where he had abandoned it.

Then came the question of what to do about Rozalia's body, still lying prone in the basement. I had promised Yuichi I would bring her body back, but Winifred argued against this, pointing out that if we did, we would almost certainly have to bury her in secret – otherwise, the Authority would know we had come back to get her.

And if they knew that, they might well get to wondering what *else* we might have brought back. There was greater dignity, she said, in leaving Rozalia where she was – in the same place that Nadia and also Oskar had met their ends.

I couldn't argue with that. At least this way Nadia and Rozalia were still together, after a fashion. So we took Rozalia's body from where it still lay sprawled across the concrete and arranged it so it at least had a little more dignity. Winifred said a few words, but I'm damned if I can remember a single one of them. Then Winifred took previously collected samples of the spoor the night patrols used to indicate which areas of the city the bee-brains should next tear apart, and she smeared it all over the basement and most of the rest of the building. That way, if the Authority ever came looking for the stage Casey had hidden there, they'd find the building razed to the ground and assume the stage had been destroyed along with it.

We drove the jeep with its cargo of field-pillars back across the city to the reservoir stage. There, we unloaded the field-pillars from the jeep and abandoned the vehicle, as it was too large to return through the stage hidden in the trawler back on the island.

We used the control rig taken from the basement as a replacement for the one smashed by Casey's drone, since the reservoir stage was otherwise unharmed. That way, when we arrived back at the trawler, it was with nearly everything we needed to have our own, secret transfer stage – without, we hoped, Bramnik or anyone else from the Authority ever figuring out the truth. Finally, we reopened the link back to the bee-brain alternate from the island, so we could fetch the functioning control rig to operate our own, secret stage.

Bramnik closed his eyes for a moment, and rubbed at one temple with his hand. 'I guess it's plausible enough,' he said, 'that I can put it in a report.'

I felt a cord of tension that had been with me all that morning slacken, just a little.

He looked at me. 'You should know,' he said, 'that depending on how my report is received, it's possible the Authority might decide to bring in replacements for the Pathfinders who died – or some of them, at any rate.'

'New people? Or . . .'

'Alternate versions of the ones we lost,' he replied, 'with at least one exception. That's not my decision, you understand. There may be others in the near future, as well. People from outside the Authority – possibly even from among the Soviets, if things pan out. There are still a lot of transfer coordinates we haven't explored yet, and we're going to need all the help we can get. We need either to find some way of programming our own destinations, if any of us are to have any hope at long-term survival, or hope to God we can at least find somewhere among all these dead worlds that isn't completely inhospitable.'

'I understand,' I said, and Bramnik turned his chair to stare out of the window towards the sea. After a moment I got up to leave.

'So did he believe you?'

Chloe and I had walked down to the old docks, near to where Nadia and Rozalia had restored the old lifeboat, where we could be reasonably certain of not being overheard.

'I don't know,' I said truthfully. 'Even as I was telling him about Haden, Selwyn and Randall killing themselves, it sounded less than believable, even to my own ears. But maybe he did believe it. I just don't know if I can ever be sure.'

'Maybe we should have come up with a better story,' she said, pushing her hands deep into the pockets of her coat.

'There isn't one,' I replied. 'Nothing that could explain the disappearance of all three of them.' I reached towards her, and she lifted a hand out of one pocket, wrapping her fingers around mine. 'Did you find somewhere safe to hide the field-pillars?'

She nodded. 'There's a well,' she said, 'not far from the fishing hut where we . . . you know.' I nodded, remembering that first time we had made love. 'We wrapped them all up in tarpaulins and dropped them down inside the well on a rope. If we ever need to get out of here fast, we can just pull them back up and set it all up in minutes. Winifred's talking about a more permanent solution, though, maybe digging a hole beneath the fishing hut where we could hide all the equipment.'

She shivered as we walked along, the sea to one side and the almost deserted town on the other. 'And you really mean what you said the other night? That Haden might be . . . one of them?'

'A stage-builder?' I said. 'Why not? Nothing else makes sense. There's no reason to imagine that the Authority are the only ones exploring the multiverse. I think that's why we never got visitors from outer space, or flying saucers landing in front of the White House. Any sufficiently advanced race probably figures out how to build transfer stages first. And it's a lot easier to go exploring parallel versions of your own reality than deep space.'

We kept walking. A breeze caught my hair, and I felt rain on my skin. 'And maybe some of those people exploring our little corner of the multiverse are friendly, like Haden, and maybe some of them aren't. But all the evidence points to something scaring the hell out of whatever civilization built our stages, after all.'

'I wonder if things can ever really go back to normal now,' said Chloe. 'Do you think they'll really bring back alternate versions of the others?'

'That's what Bramnik told me. But, to be honest,' I said, looking along the road back into town, thinking it was about time to go to the Mauna Loa for something to eat, 'I'm not sure if things were ever remotely normal here in the first place.'

Her hand held mine more tightly. 'And if things ever start to go wrong again, we can escape.'

'We can escape,' I said, squeezing back. I felt more optimistic than I had in as long as I could remember, even if I still harboured some doubts about remaining on the island. The one thing I knew for certain was that the events of the past several days had changed the dynamic between the Pathfinders and the Authority forever.

TWENTY-EIGHT

A few days later those of us who were left held a memorial service for everyone we had lost. This took place in the little cemetery past the runway, not far from where my predecessor lay buried. There wasn't a Pathfinder on the island who didn't know the truth about Selwyn, Randall and Haden. But, with Bramnik and Mayer present, we had to act otherwise. Before long, Bramnik had new schedules posted, and we prepared to return to something like our old routines.

This time, however, something was different. Some of our first missions were to retrieve people, instead of artefacts or information.

Three months after Casey tried to murder a world, I drove up to the front of the base hospital and saw Nadia and Rozalia standing together outside, blinking in the sunshine. They looked younger than I remembered. But they *were* younger, I reminded myself, than the originals by a good few years.

'There you are,' I said, pulling up next to them and climbing out. 'Name's Jerry,' I said, reaching out a hand to each in turn. 'Jerry Beche.'

'Jerry . . .' wheels turned in the new Nadia's head. 'I've heard about you. You were a friend of . . . ?'

Of the previous me, I knew she meant. 'Of both of you,' I said.

The two women looked at each other, then they both grinned and laughed as if I'd said something hilarious. 'I'm sorry,' said new-Rozalia. 'I'm still having a hard time wrapping my head around all of this.'

I noticed that the long, dimpled scar I had seen on Rozalia's cheek the first time I met her was missing. She must have acquired it some time after her retrieval, I realized.

'It takes time,' I agreed. 'Are you ready to see your new home?' I nodded towards the jeep, then held up the clipboard in my hand. 'We'll give you a couple of days to get settled in and undergo a few more debriefings, then you'll be due for your first training mission.'

'Yeah.' New-Nadia nodded, looking uneasy. 'Is it going to be dangerous?'

'It'll be a cakewalk,' I assured her. I looked at Rozalia. 'Or at least, any potential danger will be minimal. I can promise you that.'

She nodded, absorbing this information. I could see how the two of them were still more than a little shell-shocked from their new circumstances, and I remembered all too well just how it felt to be in their shoes. Winifred had already taken charge of a number of their debriefings prior to their release from quarantine, clueing them in on their new reality and helping them to adjust to the learning curve involved. Even so, I knew they would adapt quickly. People who survive global extinction events tend to be good at that kind of thing.

I got back in the driver's seat and they both climbed in back. 'Hey,' said new-Nadia, and I turned to look at her. 'You're like us, right? You were . . . someone's replacement. That's what Winnie said.'

I nodded. 'It's a long story.'

'But there are others, right? Winnie said there are other new replacements, like us.'

I mentally damned Winifred for leaving me to have to explain so much. 'Like I say, it's complicated. We're bringing back a lot of the people we lost.'

'Most, but not all?' asked Nadia, perceptive as ever.

I hesitated only briefly. 'All but two,' I said.

Because, of course, even the Authority was not so foolish as to bring Casey back. We'd already retrieved a new Randall, and a new Selwyn, and what they and all the new recruits had in common was that they had not been given any lies about retirement. They knew that, apart from the island and those alternates that the Authority was able to access, there was no going home.

Or at least, so they would know for some time. I knew the day might well come when we would take them into our confidence and share the list of coordinates Haden had given me. We could never be sure, after all, if Bramnik would always be in charge, or if one day we might want to run.

As for retrieving Haden . . . well, we went looking, but we never found him. Don't ask me how or why, but every coordinate we tried in his particular braid came up empty. I came to believe Haden had been a plant, left behind for the Authority to find, complete with a cover story to explain how he had managed to 'survive' all those years.

I turned on the ignition and drove the two of them out of the base compound, past the runway and into town, turning into the street where the original Nadia and Rozalia had lived.

'Hey,' I said, a sudden thought occurring to me as I pulled up outside. 'You like fishing?'

'Hell, yeah,' said Rozalia. 'Got any boats around here?'

I grinned. 'Maybe before I show you your new home, I'll show you a dandy little boat that's just right for the job. Sound like a deal?'

'Deal,' they both said at once.

There are risks in every walk of life. My predecessor knew that, and I've come to believe he knew there was at least the possibility that some other Jerry might one day read the pages he left behind. The more I read and reread those pages, once Mayer gave them back to me, the more I thought of it as a letter addressed to me as much as it had been to Chloe. I liked to imagine that in a way he was looking ahead, giving the newcomer some hints and tips to make his time as a Pathfinder easier.

So I figured it made sense to do the same thing, and anticipate in turn. Because you just never know.

It's been a little while now since we brought Nadia and Rozalia back to the island. They've gone on some tentative first missions, as have the new Randall and Selwyn, and we're even putting together a team to retrieve Wallace Deans. Much of what he did, after all, was under the influence of Casey Vishnevsky – and a finer case of Stockholm syndrome I've never encountered. With the right guidance, I felt sure – or hoped – his replacement might make a valuable contribution.

This morning, before I walked into town, I finished writing all of this down. It is, by far, the longest thing I've written in one go in my whole damn life. I had delayed writing it too long, always with the thought in the back of my head that something could happen to *me*. And, if it does, then a third iteration of Jerry Beche – should he be retrieved – would lack the opportunity to read the words of his own direct predecessor.

I hope that never proves necessary. But just in case it does, I want him to know everything I do. I'm going to give the letter – Christ, it's practically a novel – to someone to look after. Maybe Yuichi, or Chloe, or maybe both. And if the day comes, and some other Jerry emerges blinking into the sunshine outside the medical facility, they'll be waiting for him with these words in hand.

Dear Jerry, the story begins, *I'm you. I'm guessing whoever gave you this told you that already. But take it from one who knows, it's a hard thing to get your head around. Like the first Jerry Beche, who came before me like I came before you, I originate from a parallel reality to yours. One so thinly separated from your own that they are, by any measurable standard, identical . . .*

Acknowledgements

I am indebted to my wife, Emma Gibson,
for her continued support and encouragement.

Also in memory of Dorothy Lumley, my former and
first agent, and with thanks to John Jarrold, my new agent.
Both have long proven themselves adept at
keeping authors out of the Sarlacc Pit.

extracts reading groups
competitions books new
discounts extracts
extracts discounts
competitions extracts
books new
events books extracts
extracts reading groups
books
new titles reading groups
interviews
events extracts
discounts
new books events
events new
discounts extracts discounts
www.panmacmillan.com
extracts events reading groups
competitions books extracts new

31901056807839